THE LAZARU

By Barry J. M

Chapter 1

The music was so loud. It was the sort of volume
which made the inside of my ears tingle and itch,
and I knew this wasn't good news. At best I
risked tinnitus; at worst, impaired hearing loss.
But, hey I was happy and having the time of my
life. I glanced around to see an ocean of bouncing
bodies. Leather and denim clad teens punching
the air rhythmically to the pounding beat. Sweat
ran down faces making them shiny and red like an
orchard of juicy apples. Greasy lank long hair
fluttered in tandem to nodding heads as the ritual
of head-banging got underway. Thousands of
necks pulsed to the beat in synchronisation. In
addition to the earache, these kids would no doubt
be sporting tender necks in the morning. I could
see they were as ecstatic to be here as I was and
all thoughts of personal health and safety were the
least of their worries right now.

My gaze focused on the two loudspeaker
stacks, one each side of the stage. They rose
majestically like a great black pyramid reaching
only inches from the ceiling. I got the distinct
impression that if the ceiling was slightly higher,

the roadies would have inserted an extra cabinet or two into the stack, not just to increase the volume but to impress the crowds with the veritable sheer tower of power.

'Look at the speakers man,' shouted one teenage rocker to his buddy bouncing along beside him.

'Totally awesome – they'd sound wicked in my car,' his mate replied as he craned his neck to look up at Mount Decibel.

I gazed around to witness thousands more raucous rockers pouring over the balcony as if trying to get closer to their idols on stage. I feared the balcony edge wouldn't hold the weight of the masses pressing against it and visualised it collapsing with disastrous consequences. Morbidly I envisioned a sea of sweaty bodies piled on the floor of the main arena, blood blending with sweat, leather twisted around broken limbs.

The music jerked me back to reality. The screams and wails of Andy's guitar blending with the power and energy of Danny's vocals making the tweeter units way up top of the speaker pyramid screech as they reproduced the sounds from the stage via the plethora of amplifiers. The low frequency notes from the dextrous hands of bass player Chas perfectly complementing the pounding drum beat of skilled drummer Paul, and making the bass bins resonate like the heartbeat of a blue whale. The air from the piston-like bass speaker diaphragms making hair vibrate as though in a breeze, and succeeding in providing a slight cooling effect in the hot perspiration-filled power house of the Glasgow Apollo.

At this point in the song, it was the turn of keyboard player Mick to display his musical talent and amaze the audience with his fluttering fingers as they flew crazily across the ivory keys of his Hammond organ. His classical training was evident as he expertly blended this with his rock and roll influences making for a unique musical montage. His lanky figure rocked back and forth as his hands darted and danced left and right as each and every key was hit with precision. The crowd was loving this and so was Mick; in fact he decided that another bar was in order and made eye contact with Danny who got his colleague's message loud and clear and refrained from resuming his singing until Mick had completed yet another organ overture.

I was nearing the front of the high stage and strained my neck to see my rock and roll heroes. If the stage had been a bit lower, I would be able to virtually reach out and touch Danny's hand as he regularly bent down to be closer to his admiring audience, and give the occasional handshake. I had started out nearly at the back of the hall at the commencement of the concert but feeling like a third class passenger, I coveted the more prestigious position at the front of the hall right under the stage. So I systematically weaved my way through the throngs, filling a gap at the front of me as and when I could and excusing myself whenever the going got tough. Most of the rockers good naturedly moved aside to permit me my sneaky access to the first class floor position. I made it look as though I was trying to get to my mates who were at the front and this was the reason for my somewhat rude jostling. Unbeknown to them, I did this at virtually every gig I attended and was now an expert at skipping queues, no doubt in part helped by my lanky six foot two inch frame.

I had almost reached my ultimate goal when I bumped into a big burly biker type causing him to stumble a little. He spun around and glared at me showing a mouthful of broken teeth, angry eyes and a nefarious grin on his scarred face. He grabbed me by the lapels of my jacket and I was jerked towards him, so close I could smell the reek of alcohol and garlic on his breath. I stood helpless as I watched his right hand curl into a fist then withdraw in readiness to a launch into a haymaker punch. There was nothing I could do – I was being held tight in his clutches and unable to move due to the heaving crowds around me. I closed my eyes and awaited the inevitable.

My world seemed to transform into slow motion as I anticipated the blow to my face at the hands of the livid and drunk 'Hell's Angel'.

I could hear Danny belting out the chorus once again and the crowd responded by accompanying him, some tunefully, but most sounding like a cat's choir as they failed to match the appropriate key that Carter was leading.

But the knockout blow didn't come – I opened my eyes to see the huge tattooed fist only inches from my face, but it was being deflected by a small dainty hand before it came into contact with my jaw.

'Leave him alone – he's with me,' the female owner of the voice said.

Then I was released from his grasp and swiftly hustled away through the throngs towards safety in the arms of my rescuer – a pretty 'hippy-chick' type girl.

Fists were now punching the air in time to the shouted words and the crowd joined in with the well known lyrics.

'Lovin' life and rock n' roll,' more than three thousand voices rang out in fierce competition to Carter's powerful vocals. I was only glad the fists weren't being aimed in my direction.

We had now reached the side of the auditorium. I looked at the girl and she treated me to a lovely warm smile as wide as the Clyde. This was so unexpected – I had braced myself for a beating but got a glimpse of beauty instead.

'Hey, thanks for doing that,' I managed to say. I was feeling half embarrassed and half relieved at being spared.

'That's okay,' my smiling companion replied. 'Big Al starts a fight everywhere he goes.'

'Thought I'd be spending the night in hospital,' I joked.

She moved closer to me as though to afford me even more protection from Big Al or anybody else who dared to pound me. I felt her warm breath in my ear and caught a whiff of perfume and faint aroma of spearmint chewing gum. Her long brown centre-parted hair brushed lightly against my face, but I was not complaining.

'I'm Alison.'

I drew back to meet her eye, bending down slightly as she was not nearly as tall as I was. She dutifully turned her face and presented me with her left ear sporting a wealth of metal ear-rings, and not just on the lobe; enough to make a metal detector go crazy. I moved closer to her and could smell the leather from her jacket; obviously new, perhaps bought especially for this gig.

'Hi Alison, I'm Tony.'

Alison spun around again and, to my surprise, wrapped both her arms around my neck and pulled me closer to her. I felt I was in heaven. I couldn't believe I was in such close proximity to such a beautiful girl – and she wanted to talk to me.

'It's really difficult to hear you Tony,' she called.

I nodded my agreement and hoped she wouldn't let go. Now that we were closer we didn't have to offer ears to each other and I got the chance to examine her beauty. I gazed into her heavily made-up eyes and was treated to another award winning smile. Her face was blemish-free and her skin easily visible below a thin coating of foundation. She fit neatly into her leather biker jacket, her slim figure showing off the curves of the shiny black material.

'You been to many gigs Alison?'

'You mean: do I come her often?' was her witty reply.

I laughed at her observation of the clichéd chat-up line and nodded. Not only was the girl pretty, but she had a sense of humour and seemed to own a nice personality to match.

'Yeah. I've seen them loads of times,' she said indicating to the band, 'and I've seen Led Zeppelin, Deep Purple and Pink Floyd.' I was impressed. Here was a dedicated rock chick, plus she had a bit of disposable income! Corny as it may sound, but this was pretty much the type of girlfriend I had always dreamt of.

'I've seen Zeppelin as well, but I just love the Faceless Legions,' I replied as I pointed to Danny who was now engaging in some crowd interaction by thrusting his microphone out towards the audience.

Alison and I chatted a little more about the bands we had seen and highlights of recent gigs we had both attended, before turning out attention back to the area of the stage. As much as we both were excited to learn more about each other, we had paid a tidy sum to be here and didn't want to miss too much of the concert. Besides we could chat after the gig had ended and not have to shout to be heard.

We turned to face the stage, Alison now close by my side, her head resting lightly on my shoulder. It was as though we were an actual couple and not just rock fans who had only met about fifteen minutes ago. Again, I was certainly not complaining and actively encouraged her to stay close to me by narrowing the gap gradually until she felt almost part of me. By now all memory of my recent near-death experience had evaporated. We slowly edged nearer to the stage, hoping to get closer to our rock and roll idols; however we were careful to steer clear of quarrelsome Big Al and others of similar ilk.

The band was now between songs and the three thousand odd fans were showing their approval by clapping loudly into the air. Cheers and whistles accompanied the applause augmenting the volume and confirming to the band that their efforts were greatly appreciated.

'Who wants another song then?' Danny asked the audience, using his well-worn catchphrase. This stirred the crowd into frenzy as they chanted, punched the air and begged for more quality entertainment. In the background Paul was indicating to his watching fans by waving his drumsticks wildly in the air. Paul knew drummers were the members of a band often heard but not seen, and always liked to remind his fans that he was indeed present and correct, albeit hiding behind his fifteen piece *Premier* drum kit. The hoards noticed the small drummer standing on his pedestal and acknowledged his presence with a whoop and a cheer.

Andy Brookes was now keen to get going with the next number and began a very familiar riff. This was the trigger the crowd needed and cheers of delight erupted throughout the concert hall. Soon drums and bass had entered the song, keyboards accompanying on the eighth bar and the crowd-pleasing song was quickly underway; the tight rhythm section driving the song like a powerful steam engine. The audience went wild, arms moving up and down like out-of-control pistons. The head-banging crew got to work and the legions of fans swayed to the beat. I sang along to the well-known lyrics and I could hear Alison chanting along also. She had a decent voice by what I could make out, her face a mere inches from mine.

'I totally love this one,' Alison screamed.

'Me too,' I answered. And we both resumed our passionate accompaniment.

Danny was darting around the stage working off his excited energy like an animal released from captivity. He would run off to centre right and encourage the masses to sing along before racing towards centre left to do much the same. He never forgot the balcony though, and raised his arms to acknowledge the fans high above him.

Then Danny spotted me. He actually looked right at me and smiled – I think he was impressed by my enthusiastic singing efforts or perhaps he was thinking 'what was that gorgeous girl doing with him'. He sang the next line and pointed his microphone at me to indicate I should sing the next line. I obliged and shouted out the lyrics, accompanied by thousands of other voices. Danny sang the following line and gestured for me to continue our little game. I sang my heart out, Alison sang and most of the hall accompanied.

Then I couldn't believe what happened next. Danny invited me to join him on stage to help him sing the remainder of the song. I leapt at the chance and sprang forwards only to stop suddenly when I couldn't for the life of me find how I was to get up there; the stage was about twelve feet high! I looked at Danny for guidance and he indicated the stairway to the right of stage, as he sang the next verse. I headed to the stairway as fast as I could just in case Danny changed his mind and my chance at fame was dashed. I was stepping onto the top stair when I noticed a burly security guy look straight at me; for a minute I thought it was Big Al's twin brother. It was obvious that he had probably been looking the other way when I was officially invited onto the stage. His reptilian senses registered a threat and he sprang to life. He raced towards me with impressive speed given his bulk and huge beer belly and was about to grab hold of me when Danny spotted him and intervened, to my relief. Realising his error, he skulked off stage left with a sheepish look on his chubby goateed face. I was feeling lucky – that was twice I'd been saved on the same night.

Not only was I on top of the stage, but I felt on top of the world. Danny put his arm around me and we chanted along to the song. The lights were blinding and the heat was unbearable. At least the sound was nowhere near as loud, being behind the speaker stacks. I could hear the guitar and bass clearly, now coming from the wall of *Marshall* stacks and *Ampeg* bass combo amplifiers behind me. I gazed at the thousands of enviable faces and could not wipe the smile from my face. I was living the dream. I strained to catch sight of Alison but struggled to find her in the sea of denim, leather and long hair, plus the glare from the multicolour spotlights causing temporary blindness. I only wished she could be here with me – it would make her night.

Andy crossed in front of me, the long lead trailing from his Stratocaster like a slithering snake on a mission. Chas moved towards me and nodded as he caressed the strings and frets of his *Fender Jazz*. Being close to the band, I could see that Chas and Danny were much taller than I ever imagined, and Andy was exceptionally small. Mick and Paul couldn't leave their stations, so I didn't get a chance to see them close up. The atmosphere on stage was electric: a pulsing, throbbing surge of vibrant energy causing the hairs on the back of my neck to stand to attention.

Then the song ended; Danny swiftly thanked me for my input and showed me the way off stage. I was gutted. I wanted to do another number, but Danny had simply dismissed me like a schoolmaster after reprimanding a naughty pupil. I headed to the stairway and was met by my bouncer mate; he growled at me and indicated for me to hurry up, probably hoping I rebelled and he was given the opportunity to push me.

When I reached the bottom, my eyes took their time in adjusting to the intense glare they had recently been exposed to. Then the onslaught of the loud volume and smell of sweaty bodies hit me like a tidal wave. Alison approached and guided me back to our position in the crowd; her arm around my neck just like Danny's a moment ago, but with a touch more romance.

'I can't believe how lucky you are,' Alison shouted.

I stood there in a daze struggling to comprehend this fact myself. I was actually on stage with the Faceless Legions – one of the biggest bands in the world. I had stood on stage, sang with, and watched my heroes play. Now I was in the arms of beautiful girl who also wanted me. I really was a lucky guy.

Chapter 2

That was way back in 1978. That was a night I will never forget. It is permanently etched onto the contours of my memory. Fortune seemed to favour me in particular that night – I had not one but two dreams come true. Of course, the short gig on stage with the Faceless Legions was just a fleeting dream; the kind you wake up from wishing it never ended. The type of dream in which you fall back asleep hoping the vision resumes, but it never does.

As for the second dream, this became more of a reality. After the gig, Alison and I left the Apollo along with the sell-out crowd of three thousand five hundred delighted fans. It took almost half and hour to exit the building, but neither of us were particularly bothered as we shuffled towards the main doors in a disorderly manner. We had our arms around one another and each quietly contemplating our blossoming whirlwind romance amidst the throngs of boisterous perspiring rock fans.

We stepped out into a cold frosty November evening and shivered as the cold made contact with our sweaty skin. Having just spent nearly two hours in a musical hothouse, wet with perspiration and wearing only a t-shirt beneath our light jackets, it was like climbing into an industrial freezer. Still this was adequate excuse for cuddling even tighter into each other.

Outside, the throngs gathered for a post-gig analysis, then departed on their separate ways; herds of black leather headed in one direction towards the train stations whilst flocks of denim hurried the other way towards the bus station and taxi ranks.

My date and I wishing to prolong the evening quickened our pace to generate some heat and headed into the city centre stopping off at a chip shop. Here we shared a fish supper as we chatted about the gig and ourselves, through greasy lips and frosty breaths.

I offered to drive Alison home, and she accepted. Now I feared she me might just go off me when she seen my car. When I told her I owned a car, she looked impressed and probably thought it was a flashy sports model, but alas, it was only an old rusty *Vauxhall Chevette*. To my relief she smiled when she saw it but still looked impressed. It turned out she was amazed more at the fact I actually owned a motor vehicle than the car itself. None of her other boyfriends, it seemed, owned such a luxury and she had to travel everywhere by public transport.

After a couple of embarrassing false starts, the trusty *Chevette's* engine burst into life and we motored to the east end of Glasgow in no particular hurry, heater blasting away to heat the inside to a toasty temperature.

'I've had a fantastic evening, Tony,' she whispered as we drew up outside the terraced block where she resided with her parents and older brother.

'Me too. This has been such an amazing night.'
We engaged in the usual clichéd lovers routine: kissed, hugged and whispered sweet nothings into each other's earlobes, and still having to talk louder than usual due to the persistent ringing in our ears. My heart was thumping away inside my chest as if in competition to the course throbbing of the *Chevette's* engine. And we arranged to see each other again, and again.

I reached far into the cupboard and hauled out the off-white leather vanity case. It had a light coating of dust and smelled slightly of mildew. I stared at it trying to remember what it contained, afraid to open it and spill its secrets. This case had obviously been hibernating at the back of that cupboard for years and looked like no one had bothered to open it in decades.

I dragged the case through to the living room, gave it a cursory dusting then began to prise open the gold coloured zipper. As predicted, it was reluctant to move and I contemplated going to my garage to fetch the trusty can of *WD-40*, when at last, it yielded. It took a couple of minutes of gentle coaxing to avoid breaking the delicate artefact of a zip, before I had the case fully open and was able to reveal its hidden contents.

I tipped the entire load of photographs out onto the carpet and smiled at the promise of an afternoon stroll down memory lane. I sat there cross legged, on the floor and leafed through the photos. Some were faded, some yellowing, but all images still intact and clearly visible despite the reminiscent tears in my eyes.

There I was, clad in garish shorts and t-shirt and smiling like a lunatic; Blackpool tower clearly visible in the background and the odd donkey plying its trade across the sand with a giggling child on its back. More photos appeared of me and Martin, my older brother; some of mum and dad and the occasional one with the whole family, probably taken by some stranger who had either offered or was press-ganged into it. Some were back and white and others colour, though ranging from dull lacklustre shades to vibrant and garish hues - such was the quality in the days of film rolls and flash cubes; we seemed to be spoiled now in the digital age.

There must have been about five hundred snaps in this case and would likely take many hours to sift through them all. So I made myself a brew and settled down once again to resume my trek through reminiscence land. The photos, lying scattered all over the floor, were in no particular order and I simply lifted a small bundle and looked at each in turn. Some were of no particular interest to me – such as wedding snaps of people I didn't know or care to remember. I simply tossed the irrelevant relatives back into the musty case as though closing the door on select members of my kith and kin.

About an hour later, I came across the interesting batch: photos of me and Alison taken not long after we met. Both looking like the proverbial rock fans: clad in leather biker jackets, tight jeans, long hair and sporting Faceless Legions t-shirts, purchased from one of the many concerts we attended together. More snaps with the happy couple on a camping trip; by the seaside and many taken high up a hillside somewhere in the Trossachs.

The sight of the Faceless Legions casual-wear jolted me back to reality. What ever happened to that band? During their heyday, they were one of the biggest and most popular rock bands in Britain, if not the world. But it seems when they disbanded back in 1979, they just disappeared into oblivion. I never heard any of the guy's names appearing in other bands since, which was strange. Given the band was made up of five pretty talented musicians, I would have thought one or two of them would go on to form or join other bands in the proceeding years, but there seemed to be no trace or memory of any them; I should know – I was one of their biggest fans. Perhaps they had all had enough of the hectic touring schedule or extravagant rock and roll lifestyle. Heck, maybe they all died from a drug overdose or alcohol binge; it was certainly not unusual during the 70's as friends, family and fans of Jimi Hendrix, Janis Joplin, Jim Morrison and the like will attest.

I pondered this enigma as I flicked through more and more photos although neither my heart

15

nor concentration was in it anymore. I couldn't help but think about my favourite rock band and where they'd all gone. This triggered and idea and I went over and sorted through my CD pile, looking for the 'best of' Faceless Legions album. After a frustrating search lasting about twenty minutes, I found the case, but to my horror, the compact disc was missing! How ironic, I mused; both the band members and their CD are missing. There seemed to be a conspiracy against me.

Since retiring from the police force, I had achieved quite a lot by way of leisure time. But now the honeymoon period was coming to a close and I was starting to get just a little bored. In the last seven or eight years, I had learned a number of new skills; travelled to exotic locations around the world; had become a competent enough musician and somewhat of a DIY expert. But now I was looking for something new and different to stimulate my mind. I needed a project to keep me occupied and sane.

Then I hit upon the bizarre notion to pile all my energy and resources into trying to track down the former members of the Faceless Legions. I pondered this for quite some time and the more I thought the more interesting and exciting the mission became; I was in the grip of a large idea.

I had spent thirty years of my life as an operational police officer; the vast majority as a detective in the CID with Strathclyde Police Force. I even retired at the lofty rank of Detective Inspector. So I had a wealth of experience at my disposal and considered it prudent to channel these skills into something worthwhile – and planning and executing a mission to find the missing musicians of my favourite band of all time seemed like a pretty good use of my time and energy. Besides, who knew where it might lead? I might have to travel the length and breadth of the UK, or maybe even the world! And if I was successful, maybe I could talk the guys into reforming as a band for one last reunion concert. How awesome would that be? To see one of the greatest bands of yesteryear back on stage and doing their thing for music culture and rock fans everywhere. After all, many bands have reformed in the past and performed one final farewell gig, to much acclaim and financial gain; so why not the Legions? Perhaps I could present them with that unique opportunity and rekindle the old flame of musical mastery.

But literally, where on earth do I begin my quest? I suspected that the internet was going to be a big help in my mission, but I still reckoned it would be an immense and daunting task; however I had pretty much set my mind on the job in hand and was feeling butterflies of excitement fluttering in my stomach and my heart was quickening its pace as if in sympathy.

During my time in the CID we undertook a great many operations and it was common practice to compose an operational name to marry with the mission. For instance, I led a team where we raided an illegal cannabis growing plant within a disused warehouse, naming the mission: 'Operation Rasta' for obvious reasons. Then we had 'Operation Rambo' where we uncovered a moderate firearms cache in a Glasgow tenement block. My favourite, however was an operation in which we raided an office block to find a multitude of stolen and pirated video cassettes. Some ingenious member of the team decided to call this one 'Operation Del Boy' in honour of the wheeling-dealing Cockney character from *Only fools and horses*.

So, after a careful composition and whittling down my short list, I decided to name my own personal mission: 'Operation Lazarus'. I smiled at my ingenuity, and biblical knowledge. After all I was about to embark upon a quest to effectively raise the dead, just like Jesus in the gospel account, so this seemed like an apt enough sobriquet. I couldn't wait to get started.

Embarking upon a new experience is often daunting, but stimulating. I cast my memory net way back to 1980 when I first joined Strathclyde Police. After working with my mate as a mechanic in his dad's garage, I never felt settled and often aspired to greater things. The first sign of my latent ability to detect was when I managed to trace a fault in an engine which had baffled all the highly experienced mechanics. They were about to write the car off as un-reparable as no one could actually find where the fault lay, despite having spent a great many hours of labour on the thing. I systematically traced the fault to the high tension leads and was quickly hailed a hero. I showed them how I had methodically eliminated each stage of the chain of faults to arrive at the suspect part.

'You're a pretty smart guy' said one of my colleagues.

'You should be a detective,' added another.

'The Sherlock Holmes of motor mechanics,' suggested the boss.

I sat in a waiting room along with about twenty other nervous looking people. The room was gloomy, the lighting sparse and had about as much charm as a death-row prison cell. I eyed the guy across from me: he fidgeted with the lapels on his suit jacket and tie. The boy next to him bit his nails so much I spotted blood on his trembling hands. A girl next me quietly mouthed something inaudible. I reckoned she was rehearsing her answers to predicted questions, or maybe it was a calming mantra. By contrast I was quite calm. I had set my heart on joining the police, but was philosophical enough to accept rejection if this wasn't for me. Besides I was a bright enough guy having left school with a decent amount of qualifications and knew the world was a big place. There were plenty of opportunities to be had. If they decided I wouldn't make a good police officer, then so be it, I would simply try something else – explore another avenue or three.

The door squeaked open and twenty heads shot up, eyes bulging in anticipation. A tall uniformed officer appeared and gazed down at his clipboard.

'Tony Caulfield, please,' he announced looking demure and disinterested; he had the look and demeanour of an undertaker. I sprang up feeling my heart race and thump against my chest. Everyone looked at me; maybe they were wondering what that loud rhythmic thudding sound under my jacket was.

'That's me Sir,' I said smiling like an idiot. I hadn't a clue how to address the guy or what to say. The undertaker surveyed me from head to toe but said nothing, his expression remained unchanged and he beckoned me into his lair. I walked in briskly, my head held high and breathed deeply to keep any nerves at bay. The undertaker gestured to a lone seat and I sat. I faced a long wooden table with two uniformed officers behind, and one woman dressed in civilian dress. My escort then seated himself next to the woman and they all began their usual pre-interview procedure, some shuffling papers, others pouring themselves a drink from the water jug. None of them had looked at me yet. I moved to get comfortable on my seat and realised that it squeaked like an angry pig every time I moved. I froze as four stern faces looked back at me as though I had just interrupted their quiet contemplation; I felt like a rabbit in the path of a speeding juggernaut.

Then the show was on the road. My host introduced himself and the others, although I never really caught any of their names or rank. I was hoping I would not be tested on this later, as I would no doubt fail. The lone woman was representing the human resources department and as such, was merely a civilian, that explaining the lack of uniform.

'So why do you want to join the police Mr Caulfield?' asked a smiling uniform with silver diamond-shaped pips on his shoulder. I wasn't a hundred percent sure, but I think those pips signified the rank of Inspector.

'Well I enjoy helping people and would like to uphold the law,' I replied with all the confidence of a motivational speaker.

'So why not become a social worker if you like to help people?' asked the other uniform with the silver crowns on his shoulder. I was caught out with that unexpected retort to my prepared answer. I shuffled in my seat and it squawked again much to my embarrassment; why didn't they supply a nice comfortable plush chair like on *Mastermind*?

'I believe I would make a better police officer than a social worker, Sir.' He nodded as though satisfied with my answer and jotted something down on his notebook.

'What is your current occupation Mr Caulfield?' enquired the women as she peered at me through rimless spectacles half way down her nose. She had the look of a very strict headmistress and I wouldn't have been surprised if it turned out this is what she previously did before joining the police service.

'I'm a motor mechanic, Madam,' I said. She nodded then scribbled something on her notepad.

'Strange career move going from fixing cars to policing the streets is it not?' said the undertaker, undertones of sarcasm and incredulity discernable in his croaky voice.

Now was my chance to impress them with my intrinsic detecting skills and aspiration to someday become a police detective. So I explained my expert methodology in tracing and detecting problems and my dogmatic adherence to health and safety protocols and employment law in the workplace, not just for myself but for my colleagues also. I wasn't sure if I dazzled them: half of them looked sort of impressed, the rest just bored.

An hour later I emerged from that austere room feeling drained and relieved to finally surface and taste fresh air. That had been a long and dreary affair. I felt like a heretic after a grilling by the Papal Inquisition. I didn't have a clue if it had gone well in there – their stern faces certainly gave nothing away. Sure, I answered all questions fired at me intelligently and decisively, but whether I sold myself as potential police material, I would just have to wait.

Chapter 3

Two months earlier I had discussed with Alison, the possibility of joining the police. She approved and said I would make a great policeman on account of my calm, clear headed thinking ability and tall stature. She was training to be a nurse and thought it cute that we could both be in the industry of helping others. So with her blessing, I filled in the multitude of paperwork which made up the recruitment pack and sent it off to Force Headquarters. One month later I was invited to sit the entrance examination. Alison whooped for joy when she read the letter thinking I was almost in the force. I burst her bubble when I explained this was only one step in a long and laborious process and there was no guarantee I would make the grade. As a motivating force, Alison declared she would marry me if and when I became a police officer. That had the desired effect and I put a great deal of effort into the ensuing process. I even went and got all my long hair cut off, much to the disappointment of my girlfriend. Alison said I looked so much different with short hair and struggled initially to adapt to my new image, but soon fell deeper in love with her new improved 'soon to be police officer' boyfriend.

The exam I passed with flying colours and was now one step closer to tying the knot with my trainee nurse. The long and arduous process of background checks I endured with quiet confidence, patiently awaiting the results. Next came the home visit from a couple of officers of Sergeant rank. This too, I passed and was now on the home straight. Only the medical then the tough panel interview to go and I could well be wearing the black tunic of a member of Strathclyde Police's finest in the near future. I was raring to go, and Alison's blessing and support never faltered.

I booted up my laptop and waited on it presenting me with the desktop. I had finally found the missing Faceless Legions compact disc being mis-filed in a *Status Quo* jewel case. I fired up the CD player and my memory reeled at the blast from the past. This would be the perfect background accompaniment to my research.

I swiftly brought up my internet browser and began surfing. I tapped in 'Faceless Legions' on the search engine but it brought up only nominal information. It told me pretty much what I already knew but didn't furnish me with stuff I needed. I wanted to know where these guys were now and what they were doing, but no website offered to reveal these details. It was as if no one actually knew. It seemed more folk knew the intricacies of how to split the atom than, whatever happened to five well known musicians from a well publicised band from the 1970s. That information had to be out there somewhere; someone had to know. I would just have to dig a little deeper.

It was easy enough to bring up a whole host of facts about old musicians like Jagger, Richards, Page and Plant, but nothing much on Danny Carter, Andy Brookes and Co. It looked like the Legions were the Lord Lucan's of the music world.

I tried entering these names into the search bar. Lots of Danny Carters but none pointing to the one I wanted. Andy Brookes was next, and one entry appeared to be promising, albeit only slight. There was an entry for a guitar and music store in Birmingham, the proprietor being listed as one Andy Brookes. This merited closer inspection, so I visited Mr Brooke's website; all rather disappointing: the web told me everything I needed to know about buying a new or used guitar, but nothing about the owner. Could this Andy Brookes be one and the same? I pondered this before experiencing my 'Eureka' moment: I remembered hearing Andy talk on an interview and he had a distinct 'Brummie' accent. In addition, Brookes was an avid collector of electric guitars and admitted to owning dozens of different makes and models. This was more than coincidental, surely. One Andy Brookes, a native of Birmingham who loved collecting guitars, owning a guitar emporium in the same city? I required a bit more of a clue before I pursued this line of enquiry. I navigated to the store's gallery page hoping to find a photo of Mr Brookes, but alas, there was none.

I was beginning to lose heart and abandon my search in the shop's website when I spotted the mother of all clues – this had to be the confirmation I badly needed to kick-start my elusive quest.

I was now staring at a general view of the store. Hundreds of guitars lined the walls and others sat on stands on the floor. But on a wall in the background was a mounted guitar which caught my immediate attention. I zoomed in and enlarged this section of the photo as much as I could and smiled when I identified a very rare model indeed: not one of your common or garden *Fender Stratocasters* or *Telecasters*, but a 'Nocaster'. According to legend, when the *Fender* company first introduced their now famous *Telecaster* model, it was originally named the *Broadcaster*, however some other company already had a product using that name and threatened to sue unless the name was dropped. *Fender* obliged but continued to produce the guitar model, a small quantity being sold with no name on their headstocks until some bright spark at *Fender* decided on the new name of 'Telecaster'; the rest is musical history. So the rare models with no name were quick to pick up the sobriquet 'Nocaster'; now I knew this as a fact of rock and roll trivia that the famous Andy Brookes of the Faceless Legions owned one of these rare fish. Bingo – I had him. This had to be the same guy; only a strange set of coincidences could otherwise explain this certainty.

This was an excellent place to start. Perhaps Mr Brookes could tell me everything else I wanted to know about his former comrades. Maybe Operation Lazarus would prove easier than I first thought. If only I knew different – maybe I wouldn't have bothered.

Alison broke down and cried when I showed her my acceptance letter as a probationary officer in Strathclyde Police Force. I now had one month to terminate my current employment, get myself and my affairs in order before embarking upon my chosen career promising much action, adventure and ultimate job satisfaction. Not only that, but Alison was itching for a gold ring to slip on her finger.

I promised her I would purchase her one of her choice as soon as I received my first pay as probationary policeman.

My eyes popped when I stared through the windows of a number of jewellery shops to see the price of engagement rings. I reckoned I would require to save more than six months pay to be in the position to purchase one of these gold bands. Alison was happy enough to wait a reasonable amount of time, as she had selected a diamond encrusted ring costing over £200 and knew I would have to save to afford that. Besides, I would be away for a few months at Police College which was a residential course but allowing students to return home at the weekends. I didn't know what my fiancé-to be expected in me joining the police, but she was visibly upset and down when I told her about the Scottish Police College at Tulliallan, and the fact we could only see each other at the weekends. I think she assumed the job of a police officer was pretty much like any other where you learned on the job like an apprentice. This was only partially true, and a whole wealth of procedure and paperwork, legislation and law had to be learned and mastered before fledgling cops were let loose on the streets.

I gently reminded her that she was also attending college in training for her chosen vocation; she seemed to accept this and felt a little better all things considered.

'I'll miss you,' Alison said as she hugged me, her hand caressing the back of my head in the place where I formerly had long hair, 'I just want to spend loads of time with you.'

'Me too, babe,' I returned. 'But this is just temporary. There's light at the end of the tunnel.'

The next few months for both of us were, as predicted, difficult. Five days apart and only a fleeting weekend together was torturous for us. We wanted to spend much more time in each other's company, do more things together and fall even deeper in love. Little did we know that our current situation would be a pattern of things to come; I only wish we had realised at the time.

I rubbed my eyes trying to generate more moisture to lubricate the tired and dry organs. All this staring at a computer screen was taking its toll on me. I decided a break was in order and went to the kitchen to fill and get the kettle going. On my way I nearly tripped over the pile of photos still laid strewn all over the carpet. I stooped down to tidy the bundle slightly, when I caught sight of a gorgeous girl in a big puffy white wedding dress. Beside her was a tall smiling, quite handsome man looking like an extra from *Braveheart*. I recalled how uncomfortable that kilt felt, its rough heavy material brushing across my bare knees was a weird sensation. The collar of my shirt irritating, feeling like the lapels needed flattening, although this was how they were meant to be. The black

Prince Charlie jacket felt a little too tight and I spend most of that day pulling at it hoping to make it fit better. The laces of my shoes kept slipping down the socks and I wished I had safety pinned them earlier.

Alison looked radiant; her wide smile enhancing her attractive facial features and confirming that this was the happiest moment of her life. She wore only a modest amount of makeup and knew as well as I, that she didn't need much; Alison was a natural beauty and I was as proud as could be, standing there with my new wife.

More photos vied for attention and I glanced only briefly at some, and studied others in a bit more detail; the beaming bride with her mother; Alison with her two bridesmaids, then some with me and Martin, my best man. Each and every snap seemed to be the very definition of happiness; every one smiling and content. Every member of the wedding party pleased for the proud couple and delighted to be sharing in this momentous celebratory moment.

The Faceless Legions were still doing their thing on the CD player and my living room was filled with the sounds of their unique and legendary musical prowess. I sang along with the ones I knew the lyrics to; and hummed along when the words slipped my memory. I even performed air guitar when Andy's guitar solos came up.

I decided that I had strolled far enough down memory lane for the time being, so I unceremoniously bundled the remaining pile of photos back into their musty case. This was easier said than done as handfuls of the glossy snaps slid out repeatedly making the task frustratingly tricky. As I was shoving the last of the prints in, a couple of a young Alison fell out as though to remind me she still existed. As if by coincidence, one photo was of Alison taken within a few days of us meeting. There she stood looking tall and gorgeous her head tilted slightly and looking off to the left gazing into the middle distance; her leather jacket – the same one she wore to the gig – enhancing her slim figure. She sported a pair of leather fingerless gloves and I could see fake silver bullets adorning her belt on the hips of her tight black jeans. I really liked that photo. She looked like a true natural and the perfect poster girl for 'rock chick' clothing and accessories. I wondered how she looked now.

I took the photos and propped them up near to my workstation. Along with the Legions playing in the background, these pictures would serve as inspiration as I resumed my research.

Now that I was pretty certain I knew where to find Mr Brookes, I turned my attention to Mr Carter. As before, and despite the internet containing virtually millions of websites, blogs and links, I was rather disappointed at first glance. I already knew Carter was the lead vocalist of the Faceless Legions for the duration of their life from 1974 until their disbanding in 1979. I was also aware Danny Carter hailed from South London, was nicknamed 'Smiler' on account of his perpetual grin, but it appeared that no one knew or wanted to share with the world what happened to Smiler at the demise of the Legions. He was a good solid vocalist with a broad range, being able to span four octaves and the power of a foghorn to match. Some band must have jumped at the chance to have him as their lead man. Watching and listening to him, he always gave the impression that singing was his life, his vocation and that no other job would satisfy.

I tried the other members as well – with equal failure. Drummer Paul Dixon from Bristol was also missing in action as was his keyboardist Mick Walker. The bare-bones web pages simply sated the obvious – their dates and place of birth and the fact they played with the Faceless Legions. That was the depressing extent of my research and I was left feeling rather deflated.

Married life was good to begin with. We spend all the time we had promised ourselves with each other. We still went along to the occasional rock concert, although I felt pretty out of place sporting my short hair, although I still wore my leather jacket on top of a rock band t-shirt. To me I still was a rocker through and through. Alison had retained her long brown hair, but wore it tied back most of the time due to her job as a newly qualified nurse.

As time went on, our marriage seemed to go wandering downhill. The problem was: our jobs and they prevented us from seeing each other on a regular basis. We both worked a variety of shifts and they always seemed to be in direct conflict with each other – Alison would be around when I was working, and vice versa. Even annual leave was a struggle although we both made very effort to arrange our holiday leave to be off at the same time. We had to negotiate and even plead with colleagues to swap days to suit, but it was still problematic, and did place a big strain on our marriage. It appeared we simply shared a house and were married only in the official sense of the word.

We did make an effort to address the problem. We found the odd spare moment before one of us was about to go off to work, or had just clocked off, and we discussed and analysed the problem, but neither was prepared to admit we had a major problem on our hands. Naively, we both thought if we ignore the problem, it may just go away or sort itself out. Having established our careers were to blame, again neither party wanted to back down. She aspired on climbing up the nursing tree and I had my heart set on getting into CID and my foot on the rung of the promotion ladder.

Having no ready answer or solution to our marital problems, we ignored the issue and continued passively as though someday the genie with the magic lamp might turn up on our doorstep and solve all our problems.

I was suddenly jolted out of my revelry when my browser informed me that Chas Hannagan was now deceased. I sat back in my chair, shocked at this revelation. I didn't see that coming. Somehow I expected all my old musical heroes to be alive and well, but such is the great rock and roll lifestyle. The barer-of-bad-news entry told me Mr Hannagan had died of 'drug related' complications only a few years ago and was survived by his wife, son and daughter, still residing in south Wales.

'Chas the Jazz' attracted the nickname by his musician friends on account of his liking for the *Fender Jazz* bass guitar. Apparently he insisted that only the *Fender Jazz* was worthy of any bass player's efforts. He was once offered the alternative *Fender Precision* bass, but dismissed this as 'not a real bass'. He admired the Jazz's slim neck permitting much slicker playing and fret-work, the instrument's body-contoured curvy offset waist and full-range bi-pole pickups. He lambasted all other makes and models of bass guitar, stating he had 'tried the rest and found the best!' Surely he must have known what he was talking about, as Chas Hannagan was a fantastic and experienced bass guitarist.

In view of this depressing news, I reset the Faceless Legions CD back to the beginning and sat back in my armchair, eyes closed and focused on listening to the prominent bass guitar lines of Chas the Jazz; my own personal memorial service to the great man.

In stark contrast to many other bass guitar players, Chas's bass lines were always audible and prominent. Most bass players are rarely heard and their playing simply 'blends in' and just becomes part of the rhythm section. But not Chas – his funky bass lines were an integral part of each and every song and enhanced the melody perceptibly. He was as proficient on the bass strings as his colleague Andy Brookes was on the six strings of his electric guitar.

But did this bombshell spell the end of 'Operation Lazarus' before it had actually begun? No I couldn't let this stop me, not until I had made an effort to trace the other members. I assumed the rest were still alive and well as there was no such news of any other former Faceless Legions members dying. Perhaps an alternative bass player could fill the dead man's shoes? This was assuming my mission was successful and the

Legions reunited, which right now was looking like a mammoth task, if not downright impossible.

The end of the CD album was my cue to get myself ready for my own musical performance. I bunged a ready meal into the microwave and left it to heat while I packed my gig bag with leads, effect pedals and guitar straps. Next I polished my shiny Ibanez and laid it gently into its fur-lined guitar case before clipping it closed. I was just completing my preparations when the micro signalled to me with a decisive 'ping'.

Suitably fed and watered, I loaded my gear into my *Hyundai i40* and drove to The Regent pub in south side of Glasgow. I decided that a tribute to the Legions was in order and so I had brought the disc with me and fired it into the car's CD player. I drummed on the steering wheel in time to Dixon's drumming and sang along with Carter's vocals, although I couldn't quite reach the high notes he could. I even hummed the guitar and keyboard instrumental parts as and when they appeared.

Despite the bustling early evening traffic, I arrived at the pub in good time and pretty much the same time as my band-mates.

'All right, Catcher?' shouted Stevie, my co-guitarist.

'Yeah, not bad,' I returned.

Stevie preferred to call people by their nicknames rather than their actual names, if he could help it - and I was no exception. He was referring to the sobriquet I picked up whilst in the police. Given I shared the surname with J.D. Salinger's famous character Holden Caulfield in

Catcher in the Rye, it was not long before some cultured and literature-conscious colleague picked up on this fact and so named me. Apparently it was also on account of my 'crook catching' abilities as a policeman, but I never boasted this fact. It was a fair enough nickname and could have been a lot worse I supposed.

We extracted our instruments and gig bags from our respective cars before heading into the small lounge area of The Regent, careful to avoid banging our guitar cases on the walls and doorframes – our instruments were far more valuable than the fixtures and fittings of this old dismal pub. The interior had that distinctive pub smell – ubiquitous to every pub in the land: a fine blend of ale and stuffiness mingling with the odour from the toilets.

Next we formed into a kind of bucket-brigade as we helped ferry bits of Phil's drum kit into the venue.

'Do you keep adding to this kit?' an irritated Stevie asked. 'They get heavier every time.'

'Nah, its just you're getting older, mate,' Phil retorted as he set about impersonating an OAP, compete with stooping shoulders, hunched back and an acetic look on his face.

'You should have your own roadies to haul all this stuff about,' bass player Darren cut in.

'Why do I need roadies when I've got all you complaining gits?'

On and on went the good-natured banter until all drums, cymbals and stands had been ferried into the room. Within an hour we had set up and began to sound check.

'One, two, three. Testing one, two, three,' I spoke to the microphone and both Stevie and

Darren, like a couple of children with a toy, battled to be the one at the controls of the mixer amplifier. Then Phil rattled his drums and whacked the crash cymbals startling Darren who nearly fell over.

We performed a version of an *Eagles* song to ensure all levels were correctly adjusted then we fine-tuned the settings before heading to the bar to lubricate our vocals chords before our big performance.

Experience Counts was a respectable and predictable 'rock covers' band, performing a broad range of well-known songs from bands such as *Led Zeppelin, The Doors, Status Quo* and of course, the odd number from the Faceless Legions! We had a semi-permanent residential spot at The Regent pub, but got the impression we were merely filling the musical gap until the manager talent-spotted a better band. Not unlike the band in *Dire Straits' Sultans of Swing*, we enjoyed playing but were happy in the knowledge we would never make the scene.

Seven o'clock on the dot and we launched into *Can't get enough of your love* to get the bustling Friday night crowd sparked up. The audience was a mixed bag: some enthusiastically chanting along between mouthfuls of frothy beer while others ignored us completely as though the three hundred watts of melodic disturbance was non-existent.

The guitar solo was fast approaching in *Sharp dressed man*, so I picked up my finger slide, inserted it onto my left ring finger and replicated the iconic guitar instrumental, virtually note for note. This seemed to impress a table of middle-aged ladies who seemed to regard me as some

Eric Clapton clone. No doubt the copious consumption of alcohol was heightening their impression of me and my mediocre talents.

By now the room was a heaving mass of hot bodies; now standing room only as the band played on. The manager was happy to have bums on seats and all patrons regularly purchasing all manner of drinks. We were simply a means to a fortune for the guy. He never complimented us on our performance and simply remarked about how busy the place was, and how depleted his cellar had become. None of us cared much as we were happy for the opportunity to play a catalogue of favourite songs on a regular basis, all for modest acclaim and applause – and the occasional free drink.

I was wet with perspiration by the time we completed our set list and finally powered down all the equipment. For this reason, I always carried a towel in my kit bag, and never allowed it to be borrowed by my other begging band cohorts.

'I might have a wedding gig for us.' Stevie said as we were transporting our gear back to our cars in the rear car park, 'Are you guys available?'

'When is it?' I enquired knowing I had a little field trip pending within the next week or so.

'Probably a week or two, but I'll let you know once I've used my expert negotiating skills,' he replied as though he was Brian Epstein or similar trying to secure us a sell-out gig in the O2 arena.

'Should be okay,' was the majority vote.

Chapter 4

The next day I set off for Birmingham, with the address of Brookes Guitar Emporium scribbled on a post-it note safely housed in my shirt pocket. I only intended on being in the city for a couple of days at most, so I booked myself in for two nights in a *Travelodge* not far from the city centre where my target was located. In order to lighten the tedious drive down the M6 motorway, I let the melodic sounds of the Faceless Legions fill the interior of the car as I drummed on the dashboard just above the steering wheel, keeping a watchful eye out of police traffic cars who might just take the notion to stop and book me for a spell of careless driving.

I searched my memory bank for the charge should this occur. Was it section 2 or 3 of the Road Traffic Act 1988? No, section 2 was dangerous driving; section 3 was careless or inconsiderate driving. I recalled my early police days where I routinely pulled over all manner of bad drivers and gave them a stern talking to. I really couldn't be bothered with charging them or dishing out fixed penalty tickets, leaving this to the so-called experts: the Road Policing Department. It has been said that your average traffic cop will prosecute his own granny if the chance presents itself. Funnily enough, one particularly loathsome officer I knew actually stopped and charged his own teenage son for his 'boy racer' tactics. I later heard that the boy disowned his father and legend has it, neither have spoken to each other since - and that was way back in the 1990s!

The rain came down in torrents and my wipers struggled to repel the lashings of water to enable a sighting of the road ahead. Soon a sea of brake-lights was visible ahead through the haze as motorists everywhere panicked and slowed as thought the rain was an impenetrable wall. Needing a comfort break, I scanned the sign ahead which informed that Knutsford Services was only three miles ahead, so I steered into the nearside lane and prepared to leave the M6 at the next junction.

It was a welcome relief to be able to stretch my legs, although I was forced to hurry to the building as the rain was still pounding down from the heavens as though going for a record to rival Noah's experience. I was half expecting the waters also to 'burst forth from the deep' in keeping with the biblical event.

Now this always seems to happen to me: I arrive at a service station just at the same time as a convoy of coaches; its as though they see me coming then follow me. I joined the masses of elderly tourists as we pushed through the doors to the welcoming aroma of overpriced coffee; it always smelled different from the cheap stuff. There stood a *Costa* franchise, a *Greggs* bakery and an *M & S* shop all hungry for our money. My first stop was the toilets, but unfortunately this was also the inclination of the old boys who had just debussed five minutes ago and were probably bursting for the toilet for the last couple of hours; no one daring to use the on-board facilities. I knew I didn't stand a chance of a free urinal in the next ten minutes, at least.

Queues were massive for both the *Costa* and *Greggs* – the exorbitant prices not dissuading anyone. So, keen to be on my way before I hit the rush hour traffic in Birmingham, I opted to purchase a cappuccino from a lonely little vending machine hidden away near to a small gaming arcade. I wished I had saved my £3, as the coffee was awful, tasting more like chicory than coffee. In addition, the cup was tiny and the liquid within lukewarm. I had a quick nefarious notion to kick the machine out of sheer despair, but knew this would not make the stuff in the cup taste any better. I may even risk drawing the attention of a security guard.

As a tribute to my lifelong habit of forward planning, I had prepared and brought with me a packed lunch, but never thought to fill a flask with coffee. Never mind, I had my heart set on consuming all the free teas and coffee sachets when I got to the *Travelodge*.

The place was still awash with bodies; most of them the OAPs from the coaches. They dithered around, like me, not wanting to part with any money to the overpriced franchises. I had to excuse my way around and through them, their hearing impairments causing me to raise my voice. I wished they had all come with a guide who could herd them into the restaurants like a good sheepdog and clear the passageways so everyone else could move around.

I browsed in the *WH Smith* shop; I joined the line of sad middle aged men who like nothing better than to read virtually cover to cover a magazine of choice, then put it back on the shelves all dog eared and creased whilst muttering 'Glad I didn't pay £4.95 for that rubbish.'

It was four o'clock when I entered the urban sprawl of Birmingham. It was now time to fire up the satnav and let the pleasant sounding voice of my female guide take me to my destination. She did with all the ease of a seasoned tour guide, with only the occasional hesitation as the system flickered and announced 'Recalculating route – please wait.'

I pulled into the car park of the ubiquitous and uninspiring brick and glass building adorned by the equally lacklustre *Travelodge* logo, parked and got out stretching my stiff legs. I approached the reception desk and was greeted by a be-speckled smiling woman in her mid thirties. She looked every bit the spitting image of the mother of Greg Hefley in the *Diary of a Wimpy kid* movies. If they ever decided to run a stage play version of the films in a theatre in Birmingham, perhaps this lady should audition for the part of Mrs Hefley's stunt double.

'Hi. How are you?' Greg's mum asked. I returned her smile, as I dropped my holdall on the floor at my feet.

'Great, thanks,' I returned. Then in an effort to spare more small talk and have my new friend ask all manner of questions about my journey, the route and the weather, I cut to the chase; well I was desperate for a cup of decent coffee.

'You should have a reservation for Caulfield.' It came out more of a question than a comment.

She scanned her computer screen, tapped a few keys and looked up again. Her glasses had slid down her nose forcing her to shove them back up into place before resuming eye contact.

'Yes, two nights, Mr Caulfield; I have it here.'

A few more keyboard taps and she produced the key-card for my room. I was hoping it would work first time as I rarely had luck with these things and often had to slink back to reception within five minutes when it failed to admit me to my room.

My smiling companion directed me to the stairway where I would find my room at the end of the corridor. I thanked her, lifted my bag and walked out to calls of 'Have a nice stay, sir'.

I was well surprised when the key-card flashed green and the door opened. I hurried inside just in case the device changed its mind and locked me out. As expected, the room looked like every other *Travelodge* room in the country: same funky bedspread, same matching curtains and everything where expected and exactly as it should be. Even the hideous multi-colour abstract painting on the wall seemed far too familiar.

The first thing I did after dropping my bag was to fill up the kettle with fresh water from the bathroom. I let the tap run for ages but it still produced a milky-white shade of water; I would just have to endure some limescale with my coffee.

I poured the recently boiled water from the world's smallest kettle into the tiny cup of coffee, added a couple of UHT cartons and stirred the whole mixture. I sat back on the bed and savoured the first semi-decent cup of coffee since leaving Glasgow.

I ate alone in the restaurant looking like a fish out of water surrounded by couples and families in the spacious, brightly lit room. To relieve the look of the 'sad man with no mates', I kept looking at the door every time someone walked in, as though I was waiting on my partner or a mate to join me sometime soon. I was fortunate that the table service was rapid enough for me to guzzle down my scampi and chips in record time before retiring to my room for the night.

I passed through reception once again, but there must have been a shift change as Mrs Hefley had been replaced by a tall skinny black man, who bid me 'Good night, sir,' in the thickest Brummie accent I had heard all day.

I pondered my strategy for the next day: I was about to discover if the owner of Brookes Guitar Emporium was indeed the Andy Brookes, formerly of the Faceless Legions. I had no particular plan and would just play it by ear, so to speak. Then my thoughts turned to my ex-wife. Since finding those photos of her, I was reminded of her good looks, charming personality and fun-based approach to life.

How could I have let our marriage and relationship dwindle like it did? It seemed I did all the hard work wooing Alison until she married me, then simply let the whole affair decay and wither away like an un-watered plant. I should have anticipated the problem and addressed it accordingly, but my career was much more important. I was just one more statistic proving that an unhealthy number of police officers' marriages often end in separation or divorce. I was well aware of this fact but foolishly didn't consider it worthy of contemplation; the power of promotion had blinded me and the quest to get higher up the rank structure had wrecked my marriage to the one I once loved.

Strange how it happened, but back in 1991, both Alison and I happened to get two whole weeks off together, so we reluctantly booked a holiday in Cyprus, hoping to engage in some serious talking and perhaps sort out our flailing marriage; instead we spend most of the holiday in a very loving embrace and rekindled our mutual passion in the heat of the Cyprian climate. Upon our return to Glasgow, Alison full of surprise announced that our fortnight of passion had borne fruit and she was pregnant. I was stunned, although I should have also seen this event coming. Just like a randy teenage boy, I should have known these things tend to happen, but never anticipated it.

Lee Anthony Caulfield entered the world and the lives of his semi-detached parents nine months later; a termination was never an option for either of us and we showed brave faces and made a good attempt to look like happy parents. Our marriage may have been shaky, but neither of us wanted to compromise the upbringing of our son; it was not his fault his parents were the proverbial career-oriented workaholics.

Alison managed to alter her shift pattern slightly in order to be at home more to help raise young Lee, but it was Granny and Grandpa who did most of the rearing. I couldn't do much to modify my working hours and shifts, but did attempt to spend as much of my free time with the growing boy as practicable.

Still, Lee's somewhat precarious upbringing within the bounds of a strained marriage didn't seem to affect him noticeably. He grew to be a tall, handsome confident man, and the older he got, that more he looked like me. His main problem was what he wanted to do with his life. He did express an interest in following in his father's career footsteps, but I quickly threw down the anchor whereby halting his desire to go down the policing path. I pointed out the fact that his parents' marriage was greatly affected by my vocational choice and I loathed to see this happening to him.

Lee left school still unsure of his career route and decided to study computing at college. University did not interest him and he just wanted to finish college, get out there and find some job, whether in the computing industry or not. An additional four years of study to get a degree when he was undecided on what job he wanted seemed a wise enough philosophy, and I respected his decision.

Alison became increasingly unsettled at home owing to the strain of living with a man she was still married to though did not exactly love, and a son she loved dearly but did not know how best to raise him. Eventually, in an attempt to both further her career and her distance herself from me, she packed up, left home and headed up north for a new job at Aberdeen Royal Infirmary. The plan was to get settled, find herself a suitable home in or around Aberdeen then we could discuss and decide the best option for our young son. It took Alison a year or so to effectively get herself plumbed into the social network of her new job and surroundings; by this time Lee was settled living with me and being looked after by Alison's parents when I was working, which was pretty much all the time. Although the boy visited his mother several times a month, he preferred the status quo and so, remained in my custody and care.

Chapter 5

Bright and early next day I set off on phase one of
my quest: to find the elusive Andy Brookes. I
found the guitar shop easily enough nestled
between a phone shop and a pound store on
Corporation Street. Above the row of terraced
shops stood some austere looking red brick
buildings gazing down with disapproval on the
street below. These streets had no doubt changed
considerably since the time their red bricks were
carefully cemented into place by skilled and
diligent workmen well over a century ago.

My heart began to quicken its pace and those
pet butterflies I kept in my stomach began their
frenzied dance, as I pushed open the door to
Brookes Guitar Emporium. An old fashioned bell
pinged as I entered; strange, I thought given the
nature of the ultra modern goods on sale, I
thought they would at least have installed an
electronic door-opening alert.

I smiled as my eyes took in a veritable variety
of stringed wooden wonders; this was my kind of
place. I didn't care how long this task took, as I
was in no hurry to leave. I could gaze upon these
guitar models for hours on end. It would be a
bonus if I got the opportunity to play any of them.
The inside looked exactly like the website pages,
so I knew I was in the right place.

I strolled past the wall of guitars which seemed
to represent all makes and models I had ever
heard of, plus a few I hadn't. From *Fender* to
Fernandez; *Gibson* to *Gretsch* and *Martin* to
Musicman, the discerning guitarist had no
shortage of choice. I admired the shiny finish on

the guitar bodies but balked at the high price tags, but I supposed Mr Brookes, whoever he was, had to pay his rent and rates.

The shop was pretty quiet although I was not the only patron gracing the place with their presence. A young girl with an older man browsed the acoustic guitars. Perhaps the man was the girl's father about to part with some money to buy his daughter a means to fame and fortune. A middle aged baldy man milled around gazing up at a Gibson Les Paul: it looked resplendent in an attractive, shiny lacquered sunburst finish. I didn't blame the guy his coveting look – it was a beauty; pity about its £1500 price tag. By the looks of the guy, he would never be able to afford this item, not unless he re-mortgaged his house or spent the next ten years paying it up on some pricing plan with exorbitant interest rate.

'Hi, how are you today?' asked a voice behind me. I had anticipated this moment with dread. It never takes long before your contented browsing is interrupted by some nosey salesperson wanting dearly to be your best friend and lighten the load in you wallet. It always seemed to happen: when you want an assistant, there's none to be found; then when you want peace and quiet to browse, their all around you like a herd of hungry midges on a humid evening.

I turned around to face a pimply long haired young guy. He smiled showing shiny braces binding his teeth. He wore a plethora of ear-rings on every conceivable part of his left ear. I wondered how much this guy had forked out in the past to have someone stick needles into his flesh like a kebab.

'I'm fine,' I replied returning his smile. I looked down at his name badge which announced the salesman as 'Wayne'. He was sporting a black *Megadeath* t-shirt and tight jeans and looked every inch the clichéd guitar salesman.

'Can I help you with anything?' Wayne said as he gestured around the shop as though he was king and this was his domain. 'If you want to try anything, just give me a shout,' I nodded at this suggestion and turned back to resume my browsing. To my annoyance, Wayne didn't move away to pester any of the other customers and remained close behind me like a bodyguard. Every guitar I looked at, Wayne would launch into a spiel telling me everything I never knew about the make and model – from its pickup configuration to how low the playing action was. He even gave me a breakdown on the monthly payments if I chose to buy the instrument on a payment plan which, no doubt, he was keen to scoop the commission.

My new found friend never left my side, but I endured him; I didn't want to fall out with the guy as no doubt I would need him soon. Unbeknown to Wayne, he had now become part of Operation Lazarus. Now was the time to ply him for information, pertinent to my mission.

'So how long have you worked here, Wayne?'

'A couple of years, since leaving school,' he sang in his thick Brummie accent.

'It must be great working here?' I said.

Wayne nodded his head so vigorously, I thought it may detach and fall off.

'Totally awesome job, man,' he beamed, 'I get to play all these guitars for free!'

I faked looking impressed. I doubted the manager would let young Wayne here loose with a guitar worth thousands, for fear he scratched the finish forcing the price down by a few hundred quid. Then I launched my probing question:

'So do you own this guitar shop, Wayne?'

'No way, man. I'd love to. Maybe some day eh?' Wayne was now excited at this prospect and beamed like a prize winner.

'So owns the place then?' I ventured.

Wayne then changed; it was so blindingly obvious I had said something taboo. He suddenly averted eye contact with me and became interested in the other customers still milling around.

'The manager is Mr Brookes,' he answered a tad too dismissively, I thought.

I picked up a *Stratocaster* from a stand on the floor, crouched down and began to strum the instrument; this was a cover to make my questioning as innocent and nonchalant as possible.

'Andy Brookes?' I asked as I looked up at Wayne watching for a reaction.

Bingo – my new mate revealed his hand like a bad poker player. He avoided eye contact and shuffled around trying to look confused; he was clearly uncomfortable.

'Yeah, that's his name. If you don't mind, I'll leave you to it.' With that he hurried off to see if his services were needed with the girl and man, still undecided on which acoustic guitar would suit.

I reckoned I knew what was going on here; my theory was thus: Andy Brookes, the guitar genius with the Faceless Legions owned this shop, but in order to remain anonymous and live a quiet life away from the constant probing of nosey parkers, had instructed his staff to fend off the question of his true identity. This was exactly what happened with Wayne. He was happy to talk until I chanced upon the query of the shop's ownership, and Wayne had panicked and fled before I could probe even further.

In my career with the police, and especially as a detective with CID, I had faced many an obstinate person. But I had the skills, training and experience to know when they were telling the truth and how to get them talking if they decided on the 'no comment' strategy. I never believed in the clichéd 'good cop, bad cop' routine; this seldom works expect in the movies, and suspects everywhere seem to know that. No, I employed all my charm and friendliness to gently coax out what I wanted to hear and it worked most of the time.

I recalled a housebreaker I once arrested. He was interviewed under tape recorded conditions and was adamant he was not talking to me or my colleague.

'Can you tell me where you were about 5 o'clock this morning?'

'No comment.'

'Were you in the vicinity of Melrose Court then?'

'No comment.'

'Did you break the window to, and enter the dwelling of number 78 Melrose Court?'

'No comment.'

'Did you steal a quantity of jewellery and games console from this dwelling?'

'No comment.'

Then I went in for the kill.

'You also lifted a set of car keys on your way out. Why didn't you steal their car?'

My suspect sat bolt upright in his plastic chair, his eyes bulging, and fists clenched tightly.

'I never stole their car keys. I didn't want to nick their car.'

I smiled at how well my trap had worked. As if a light switch had suddenly been flicked to on, my suspect realised his error and shook his head in disgust. He hunched up in embarrassment and his face fell as he envisioned a few years of quiet contemplation at Her Majesty's pleasure. Just that sneaky false question was enough to bring him out of his obstinate trance and he handed me his confession on a platter. He was duly convicted and spent some quality time in HMP Barlinie.

I stood below the famous *Fender* 'Nocaster' and gazed up at it as though it was a gold idol. This was indeed the one I saw in the photo on their website, and the main motive for bringing me here today. Wayne saw me looking at it and I gestured for him to come over. He had no other customers at the moment demanding his advice, so he had no choice but to saunter over to see what other awkward questions I may have for him.

'Wayne, this guitar,' I said gesturing to the 'Nocaster,' 'was owned by a famous guitarist, ironically called Andy Brookes.'
Wayne once again did his little nervous shuffle and looked for a means of escape. Sensing the inevitable, he nodded slowly.

'Yeah, Andy Brookes used to be a famous guitarist.'

'The Andy Brookes of the Faceless Legions?' I probed.

'Yeah, the same guy,' Wayne admitted before hastily adding, 'but he doesn't like to talk about it.'

This was a result. Now the next phase would involve trying meet the shy and private Andy Brookes, and more importantly, could my long-haired multi-pierced friend help me realise my dream?

'Oh I respect that, Wayne,' I said attempting to finesse him into submission. 'What's the chances of meeting him, just for a moment?' Wayne was quick with his come back.

'Nah, he doesn't want to talk about his past.'

'Well what about talking to me in his managerial capacity?' Wayne's confused look forced me to elaborate.

'Wayne, I'd like to speak to your manager, please. Will you go get him?' Wayne looked like a deer caught in a trap and surrounded by his captors; escape was pointless and he might as well just give in. He played with his long hair, twisting strands around his fingers whilst pondering the dilemma.

'I'll go and see if he's busy,' he said and trundled off towards a door marked 'Private'.

I was performing a rapid run of pentatonic scales on a *Jackson Performer* when my new buddy returned looking all flustered and red faced. I knew exactly what would have gone on in that private office, something like this:

Wayne: 'Boss, there's someone wanting to see you.'

Andy: 'What's it about?'

Wayne: 'Well he actually wants to speak about the Faceless Legions.'

Andy: 'I've told you Wayne, I don't want to speak about that. Get rid of him.'

Wayne: 'I've tried and he insists on speaking to you.'

Andy: 'Why did you tell him I was in the Faceless Legions?'

Wayne: 'I didn't. He just guessed.'

Andy: 'You must have let slip, surely?'

Wayne: 'No, honestly. He knows your name and he saw your 'Nocaster' on the wall.'

Andy: 'Tell him I'm really busy and can't see him.'

Wayne: 'I'll try, but I don't think it'll work.'

'The boss is dead busy and can't see you today,' Wayne lied.

'Oh come on, Wayne. I know exactly what's happening here,' I answered, 'go get him and I'll not keep him long, I promise.' Wayne stood still as a statue and refused to budge, just like stubborn mule. I reckoned he needed a bit more encouragement.

'Come on Wayne. I've come all the way down from Scotland to meet Andy Brookes and I can't go back home until I've done that.' Wayne sighed and headed back to the office to deliver the tidings of joy to his boss.

I placed the *Jackson* back on its stand and selected a *BC Rich Gunslinger* to try next. I glanced over to the office; the door was closed. I wondered how Wayne was getting on now. If I was Andy Brookes, I would give in and give this Scotsman five minutes of his time then throw him out. I was caressing the low action and smooth maple fret-board of the *Gunslinger* when I could hear voices behind me. I was half expecting to have hands laid on me and swiftly frogmarched out the door and thrown into Corporation Street. Instead, I got the shock of my life.

Chapter 6

Standing next to the *Megadeath* t-shirt wearing Wayne, was a small dumpy man with a rather large belly and heavily receding hair on top with straggly shoulder length hair at the back. He approached me looking like he wanted to hit me over the head with a baseball bat. I rose to my full six foot four inch height and the dwarf-like man backed off slightly. Then he smiled and extended his hand towards me.

'Andy Brookes. I'm the manager. How can I help you?' his accent was unmistakable Brummie and as thick as ever. Wayne stood behind the bulk of his boss as though frightened to come out from hiding.

I introduced myself and returned his shake. If I was to get any kind of quality time with this guy, I would have to tread gently. I looked at Brookes as though trying to work out if he really was the guitar guru and one of my all-time heroes. There was something familiar about him. The face, although weathered with age and no doubt stress, had not changed drastically. I could see it was

The Andy Brookes. But his height; or more precisely, lack of? Then I remembered the time I was on stage with the band at the Glasgow Apollo singing along with Danny Carter. I was surprised at the height of Brookes; he always appeared taller when on posters, album covers and promotional materials, but maybe this was just an illusion.

'Hi, I'm Tony Caulfield. Thanks for seeing me. Do you have a minute for a quick chat Andy?' I asked looking hopeful. Andy sized me up and, content I was not a raving lunatic nor deranged fan agreed to my request and ushered me towards a soundproof practice room. Fantastic, now I would be able to talk in private, and possibly for a reasonable length of time. Wayne looked visibly relieved that there had been a peaceful end to a potential drama and slinked off towards a new customer to irritate.

Andy slid the soundproof door closed and we sat down on a comfortable sofa.

'So you really are the famous Andy Brookes of the Faceless Legions?' I asked.

'Yup, that's me, for my sins.'

'It's a great honour Andy. I've always been a big fan, well in my days of youth, you know?'

Andy nodded knowingly.

'So whatever happened to the Faceless Legions anyway, Andy?' I said.

Brookes shook his head slowly as though he had answered this question countless times and could not muster the energy nor enthusiasm to speak. He let out a long slow breath before answering.

'We, eh, just went our separate ways.'

'Yeah, but none of you ever joined or formed other bands. You all just disappeared as it were.'

Andy just shrugged, his head still shaking as though this trip down memory lane was more than he could handle.

'I can't speak for the other guys. Personally, I just had had enough of the,' here he searched for the right word or phrase to sum up his experience, 'rock and roll lifestyle.'

I nodded in agreement. I hadn't actually planned on what I would say to, or ask Andy in this situation, so I just used my years of interviewing techniques - and winged it.

'So why are you effectively hiding, or keeping a low profile?' I asked, leaning forward to get comfortable in my seat. 'Surely the fact a famous guitarist owns a guitar shop would be a great selling point?'

Andy shook his head once again; I feared he may go home tonight with a painful neck.

'I'm quite a private guy. I like my privacy.' Here he paused for emphasis, 'I've had enough of people asking the same old questions and saying the same old boring stuff. Don't get me wrong, I enjoy playing guitar, but when we got big, that's when my privacy got invaded and I hated that.'

'Most artists thrive on fame, but I suppose it would be an inconvenience as well,' I commented. Andy chuckled at this observation.

'Yeah, you're right. It was an inconvenience. I just wanted to play my guitar in a band, make a living out of it and go home at night happy.'

'So that's why you disappeared and tried to lie low?' I asked; He nodded in agreement.

'Yeah, I just wanted my private life back. Hey, I'm not complaining; I made a tidy fortune out of

being in the Legions and it has bought all this.'
He extended his hands in a sweeping motion to
indicate his guitar emporium; his domain.

'Oh yeah, I totally get that Andy,' I said.

At this, he looked down at his watch as a
subtle indication that our meeting was now over.

'Sure, I don't want to detain you. I know you
are a busy man,' I observed as I rose from the
sofa in tandem with Andy.

'Listen Andy, it was great talking to you, but
I'd like to chat a wee but more if that's okay with
you?' I asked with a hint of pleading in my voice.

'Maybe we could go for a coffee or a drink
once you've finished work?'

Andy thought about this before nodding in
agreement.

'Yeah, I suppose. I could meet you in the
Wetherspoons on the corner.' He indicated in the
direction of the pub, 'Say about 6:15?'

'That's perfect Andy, thanks.' We shook
hands like long lost mates and I left the store a
happy man.

I was elated at finally achieving my goal – or
at least part of it anyway. I had tracked down and
met the guitarist of one of my favourite rock
bands of all time. But the next phase would be a
tad difficult. I had to persuade Mr Brookes to
reunite with the rest of band if and when I
managed to trace them. For this he would have to
forego his privacy and step back into the
limelight.

I ate lunch in a small café and powered up my
laptop taking advantage of the café's free *Wi-Fi*
service. Again I searched for any snippet of
information which would cast light on the
whereabouts of the other missing members, with

the exception of the now deceased Hannagan. Judging by Brookes' reaction, I didn't think he had any clue of the whereabouts of his former band-mates. It seemed none of them kept in touch.

I carried out a search on *Ebay* and *Amazon* to see if anything of significance surfaced, as I munched on a coronation chicken panini.

A couple of vintage music magazines featuring interviews with the Faceless Legions appeared on the *Ebay* search. They were on a 'buy it now' listing for only £5 each plus postage. I didn't know if they would be of any use to me, but every little helps and it certainly wouldn't break the bank. I purchased the two publications and paid through my *PayPal* account.

I recalled how I once traced a missing girl after trawling through all manner of diaries, newspaper cuttings and scrap books. We had quite a team on the task searching high and low for the vulnerable teen and we were getting nowhere; it seemed she had simply vanished off the face of the earth. Officer's visited all family members, friends and associates, but to no avail. I was a detective constable at the time and spent hours in the girl's bedroom with my sergeant searching for any fragment of information or hint of a clue. Eventually I pieced together snippets from her personal belongings and diary entries, and traced her to an address in Northumbria. The girl had wanted to meet her long lost Grandfather and so set about tracing him. She eventually located him, and in an attempt to escape her tyrannical and abusive mother, she sought sanctuary with her newly-acquainted relative.

I was congratulated on my expert detective skills in managing to piece the fragments together to form a cohesive picture of the girl's recent movements and intentions. My sergeant said that promotion would be inevitable if I kept up this level of commitment to the job and honed my impressive skill base.

I selected a table in a strategic position where I could keep an eye on the door. The layout of the place was typically *Wetherspoons*. This one had a high ceiling with retro lampshades dangling down but not giving off much light. The walls were a garish maroon colour and the painters had gone to town by adding all manner of decorative touches to the borders and walls, trying to make it look like a palace or similar. On the floor was the most hideous carpet I had ever seen; it looked like something out of an Escher drawing. Its wild interlocking geometric patterns stood out like a stereoscopic picture. Just staring down at it for a few seconds gave me a headache.

The place was not overly busy, but I suspected it may start to fill up soon now that the working day was drawing to a close. The odd table near me was occupied by couples talking about their jobs; another table had four burly workers hunched around it; they had obviously just come straight off the building sight – their clothes and footwear were filthy and I could see their grimy unwashed hands as they gripped their lagers.

I looked at my watch – it was 6:15pm. My gaze switched to the main door and could see no trace of Mr Brookes. I supped my drink and surveyed the other patrons. A couple of loners like me sat at tables alone and played on their phones. A couple sat at a table just off to my left. Although they had probably met to spend some quality time with each other, both sat, heads down and fingers running frantically up, down and across the screens of their mobile phones. They hardly looked at, nor acknowledged each other. It appeared that their virtual mates got more attention than they gave to each other.

I examined my wrist yet again: the time was now 6:30pm and Andy was still a 'no show'. Perhaps he had stood me up. Maybe he had a change of heart and decided that he had had enough of his journey into the past for one day. Then the main door opened and Brookes waddled in. I waved to him; he acknowledged and came towards me. He was out of breath, possibly after rushing to get here, or maybe it was just all the weight he had piled on in recent years.

'Sorry I'm late; had a few admin things to sort out before closing up.'

'That's okay. I understand,' I replied, relieved and happy to see the guy again.

I indicated to the watching waiter and he bounded over to our table. Andy ordered his drink and I indicated I didn't need of a replacement at the moment. The waiter nodded and hurried away towards the well stocked bar.

'So what else do you need to know, Terry?' Andy began. I corrected him on the name; he looked slightly embarrassed, apologised and slumped back in his seat.

I then launched into my story about how I was a retired detective and hit upon a crazy notion to track down the elusive members of the Faceless Legions. Andy chuckled at this, shaking his head

59

as though in full agreement at my peculiar quest. I felt the need to clarify my actions.

'You see I needed a project to keep me occupied, otherwise I may go off my head.'

'And you chose us as a project?' Andy said.

'Well I was sorting through some photos and some of them reminded me of the Legions. In fact, I met my future wife at one of your gigs at the Glasgow Apollo.'

Andy closed his eyes and tried to picture the venue. He nodded perceptibly as he recalled the former famous Glasgow concert venue.

'The Apollo! You know we all hated that high stage.' I nodded my agreement; I had heard many a musician complain about that stage.

'So that's my mission, Andy,' I said sounding professional, 'to track you guys down and find out what happened, and how none of you ever made it big again.'

'How have you done so far?' Brookes asked.

'Well you're the first, actually,' I admitted.

'So how did you find me?'

'Brookes Guitar Emporium – that was the place to start. I remembered you were from Birmingham and figured you might still be here. Plus I know you were a big collector of guitars – so I put two and two together and my hunch paid off.' Actually the 'Nocaster' was a very big clue – in fact, the clincher, but he really didn't need to know that.

Andy smiled at my ingenuity and fine detective skills; he looked suitably impressed. He took another drink from his beer, then lent forward and looked me in the eye.

'How are you gonna' find the others, then?'

I spread my palms out to indicate my lack of progress in that department.

'I was hoping you might be able to shed some light on the whereabouts of the others.'

'Haven't a clue, mate. Sorry,' Andy said shaking his head in disappointment.

'So you never stayed in touch or had any contact with each other since the split-up?'

'Nope. I think we were all happy to be going our separate ways. None of us were interested in swapping phone numbers or stuff,' Andy recalled.

'You know Chas Hannagan passed away, right?' I said. Andy nodded, knowingly.

'I think his son plays bass guitar, I remember hearing something after the funeral,' Andy informed me. This was interesting news. Perhaps the son might be as suitable replacement for his father.

We spent the next half hour talking about the former band, but Andy could offer no further information of interest.

'So where do you go from here?' He enquired as he supped from his glass, leaving a white frothy moustache.

'Don't know really. I might dig around a little to see if I can find Danny.'

Andy looked pensive, desperate to recall something which may be of use to me and my quest.

'Danny used to go out with a girl from Scotland; from one of the islands I think.' I looked only slightly interested. I didn't think this morsel would be of much use. He had more to say.

'He was always heading up to Scotland when we had time off. He would come back raving about how lovely the place was and how he could see himself settling down there someday.'

Now this really was interesting. I tried to coax more from him, now that he was on a roll.

'Have you any idea where in Scotland; one of the islands you said?' His head shook.

'Sorry, I have no idea. I don't know much about the Scottish isles. He said it was way up north.' His hand came up to his face and he stroked his chin in a pensive manner attempting to tease a further fragment from his memory.

'I remember reading somewhere that he married the Scottish lass, so maybe he settled down up there. You can maybe start your search there?'

This was an interesting development, and he was right – this was a good place to start – after all I had nothing else. I thanked him for his efforts, and then decided on addressing the next issue. I sat back in my chair and hit him with the killer question.

'As well as tracking you guys down, I also wanted to talk you into reforming as a band for one last reunion gig.' I awaited his reaction. As usual he shook his head. His bushy shoulder length hair fluttered.

'I doubt that will ever happen,' was his negative reply.

Chapter 7

I was cruising along the M74 heading back home and I recalled the conversation with guitar guru

Brookes last night. His reckoning was: should I be successful in finding the other lost members of the Legions, the chances of getting everyone back on stage as a band were extremely slim. His distinct and lasting impression way back in 1979 when the band split, was that they had all had enough of each other and would die content if they never crossed paths in the future. Given the decades which had now passed and still no contact between each other, I was beginning to see his view of things, and share his pessimism. But I still had to try. This was my mission and I would see it through; I knew it wasn't going to be easy.

'Would you be up for reuniting as a band if the others were game?' I had put to Andy. He agreed he would definitely be interested if the virtually impossible happened, but I could see he wasn't holding his breath. Andy and I parted company as best of friends and we swapped mobile phone numbers promising to keep in touch and pass on any information if and when it became available.

When I drew into and parked the *Hyundai* in my driveway, it was starting to get dark. I extracted my holdall from the boot and entered my home. I stood on a pile of mail scattered over the hallway just behind the door. I had only been away for two days and I came back to a pile of mail, most of it junk by the looks of it.

I wasted no time in firing up the laptop and launching my research into the whereabouts of Danny Carter. It was a stroke of good fortune Andy's sudden and belated recall of Carter's connection with some Scottish island or other. I looked at a map of the northern part of Scotland: there were a lot of islands. The reference to a

Scottish island was quite vague – it could be the Isle of Arran located in the Firth of Clyde or perhaps the nearby Island of Bute. I pondered and recalled Andy's reference to 'way up north'. Surely this narrowed it down a bit and ruled out islands in the Firth of Clyde area – they could never be referred to 'way up north', being only a stones-throw from Glasgow. But even narrowing the search down still presented a great many islands: the Orkney Islands; the Shetland Islands; Isle of a Skye and all the islands which made up the Western Isles including the Isle of Lewis, Uist and Barra; so much choice and so little clue on where to begin. According to a website entry, Scotland has over 790 offshore islands; this was an interesting and unknown fact to me, despite being a native of this country all my life. The thought of this mammoth task made me thirsty so I headed to the kitchen to fill and boil the kettle.

As I was filling my mug with coffee, I deliberated this conundrum. What would a guy like Danny Carter be doing on a Scottish Island? What would he settle down to do? I knew he was London born and bred, so to move to the relative tranquillity of an off-shore island was curious. My impression of him was that of a showman; an extrovert; and I couldn't imagine Danny herding sheep or performing game-keeping duties to some Lord of the manor. Surely this narrowed the choice down somewhat – to an island nearer to the mainland; one in which civilisation would be easily accessible? If Danny regularly made trips 'way up north', I assumed he drove. I'm sure Brookes would have stated if he took a plane. So did this exclude the more distant Orkneys,

Shetlands and Western Isles? I hoped so, as this would make my search a little bit easier.

I poured over the map of Scotland again. If I excluded the aforementioned island groups from my search and also ignored the islands not being considered 'way up north', then I was left with a much smaller and more manageable area; that left me with the Islands of Mull, Skye and Islay. I wondered if Mr Carter was residing happily on one of these places.

I performed a search of the surname Carter with a few telephone directory search engines, and one revealed a Carter in Portree on the Isle of Skye. I zoomed in on Portree in an effort to narrow my search further. I spent the next hour searching for any reference to the surname Carter in or around the town of Portree, before feeling my thumping heart race when I was informed that a bed and breakfast establishment just outside Portree was owned by a Mr and Mrs D. Carter. Could this be a result or a false start? I checked out photos of the Tigh-na-Bain bed and breakfast establishment. It showed exterior shots of the building and a few of the various rooms including the lounge and dining room; but nothing showed the proprietors of the place; nothing hinted at having any connection with the Danny Carter formerly of the Faceless Legions. I decided to give them a ring and see if I could ascertain anything over the phone.

'Hallo, Tigh-na-Bain bed and breakfast. Shona speaking,' announced a pleasant sing-song Scottish female voice.

I enquired about a room for a couple of nights in the next day or two, but Shona disappointed me almost immediately by telling me she was fully booked and would have no vacancies for the next few weeks, on account of a 'large group of American tourists' who had chosen Tigh-na-Bain for their stay. I expressed my disappointment as though her B&B was the place I had my heart set on, and no other would do.

'You could try the Kingarth Hotel,' Shona suggested, then proceed to rattle off the phone number of the hotel. I thanked her and was dying to come right out and ask her if she was married to Danny, but didn't think it prudent to do so. Besides it may just scare Danny off if he was indeed living here. I knew how elusive Andy Brookes had been to meet with, so Danny might just have the same idea. I made a reservation at the recommended Kingarth Hotel and was in luck – they were able to accommodate me for a couple of days and looked forward to seeing me. Field trip number two was about to get underway.

Those photos of a young Alison prompted me to yet another wild notion and I decided to call her next. I had weighed up all the pros and cons of doing this on my long laborious journey back from Birmingham. I was excited about having made a success in tracing and meeting one of the members of the Legions, and I thought she'd be impressed and want to know about it. Whenever we went to a Faceless Legions gig, Alison would continually speak about wishing to meet the band and we discussed how to go about getting hold of a backstage pass. Neither of us knew the procedure in obtaining such a thing, so we just dreamed on.

I remember one gig at the Edinburgh Playhouse; right after the band had performed their very last encore and everyone knew they wouldn't be back out; Alison grabbed me and hurried me out of the hall before the majority of fans joined us. We raced around to the backstage door where we gathered with a crowd of eager fans all wanting a glimpse of their idols. Every time the door opened the crowds would erupt into excited cheering, eyes glued to the doorway to see which one of the Legions was coming out to shake hands and sign autographs. Each and every time, it turned out to be a roadie or someone else totally irrelevant and the disappointed atmosphere was almost tangible. We must have stood there for nearly an hour along with the other sad hopefuls before having to run up Leith Walk to Waverly train station to catch our train home.

So Alison never got to meet her idols and was always raving about some lucky fan who happened to bump into the band and then get themselves invited to tea with them. She even joined the fan club hoping this would be an easy way through the backstage door, but of course, that was easier said than done.

I found her home phone number in an old dog-eared phone book in a drawer, but was unsure if this was her current number. Given the state of the book, it was a good chance she had since changed her number, but I would try it anyway. I had other ways to find out her correct number if this failed. Lee could supply it, no doubt.

I dialled the Aberdeen number and it rang out a few times before going onto the answer service inviting me to leave a message – I declined the offer as I wanted to speak directly to Alison and not a machine. Besides, she might panic if I left a message, not having spoken to her in years. She might think I was phoning with news of the death of a family member. I would just call back later.

I emptied my holdall, tossing my worn clothes into the washing machine, and filled the bag with more clothes for my next trip. I had booked two nights at the hotel on Skye although I didn't know how long my trip would take. I hadn't a clue how I was going to go about checking if Danny Carter lived at the Tigh-na-Bain B&B. It's not as if I could just waltz up to the front door and ask if Danny from the Faceless Legions lives here. If he was being as private as his former band-mate Brookes, he wouldn't make it easy for crazy stalkers like me to find or identify him.

I eventually got a live Alison on the phone, and she sounded confused as to my call. In fact I had to tell her who is was as she seemed to have forgotten she used to be married to me.

'Hi, how are you Tony?' she asked. 'Is everything all right?'

'Yeah, everything's fine. Just thought I'd give you a ring that's all,' I replied. She still sounded hesitant as though expecting me to impart some sad news. I felt the need to clarify and put her mind at ease.

'I was cleaning out the cupboard in the hall and I found the old vanity case full of photos,' I explained. 'There were lots of us when we first met and they just reminded me to give you a call to see how you were.' She seemed more at ease now that I had offered a genuine explanation.

'So how are things; how is retirement?' Alison enquired.

'Yeah, things are fine. To be honest, I'm getting a tad bored being retired though.' I was easing gently into telling her about Operation Lazarus.

'I thought you would have loads of time on your hands. Time to do anything you want?' Alison said, but not sarcastically.

'Well that's the problem – nothing to do and all day to do it!' She laughed at my cliché and sounded relaxed. Then I decided to tell her all; she can think me a nut of she wished.

I revealed all my planning and phases of the operation, plus the fact I had actually met the renowned Andy Brookes.

'No way. I can't believe you met Andy Brookes,' she exclaimed excitedly, 'wish I had been with you.'

I told her I was now about to embark upon the next phase – to find Danny Carter, and she whooped like an excited child at this prospect.

'Look I'm going up to Skye for a couple of days tomorrow; maybe we could meet up when I'm done?' I chanced. Alison rose like a trout to the fly.

'Yeah, that would be great. It would fantastic to see you again.'

'Great. I'll tell you all about my meeting with Brookes when I see you.'

Alison gave me her address and mobile number and I promised to phone her when I was on my way back from Skye. It was really good to speak to her and I got the distinct impression she enjoyed hearing my voice. At least she didn't laugh at my quest to hunt down the missing Legions; in fact she seemed almost as enthusiastic as me.

Chapter 8

The drive 'way up north' was a pleasant and scenic one. The route took me up the side of Loch Lomond – 'the largest inland stretch of water in Britain by surface area' being its claim to fame. This was the route Alison and I regularly took in the winter when we would set off early in the morning and head up to Glen Coe for a spot of skiing. Our skiing was laughable though, and we spend more time lying spread-eagled on the snow, one ski still attached to a foot, the other half way up the slope. Those were the days when we spend a lot of time together and really enjoyed the company of one another.

As usual for this scenic area of Scotland, the tourists were out in their hordes. Buses stopped by the wayside and disgorged dozens of stiff and weary passengers into restaurants, whisky distilleries and bagpipe makers. I spotted a few hired cars being cautiously driven, probably by elderly American couples, totally unsure of the rules of the road and wondering 'Why these stupid Brits had to drive on the left hand side.'

To my left were boats cruising up and down the loch; some of them privately owned yachts and some commercial tourist boats offering to show you the sights of the Trossachs National Park for an outrageous fee which virtually every gullible tourist seemed happy enough to pay. The sight of a large private motor yacht reminded me of a call I once attended in my capacity as Detective Constable.

The owner of a gigantic private yacht - supposedly valued at over two million pounds wished to report that his boat had been broken into and items stolen. I drove to the marina and, after a period of frustrated driving around trying to find this particular boat, I located it and went aboard, along with my colleague. We were floored by its immense size and bowled over when we entered the interior. It was a veritable floating five star hotel. Plush teak wooden panels adorned the walls and the pristine paintwork was immaculate. The couple who owned the boat welcomed us aboard, shaking our hands like we were business partners. They gave us a tour of the boat, all two floors, pointing out the myriad rooms and storage areas where you could live comfortably for months at sea; this thing was bigger than my entire house.

The couple were exactly as you would expect being millionaire boat-owners and predictably dressed to match, both in their late sixties. He sported a handlebar moustache, slicked back hair and wore expensive looking chinos and designer shirt. His wife sported a designer leisure suit, her greying hair big and bushy sat atop a suntanned, though heavily made up face. Curiously, both wore what looked like a cheap pair of blue and white canvas deck shoes; maybe *Dolce and Gabbana* didn't make expensive deck shoes and the couple were forced to shop at *Shoe Zone*.

Mr Millionaire then pointed out the point of entry the rascals had used to enter his ship. The forward starboard side porthole had been forced open and the perpetrator had squeezed in, and then gave himself a tour of the boat. He had helped himself to the liquor cabinet and pantry before attempting to free and steal the life boat, which Mrs Millionaire informed us, was worth 'many thousands of pounds'.

Having no luck untying the plethora of knots and locks in the dark, the scallywag had left the boat, probably by the same entry point. I examined the interior in detail and could see a multitude of fingerprints, footprints and most probably DNA on the discarded bottles of whisky and wine. When I requested the couple did not touch anything until a full scenes of crime examination was carried out, they looked at me horrified, as though I had just asked them to donate their entire fortune to charity.

'We can't refrain from touching our own vessel,' exclaimed the man, shaking his head as to a wayward child.

'What do you mean scenes of crime examination; what does that entail?' asked his wife, sounding like she had a mouthful of marbles.

I patently explained the procedure: that a team of highly trained personnel would descend upon their boat and carry out a thorough examination, and gather the necessary evidence which should secure a detection and subsequent prosecution of the nefarious perpetrators. Once again, the millionaire couple stared bewilderedly at me as though I had suggested hiring their vessel for a booze-cruise.

'What will that involve?' asked the husband cautiously.

'Well they'll dust for fingerprints on all surfaces, check for DNA, photograph the scene and attempt to lift a copy of the shoeprint,' I explained. At this they both looked like I had tazered them; the shocked look on their faces was worrying.

'No, no, no,' pleaded the husband, 'we can't have that.'

With that he dismissed us from his boat and told us to forget the whole thing. He probably didn't fancy a team of police agents messing around on his craft, trampling muddy boots all over his expensive carpets, sniffing around his private places and making an almighty mess with fingerprint powder. So that was it – he decided not to report the crime after all just because it may entail a bit of inconvenience!

We called into the security office on our way out of the marina just to check but, typically, no night watchman or sophisticated CCTV system saw a thing!

I stopped off in Fort William to have lunch, this being just over half way to my destination, as I estimated. I spend the rest of the journey, half admiring the awesome views of the magnificent scenery – from the Grampian mountains rising majestically from dense glens and forests to the regular sighting of lochs and sea inlets; and pondering how I would go about trying to ascertain if the Mr D. Carter of the Tigh-na-Bain B&B was indeed my man.

After Fort William, I continued on the A82 up towards Invergarry and then swung a westerly course onto the A87 all the way to Kyle of Lochalsh where the Skye Bridge was waiting for me. This concrete non-descript structure looked like a giant hump-backed bridge, and was the home straight for me – my destination of Portree only about thirty five miles away. I really should have had the old Scottish folk song *Speed bonnie boat, like a bird on the wing; over the sea to Skye,* playing on my car stereo; instead I had the Faceless Legions belting out at considerable volume, just to get me in the mood.

'Hello and welcome to the Kingarth Hotel,' sang the middle aged receptionist. She smiled what I guessed was a genuine smile, and revealed a mouth of almost perfectly white teeth, which seemed all that bit whiter given her suntanned face. Either this part of Scotland got more than its fair share of sunshine, or this dear was heavily into sun-beds. She was attired in an immaculately pressed bright tartan waste coat over a white open collar blouse, matching tartan skirt and even a tartan bow in her hair. I supposed the management of the hotel were wanting to appear traditional after all, this being just what the tourists want and expect, but it seemed a bit clichéd to be dressed all in tartan just because they worked in a Scottish hotel. After all, I wondered if you would find a receptionist dressed in lederhosen in Germany, a Leprechaun look-alike staffing an Irish hotel, or a hotel manager dressed as an Eskimo in Greenland; I doubted it.

I furnished my tartan friend with my details and she clicked away like mad on her keyboard, looking up occasionally from me to her screen. Then she handed me an old fashioned set of keys with a wooden key ring in the shape of a bottle of whiskey. This place was bound to get bonus points from the Scottish Tourist Board for sheer effort.

Formalities over, I climbed the staircase to my room, entered and flopped onto the bed. As usual, tartan was also the theme of the room: the bed-spread was a horrible dark brown tartan to match the equally drab curtains. Although the room was spotless, it smelled of cleaning fluids and *Shake 'n' Vac*. I was feeling drained after my long, though interesting drive up from Glasgow. Scotland was a bigger place than most folk think.

I wasted no time; after a short spell of rest and recuperation on the firm but comfortable bed, I was back in my car and priming the satnav to guide me to the Tigh-na-Bain. I had decided I would attend and pose as a tourist looking for a room for the night – even although I knew they had no vacancies.

The B&B owned by the ominous Carter's was only a short drive away and just a mile or two outside Portree. I drove past rows of quaint, brightly coloured houses, looking like larger versions of doll's houses; from vibrant pink, bright blue and garish green to a multicoloured building sporting a range of colours including yellow and orange. It seemed the entire spectrum was represented here. The rows overlooked an idyllic harbour with the occasional moored boat bobbing up and down in the gentle swell.

I located the B&B and pulled into the car-park. I was presented with a large sign warning me that parking was for residents only and I was liable to have my car towed away should I fail to comply. Yeah, I thought, I bet that happens regularly!

My heart was beginning to speed up as I locked my car and walked towards the front door of the Tigh-na-Bain. It was a detached functional looking dwelling with pristine whitewashed walls and matt black roof. Mahogany window frames and doors gave it an air of elegance. A wooden hand-carved sign with the dwelling's name was attached to the side of the building.

I pushed the open door and went inside. Typically it smelled like a B&B: the persistent lingering of cooking was heavy in the air and the place was toasty-warm.

I approached the small reception counter which was un-staffed, and tapped the bell to indicate my presence and request attention. One ping and a smiling woman appeared through the door behind the desk. Either she was working just behind the door as I entered, or she had spotted me driving in and was ready to pounce.

'Hello there and welcome to the Tigh-na-Bain bed and breakfast,' said the middle aged lady. The voice sounded familiar and I guessed this was Shona, whom I spoke to on the phone yesterday. I thought of disguising my voice slightly to throw off any scent, but figured Shona probably heard hundreds of voices every day, and would be unlikely to recognise my particular timbre.

'Hi. I've just come up from Glasgow and was wondering if you had a room for a night or two?' I enquired, feigning mock tiredness as though the journey had been overwhelming.

Shona frowned showing a mass of wrinkles on her face. Her long blonde, but rapidly greying centre-parted hair, accentuated her pleasant features. A streak of hair slid over her mouth and she brushed it away.

'Oh, I'm sorry; we have no vacancies at the moment,' she said. Then as if to clarify her statement added, 'You see we have a load of American guests with us at the moment, and there's not a room to be had.'

I feigned disappointment, as though the Tigh-na-Bain was the one and only place to stay. I discretely scanned the walls looking for some indication as to the identity of Mr Carter, but I could see no trace of photos of the couple.

'I could give you the addresses of other recommended B&B's and hotels in the area,' Shona suggested. I hated winding this nice lady up and taking advantage of her hospitality, but had to go along with the ruse. I smiled.

'That would be great, madam,' I said hoping to extract her name.

She looked embarrassed, brushed some hair way from her face with her hand and replied.

'Oh, call me Shona. Madam is a wee bit posh,' then she giggled at her own joke. I joined in just to be polite.

Shona then began scribbling a series of names, addresses and phone numbers on a *post-it note*. As her head was down, hair covering her face, I took advantage and gave the place a good look over, but could see nothing of any value: no framed photos of the once-famous Danny Carter, if indeed he lived her and was married to Shona. I wished I had asked Andy Brookes if he remembered the name of Carter's girlfriend, who became his wife.

Then she looked up handing me the note as she tucked some wayward strands of hair behind her ears. I looked at it as though interested. Little did she know this slip of paper would find its way into a nearby bin. The handwriting was elegant but totally unreadable; it was just as well I didn't need it. At least I had the decency to feel a twinge of guild for wasting her time.

'Thanks for that Shona. You've been most helpful.' I wanted to keep her talking as I thought how best to extract information from her. I just wanted to know if The Danny Carter of the Faceless Legions lived here, but I couldn't just come out with the question. Besides I was hoping that maybe the husband would walk into the reception to see if his wife needed a hand.

'I'm wondering if you have any leaflets with things to do on Skye, Shona. I want to spend a wee bit of time exploring the sights?'

Shona was as helpful as ever. She dug below the counter and produced a pile of glossy leaflets offering all manner of services and activities: from fishing to hill climbing and visits to museums and castles.

'Actually, my husband does guided hill walking tours, if you're interested,' Shona said as though the thought had just occurred to her. Fantastic – this was a result. I begged for more information.

'Yes, that would be great, Shona. I fancied doing a bit of hill walking while I was here.' I sounded really keen. 'So does he do them regularly?'

'Well depending on the weather, maybe one or two a week.'

'So when's the next one, Shona?' I was gagging to get going. This way I would get to meet Mr Carter and reveal his true identity.

'Well,' she thought, her eyes darting upwards as though the ceiling had the answer, 'he's taking our group of Americans on a walk tomorrow. I think it would be okay for you to tag along if you don't mind the Americans – they can be a wee bit boisterous and loud.'

I didn't care. I'd tag along with a group of terrorists if I got to meet this Mr Carter.

'Yeah, that would be fantastic, thanks.' Then I thought of a strategy.

'Maybe you should ask your husband if that would be okay with him.'

'No, I'm sure Dan would be okay with you joining the group; one more hiker won't make much difference'

This was indeed interesting. Mr D. Carter had now a first name and it was looking promising. The adrenalin coursed through my veins as I tried to hide my excitement to avoid looking like a maniac in front of Shona and have her cancel my authorisation to join the group.

Chapter 9

I left the B&B establishment feeling like a child on Christmas Eve – full of eager and excited anticipation. The only slight let-down was the fact I would have to wait until tomorrow to confirm my suspicions about Dan Carter. I was now at a loose end and felt the need to do something constructive to my operation. Although I tried to finesse as much information from Shona as possible, it yielded virtually nothing, except the name Dan. I wanted to know if Dan was at home; any sighting of him would be enough to confirm if it was the Dan I was seeking. If not, I wouldn't waste my time on the hill climbing trip tomorrow.

I drove back into Portree and located a hard-wear store. Inside I browsed until I found a pair of binoculars. They were quite cheap looking, but fortunately the price tag reflected this. I was not interested in purchasing an expensive pair as I would have little use for them after I left Skye.

Next I located a second hand bookshop and went inside. No sooner had I started looking for the appropriate section when the elderly owner appeared as if from nowhere.

'Can I help ye, sonny?' he asked, 'Is there a particular book ye were lookin' for? My first instinct was to reply 'No thanks, I'm just looking,' but I figured it may save a bit of time in having the guy help me.

'I was after a book on birds,' then I clarified, 'well bird-watching specifically.'

His face lit up like an angel. Not only had he such a book, but he knew exactly where to find it. He beckoned me to follow as he stepped over piles of unsorted books and squeezed through narrow gaps in the overflowing bookcases to find the appropriate section. The shop was gloomy and smelled musty; it was in serious need of a makeover. I supposed the lack of light and unhealthy smell deterred most visitors from using his shop as a library. The old guy knew what he was doing.

He produced a handful of books and fanned them out like a game-show host with a hand full of banknotes. He then proceeded to read the titles out to me as though I was blind or illiterate. When he had finished, I asked to have a quick look through each. I wasn't particularly bothered about what bird book I bought – I was more concerned about the price. I had no intention of becoming a bird expert.

In the end I purchased *Birds of the British Isles*: a nice pocket sized book with glossy photos of all the birds, as opposed to the other books which had drawings of the birds which didn't look very accurate; and I only paid £2.50 for it!

Next on my list was an outdoor clothing shop. The town of Portree had exactly what I wanted, being on a hilly and mountainous island attracting hordes of hill walkers. At last I managed to browse in peace. I selected a pair of waterproof combat trousers with khaki pattern and a matching waterproof jacket. I also treated myself to an expensive pair of hiking boots, not having packed such a luxury when I left Glasgow. If I was to join this hiking party, I would need to look the part. I recalled Shona's slant on the loudness of the Americans, and wondered whether I should also buy a pair of earplugs.

I ate a hurried lunch in a small café before heading back to my car and driving back towards the Tigh-na-Bain B&B. I parked the car a short distance away in a small car-park, accommodating about a dozen cars. There was no one around so I changed in privacy into my newly purchased wardrobe, locked the car and headed for the hilly area overlooking the target building, my new binoculars swinging on their lanyard around my neck. I stuffed the bird book into my pocket making sure it poked up and was visible to anyone I passed. I wanted to look the part: a sad old bird watcher with camouflage clothing and all the accoutrements to match.

I found a great spot in tall grass with a panoramic view of the property. From here I could see the front and side doors and the car-park. I could easily monitor all comings and goings to and from the house. As a bonus, I had a fantastic view of the Sound of Raasay; its light blue rippling waters contrasting with the dark foreboding distant mountains. I peered through my binoculars and studied the house. I could see the windows, but net curtains on virtually every window hampered my view of the interior. A lone silver Volvo sat by the side of the building. I wondered if this was one of the Carter's cars, maybe Dan's.

I congratulated myself on choosing waterproof trousers as the long course grass which I lay on was damp, but I knew I was pretty invisible to almost anyone who chanced to pass by. The pathway was about ten metres to my left; hopefully any pedestrians would stick to that unless they decided to venture onto the grassy area like me. Even if someone from the B&B came out and happened to look up to the hill, it was confident I wouldn't be spotted. I felt like a sniper on stag patiently waiting my quarry to emerge before firing a bullet in the direction of their occipital lobe.

I waited and waited, but nothing happened; no one came out, no one arrived. I scanned again through my binoculars but could detect no movements from within. Perhaps the couple had gone into town to do some shopping whilst their American guests were out causing chaos elsewhere; however the parked Volvo could mean someone was home.

I was continually forced to move position to remain comfortable. The damp grass and weeds below me squeaked every time I turned. I began to browse through my bird book to pass the time. Ironically, the area was quite devoid of birdlife, save for the odd seagull or two squawking their way over the bay looking for thermals to enjoy, and occasionally checking out the bin area at the rear of the Tigh-na-Bain for any spilled morsels.

Then I detected the sounds of human voices in the distance behind me; faint though growing steadily louder as they approached. I froze, hoping to minimise my own noise and not draw attention to my presence. I remained hopeful I would stay undetected, but a sense of unease swept over me. If I was seen, I would just act like a typical twitcher and start waffling about birds and recite a few of the name of birds from my book. Hopefully, that would be enough to cause anyone to go running off to get away from the weirdo.

The voices were loud now; they sounded like a family of two adults and two or three children. I kept low in the grass until they passed, then relaxed and let out the breath I was holding. Soon the nearby pathway became almost as busy as Sauchiehall Street on a Saturday afternoon. All manner of people walked past. I couldn't see them but I could hear the voices: from giggling children to couples sharing romantic thoughts; and from serious hikers bemoaning the lack of decent facilities on the island to old folks bedazzled at the sea view. Still no one spotted me and I continued my observation of the house below.

It had been a long day. We had stood for hours keeping vigil on a shopping precinct as intelligence had revealed this was a busy location for the sale and purchase of illegal drugs. As we peered through a hole in the wooden boards covering the broken windows of a disused factory, nothing happened. No sightings of any suspect types wishing to sell their 'tenor' bags of heroin, nor of any junkie-type potential buyer. We were cold, tired and hungry and about to call it a day when a dealer turned up and inserted himself into a nearby doorway. He thought he was perfectly hidden, but we could see him clearly, being only about six or seven metres away from our elevated vantage point. His eyes darted left and right as he sought his regular customers and some new ones who were told where to look.

Soon all manner of addicts turned up and the marketplace for banned substances was in full swing. Bags of heroin were sold by the pocket-full; tablets were meticulously counted and handed over, and packets containing cannabis resin and grass were purchased in a buying frenzy. And we captured all the sordid details on camera right under their noses. My colleague radioed for assistance of his uniformed colleagues and the buyers were quickly stopped, searched and arrested for numerous charges under the Misuse of Drugs Act 1971. The 'big time' dealer was later arrested when my team and I attended his flat and searched it under warrant finding all manner of drugs and associated paraphernalia.

I was jolted back to the here and now with the sound of a barking dog. Now I was in trouble; I didn't plan for the possibility of a dog, and now my cover could be blown. I braced myself as my blood pressure rose and adrenalin flowed to equip me for fight or flight. The barking grew louder as the dog got nearer to my hide. What if the dog lunged at me; what if he decided to sample a piece of my flesh? I didn't have anything I could use to defend myself. I would just have to come out of hiding, reveal myself and launch into my avid bird watcher act. I stayed silent and held my breath – not that the dog would be fooled by that. He had a sensitive sense of smell and had probably detected me about a mile away.

The dog seemed almost upon me. I couldn't see him but could hear the rapid sniffing probably only a few metres away. I heard the dog's owner call to him; it sounded like there were at least two people.

'Rabbie, no come on.' But Rabbie wasn't interested in coming on. He had a fascinating scent and was keen to investigate. I braced for the impact of Rabbie's teeth on my leg. The rustling grass and sniffing of the dog's nose was loud in my ears. Then I caught sight of movement on my surveillance target area. Typical, I thought – no movement for hours then it happens at the exact time I least wanted. Just when I was about to wrestle with an inquisitive dog and reveal my position, a male emerged from the Tigh-na-Bain, but I couldn't spare the time to look through my binoculars to see. This was a nightmare – the stupid dog couldn't have come at a worse moment. My eyes darted between the house and the direction of the dog; I could still hear Rabbie but couldn't see him. His owners were shouting to him and a bit of a struggle ensued. Then the sounds of Rabbie's wild barking and sniffing faded away. I rose up slightly and could see the dog being tugged away as he strained on his extendable leash. Luckily the owners had managed to attach his leash before he could get any further into the bushes and maul me.

Robbie's walkers probably thought he had stumbled across a rabbit or some other creature hiding in the damp grass; they were partially correct.

I turned my attention back to the house below. I scanned the male who had emerged a moment earlier, through the binoculars. He was carrying a couple of full black bin bags in each hand and was heading to the enclosed bin area. I studied his face as he moved but the jerking movement with my unsteady hand made any scrutiny difficult. Only when he stopped and dropped the bags at his feet was I able to study his face in detail. He wore a woollen hat but I could make out strands of long hair protruding from the rear, and the unmistakable outline of an ear-ring in his left ear. The face was definitely familiar, although creased with age, it was still identifiable as Danny Carter formerly of the Faceless Legions; I was very, very sure.

Carter wasted no time in chucking the black plastic bags into the large receptacle before hurrying back to the warmth of his abode. Now I could only see his back, but that tall, slender figure and familiar swagger made me more or less certain I had my man.

I figured I had seen enough to move onto phase two of my plan – trying to get close to the guy, confirm his true identity, and then ply him with all manner of questions. Besides it was growing increasingly dark plus the midges were starting to come out to play. I had narrowly escaped being bitten by Rabbie, now I didn't want to present myself as dinner to a squadron of ravenous midges. It was now time to head back to my hotel for a well earned rest after a successful

day; after all I had yet another big day ahead –
part of which I was looking forward to and part in
which I could see far enough. I hoped my
American comrades would not be as obnoxious as
Shona had made out.

Back at the Kingarth, I dined alone; afterwards as
I sat in the bar nursing a coke, a foreign couple
approached and began making conversation. I
learned Werner and Agatha Krüger from near
Düsseldorf were having a splendid time in
Scotland. They had driven over from the
Fatherland two weeks ago and were doing a tour
of my homeland. They pressed me for all the best
sights in Skye and looked shocked when I told
them I didn't really know the island as I was a bit
of a tourist myself, having journeyed up from
Glasgow. They chuckled at this revelation as
though I ought to know the whole of Scotland like
the back of my hand because I lived here. I
wondered if they would be able to tell me all I
wished to know about all the places in Germany
from Munster to Munich and Hanover to Halle.

Chapter 10

I locked the *Hyundai* and strode into the car-park
of the Tigh-na-Bain. The time was 0800hrs and,
although I had slept well the previous night, I was
still in need of an extra couple of hours. My
muscles ached due to my previous evening's
rolling around in damp grass and mud; but it was
worth it – and now I was about to confirm my

87

suspicions and make a positive identification of Dan Carter.

In the centre of the car-park stood about ten people, all huddled round like very close friends and chatting animatedly with each other. I could hear the distinct drawl of the American accent and the guffawing whenever someone said something remotely funny. I doubted I was going to gel with this group today. I stood around with my backpack on over my khaki waterproofs and brand new hiking boots. One of the group noticed me and pointed me out to his mates.

'Hey look guys, its GI Joe.' As predicted, the group turned around, gave me the once over and roared with laughter.

'Is Scotland being invaded? Is there a war on?' cried another.

A tall back guy, obviously the brains of the team, observed.

'It he stands in a forest, we won't be able to see him; he'll just disappear!' There erupted more laughter and all at my expense. I was regretting buying the camouflage outfit, but it did serve me well the previous night. Then the team changed as though someone had flicked a switch.

'Are you the guy who's coming on the hike with us?' asked a lanky female. I nodded.

'Well welcome along partner,' called another.

Then a bunch of hands shot out in my direction. I shook each and one of the team introduced me to his comrades. I knew I wouldn't be able to remember all the names.

'I'm Tony,' I returned.

'So Tony, are from the Isle of Skye?' a young guy wearing a blue Gore-tex jacket enquired.

'No, I'm from Glasgow. I'm just here for a few days.'

They thought this was great meeting a guy from a place in Britain they had actually heard of.

'Good morning guys and girls,' called out a familiar sounding voice from behind, 'are we all ready to rock and roll?' This was surely proof positive of the man's credentials.

There followed a whoop of excited cheering ringing out in the still of the early morning. This group probably thought they were at a cub scouts meeting. Carter spotted me, looked me up and down before extending his hand towards me. I grabbed it and we looked each other in the eye.

'Hi, you must be Tony? I'm Dan Carter,' he said in his unmistakable south London accent.

'Pleased to meet you, Dan. Yeah, I'm Tony.' I was now convinced beyond all doubt. Here I was, once again standing beside the famous (or once famous) Danny Carter. The face was the same as I remembered albeit older, more wrinkly and suntanned. Perhaps my theory about the quantity and quality of sunshine on Skye was correct after all; or maybe Carter went to the same tanning salon as the receptionist at the Kingarth Hotel. He still wore the same woollen hat as last night, and still his long hair poked out from below. It was definitely him, but what was all this Dan business? He had always been Danny to his fans and followers, but perhaps this was his 'breakaway' strategy: new life, new surroundings and new name.

'Thanks for letting me join you and your group,' I said.

'No problem Tony; the more the merrier as they say,' replied Danny. He hadn't lost his confident nature and he was still at ease with an audience. He turned to the group.

'Is everybody feeling fit today?' He was met with more whoops and cries of 'All right.'

'I can't hear you guys. Is everyone ready to go?' The cheers got louder. Carter was loving this and doing what came natural to him. This is exactly as he was more than three decades ago and I wondered why he seemed to quit the music business and simply vanish.

'Well let's get our selves on the bus and get going,' Carter sang with a mock American accent. This stirred the hikers up into a near frenzy. They high-fived each other and bumped fists; I was offered neither a fist nor a hand.

Carter indicated to the white mini-bus parked in the top corner of the car-park with the name of the B&B emblazoned across it in plain blue lettering, and the team surged towards it, keen to get inside and on their way. I waited until last to board the bus, but fortunately the only seat left was the front seat passenger. This meant I could chat up Danny as we drove to and from wherever it was we were heading. Besides, I wasn't bothered about bonding with the American mob in the rear.

Carter seated himself in the driving seat, started the engine and turned towards his passengers.

'So people, today we are going to visit a spectacular rock formation called…' here he paused to let the anticipation mount, 'The Storr.' The passengers went wild with excitement as though they had never seen a rock formation before. Someone should have told them their country is full of spectacular natural geologic features, ones which would make The Storr look like an ant hill.

Carter then drove out of the car-park and onto the A855 for our short journey to our destination as he sang in an impressive operatic voice.

'I to the hills will lift mine eyes.'

At the end of his extempore performance the Yankee gang burst into raucous applause and cheering; one guy even whistled which made the noise unbearable in the close confines of the vehicle. Now I could appreciate what Shona meant about her oversees guests. Carter smiled at his audience; he certainly still had that showman ability and I wondered if he ever missed the big time.

I pondered how to go about striking up conversation. It was not as if I could just come out and ask him 'Were you once in the Faceless Legions?' He may just stop the van and toss me out in the middle of nowhere if he guessed what I was up to.

'So how long have you been living up here, Dan?' I asked. 'You're obviously not from around here.'

Dan concentrated on the road ahead whilst struggling with the heavy gearbox, the van jerking as the gear cogs crunched into position. He turned to glance at me.

'Oh, I fell in love with this place years ago - and one of its locals – Shona, who you've met.' I nodded. Then he continued.

'I just fancied moving out of the big smoke and up here into the country.'

'Do you miss London?' I enquired.

'Nah, only been back a couple of times since moving up here,' Dan said as he checked left and right before pulling away from a junction. Before I could quiz and probe even further we had arrived at the parking area for our hike up to The Storr. Dan tugged on the handbrake and it ratcheted up into place. No sooner had we stopped when the side door slip open and the eager Americans all bailed out like a crack team of paratroopers from a plane. I got out and mingled with the team who were fully excited and motivated, pointing to the distant mountains and nearby Sound of Raasay. There were gasps of 'Wow' and 'Awesome.'

Despite the early hour, the car-park was busy with other minibuses and cars. Numerous groups, couples and families changed into their hiking gear. Some folk were sitting in the boot area of their estate cars to pull on muddy, well worn boots whilst others sat on the dry grassy area and sorted out all the things they might and might not require for their adventure into the hills. One guy seemed to have a 'Captain Jack Sparrow' compass; he swung around in a full arc trying to get the red needle aligned with magnetic north, but the needle refused to cooperate and seemed to point in any random direction; he tossed the compass back into the boot of his car to the whoops and laughs of his mates; one cried.

'Shouldn't have bought it at the pound shop.'

Dan Carter cut an impressive figure as he strode along the long and winding pathway as though he walked this route everyday. I was just behind him and could sense his confidence and exuberance of a man at peace with the world. His tall slim figure certainly hadn't gained any excess weight during his venture into middle age, although his face was certainly showing signs of aging. Although he wore his black woollen hat which made it difficult to see his hair, it was still long, but probably greying. I remember him in his heyday having a voluminous mane of thick wavy blonde hair, enough to make a supermodel envious. Perhaps when he generated some heat, he might just take off his hat and we can all see how his hair had faired over the years. I caught up with Carter and we walked together.

'So you're up from Glasgow?' Carter asked as he noticed me by his side.

'Yeah, just visiting a part of Scotland I've never been to,' I replied.

'Are you just here yourself, or with your family?' He probably knew the answer to that one having been briefed by Shona.

'Yeah, just me and myself,' I said, 'that way I get a bit of peace and quiet.' Carter laughed at my observation.

'You won't get any peace and quiet with that lot,' he replied discretely indication to the noisy Americans behind us. We laughed and increased our pace in an effort to distance ourselves considerably.

Before we set out, Carter had gathered us all round in a huddle and gave us a pre-hike briefing. This consisted of a bit of health and safety mixed with the pertinent points of the country code. He insisted we all stick together as a group, although each could go at their own desired pace, as long as we all stopped periodically to let the slower groups or individuals catch up. With that he delved into a large rucksack and extracted packed lunch boxes (all carefully prepared by Shona) and tossed one to each member of the posse. I even got one, which was just as well as I hadn't really thought about lunch. I think I was expecting to find a café or fast food restaurant at the top of the mountain.

The ten Americans had now divided into two smaller groups and were chatting away to each other; I couldn't decide whether they were all students or work colleagues but they seemed to bond and get on well. Mob psychology ruled them though – whenever one of the gang laughed, they all did the same.

It was shaping up to be a nice day; azure skies with only the occasional broken cumulous cloud promised a rain free adventure. The pathway was starting to rise gradually and the perspiration and increased breathing rate gathered pace in tandem. I was still trying hard to compose an appropriate way to come out and ask Carter what I had come here to do, but for the life of me, I didn't know how. Funny how I had been in the business of asking questions for the last thirty years, yet when it mattered, I was somewhat unsure. I still had to be cautious as I didn't want to have Carter clamp up and refuse to cooperate. For all he knew, he was managing to remain anonymous and nobody had yet sussed out his antecedents. I didn't want to burst his bubble too much.

Soon Carter called for us to halt and declared a short comfort stop. We all flopped onto the grassy area, pulling off rucksacks and dumping them on the ground. I extracted a water bottle from my rucksack and drank sparingly from it; the lukewarm water hit the mark and went someway to relieving my parched throat. To my side a few metres away, Carter opened a flask and poured the steaming brown liquid into the tiny cup which doubled as a lid. As he supped, he studied an OS map, his finger tracing a line along the printed route. He was clearly feeling the heat as he took off his hat and tossed it onto his lap. His long greying hair tumbled down his face and he sorted it out with a flick of his hand. Yes indeed – this was most certainly the famous rock and roll front-man.

To my other side several of the Yankee gang were carrying on and messing around. One was pretending to push his comrade over the edge of the steep slope whilst the main group divided into those who thought the prank was funny and those who looked appalled at the behaviour.

Carter caught sight of the tomfoolery and shook his head in disapproval. His look said it all and the messing abruptly stopped. Had none of them remembered the team talk prior to us setting off?

We were soon off again; Carter acting like the proverbial sergeant major commanding his troop onward without mercy. This time I caught up with the long and rapid pace of Carter and we marched in step. It was time to begin finessing him for information.

'Hey Dan, anyone ever tell you that you look like a rock star with your long hair?' I asked.

He stared straight ahead as though focusing on the distant horizon and too busy to listen to me prattling on.

'Oh yeah, only about ten times a day,' was his witty reply. I pressed ever further.

'You know, you remind me of someone famous.' Still he didn't reveal his cards.

'Yeah, I get that all the time as well.' He was proving to be as uncooperative as a 'no comment' suspect in an interview room. I now decided he was suitably primed for me to launch straight into the killer question. This would be like the ending of a Scooby Doo episode where they finally unmask the monster in the costume, but this time it wouldn't be 'old man Withers from the fairground', it would be Danny Carter of the Faceless Legions.

Then one of the American women stepped forward and called to Carter.

'Say Dan, what is that lake over there?'

'That's the Storr Loch', Carter replied pointing to the deep blue waters far below.

The Americans then had a giggle over their attempts to pronounce the word 'loch'. They competed with each other to vocalise the word, producing a blend of stomach churning noises from the backs of their throats.

Carter then went on to point out other features which were visible in the near and far distance, impressing everyone with his vast local knowledge; when we set off, the same woman had now become Carter's walking buddy and I was forced to tag along behind. She clearly fancied the man as her flirting body language was evident for all to see. Carter remained professional and surged ahead; he probably got this a lot from the female members of his hiking troop, but appeared to take a dim view at mixing business with pleasure.

Chapter 11

We now stopped for a well earned lunch break. We had reached the summit of our conquest; the Old Man of Storr. We flopped down leaning against clusters of ancient rocks protruding out of the earth like giant gravestones. We puffed, panted and gulped large quantities of fluids as sweat ran down our faces and backs. Soon the packed lunches were opened and our group of ravenous hikers ate like vultures. It was just as well there wasn't a café up here otherwise our group might be asked to leave when the management witnessed their eating habits, I mused.

Carter's love interest had now taken the hint and slinked back to her clique. I moved in to fill the gap.

'I think I know who you look like, Dan,' I said, 'it's been bothering me for hours now.'

He turned to face me and I could detect a hint of expectation in his face, as though he knew what was coming next.

'Danny Carter, formerly of the Faceless Legions,' I announced as I watched his reaction. He nodded slowly and a slight grin broke out over his face, the laughter lines as prominent as the craggy rocks we sat around.

'Got it in one. Well done mate,' he replied – and I was elated.

We ate in silence for a period, each pondering our own thoughts. I let my brain digest this information as my stomach got to work digesting ham and cheese sandwiches.

'Don't you miss the music industry, Dan?' I enquired.

He shook his head gently, 'Nah, been there, done that and made a packet out of it.' Then he twisted around to look at me.

'So how did you find me? Is this just coincidence?'

'Not really,' I said, 'I'm actually a retired police detective, so I just done a bit of clue hunting, so to speak.'

'So you set out to find me, track me down?' Danny replied.

'I set myself a mission – to find the elusive members of one of the biggest rock bands of all time.' Danny found this slightly amusing – that I would waste my time on such a pointless quest.

'So have you found the rest of the guys?' Danny said; his eyebrows rose in anticipation.

'No, you're only the second, but I did meet Andy Brookes.'

Danny's face reflected surprise. I could see his eyes glazing over as his memory ventured into the past.

'You met Andy?' he said after a long pause.

'Yeah. He's alive and well, living in Birmingham.'

I thought Danny was going to say more, but all he offered was, 'Wow!'

Then as though Danny had ventured enough into his past life, he seemed to snap out of his trance, look at his watch and rise slowly to his feet. He ambled over to the edge and stood tall and proud admiring the spectacular scenery as though he was king and this was his domain. His head swept left as he gazed down upon the Sound of Raasay and the distant Island of Rona, then he took in the breathtaking panorama of the Island of Raasay. I could see the smile break upon his face;

he was happy here and didn't seem to miss his past life. I could see I may have a problem trying to talk him into a reunion.

'Is everyone suitably fed and watered?' he shouted as he turned towards his gang. There were weak cries of 'Yeah, suppose,' from the weary warriors.

'We better get going; it's a long way down,' Danny advised.

Slowly the team rose to their feet, brushing grass and weeds from their clothing and groaning as their aching muscles flexed into position.

Danny then led his gang of intrepid hikers down the steep slopes with all the ease and confidence of a Nepalese Sherpa. I was just behind him, struggling to keep up with his relentless pace. Behind me were the chatty Americans, although tiredness had seemed to zap them of much conversation, which was a good thing. Danny turned to check the progress of his merry band. He could sight of me and slowed his pace so I was able to catch up with him and we descended side by side. The brisk breeze coming from the Sound of Raasay provided a much welcomed cooling effect for our hot, perspiring bodies.

'So, do you miss being in the police?' Danny asked.

'Not really. Thirty years in the job is enough for anyone.'

'So are you a private detective now?' I shook my head.

'No, I just got a bit bored and needed a project to keep me busy,' I said with a grin.

'And finding the Legions was your project?' Danny asked with incredulity.

'Yeah, why not? After all you guys seemed to just disappear into oblivion,' I replied, 'what was all that about, Danny?' Carter seemed to chew this one over before he answered.

'Don't really know mate. Me personally, I just had had enough of the so called rock and roll lifestyle,' with this he framed the words 'rock and rock' with raised twitching fingers, 'It was killing me – all the touring, rehearsing, performing and trying to sleep on a tour bus.' He was on a roll now and I sure wasn't going to interrupt.

'You know, the record company were relentless. They drove us hard. We played seven nights a week, with only the odd day off. They refused to book us into hotels and we had to sleep on a tour bus, which was a nightmare. No comfortable bed, no privacy, no decent meals.' His head was shaking in disgust. I hoped he wouldn't turn on me for bringing up the subject and forcing him to relive his incubus.

'So it's no wonder I got out when we had the chance, and I came way up here to all this amazing scenery,' Danny said sweeping his arm in an arc over the immense panorama spread before us. He paused to let his words of wisdom sink in before continuing.

'I don't know about the other guys, but we were all glad to be splitting up and going our separate ways.'

'So you don't know what happened to the others?' I asked. I could detect a shrug from Carter below his bright red ski jacket.

'And you never kept in touch?' I probed. Carter shook his head.

'I know I didn't. I came straight up here and me and Shona got married.'

We strolled on in silence for a while. The craggy path was now demanding all our efforts of concentration to avoid tripping or spraining an ankle. I pondered what Carter had told me and, no doubt he was lost in his own thoughts of a life once lived.

The sun was laying low in the sky by the time we arrived back at the car-park. I surveyed the group: they looked like the stragglers at the end of a marathon; faces red as healthy tomatoes, sweat soaked hair and the vigorous rubbing of limbs. By contrast Carter looked quite fresh as though he could do the entire trip again with ease. Given he did this on a regular basis, his fitness and endurance levels were amazing – despite his age.

'That's the guy there, officer!' shouted the heavily made-up teenage girl as she pointed to a male now running off in the opposite direction. 'He assaulted my boyfriend.' Beside her stood a young teen boy, blood pouring from his nose and smeared over his face. I felt compelled to run after the culprit although I couldn't be bothered, but the watching crowd expected me to give pursuit to the escaping thug.

I ran after him, but he was a good fifty metres ahead. Now I used to be an expert at the hundred metre sprint, setting many records at my high school, but this seemed an impossible task given I was hampered with a my tight police tunic, the bulky wooden truncheon and handcuffs hanging off my belt. I was the rookie and wanted to impress my colleagues and supervisors, so I ran for all I was worth, but it seemed my quarry was gaining distance. My mind was telling me to abandon the chase but my heart was egging me on.

'Suspect has gone up Crawford Street,' a firm voice barked from my radio.

I turned into Crawford Street and, to my horror it was a steep incline. So I ran and ran, my quarry looking over his shoulder every so often to check if I was still in pursuit. My lungs screamed for oxygen and my legs ached so much I thought they would collapse. I caught sight of faces at tenement windows watching the scene; this was quality entertainment – the cop chasing the robber up a street; it must have looked like a scene from a slapstick movie.

My pace was now slowing; I was rapidly running out of energy and motive. Fortunately, so was my suspect. About twenty metres ahead, without warning, he stopped and sat down on the pavement, panting like a winning racehorse. I caught up with him, but fully expected him to get up and continue his escape. To my amazement, he didn't budge. I stood over him panting as much as he, and tried to catch my breath to utter the ominous words 'You're under arrest,' but it took a while. We both looked like a couple of boxers after twenty rounds. We locked eyes and we both burst into laughter, giggling like schoolboys. My suspect extended his palms outward to be handcuffed. He knew I had earned the right to make my arrest and he was quite happy to come quietly.

This was the event my memory was playing as I descended the slope to the welcoming sight of our four wheeled transport. Although no where near as exhausted as that day in my fledgling police days, I was now feeling my age and looked forward to a seat on the minibus, if only for the short trip back to the Tigh-na-Bain.

We all piled into the bus and dirty rucksacks were dumped on the floor. Again I took the front passenger seat next to my new mate. Danny started the engine and the big diesel throbbed into life; a clunk of the heavy gearbox and we were off and heading back home in virtual silence. Only the occasional word was muttered in an American accent, most being content to gaze bleary-eyed out the windows. Danny ignored me and drove with all the concentration of a police pursuit driver; I hoped he was still talking to me and wasn't too annoyed at my intrusion into his life. Besides, I still had phase two to deal with, so I did want to talk to him further; at least I knew where he stayed!

'Okay people, dinner should be about ready. You guys have a quick clean up and I'll see you all in the dining room in ten minutes,' Danny called to the team. They acknowledged with a nod as they gathered up their possessions and headed to the B&B. I extended my hand to Danny.

'Look thanks for letting me come today, and it was great meeting you.' Instead of returning the handshake, Carter put his arm around me, just like the time on stage at the Apollo.

'I would like to chat a little more about this crazy project of yours, Tony. Why not join me and Shona later on for a drink.' I was thrilled; this was exactly what I wanted. I tried to suppress my eagerness not to appear like a madman.

'Thanks; that would be great. Where do you want to meet?'

We arranged a suitable time which would allow us both to eat, shower and change before our rendezvous, not in some local tavern as expected, but in the lounge of the Tigh-na-Bain.

Two hours later following a refreshing shower then dinner at the Kingarth, I drove back to the Carter's place. I was excited at having positively identified and even met the great Danny Carter. All that remained was to talk him into a little reunion with his former band-mates, assuming I managed to trace and persuade the others.

There followed a pleasant evening in the relaxed and quite confines of the lounge area with Shona, Danny and I sitting around a dark mahogany coffee table. Subdued background music played from a couple of wall mounted speakers as Eva Cassidy serenaded us on the virtues of lost love.

'Dan's told me all about your wee…project, Tony,' Shona said beaming, 'and I think it's a great idea.' I smiled in return.

'It's kind of a personal challenge,' I replied, 'to see if I could actually do it.'

'No I think it's admirable.' Shona replied in her pleasant Highland lilt.

'You've certainly proved your detective credentials by managing to track down Andy Brookes, then me,' added Danny. I smiled but tried to appear modest.

We chatted away for an hour about the band, the aftermath of the band and how different life is now living on the Isle of Skye. Shona revealed she was unhappy about Danny giving up the music business hoping he might take a short break then resume with another band, however had got used to the relaxed life they both shared now. Incidentally, it was Shona who insisted he change from Danny to Dan as a way of signifying a change, and to go someway towards guarding his privacy. I would always know him as Danny, and he seemed happy enough to answer to either.

'So Dan, the big question is.' I paused for emphasis. 'Would you be up for reuniting the Faceless Legions for a one-off come-back gig?'

Danny sat back in his seat and presented me with a wide, warm smile.

'Yeah, that sounds like a plan. I'd be up for it.' Shona grabbed her husband's hand and cradled it in her own. She beamed also. I revealed that Andy Brookes was certainly keen to reunite.

'I'd love to see Dan up on stage again, it would be fantastic.'

It was a delight to study them both. They seemed a happy couple, well matched and complimented each other nicely: his south London accent contrasting with her quiet sing-song highland voice, and his tall confident manner a distinction from her small-framed mousey mannerisms.

'Mind you,' Danny said, 'I doubt you'll every get everyone back on stage again, even if you manage to track them down'. I held out my hands submissively.

'I can but try. I'll see what I can do.'

'Didn't one of the members die recently?' Shona cut in. We both confirmed the sad demise of Chas Hannagan, and Danny looked surprised and slightly bemused when I told him about his son being a semi-professional bass player.

'Is your plan to ask him to replace his old man?' Danny enquired. I nodded.

'I'll certainly put the proposition to him, but I don't know.'

The relaxed Danny was looking lost in yet another memory trip. I could almost see the scene playing out in his mind: the Faceless Legions back on stage and doing their thing, only this time they were older, greyer, balder, fatter an sporting many more wrinkles.

'So what's your plan now?' said Shona.

'Well the next step is to find Mick Walker and Paul Dixon.' I replied. Danny let out a snort of derision as he shook his head.

'See, that's gonna' be the major problem.' Danny explained. 'Paul and Mick practically hated each other. The problem was mainly Paul; he had a ferocious temper and always seemed to be in a pig of mood.' He went on reminiscing.

'Him and Mick were always arguing, and on a few occasions, they came to blows with each other. Me and Andy had to step in and separate them. So I doubt either of them will want to share a stage with each other again.'

This was something I wasn't aware of and could be a problem; however I was hopeful the time span and move into middle age might have mellowed them both. At this point I didn't consider it a spanner in the works. If it took all my negotiating skills to talk them into it, I would do it.

'I need to start looking for them both, so any info you can give me to work on would be appreciated,' I said. Danny sat back again in his seat and crossed his arms.

'I haven't a clue, I mean we never kept in touch and I've never taken the notion to look them up,' Danny replied with a look of helplessness. He unfolded his arms and extended his palms upwards.

'Sorry, but I know that's not any help at all.'

I nodded in acknowledgement; I needed anything he could offer, even the smallest snippet of information – something no matter how miniscule to go on. I pleaded with Danny for any distant memory which could shed light on the whereabouts of the missing musicians. He resumed his pensive position: head back, eyes closed and he delved deep into his memory. I could tell he was keen to help and wanted to offer me something. I looked at Shona as she studied her husband; she too was keen to assist and was probably willing Danny to come up with some morsel I could work with.

Chapter 12

I left the Carter's place after swapping phone numbers and promising to keep in touch; I would update Danny on any significant developments, and he pledged to contact me should he think of anything which might be of help. The only thing Danny could offer was that Paul Dixon had relatives in Australia, although where in that vast country, he was unable to narrow down. Apparently during one of the Faceless Legions tours which took them to Australia to play the major cities, Dixon had the band meet his relatives, sign autographs and pose for photographs. Carter then suggested that perhaps Dixon had emigrated down under to be with his family; besides he hated the British weather and was continually complaining and bemoaning the fact he wished he lived somewhere warmer and dryer.

I pondered this, but felt it was too vague a clue. Australia was indeed a vast place, being the world's sixth largest country by area - nearly 8 million square kilometres. To search for one person here would be like searching for a toothpick in a haystack; besides it was only a mere suggestion that Dixon could have gone here and there were plenty of other destination which could satisfy Dixon's craving for a warm dry climate.

As for Mick Walker, Danny could offer nothing at all. He claimed he didn't really know Walker terribly well despite spending quite a few years in close proximity. Given Carter's rant about the conditions he and his colleagues were forced to live in, I figured all the guys would be like brothers and might just know each other's deepest, darkest secrets; however I could only speculate. I couldn't tell if Carter was telling me everything he knew, or holding back crucial points, but perhaps he would phone me at some point in the future and offer me something interesting.

I chewed over all the events of the last two days, and I felt good. My hunch to come to Skye had paid off. Certainly I had to work to uncover Danny Carter; I had lain in damp grass whilst spying on the guy's house, posing as a bird watcher and nearly getting mauled by a nosey dog, and I had endured a exhausting hike up and down a hill – but it had paid off well – I had unmasked the famous Faceless Legions front man. As a bonus he had agreed to be part of the hypothetical reunion of the once famous rock band. So now I had two ticks in the box: Brookes and now Carter. Operation Lazarus was proving to be a tad easier than I had first envisioned, but I knew better than to get too confident; I still had a long way to go to complete the mission.

As my journey to find the missing members of the Legions would be a long and wearisome affair, so was my current journey – I was now leaving the Isle of Skye and heading to Aberdeen to see my ex-wife. Miss Satnav told me the distance was 215 miles and would take me about five hours. I had a quick glance at my old battered UK road atlas and made a conscious note to stop at Inverness for lunch.

I thought back at my life in the police; it was always good when you 'got your man' and secured a conviction. The sense of achievement and job satisfaction was rewarding; and this is how I felt at the moment.

I once had a case where I had tons of evidence against the accused – from fingerprint and DNA evidence to dozens of eye witness statements and CCTV recordings, yet I still did not have the accused in custody. A warrant was issued for his immediate arrest should he be sighted and every cop in the area was vigilant for a visual on the guy, however he seemed to elude us. Weeks went by and hope was fading when one day he pinged one of the town's CCTV cameras. An on-the-ball observer spotted him coming out of a shop and called in the cavalry. Soon he was surrounded by the boys in blue and, following a valiant struggle, he was finally arrested – and I had my man. It felt fantastic to tie up the case and finally turn my suspect into an accused.

I glided along the A82 running parallel to Loch Ness whilst my *Rock Driving Hits* CD blared way out of the car speakers. I scanned the dark cold waters of the vast foreboding loch, but could see no sight or sound of the infamous Loch Ness Monster. I figured it may prove easier to locate Nessie than Walker or Dixon; if Nessie did exist, at least they knew where he was; it was just a matter of seeking and finding, employing all manner of sophisticated equipment for the task; but Paul and Mick could be anywhere in the world and I didn't have any specialist gear to help me find them. I would just have to rely on my tried and tested detecting skills.

At Inverness, I partook of a fast food lunch, courtesy of the local *Subway*. My foot-long sub laden with Teriyaki Chicken and dripping with sweet onion sauce was delicious and filling, if still overpriced. Thoughtfully, the staff gave me a bundle of napkins, and I used them all wiping the smear of sauce and salad juice from my hands, face and clothes. I then gave Alison a call to tell her I was on my way, as promised. She answered almost immediately as though sitting waiting for my call.

'So how was your mission to Skye?' she asked as excited as a child, 'was it a success?'

'Yeah, it was – very successful,' I said with all the air of a General after a victorious battle. Alison whooped like a hyperactive child.

'You mean you met Danny Carter?' she asked, having calmed down enough to breath again.

'Yeah; me and Danny hung out for the day.'

'I…I...don't believe it,' she stammered, 'you actually met the famous Danny Carter?'

I assured her I was not jesting and had indeed met the great man. She demanded to know all about my meet and what Carter was like now, but I informed her all would be revealed when I saw her in person. She said she would wait my imminent arrival with eager anticipation. I was hoping she was as keen to see me as to hear about my adventure with Carter.

The satnav calculated I still had about 105 miles to run, and worked out this would take just under three hours, so I pushed on intending to be at Alison's place in Aberdeen before rush hour.

My route took me past the towns of Nairn, Forres, and then Elgin. At one point on the dual carriageway road, I spotted a police car trying to hide by the side of the road, the dual crew hoping to catch the wary speedster out and empty their 'conditional offer of fixed penalty' books before their shifts-end and get a triumphant pat on the back from their supervisors. In my police days, the traffic department always seemed to think highly of themselves, emanating an air of arrogance and considering their skills and pristine cars not worthy of attending non-traffic related calls and incidents. It was always a delight to hear a sergeant or higher rank order them to attend calls such as a fight outside a nightclub or housebreaking in progress as they were the closest unit to the incident and drove those big powerful fast cars.

On more than one occasion in my service, I recalled Road Policing Department cars driving away from a disturbance or serious incident when myself and colleagues were heading to the call. Frustratingly, they never seemed to be reprimanded for the obvious neglect of duty; it's not as if a normal police patrol can turn their backs on a road traffic accident saying 'That's not my remit!'

I knew a colleague who had a minor crash with one of the marked police cars as he was driving to an urgent assistance call, which caused minor damage to the bodywork. No one was injured and no other property was damaged; however the traffic sergeant swiftly arrived on the scene in his shiny *Mercedes* and proceeded to breathalyse then charge the cop for careless and inconsiderate driving. A prosecution report was sent to the Procurator Fiscal, who fortunately had more sense than the sergeant, and sent the report to the security shredder.

Once again my satnav girlfriend impressed by guiding me straight to Alison's address with only the occasional hiccup in directions. As I applied the handbrake and extinguished the engine, bang on cue, my heart started its wild race and my mouth went dry. This would be the first time Alison and I had seen each other for quite some years; how many exactly, I did not know. I expected she would be just as nervous as I.

About six or seven years after Alison packed up her troubles in her old kit bag and left Glasgow for Aberdeen, she had met and later married a doctor at the hospital where she was now a senior staff nurse. Married life was good to begin with, then gradually deteriorated as it was discovered that Doctor Charming was a control freak with a propensity for regular bouts of violence. He hit Alison: the beatings being moderate to start, then with increasing ferocity as he learned that he had her under his thumb and was in a position to manipulate her and dictate his philosophies at will – and she never resisted. Alison was too fearful to call for assistance of the police or any other helpful agency and merely tried to ignore the problem thinking it might just disappear.

She suffered not just physical violence but an equal share of emotional turmoil. She regularly sported cuts and bruises and went to great lengths to cover them up cosmetically and explain them away by a series of stories and lies from the old 'walking into a door' routine to the rather creative 'I fell off the treadmill at the gym.'

Alison's nursing colleagues worried about her and did not believe her cover-up stories; however her doctor husband was in a senior management position at the same hospital and the consequences of interfering actions were enough to deter the nurses from taking action. It was one of Alison's worried neighbours who finally put an end to her living hell. The neighbour heard the disturbance which was louder then usual and hit all three nines on her telephone to report the urgent matter to police. A team of Northern Constabulary's finest attended and witnessed Doctor Charming practicing his boxing skills on his wife-shaped punch-bag. He was soon dispatched in handcuffs to the local nick, then Aberdeen Sheriff Court before ending his journey in Peterhead Prison. A relieved Alison took quite a few years to finally recover from her emotional and physical turmoil.

I only learned all this from Lee who used to make regular trips up to stay with his mum on the odd weekend and school holidays. He never liked the doctor husband and could sense his controlling nature and arrogant demeanour behind the façade of charm and sophistication. The doctor couldn't wait for the teenage Lee to leave after his stay so he could resume his tyrannical behaviour towards the boy's mother.

I remember hearing of the beatings administered to my ex-wife from Lee and was poised to race up to Aberdeen, confront the doctor and make sure he spent some quality time in the Intensive Care department of his own hospital, hooked up to all the machines the ward could find.

Lee had to calm me and try reasoning with me; I was furious with the husband. Although ours was largely an estranged marriage for the best part, I never once laid a finger on Alison and would not dream of such a course of action. My son had to restrain and continually remind me that I risked jeopardising my police career if I sought to vent my anger on the violent doctor.

Alison must have watched me arriving on her street as she was at the door to meet and greet. I considered the possibilities of what to do when meeting: do we shake hands? But that seemed too informal, or do we hug? But that was a bit too intimate considering the length of time since we last met. When I ascended the top step to her front door, she had obviously decided that a hug would be in order. She outstretched her arms like a scarecrow and flung them around me as though meeting a long lost relative with a healthy bank balance in his will. We kissed briefly on each other's cheek and that was the meeting formality over.

'You're looking well. Tony,' Alison chirped.

'And you Alison, gorgeous as ever.' I returned with a smile and watched her cheeks redden.

'Come on in out the cold, Mr Caulfield,' she said and led me along the long corridor to a comfortable, well furnished living room.

I could see she had not changed much as far as her taste in décor was concerned. There were candles on every conceivable ledge and shelf, homely nick-knacks on the walls, and an abundance of cushions on the sofa and chairs. She took my jacket and I watched her walk towards the coat hooks in the hallway – she was indeed looking good. She had kept in shape and now suited the short centre parted hairstyle she now sported; plus she hadn't lost that wide genuine smile of hers. When she returned I had taken the liberty of sitting down on the sofa, after moving around some cushions to make room; some were heart-shaped and some frilly, but all in a dark magenta colour. She took a seat on an armchair and we faced each other. I could see the bruised and cuts had now healed and luckily did not spoil her still youthful facial features.

'How are you doing Alison; is it good to be single again? She looked dismayed and avoided eye contact.

'I'm fine Tony, in fact I'm great since I got rid of him.' I didn't need reminding to whom she referred.

'I'm sorry you had to go through that, Alison,' I responded. 'I was all set to come up here and sort him out.'

'Yeah, I know. Lee told me. But look, its all in the past now and I don't really want to talk about it.' Alison said with a smile while she rubbed her hands together.

'So tell me all about meeting Andy Brookes and Danny Carter.'

'I'll tell you everything over a cup of coffee,' I replied.

Off she went to the kitchen and returned minutes later with two matching mugs of steaming liquid and a plate of assorted biscuits. We settled down on our seats and I told her all.

I recalled how I pieced together the fragments which led me to Birmingham and finding Andy Brookes. Then I impressed her with my detecting skills by narrowing down the search net to the Isle of Skye in the hunt for Danny Carter. She was amused at my rolling in damp grass posing as a bird watcher in order to spy on Carter's place, and actually getting to hang out with him for a day, finally culminating in him agreeing to a reunion of the Faceless Legions for one last come-back concert.

After an hour of talking, we decided on a takeaway for dinner. Out came the takeaway menus and we opted for a Chinese meal. A quick phone-call to the local 'Orient Express' and we were promised delivery within the hour.

'So what's next then? How do you plan on finding the others?' Alison enquired. I shrugged and threw up my hands.

'It's going to be hard. I've very little to go on. I haven't a clue where to start searching for Paul Dixon and Mick Walker. You know that Chas Hannagan died?'

'Yeah, I heard about that a couple of years ago. Look, I'm sure you'll do it Tony. I have every faith in you,' Alison replied with a cheerful smile.

By now we were totally relaxed in each others company. I was very glad to be here and talking to her, and I'm sure she was delighted to see me. Gradually throughout the evening, Alison had moved closer to me as though learning to trust me again. She moved from her armchair to the opposite end of the sofa, claiming that she needed to be nearer to me to hear all I had to say, but I detected the proximity was more than just a hearing issue. That was fine by me.

Chapter 13

When the hot food arrived, we dined in the kitchen at the small dining table. Alison even lit a couple of candles to hint at a slightly elegant and romantic mood, and she opened a bottle of wine. We chatted as we ate and covered a wealth of ground from our past, recalling how and when we met; the places we went on our first dates up to getting married. The mention of this seemed to trigger a slight melancholic mood in the proceedings. We brooded over how we both transformed from happy couple madly in love to practically living as friends or housemates. We each blamed ourselves for the marital breakdown, citing work commitments and career advancement as the mitigating factors. Then the apologies flew thick and fast. Funny how it had taken so long for us both to admit we were mutually to blame, and make our apologies.

Soon evening gave way to night and it dawned on me that I didn't have a plan for accommodation. I was figuring I would only be at Alison's for a flying visit and would then motor on home down the A90; but now it was rather late to be setting off on the 150 mile journey back to Glasgow. Besides I was tired with the driving from Portree, plus I was still recovering from my hiking aches from the previous day.

'I can give you a sleeping bag and you can kip on the sofa,' Alison offered.

'No, it's all right, I'll go and see if I can get a room at a *Travelodge* or somewhere,' I returned, although I quite fancied taking her up on her offer. 'I don't want to intrude.'

'Don't be daft, Tony.' Alison said with a dismissive swipe of her hand. 'It's not as if we're strangers.' I admired her logic and jumped at the chance to kip on the comfortable sofa; besides I wouldn't be short of a cushion or three. So I acquiesced and stayed the night.

I was on the road by 10am the following day after consuming almost my entire bodyweight in carbohydrates: Alison showing she still has the makings of a wife presented me with a full cooked breakfast. Initially I recoiled at the plate load placed before me, but I must have been hungry as I cleaned the plate and enjoyed the feast. Then Alison provided me with a bath towel and pointed me towards the shower. I don't think I was smelled bad, I reckon she was just being helpful; after all that's what you do when you have a friend for a sleepover.

Spending the evening and next morning with my ex-wife was surreal; as though we had never parted and seemed content and relaxed in each other's company – plus I think she still felt as much attraction to me as I did to her. I really wouldn't complain if we began a fresh relationship, although the strategy would have to be: slow and easy, no pressure, no hassles just see how it goes.

Alison kissed me goodbye after insisting I keep her up to date with my mission progress; I promised I would. She was now a big supporter of my quest and wanted to contribute in any way she could. She even revealed she had a couple of weeks annual leave coming up shortly and would be happy to keep me company on my travels if I so wished. I bore that in mind; I may just take her up on her offer.

So I buckled up, primed the *Hyundai's* engine and headed for the Scottish lowlands. The A90 was practically downhill all the way with the grey restless North Sea on my left. The occasional sighting of a container ship or oil tanker was mixed with the drone of helicopters plying their trade across the busy shore-to-oil platform airway corridor, with gangs of workers being transported to and from their jobs on the various oil rigs and platforms dotted along the sea between Scotland and Norway. The oil industry being an essential and lucrative revenue earner for Scotland, the proceeds of which were swiftly taken from them to pay the bills at Westminster - allegedly!

I called into Perth for a comfort break; although it was lunch time, I certainly didn't need lunch as Alison's huge breakfast would be enough to see me through to supper time.

I recalled an incident many years ago when Alison and I, prior to being married, went over to Belfast to visit a relative of hers. We stayed overnight with an aunt, who served us a Northern

Ireland breakfast special. The plate was extra large and needed to be to accommodate the myriad of food items. Upon it sat link sausages, square sausages, bacon, a pork chop, tomatoes, mushrooms, beans, fried eggs, fried bread, soda bread, wheaten bread, potato bread and a whole load of grease to lubricate the food. We stared in disturbed horror at the feast before us, knowing that sweet Aunt Nellie would expect us to polish off the lot. We eventually did, although it did take a while. After the belly-aching breakfast, we decided to go for a walk in an attempt to burn off the excessive calories before it went straight to our thighs and hips. On the way, we passed yet another of Alison's relatives, and we popped in for a quick visit. After a brief catch up, the elderly women went through to the kitchen, which we assumed was to fire up the kettle; she emerged about forty minutes later beckoning us through to the kitchen.

'I've made you both a little something to eat,' she declared, 'it's a speciality here in Northern Ireland.' She pointed at two laden plates of food on the kitchen table – and it was almost identical to the heart attack we had just consumed about an hour ago!

'Enjoy,' she sang in her Northern Irish lilt and studied both our faces expecting us to be stunned by the culinary masterpiece. We were not so much stunned as horrified at the sight of yet more food, but managed, I think, to look impressed as we took a seat at the table. None of us had the heart to tell the old lady we had just recently partook of one of the legendary Northern Ireland breakfast specials.

I was back in Glasgow by mid afternoon. Heaving open the door to Castle Caulfield, the door snowploughed a pile of mail into the hallway. I picked up the letters and pondered the sight of an A4 envelope with a hand-written address label. Tearing open the package, I caught sight of some familiar faces. I had forgotten I had bought these nearly a week ago – it was the vintage magazines purchased on *Ebay* – the ones featuring articles, photographs and interviews with the Faceless Legions.

Half an hour later, after tossing my worn clothes in the washing machine and emptying my bag, I sat down with a refreshing cup of coffee and studied the old magazines for any hint of a clue which would be helpful with my ongoing quest.

As suspected, the glossy pages yielded nothing by way of new or useful information about the Legions, although I did enjoy reading the articles and it was interesting to see photos of the band I had never seen before. One showed the band posing for an official photo-shoot; it looked like they had all been in the hairstylists shop just prior to the shoot: the pose was very clichéd rock and roll – that macho look, half smiling, half trying to look mean, and all dressed in various articles of denim and leather. Danny, having a reputation for smiling a lot, looked the coolest and most natural of the bunch; Paul being the grumpiest did not have to try too hard to look tough.

Other photos showed the band playing live on a variety of stages around the world – from London to Lisbon and Rome to Rio. They were in their prime and doing what they loved – it was a pity that all ended so abruptly and the band migrated to the four winds. Still, I had, so far succeeded in tracing two of the musicians and was now setting my sights on the next candidate – drummer Paul Dixon.

I fetched my world atlas and spread it before me. I stared down upon Australia – it was indeed a vast place. Danny's unhelpful suggestion to begin my search for Dixon in Australia was looking like a non-starter. I didn't even have an area, or a city with which to start my hunt. If Dixon had indeed emigrated here, he could be anywhere from Western Australia to New South Wales – heck, he could even be living like an Aboriginal in Tasmania for all I knew.

Then it dawned on me that, unlike most other countries in the world, Australia actually had a modest number of cities in the vast country, partly due to desert claiming a good chunk of the place; or so my map revealed. Out of all the major cities displayed, I could identify: Perth, Adelaide, Melbourne, Canberra, Sydney and Brisbane. Suddenly the country shrank in size and I began to feel hopeful. If I was to pursue the line of Paul Dixon and Australia, I would need to narrow the search down to a much smaller area, and right now, I had nothing to go on.

I thought of Mick Walker, but Carter could offer nothing by way of clue to where he could be presently. I recalled from one of the magazine interviews Walker stating he hailed from London; but could he still be resident in the city? According to Brookes, all the guys made a small fortune from being part of the band, so none of them would be forced to remain living in Britain if they fancied moving to sunnier climes. Maybe Walker had used his wealth, like his colleague

Brookes and bought a piano shop or studio or something similar, perhaps still in London?

It was time to fire up the trusty laptop computer to see if it could be of assistance. Although elated at meeting and managing to persuade both Brookes and Carter to sign up for a band reunion, my mood was beginning to ebb when I thought of the almost impossible task of finding the other needles in the vast haystack of the world. Perhaps I should target Chas Hannagan's family; they might well be able to provide some information worthy of my consideration. Hannagan's family, I knew wouldn't be particularly hard to find – I knew there was a wealth of newspaper stories online reporting the death and subsequent funeral of Chas; and I knew he died at the family home somewhere in south Wales.

Windows had now booted up, so I brought up the internet browser and began my search for the news stories on Hannagan's demise. Quick as a wink, I was presented with all the info I needed in glorious black and white with the occasional colour photo showing grieving members of the Hannagan clan, smartly attired in drab black and dark blue clothing and sporting white handkerchiefs which dabbed at tear stained eyes and dangled below running noses. I read the article:

'This was the scene today as hundreds of mourners turned out to the funeral of Charles 'Chas' Hannagan, musician and former member of the British rock band the Faceless Legions. Hannagan died in the early hours of Tuesday morning at the family home in Carmarthen, South Wales, after suffering a heart attack. A spokesman for the family stated that, although Hannagan was a self-confessed drug addict, he had acknowledged his dependency and was actively seeking help'. The article went on:

'Hannagan is survived by his wife Rita; 28 year old son, Dale and 30 year old daughter Rhonda. None of Hannagan's former colleagues from his music days appeared to be in attendance at the funeral. Fans paid tribute to the musician saying he was a fantastic musician, a great personality, loved his rock and roll and would be sadly missed.'

I didn't know if Hannagan, prior to his ill health and subsequent death, still played professionally – the so-called tribute by fans would suggest he was playing up until recently; or perhaps they all had long vivid memories.

Carmarthen - I checked my UK road atlas to check exactly where it was; I had heard of the place but needed confirmation as to its precise position. I sighed when I performed a rough calculation on the distance to Carmarthen: it looked about 400 miles away and would likely take me about seven or eight hours of travel. If only I had thought of this earlier – I could have tied up a visit to Wales with my trip to Birmingham. Who said this mission would be easy?

I deferred my decision on a trip to Wales for the moment and turned my attention to a more in-depth search for some fragment that could help me narrow down my search for Walker and Dixon.

As before, I performed a search for the Faceless Legions – and got more or less the same sparse data as before. I narrowed the search further and tried differing keywords. Still more of the same; most of the results were simply links to the same websites, but different pages. I trawled and trawled, page after page I sifted through. I was descending into my own personal doldrums when I struck gold. Off went my heart on a sprint and my hand shook like an earth tremor as I clicked on the website entitled 'Legions of Fans.'

Chapter 14

We didn't have computer systems in the police - well not at first anyway and not in my early days. Then they introduced a crude system but only for the higher ranks to access police data and reports. Eventually came the PNC: Police National Computer, then smaller systems like the Crime Management system, Prisoner Processing and the Scottish Intelligence database. All these system were helpful, though slow, but the main problem was they were not linked in any way; this caused countless hours of tedious repetition in entering the same information when you wanted to perform a search for a suspect in connection with an ongoing enquiry.

As I was retiring, the police now had a great many computer systems in place, but the same problem remained – they still had no actual connection allowing simple searches on multiple systems. So this involved tedious duplication of data into each and every system – a long, laborious and frustrating task; and the public wonder why they never see the police on the streets! After all these years, police forces had failed to embrace the technology adequately for the greater good. If only *Google* or the like got invited on board, perhaps the police forces of the world would be much more efficient. If I was using a police computer system to carry out my research as part of Operation Lazarus, I almost certainly would have given up a while ago.

That was the thought that struck me when surfing the net on my own personal quest. I smirked when I remembered a PC who worked at my police station. PC Henderson was the office joker and was always busy with one prank after another. His favourite trick was to swap the N and M keys around on all computer keyboards, causing untold frustration and misery. He had the entire station thinking they couldn't spell and convinced they were dyslexic, and no one every noticed the deliberately juxtaposed keys.

Why had I not found this goldmine of a website before? What were the sophisticated and complex *Google* algorithm systems playing at? This was the most relevant site I had found – a website dedicated entirely to the band itself, and run by bona fide fans.

I browsed the pages, and was treated to loads of information and pictures of the band, but annoyingly I didn't learn anything new; nothing to assist me and advance my research much.

Then I found the forums page – and this was exactly what I sought. Page upon page of burning questions and knowledgeable answers from dedicated fans of the band. I ran down the list of discussions; nothing much of interest so far. Then it jumped out the screen and hit me. The discussion was entitled 'Whatever happened to the Faceless Legions?' I clicked through the threads but could find no useful answers from the recipients. Pretty much just the usual speculation and guesswork, though none had suggested that Danny Carter was alive and well living on the Isle of Skye and Andy Brookes was the proprietor of a guitar shop in Birmingham. I certainly wasn't going to reveal this nugget of information.

Someone with the unlikely username of 'rocknroller332' provided the mother of all clues to the whereabouts of Paul Dixon. If I could have met the guy, I would have shaken his hand clean off. The reply read like this:

'I saw (or at least I think I saw) Paul Dixon while on a recent holiday in Perth, Australia. He was playing drums with a blues band in a pub in the city'.

I reckon my eyes must have popped out of their sockets for a moment. I couldn't believe how valuable this information was. This was one huge helpful clue. With a bit of perseverance and manifold mouse clicks, I had confirmed the theory of Dixon and Australia; plus I had his whereabouts narrowed down to the city of Perth in Western Australia. It was like looking at a view of Earth from space and zooming in on Australia, then more zooming until you had Perth, then zooming even further right down to street level. I had no doubt the city of Perth was large, but this was certainly a promising place to start.

My elevated mood fell slightly when I noticed that thread entry was over a year old. I hoped this did not matter, as I was sure Dixon would still be there. Given the fan stated he witnessed Dixon playing in a band, I was sure this could only mean the man resided there; I doubted he had happened to secure a guest spot while on holiday.

My appetite was whetted and I craved more information from this source. I intended sending the guy (I presumed it was a guy) a message hoping to gain more info on his sighting of the drummer, but the website stated I needed to create an account in order to send messages and participate on the forums. So I duly created such an account in a matter of minutes and was soon welcomed to the site as an official user and reminded of the usual protocols for behaviour while participating. I felt very special indeed.

I sent rocknroller332 a message asking if he could provide any more details on his sighting of Paul Dixon – the pub name, address and anything else relevant. I was praying this username was still active on the forums and would receive my message. More importantly, I hoped he would reply with more information, something I could utilise to help narrow down the search net a bit.

I wasn't expecting a reply anytime soon, so I left my research station and rocknroller332 to chew over my questions, and went upstairs to the bathroom where I ran a deep hot bath with the intention of soaking my still aching muscles following my recent hiking trip.

As I lay in the warm comforting arms of the foamy bathtub, I planned my next phase of Operation Lazarus. My mission would now require yet another trip down south, but I knew it would be easy enough to find the Hannagan family and try to talk Chas's son Dale into joining the reunited band. I would tell him I had Carter and Brookes already signed up, so that should grease the axles somewhat.

However I really needed a rest – a day or two off in which to recuperate so I would be fit, able and fully energised to continue my quest. Besides I had achieved more than I had hoped or expected. So far, it had been taxing on my brain and required full use of my detective abilities, but I had accomplished so much. At first I thought my operation would be doomed from the start and end up with a truckload of hassles, grief and frustration, but now Operation Lazarus was beginning to look more like a brilliant idea than a hair-brained scheme – and I felt good about the whole thing.

The next morning brought some very welcoming news: my new forum buddy had posted a reply:

    'As I said, I'm pretty sure it was Paul Dixon, but please don't quote me on that...I'm not 100%

sure, probably only about 90%!!! The band (sorry I don't remember the name) was the resident band playing every weekend in the bar. I can't recall the name of the bar but it was a 'rhythm and blues' themed place with pictures of old blues guys on the walls! Sorry I can't be of any further help. If I remember anything else, I'll send you a message.'

Fragments they may be, but they all went somewhere to contributing to the overall picture. My forum contact may have thought he hadn't been very helpful, but he had provided enough detail to help narrow down my search to a specific area of the city. I wondered if I could tease any further info from him; perhaps he just required asking specific questions.

This was something we routinely did with suspect interview in the police. Ask them basic closed questions and all you'll get are head nods, shakes or mumbled yes or no replies which aren't always helpful. But ask a suspect an open-ended question and they'll have to provide an answer other then an affirmative or negative; that's unless they decide on the good old 'no comment' reply.

'Sorry to trouble you, but any chance you could narrow the pub down to a specific area of the city?' I typed in great expectation. The reply was swift in coming.

'Yeah, it was in Guildford – I remember that because that's where I live in London! Freaky or what?'

Yes indeed, it was all rather coincidental, but that information was of great assistance and helped progress the operation along nicely. I thought that would be it from rocknroller332, but he (or was it she, I still hadn't been able to ascertain) came back with a nugget of a clue: a photo of the band playing in the blues bar in Guildford, Perth. Certainly it was not the best quality photo given it had been taken on a mobile phone in a gloomy pub with the band moving around the small stage, but it was worthy of closer scrutiny. I thanked my contact for this helpful piece of evidence then began to study it in detail like a zoologist studying a fossil.

The scene showed most of the band: I spotted a bearded guitarist playing a semi-acoustic guitar, the singer was female and was dressed more like a country and western singer than a rhythm and blues one, in a frilly skirt and cowboy boots; I could only see part of the bass player's instrument as he was not in the shot, then the drummer in the background – was this Paul Dixon?

Sure enough, in the background hanging on the walls were the aforementioned photos – I couldn't make out many of the stars in the frames, but one or two stood out. One, I was certain was BB King, perched on a seat and strumming away on his *Gibson* ES-355. Next to BB was the unmistakable pose of Chuck Berry: semi-acoustic guitar practically touching the floor as he hopped on one leg whilst playing.

I zoomed in on the face of the drummer; I could see how rocknroller332 was uncertain – it was difficult to tell. I grabbed one of the recently acquired magazines and flicked it open to a photo of Dixon playing the drums in what looked like a recording studio. I held up the picture alongside the screen and studied both – there was a marked difference in the two drummers. One had long flowing brown hair, the other grey, almost white hair which was seriously receding on top but slightly long at the back. Both sat atop their drum stool unsmiling and looking gloomy as though drumming was a chore or the photographer an intrusion. I compared the nose shape between each photo – similar I had to admit: slightly bulbous and rounded at the tip, not pointed; then the lips – now they were more obvious – both drummers had a marked protruding lower lip, slightly fatter than the top and very distinct.

The final confirmation came from the glasses worn by the possible Paul; I remember he always wore glasses with a tint in the lenses; this was probably to help protect his eyes against the glare of the spotlights; but the drummer playing in the recent photo also wore glasses and I could detect a definite purple-ish tint over his eyes. I sat back and exhaled a long breath of triumph; I was more than convinced this was Paul Dixon and was happy enough to pursue the matter.

Just to ease my path before I contemplated heading to Australia, I decided to narrow down the net even further. I counted the pieces of information I had: a resident blues band in a rhythm and blues themed bar in Guildford, Perth, Australia. That shouldn't be too hard to find, but I thought if I had an exact address, this would ease my path when I got to Perth and save a bit of time and frustrated messing around.

I performed a search of bars in Guildford with regular live music programmes – the result was an unhelpfully large list of venues. I noticed not all satisfied my search criteria: some unhelpful entries having slipped through and around the search engine filters. I utilised the advanced search and narrowed the list down to a handful of bars.

More clicking and more risk of repetitive strain injury to my wrist, and I had a manageable list of bars which had a resident band playing at weekends. I dove even further pushing the advanced search to its limits, requesting it to furnish me with blues bands or blues themed venues – and soon I had a nice short manageable list presented before me.

I visited each bar website; here I was given a whole bucket-load of information about each bar's history, its famous patronage visits and all their drinks promotions – but none of this was of any interest to me; besides, Paul Dixon wasn't on the list of famous people to have paid the bar a visit!

It was photos of the interior of each venue I was after. I was happy to see the majority of the bars had some photos on their websites showing a busy bar area and the odd blurred photo of the resident band. I trawled through each site in turn, studying the live bands; so far none of them looked like the photo supplied by my forum friend; however I persevered.

Then like an Arab digging deep into the ground, I struck oil, so to speak. The aptly named 'Johnny B Goode Bar' showed a band playing on a small stage in the corner of the lounge; although the band were too far way to identify the members, my eagle eye at once caught the sight of the photos of the Chuck and BB adorning the walls – this had to be the place. I compared photos and was certain this would be where I could meet the once famous Paul Dixon.

Then a moment of uncertainty washed over – my forum contact had taken the photo over one year ago; what if they had a different resident band playing now? Maybe the bar employed a policy of regular changes in its entertainment billing in order to keep its image fresh and, more importantly, encouraging the masses to keep coming through its doors to buy drinks. Still if the band in question were any good, they might remain the star billing.

I reasoned this was sufficient enough evidence to warrant a long, laborious and expensive journey down under. Besides, if it was indeed Dixon who was the drummer of the in-house band in the Johnny B Goode but no longer played, then surely the staff in the bar would be able to tell me where he had gone. If he had moved on, I was betting it was to another bar, probably in the area.

I noted the address from the 'contact us' page and added this to my folder which now housed all the information I had so far gathered in connection with my mission – I gave the folder a title: Operation Lazarus – files and information.

Chapter 15

Suddenly the operation was becoming very expensive. Granted, I had clocked up a fair mileage so far with my journeys to and from Birmingham; then to Portree, across to Aberdeen, then back to Glasgow; I felt like a touring musician. My expenses so far had been moderate with only the cost of diesel for my fuel-efficient car and reasonable accommodation charges; but now the cost of the operation was about to skyrocket I suspected. Not that money was a real issue – my police retirement pay covered all my bills easily and left me with a reasonable amount to live on, plus I had a healthy reserve in a savings account in the event of an emergency; not that I had a very extravagant lifestyle: my mortgage was fully paid off, I owned a very economical car and didn't exactly throw money away. When retiring, it was suggested I go out and buy a set of expensive golf clubs and join a prestigious club, but I was never much interested in golf before retiring, so I certainly didn't crave the challenge now.

Yet again the world's friend *Google* came to my assistance and provided me with a quick flight price search engine. I knew *Emirates* operated a daily service from Glasgow airport to Dubai International. I researched this and within seconds got my answer – and a shock into the bargain. I recoiled in my seat and stared horrified at the screen. *Emirates* would be happy to take over £950 from my wallet to fly me to Dubai. I didn't want to buy the plane – I just wanted a seat on the thing.

Once I had recovered, I searched for a connecting flight from Dubai to Perth, Australia: another eye-popping price – over one grand! A quick addition sum revealed a trip from Glasgow to Perth would cost nearly £2000 – and that was just one way.

Besides the price, I couldn't be bothered messing around in different airports and would have preferred a direct flight; but at what cost? I changed my search criteria and nominated London Heathrow as my departure point, specifying a round-trip price. The displayed prices were still high though no where near the previous shockers. The multitude of airlines offering to fly me the vast distance to the other side of the world were as varied as their prices. I guessed this was largely due to the aircraft type each operated; *Qantas* operating their super fuel-efficient *Boeing 787 Dreamliner* naturally were the cheapest.

With a bit of time and perseverance I got the price of a return trip from London to Perth for a very reasonable cost and my hopeful mood returned. The next dilemma was when to go; I wanted to keep up the continuity of the mission and strike while the iron was still blazing. This was Thursday and I wanted to get away as soon as possible, but the flight prices increased for weekend travel, so in order to remain on a tight-ish budget, I had no option but to wait until the beginning of next week.

Accommodation – this was the next mission: to find a reasonably priced hotel in or near to Guildford, Perth where I would be near to my target area in the event I had to make multiple visits to the Johnny B Goode bar. I would avoid, where possible, having to rely on taxis and public transport and use my legs instead. Then the unanswered question rang inside my head: how long would I be away for? I couldn't answer this one. If I was lucky, then as little as a couple of days ought to do it; then again, if tracing Dixon was going to prove more problematic, then it may well take a week or more. I would seriously risk blowing my hypothetical small budget.

I was trawling through hotels in the Guildford area when my mobile, which was lying on the table beside me, buzzed and began a shuddering expedition across the table top. I grabbed it before it reached the edge and gravity took over. I looked at the screen prior to answering it – it was Stevie, my band colleague.

'Yo, Catcher how's it going?'

'Not too bad Stevie,' I returned in a cheery mood.' What can I do you for?' I could sense excitement and pride in his voice.

'Remember the wedding gig I told you about?' I thought back - then recalled the conversation outside the Regent pub. I became slightly irritated; being so caught up in my own little quest I hadn't given the conversation a second thought.

'Oh yeah, that gig?' I replied with all the enthusiasm of an undertaker. He must have sensed my apprehension and replied.

'Have I caught you at a bad time, mate?'

'No, no problem; I'm just a bit busy at the moment,' I said. He cut through my despondency hoping his news would instantly transform my mood.

'Well the gig – it's a go!'

'Great – when is it?' I asked wondering if I would be back from my planned trip to Australia in time.

'Saturday – it's on this Saturday evening,' Stevie said, 'Tell me you can still do it Tony. The rest of the guys are up for it. I know it's a bit short notice but the other band pulled out at the last minute.' I could detect a slight hint of disappointment creeping into his voice as if expecting me to let the team down.

'Yeah, that's no problem, I can do it.' Then by way of explanation I continued, 'I'm just a bit distracted right now.' He seemed audibly relieved by the news that I would be on board.

He provided all the pertinent details, the when and where. I noted the reception venue and time where we would be permitted access to set up and sound check; then we swapped our goodbyes.

I thought it fortunate that I hadn't gone ahead and booked the flights and hotel, otherwise I would be facing the dilemma and hassles of changing flights and reservations, or pull out the gig letting the others down. But that would work out nicely – the gig was two days away and I would aim to fly out to Perth perhaps Tuesday or Wednesday. That would give me adequate time to prepare and pack.

The next thing on my list to consider and decide upon was how I would get down to London. My options were: catch a shuttle flight from Glasgow or drive down and leave the car in a long term car-park; alternatively, hire a car, picking it up in Glasgow and dropping it off at Heathrow. I was all rather undecided at the moment – too many unknowns to make a proper decision.

I was still mindful of the need to visit the Hannagan family in Wales, so I considered it may be economically viable to drive to Carmarthen where, all being well, I would be able to speak with Dale Hannagan, then I could drive over to London in time for my flight. But was it better to call into Wales on the way back from Australia? I would have to carefully think about and weigh up each option before making my final decision and going ahead with the expensive hotel and flight bookings.

Later that evening I called Andy Brookes to update him on the progress of Operation Lazarus. He answered after a couple of rings.

'Hi Andy, its Tony Caulfield here.' There was a slight pause as he ran the name through his memory bank. Either he hadn't entered my name along with the number into his mobile phone, or he had a very poor short-term memory.

'Oh Hi, Tony,' he replied, but I could tell he was still trying to ascertain my identity. I thought I would help him out.

'It's Tony from Glasgow. We met recently in your shop.' Still there were only hums of uncertainty coming back through the speaker, so I elaborated.

'You know, about getting the Faceless Legions back together again.' Suddenly the penny dropped; I was beginning to get worried. If his memory was that bad, then maybe he would forget to turn up to the big Faceless Legions reunion gig!

Now that he was back to normal, he became enthusiastic and wanted to know how I was progressing with my quest. I told him my success in finding Danny Carter alive and kicking on the Isle of Skye and thanked him for the snippet of information which was instrumental in leading me up north to the island.

Brookes was overjoyed when I told him that Danny was up for reuniting; he had half expected me to be unsuccessful considering it an almost impossible task. Now I had proved my worth and he could now take me seriously. I had demonstrated that my detective skills were still as sharp as ever.

'It would be great to speak to Danny. Any chance you could give me his phone number?' Andy asked.

'Well I don't want to give out his number without his say so,' I replied apologetically. 'But you can send him an email through his business website.' He murmured his agreement and I heard him rummaging around looking for a pen and bit of paper; eventually he gave me the go ahead and I told him the website address being sure to spell out letter-for-letter the complex Gaelic words: Tigh-na-Bain.

Andy scribbled the details down and I told him I had a possible sighting of Paul Dixon in Perth, Australia and was intending to head down there to follow the lead. He was over the moon at my enthusiasm and temerity to travel to the ends of the earth in search of his former comrades. This information should keep him suitably enthused and energised for a possible reunion gig, and go some way to demonstrating I was serious about the operation to resurrect the dead band.

The next day brought a surprise, and was instrumental in assisting me with my dilemma. I was hunched over the laptop checking hotel prices in Guildford, Perth when the front door was knocked. My first thought was it had to be the postman, but the items I had ordered recently had been delivered. Next on the list was an unsolicited call from a cold caller; perhaps even a couple of Jehovah's Witnesses eager to recruit me into their fold. Enough pondering, I would never know unless I answered it.

I glided over to the front door preparing to take on the cold caller and send him packing before he could launch into his spiel. I flung the door open and stared in disbelief at the figure standing on the doorstep. The young man stared back at me; it was like looking in a mirror. He was as tall as me; same short neatly cropped hair, albeit his was brown where mine was tinged with grey; same blue eyes and clean masculine facial features.

'Hi dad; any chance I can come in?' I burst out laughing; half from sheer surprise and half from how silly the question was – of course my son could come in. I stepped aside and beckoned him inside.

'Lee, what a pleasant surprise.'

He stepped over the threshold and we hugged like playful bears. His grip was as strong as mine;

140

no surprise given his muscular physique. I could feel his broad shoulders and firm pectorals as he squeezed me firmly. We withdrew from each others embrace and I pushed the door closed as he moved into the hallway.

'So what brings you to town, son?' I enquired, the obvious pleasure beaming from my face.

'Just up for a flying visit. Thought I would visit you, then head up to Aberdeen to visit mum.'

I pondered when I had last seen my son – it must have been about a year ago. Lee worked in the construction industry and was living in London. He returned to Scotland at least once a year and generally called in to see me before heading up to visit with Alison. Normally his visits were fleeting and left no real chance to spend time with him. It would be good if he was up for a little longer this time, although I was mindful of my planned Antipodean excursion.

I left Lee in the living room whilst I went to the kitchen to boil the kettle. When I turned around to fetch the cups from the mug tree, he was beside me.

'So how's things dad?' he enquired looking around the kitchen trying to spot anything new or different. I spoke as I prepared two cups of coffee.

'Yeah, things are great son; can't complain.'

'Well you could, but no one ever listens.' Lee responded with his usual brand of humour.

'I assume you drove up?' I said. It was Lee's usual practice to phone from the airport looking for me to drop whatever I was doing and pick him up. He had the irritating habit of not giving any notice and simply appearing like a magician's rabbit. I didn't mind that much; it was good to see him.

'Yeah; left late last night. The roads are a bit quieter, but full of crazy lorry drivers,' Lee explained.

I stared at him but he didn't look like a man who had driven through the night for seven or eight hours. Mind you, by the way Lee drove it probably hadn't taken him that long – he was the proverbial 'boy racer'.

'You must be exhausted?'

'Nah, not really,' he replied with a dismissive shrug, 'had a few cans of *Red Bull* and a couple of coffees to keep me awake.'

I laughed and shook my head as I stirred the hot drinks.

'You must be rattling with caffeine then?' He took this suggestion as a cue and headed for the toilet.

'Yeah, I'll just go and pee it all out now before you give me a drug test.' I laughed at the boy; he hadn't lost his sense of humour and enthusiastic outlook in life. He was also looking well – slim, muscular and strong; probably on account of all the heavy lifting required on the many building sites where he worked.

When he returned I had the coffee mugs parked on the table along with a newly opened packet of *Jaffa Cakes*. Lee returned a few minutes later and I could see he had washed his face and wet his hair. He clocked the biscuits like a beggar notices a dropped coin on the pavement.

'Fantastic, dad. I love *Jaffa Cakes*, me.' He picked up the box and extracted a handful of the chocolate coated treats and fed them one-by-one into his mouth.

142

'I can see that. Mind leaving me one?' I asked with mock sarcasm. He merely nodded, being unable to speak at this moment.

'Tell you what. Once we've had our coffee, I'll go and make you something to eat,' I suggested, to which he shrugged.

So we settled down to chat and catch up. This was only possible once his mouth was finally empty. He appraised me of his life in London, his busy working schedule being involved in construction projects all over London and the amount he earned for his hard work, which was impressive. He was currently involved in the building of an office complex in the Docklands area, near to London City airport.

'When the planes come in to land, they practically skim right over your head,' Lee said demonstrating the low flying aircraft with a sweep of his outstretched hand over his head, narrowly missing his hair.

'Just as well you have to wear a hard hat!' I returned. He liked that one and laughed at the observation.

In our ensuing conversation, we covered a wide area of subjects from politics to showbiz and terrorism to religion. I then told him that I had seen Alison recently; his eyebrows shot up as though I had told him I had dined with the Queen. He knew his divorced parents never really communicated with each other, let alone visit.

'So what were you doing up in Aberdeen,' Lee asked. I remained vague for the time being, not wishing to tell him about Operation Lazarus at the moment; the time would come later on. Besides I predicted he would laugh at my mad ploy and probably accuse me of experiencing a mid life crisis.

'Oh, I was just touring in that area and thought I would pop in to see how she's doing.'

The scene was now set to lambaste the former second husband of Alison. We discussed how he must be fairing behind bars and whether he had been stripped of his doctor's qualification owing to his conviction.

I gathered up the empty mugs and transported them through to the kitchen. The *Jaffa Cake* box was now empty so I tossed it into the swing bin. I rinsed the cups and went back through to the living room, to see Lee standing over my little workstation – the Operation Lazarus control centre, leafing through my notes and print-outs. He looked slowly up at me.

'What are you up to dad?'

'Oh, just a little project of mine; nothing much really,' I replied trying to dilute the intensity of the planning and preparation of the mission; however Lee wasn't prepared to be kept in the dark. He knew this was something interesting I was working on and demanded to know more.

Chapter 16

My son and I had a meal in a local Mexican restaurant before heading to an old haunt of Lee's – a pub where he spent a chunk of his student days playing pool with his mates. Over dinner I told him about my mission. To my surprise, he didn't brand me an old fool and time waster, but congratulated me on my ingenuity and drive. He was instantly energised when I told him the extent of my planning and execution of the operation; and the unprecedented successes so far.

Lee was well aware of who the Faceless Legions were, having been brought up in a home with two of the band's biggest fans. Between me and Alison, we probably had every album they produced and all manner of branded merchandise. It was not unusual to see us both as a young couple attired in our Legions t-shirts and pushing a pram with the baby Lee snuggled up inside.

Lee swamped me with a constant salvo of questions relating to the mission. How did I manage to trace Brookes and Carter? How did I think my chances of finding Dixon in Australia would be? What if Dixon refused to cooperate? What if I failed to find Mick Walker or Chas Hannagan's son was unwilling to play along? I answered as best I could; the mission to reunite the band was still merely a hypothetical wish; it may or may not ever happen, but I was determined to give it all I could to ensure at least it stood a chance. As the famous Magnus Magnusson used to say: 'I've started, so I'll finish.'

Lee buzzed with excitement as he involved himself with thoughts of the next phase of planning. He did offer a wealth of words of encouragement and a few avenues of exploration which I hadn't yet thought of. I got the distinct impression that if he wasn't residing so far away, he would actively involve himself in both the planning and execution of the operation, such was his infectious enthusiasm.

By the time we drove back to the house I had practically planned the next phase of the mission with the assistance of Lee. As he was intending driving back down to London on Monday morning but didn't start back work for a day or two, so I would hitch a lift with him, we would call into Carmarthen and attempt to speak to Dale Hannagan before heading over to London where Lee would drop me off at Heathrow airport. We figured an overnight stop in Wales before driving to London would be essential. My uncertainty of the last day had now been resolved and I could move forward with the next phase of planning.

I booked us a room in the old faithful *Travelodge* in Cardiff then booked my return flight to Perth for the Tuesday afternoon. I toyed with how long I would require in Perth; less than one week ought to do it, I reasoned. I know it seemed crazy going all that way to spend less than a week in the country, but this was going to be more of a business trip than a vacation. In the end I opted for a five day trip to Perth. My logic was simple: given I had the address where I was fairly confident I would find Dixon, or at least learn his whereabouts, I figured it wouldn't take much time to find the man, convince him to join the team, swap phone numbers and email addresses, then get out of the country. I didn't intent on doing many touristy things; if I got the chance, then perhaps, but my priorities were to the mission.

Reservations all complete and my credit card had taken a beating. I now had all manner of printed receipts and confirmation papers being spewed out from the overworked printer.

Lee's lack of sleep had finally caught up with him and he retired to his old room not long after we returned from our pool session. Perhaps it was his fatigue, but I beat him convincingly at the game he was such an expert at.

The smell of the cooked bacon, eggs and potato scones I was frying was enough to wake Lee from his deep slumber. He drifted down the stairs still bleary eyed and sporting some impressive 'bed hair' and into the kitchen where I was dishing up the cholesterol-rich feast onto plates. His plan was to eat, shower then commence his drive northwards to Aberdeen. My plan was to get my guitar gear together and sort myself out for my wedding reception gig later that evening.

The sheer quantity of planning and preparation I had carried out in the last week or two was impressive and daunting; mind you planning and preparation no matter how thorough is no guarantee of success. This coaxed yet another memory from my long lost police days and I smiled at the recollection:

I was a Detective Sergeant and was temporarily seconded to the local Crime Unit to gain some experience in planning and executing operations. We had strong intelligence that a house in the east end of Glasgow was being used for the storage and distribution of illegal drugs. I sat down with my team and we analysed the intelligence and evidence, before concluding it was sufficient enough to warrant a raid on the house. We meticulously planned and discussed how best to perform the operation, and considered every conceivable snag and problem, and composed possible solutions. It seemed that everything had been planned and catered for and a success was inevitable.

On the morning of the bust, we divided into two teams – one team would approach the front door and try to gain entry as quick as possible whilst the second team would monitor the progress from the rear in the event the occupants spotted us coming and decided to jettison their narcotic cargo out the window. We went in two separate unmarked cars and drove towards the target, all dressed in casual clothing with our police warrant cards on lanyards around our necks, though concealed under our jackets.

About a mile or two from the target we stopped to have one last pre-raid briefing so every member of the teams were fully conversant on what was about to happen – like a carefully choreographed show, each officer had a designated task and position and we had to ensure everyone knew their duties. We selected the empty and secluded car-park of a restaurant in which to carry out our briefing. Given the early hour, we figured the restaurant would be closed and we gathered around the cars to discuss and prepare. Not long after we had completed the team talk and were about to get back into our respective cars, a marked police car drew up. The two cops emerged and strode towards us looking menacing.

'Can I ask what you guys are up to?' enquired one officer trying to look mean and intimidating; an impressive attitude despite a car-park full of big burly males. I approached them and tried to reassure that we were not a threat and merely a group of friends meeting up for a get together; I didn't want to identify ourselves as plain-clothes police officers if I could help it – it may just compromise the operation. But *Robocop* number two was having none of it.

'We had a report that you lot were acting suspiciously; now you better had a good reason for being here.'

Seeing that time was running out and we were getting no where with these two, I was forced to reveal our identities as fellow police officers and our reason for being here; however I was careful not to reveal any detail of the operation and its locus.

Looking thoroughly embarrassed both retreated back to their panda car nodding apologies like naughty schoolboys. We had a laugh as we drove to the target house; apparently the chef was on duty at the restaurant preparing food for the lunchtime specials and spotted ten men lurking around his car-park. He freaked and telephoned the police fearing we were a group of armed bandits about to hit his restaurant, rob the safe and maybe even raid his pantry.

When we finally arrived on target, we were all sparked up and ready to go. I led my team stealthily to the front door, keeping as low a profile as possible to minimise being seen. Team two dispatched with the speed and movement of a crack SAS troop to the rear of the property to take up their sentry positions.

I had the search warrant in my pocket and knocked the door loudly. My troops gathered at each side of the door ready to affect entry on my nod. Big John held the *Ramit* – a heavy metallic battering ram with a couple of handles for ease of use, firmly in his gloved hands ready to batter the door down should we get no response. No sound was audible from within, so I lifted the letterbox and called inside.

'Police – open up. We have a warrant to search these premises.' Still there was no sound, no movement, or signs of occupation.

Wishing to waste no time, I indicated for Big John to do his thing and smash the door down. He happily obliged and had the heavy wooden door in pieces in less than a minute. We squeezed inside waving our warrant cards like flags at a VE day parade and identified ourselves as police officers, in the event we ended up staring down the barrels of a couple of shotguns.

Then a young couple appeared, the woman carrying a baby cradled in her arms. They stared at us as though we were aliens from another planet. The woman let out a shriek; the baby woke and howled and the man stood shaking in his tartan slippers, unsure what to do.

Something was not right. This was not the home of a notorious drug baron. I extracted the warrant and looked at the name and address. I asked the quaking man to confirm his name and address. He answered through quivering lips – and I nearly exploded with rage. We had the wrong house. The raid should have been made on the house next door. Big John had assured me we were at the correct house and I foolishly did not double check the details.

Now the operation was over before it began. We spend the next hour trying to calm the fearful family down and offering all manner of apologies for our gross incompetence. A joiner had to be summoned to replace the destroyed door, and we witnessed a great deal of movement and curtain-twitching from the house next door – the one referred to on the search warrant!

I tuned up my *Jackson Performer* and looked at the other guys: Phil was sitting behind his drums, sticks twitching as though raring to go; Darren was poised ready to strike the first note of the song on his bass and Stevie approached the microphone and welcomed all the guests to the event. He signalled to us, Phil counted a beat of four using his drum sticks and we launched into the old wedding favourite, Dire Straits' *Walk of Life*.

The dance floor remained empty until the second chorus then one brave couple appeared and began swaying to the beat before being joined by another couple. Gradually the dance floor filled up to near capacity and that was a good sign that we as a band were doing well.

Earlier that day, Lee had gotten into his clichéd boy racer *Mazda MX-5* and drove to Aberdeen. I watched him disappear in a cloud of dust and burning rubber as he sped out of the street in his usual poor driving manner. I was beginning to dread accepting a ride down to London with him, given his choice driving style, but maybe it would be beneficial in getting us to London in record time. I only hoped we survived the journey.

It could have been a lot worse; Lee in his younger days had an unhealthy interest in fast motorbikes – the faster the better, seemed to be his motto. Alison and I were worried that one of his two-wheeled beasts would kill him some day. We tried to talk him out of his craze, reasoning that a car would be better for him and more conducive to road safety and preservation of his life. But like many a rebellious teen, our mature logic fell upon deaf ears and the motorbikes he bought got bigger, faster and louder. He had a few close shaves and near-death experiences before he finally saw sense and traded the bikes in for a sensible car. Just when his parents were beginning to relax, his sensible *Seat* was traded in for a gas guzzling *Subaru Imprezza*. Still he failed to learn his lesson and slow down, and was awarded with a regular supply of fixed penalty tickets for his speeding efforts. The moment he was at risk of losing his licence was the moment he received a dose of common sense and decided that his wild young days should be curtailed somewhat, though not necessarily concluded.

As the evening wore on, so did the effects of the alcohol. From the slightly elevated stage area we could see tipsy dancers swaying and falling over, arguments breaking out between family members sitting hunched around tables cradling their drinks and, as expected: the ubiquitous drunk uncle staggering his way around the dance-floor bumping into couples and feeling the bums of all the female dancers. I was reminded of the reason for us only taking the very occasional booking for this type of event. Certainly the money was good but the crowd were wearisome to watch and rude in their requests. Quite frequently fights broke out when the toxic effects of the alcohol possessed the alpha males or the fickle females and all hell would break loose.

According to Stevie, the bride's parents wanted a traditional Ceilidh band and booked and paid for a reputable one. The bride and groom being rockers did not fancy such entertainment and craved a rock covers band, but were continually vetoed by the pedantic parents. However this backfired on them when the booked Ceilidh band pulled out at the last minute requiring a frantic serious of phone calls to secure a band to fill the void. That's when Stevie's mobile rang and the desperate pleading was made.

'That must be why the bride's parents look like they're at a funeral rather than a wedding,' Darren whispered to me between songs.

I looked over at the glum couple who sat at a table in the corner; sure enough she looked like she wanted cry and he had the look of someone spoiling for a fight. They should have been up jigging to the Gay Gordon, instead they found themselves being serenaded by us doing Aerosmith's *I Don't Want To Miss a Thing*. The only thing this pair was missing was a good old fashioned knees-up Ceilidh – but that wasn't going to happen.

At the last hour, the cocktail of alcohol and testosterone finally claimed its first victim. A tall muscular action man figure with shaved head and bulging biceps got fed up with the bride's male cousin hitting on his girlfriend and lashed out at the shocked victim. Soon chairs were falling over and drinks spilling on the floor as people fought to separate and control the fighting parties with minimum bloodshed.

I looked at each of my band-mates in turn seeking some consensus as to whether to continue or abandon all hope. We only had a couple more songs on our set-list and could easily get away with stopping and packing up now. Besides, no one was listing; the riot was in full swing now all attention was centred on the battling teams rolling around in the corner of the room. Guys in suits and kilts were punching each other while females in frilly dressed tried to prise them apart before the boys in blue were called and they all spent the night in a police cell. The venue manager darted frantically around the melee pleading for them to stop, fearful he might lose his liquor licence.

'Do you think we should do *Kung-Fu Fighting* to finish?' I shouted to the others, and we all laughed like idiots.

I recalled the series of events to Lee as I sat in the passenger seat of his little white *Mazda MX-5*. He laughed when I told him we stopped abruptly in mid-song, unplugged our instruments and started packing up. We were lugging out gear out to the car-park before someone noticed we had stopped playing.

'The Elton John song *Saturday Night's Alright for Fighting* would have been perfect for that gig,' Lee offered; we laughed together.

As we sped down the M6 I looked across at the speedometer – it was edging towards the 90mph mark. Although a fast driver, Lee was actually a careful one; he kept his eyes on the road and I could see the concentration on his face as he surveyed the road ahead and continually kept an eye on other vehicles, anticipating any aggressive moves which may compromise our safety and cause him to perform an evasive manoeuvre or two. I hoped he was paying attention to all speed cameras and keeping an eye out for any police traffic cars.

I was starting to nod off now with the gentle rumble of the tarmac beneath the wheels and the very comfortable leather seats. In addition we had an early start, setting off at 0730hrs. Lee saw me struggle to stay awake.

'It's okay old man; just you have your little nap. I'll wake you up if anything interesting happens.' I didn't dignify that comment with a response. Instead I turned over and let sleep wash over me.

When I awoke, my head hurt and my neck was stiff; so much for Lee's plush comfortable seats. We had stopped moving and the interior was eerily silent. I tried to focus outside but my eyes were blurred and required a moment to adjust. We were in a car-park, jammed between a couple of people carriers.

'Wakey wakey Dad,' Lee's cheery voice rang out.

'Where are we?' I said looking around.

'Chester. Chester services,' Lee announced. 'Do you want to go for a coffee?' I nodded my stiff neck and it hurt. Wow I must have been asleep for a couple of hours to get this far; then I remembered Lee's speedy driving habit.

We had a coffee and quick bite to eat in the café with the smallest queue before heading back to the car and driving the short distance to the petrol station to fill up the *Mazda's* fuel tanks for the next phase of our journey. I was hoping to get to Carmarthen by late afternoon and looked like we were on track to do so. It was only 1130hrs and I was happy with our progress so far. But now the *Mazda's* satnav was saying the next stage of the journey would take us over three hours to cover the 140 miles: this being on the slow A843 which was dual carriageway only until the town of Ruabon, thereafter single carriageway. We only needed to encounter a road accident, road works or be stuck behind some slow moving traffic and this would push our arrival time into Carmarthen way back.

I offered to drive the *Mazda* and let Lee rest but he was having none of it. This was his pride and joy and no one was allowed to drive but him. I was actually glad with his decision as I knew if anybody could get us to our destination in record time, it was the *MX-5's* owner.

Chapter 17

'Are you just going to turn up at the family's door and ask to speak to Hannagan's son?' Lee asked interrupting the music emanating from the speakers. Now I hadn't given this phase much thought until now.

'Yeah, I think so, unless you have a better idea?' Lee pondered this before answering.

'I don't know if that's the best thing. They might think your some weirdo fan come to pay homage.'

'Not if I explain the reason for me calling,' I countered.

Lee considered this and we both lapsed into silence to rethink our strategy. He might be correct; if I was turned away at the door that would be my chance blown as time was at a premium; I had to be at Heathrow by lunchtime tomorrow to catch my flight.

'You could say you're the police. Have you still got that fake warrant card on you?' Lee said. He was referring to a homemade warrant card I produced on a computer and printer; I modelled it on my former Strathclyde Police warrant card and I had to admit it looked pretty convincing. It had a photo of me embedded on the card but omitted any particular police force – it just stated POLICE and a fancy official-looking logo. I still retained my rank of Detective Inspector of the CID. The card had come in handy on a few occasions in the past when I needed to get in somewhere or speak to someone, but it could only work if I was wearing a suit and looking like an actual police detective. Today I was attired in jeans, sweat shirt and trainers. There was no way I could convince someone I was a police officer on official business.

'Nah, I'm not even dressed for the part, but I do have that card in my wallet.'

'So, go buy a suit then,' Lee suggested, then went on, 'or just say you're a plain-clothes cop.'

'No its okay. I'll just use all my charm and charisma to get me in,' I replied with a smirk. Lee was quick with his reply.

'That's what all con-men say.'

I laughed at his witty remark. He was right of course. I couldn't risk blowing my chance to get to Dale Hannagan and scaring him off, besides I probably would have to go through Chas' still grieving wife and she might not be interested in my proposal. Whatever way I went about it, I would have to appear bona fide and not some crackpot, in order to have any chance of success.

As predicted, our average speed had now dropped and the satnav display had updated its estimated arrival time – and it was getting later and later.

Brake lights lit up the road ahead and we both strained to see what the hold up was. Nothing was obvious at first then as the road curved to the right we could see the ominous sight of a farm tractor with about seven or eight cars behind all driving very close to each other as though trying to coax a bit more speed. The road was not conducive to overtaking given the winding curves. The driver immediately behind the tractor kept manoeuvring his *Renault* out to the centre line to check for oncoming vehicles. Clearly he was uncertain about undertaking such an overtaking and held back. The car behind him decided that there could be no undue hesitancy and pulled out to overtake both vehicles. This must have put immense pressure on the *Renault* driver but still he was cautious about overtaking.

Lee moved out to the white lines to peer ahead. I studied his face: he was desperate for a chance to overtake and knew his powerful car could meet the challenge. His hand rested upon the small gear-stick; this looked more like a joystick on a games console than the gear shift on a fast car. He must have decided; before I could react or question his decision, we were on the other side of the road whizzing past the long line of slow moving cars. I glanced at them as we passed – their faces said it all – some were probably commenting on how irresponsible the mad *Mazda* driver was in performing such a suicidal manoeuvre, while others may have been admiring Lee's courage and determination in deciding to overtake.

I glanced at the speedometer and the needle registered 70mph. My eyes rose above the dashboard to the road ahead – and I shuffled uncomfortably in my seat as I spotted a car racing towards us. It was still about fifty metres distant but we were only alongside the tractor and required perhaps twenty metres more to complete the overtake and pull safely in. Lee pressed the accelerator a bit more and the rev counter needle rose towards the red area. The noise was uncomfortable as the engine roared in response to the demands placed upon it.

We pulled into the left hand side with only seconds to spare before a sleek black *BMW* roared past, the driver sounding his horn in disapproval at the outrageous manoeuvre. I saw Lee grinning as he took pride in his accomplishment – six cars overtaken with minimum visibility of the road ahead. He had rather an unhealthy confidence in both his abilities and his machine; I only hoped he wouldn't come a cropper one of these days.

Now that the tractor and all its followers were far behind us, the road ahead was clear. Lee took full advantage of this fact and floored the *Mazda*. As testament to the *MX-5s* solid engine, it seemed to have recovered quickly from its high performance demands of the last minute or so with no complaints, and now responded contentedly to the gentler requirements of the driver.

I remembered my first ever fast drive in a police car. I was just a rookie fresh out of college and on my first day with the shift. I was paired with Eric an eager young constable with about eight years service. We were patrolling a neighbourhood, having resumed duties after a short break for lunch. The radio buzzed into life and I responded with cautious and uncertain phraseology. The excited controller requested we respond to a raid alarm coming from an office in an area of the town several miles away. Eric slammed the car into gear, spun the tyres as he performed an impressive one-eighty degree turn and we hurtled towards the given address as though our lives and careers depended on it. He must have nudged the aging panda car towards 75mph most of the way and we bounced over potholes and uneven road surfaces with the small engine screaming in protest. My stomach lurched and I was certain I would part with my recently consumed lunch. The feeling of nausea was overwhelming, but I tried to conceal my pale face and queasy disposition; it was not as if I could ask Eric to pull over to allow me to vomit then inhale some fresh air. He was a man on a mission and would not stop for anyone. Whenever we approached traffic lights or junctions, Eric would become livid when drivers failed to move aside to allow him clear access; despite the 'blues and twos' announcing our presence loud and proud, many drivers, through lack of concentration and spatial awareness, failed to notice us. A frustrated Eric leaned on his horn and gesticulated angrily for divers to move aside without delay.

Eventually we arrived at the locus and ran inside. I was not feeling great, but welcomed the fresh air once I stepped out of the car. Fearing a robbery was in progress Eric drew his truncheon and wielded it like a crusader facing the Saracen hordes. The startled secretary gazed at us in horror, her jaw hanging low in disbelief.

'What seems to be the trouble officers?' she asked through quivering lips.

'Your panic alarm has been triggered,' Eric replied as he lowered his menacing baton. The girl lowered herself to look under the table and noticed the big red button had been accidentally activated. She apologised, as did her manager who was out of his office in a flash when he heard the siren of our car approaching and the boys in blue hurrying inside.

Relieved at not having to confront armed robbers, we trundled back to our patrol car and I let my stomach settle. Eric drove for the remainder of the shift with a smug look upon his face as though proud of his driving skills and having impressed a rookie.

We were now passing Builth Wells and the satnav was teasing us by displaying an ETA of nearly one and a half hours to go. Why did Hannagan have to live so far away? I lamented as we drove along the A843 passing between imposing mountains with unpronounceable names. We knew we were deep in a pseudo-foreign country now as the road signs were multi-lingual – telling Lee to 'Slow' and also 'Araf' in the event he preferred Welsh. We did have a laugh attempting to pronounce some of the Welsh place names – our efforts sounding more like a spitting contest, especially with the ones beginning with a double L.

Feeling helpless and not being able to control my situation, I decided to lie back and let Lee do all the hard work. I closed my eyes and contemplated how I would get on in Perth. I envisioned it would be easy: simply walk into the

161

bar when Dixon's band were playing, wait until they stopped for a break, then approach the man, explain my mission and get him to sign along the dotted line; however I was not that naïve and knew it would present its own set of challenges. I would just wing it as usual and make it up as I went along.

Lee was presented with many more opportunities to push his pride and joy to the limit, and he rose like a trout to the fly at every chance. None of his overtaking manoeuvres were as hairy as the one behind the tractor, but I still cringed when I saw the risks he took.

I thought it would never happen, but we saw the buildings springing up as we approached Carmarthen from the east along the A40. We had made it and it was still light. The *Mazda's* built-in satnav guided us to the address of the Hannagan household with ease.

I stared in bewilderment at the large two story house which loomed ahead. It was a modern building but designed and built to look like an old solid one. Its unique design comprised a clean smooth white finish to the two ends whilst the middle section was a rustic Flemish-bond brick affair. An oval window was encased in the upper section and below it stood a burgundy coloured wooden front door. Four huge bay windows jutted out looking like four large eyes surveying us intruding along its paved driveway. I couldn't decide whether I liked the house or not; either way, it looked like you wouldn't get much change out of three quarters of a million pounds to buy it.

'Wow. That looks like the house in that animation, Monster House,' Lee exclaimed as he drew up outside the austere mini-mansion.

162

There were no cars on the driveway, but a garage off to the left hand side was closed, possibly indicating a car was inside. I hoped someone would be in so my arduous journey was not made in vain. It was now late evening and the sun was thinking about retiring soon.

I eased the door open and got out, my stiff legs protesting at their sudden wake from slumber and demands to move. I strode towards the red door and peered inside as I passed one of the ground level bay windows; there was no hint of movement from within. I rapped on the brass knocker and stood back smiling like your friendly neighbourhood cold-caller. I turned around to see Lee monitor my progress through the car windscreen, the wipers screeching across the glass as he attempted rid it of the impressive collection of dead flies we had gathered on our epic journey from Glasgow earlier this morning.

No reply and no indication of activity from within; not even a dog barking. I tried again, this time louder. The brass knocker hit the plate with an almighty whack, which was harder than I intended; if there was someone currently home and hadn't heard the door, they were now left in no doubt they had a persistent caller. Still nothing – my heart sank and I shook my head in annoyance. Typical to have come all this way to find no one was at home. I tried one last time knowing it was now hopeless; it was not as if I could come back later as we had to head to Cardiff to be ready for our early morning start to Heathrow.

I turned to head back to the car my arms outstretched in defeat. Lee returned my disappointed look and shrugged. It was now

163

beyond my control and I had to accept defeat. As inconvenient as it may be, I would just have to come back here on my return from Australia. I looked around but could see no neighbours from the other nearby detached properties.

I was about to get back into the car when I heard a croaky old voice calling from behind. I spun around to see an old lady dressed in a gingham apron and furry slippers trundle towards me; she had appeared from the side of the building.

'Can I help you sonny?' she asked looking at me through glazed eyes.

'Yes, madam. Are you Mrs Hannagan?' I asked trying to look friendly but professional, despite my creased shirt and crinkled jeans. The old lady shook her head, her curly white hair rippling.

'On no. I'm Mrs Rosser.'

An air of frustration swept over me. I couldn't believe I had got the wrong house; I was reminded of the drugs bust scenario when we wrecked the door to the wrong place.

'Oh, I'm sorry,' I said apologetically. 'I was actually looking for Mrs Hannagan. Do you know where she lives?'

'Rita?' she asked in her old croaky Welsh accented voice. I remembered that was the name of Chas's wife, from the funeral coverage in the online newspaper story.

'Yes, Rita Hannagan. Does she live nearby?' The excitement was starting to rekindle in me. Perhaps I would succeed after all. The old woman pointed to the Monster House.

'Yes, Rita lives there, but she's not home at the minute. Can I help you at all?' I guessed the lady was a grandmother or some other relative living with them or maybe she was the cook or cleaner.

'Well, it was actually Dale Hannagan I wanted to speak to,' I said hopefully, 'does he live here too?' She shook her head again.

'No, young Dale lives in Cardiff. He works there too. He owns his own music studio there,' she said with pride as though Dale owned a blue chip company. I was about to respond but she hadn't finished.

'Dale is my grandson.'

Fantastic, I thought: I am making progress here; slow but sure. Then Mrs Rosser turned and shuffled back the way she came, and beckoned me to follow her.

'Come on sonny, best come inside.'

I looked over to the car and saw Lee laughing at my awkward situation. I extended my hand spreading all fingers outwards and mouthed 'Five minutes.' Lee responded with a thumbs-up sign.

I followed the old lady as she hobbled in her slippered feet towards a door at the rear of the property. This looked like a traditional granny-flat; it was moderate in size and probably half the size of my own house. She indicated for me to step inside. I entered the spacious living quarters – it was spotless, tidy and smelled of potpourri. She had everything she needed: a full kitchen with every electrical appliance she could think of; a comfortable looking living room plus easy access through to the main house if she needed anything.

'Do you know Dale?' she asked turning to face me. I shook my head. I had no idea who she thought I was. Then her face turned suspicious.

'You're not one of them reporters are you? We've had it up to here with all you lot snooping around asking about Mr Hannagan's death. We're fed up with it all.'

'No, no. I'm not a reporter Mrs Rosser,' I said to reassure her before she kicked me out.

'I'm looking to speak to Dale. Do you happen to know where he lives or works?'

'Dale is my grandson, did you know that?' the Welsh lady stated. She was just as I suspected – fairly senile and having the memory span of a virus.

'Yes, Mrs Rosser. Are you able to tell me the name of the studio he owns?' I asked trying to keep the frustration from my voice. If I could get this information, then I knew where to head next.

'Yes that's right. Dale owns his own music studio in Cardiff. He's at work at the moment. He also lives in Cardiff,' she reiterated. I knew this wasn't going to be easy, but I had to persevere.

Chapter 18

Old Mrs Rosser trundled over to the sink and began to fill an old fashioned whistling kettle; her rubber-soled slippers squeaking on the tiled floor. I had to extract some information from her. She had teased me by telling where Dale lived and worked; this was a start but I need a lot more; the clock was ticking away.

'Mrs Rosser, I don't want to detain you any longer. If you could tell me the name of Dale's studio in Cardiff then I can leave you in peace.'

The sound of the rushing water into the metallic kettle was loud and she failed to hear me. I raised my voice and repeated the question.

'You don't have to shout. I'm not deaf,' the old lady responded.

'Sorry. Do you know the name or address of the studio please?' I said still trying to control my agitation.

'Oh no. I don't know what it's called. I only know it's in Cardiff.'

That was of no use to me. If I could at least get a business name or street name then I could look it up. A sound studio in Cardiff didn't narrow it down much. There was likely dozens of recording and rehearsal studios in Cardiff, like most other cities. I wasn't prepared, nor had the time to ring each of them asking if Dale Hannagan worked there.

Mrs Rosser busied herself with two cups. I surveyed her granny-flat looking for anything of use to my quest. Then I spotted a cork notice-board hanging from one wall near to the fridge. It was decorated with a plethora of business cards and post-it notes. I went over to investigate as the old lady hummed an old favourite tune of hers.

There were business cards for all manner of services from plumbers to painters and electricians to embroidery suppliers. I scanned the board whilst keeping an eye on the lady. I didn't want her to suddenly suspect me of being a confidence trickster and panic. This lady was far too trusting – within a couple of minutes of meeting me, she had invited me in to her abode. I could have been anyone; a conman, crook or killer; or maybe I just had a trusting, friendly face.

Mrs Rosser turned round slowly and looked at me. She caught me looking over her notice-board and I feared she may take offence to me prying at her personal stuff like family member phone numbers.

'What do you take in you tea sonny?' she enquired. I hadn't realised I had been asked if I wanted a cup of tea; not that I had the time to sup tea, munch biscuits and have a chin-wag with my new friend.

'I don't actually have time for a cup of tea Mrs Rosser,' I replied.

She ignored me and shuffled back round to the worktop and stared opening jars with 'Tea bags' and 'Sugar' hand-written on white labels and applied at a jaunty angle. I resumed my snooping and found what I was after. It was a business card emblazoned with clipart images of drums, guitars and musical notes. Along the top of the card in big bold lettering was 'Dale's Music Box'. Under this was the subtitle 'Cardiff's premier rehearsal and recording studio'. Well who could argue with that definitive statement?

'I have only red milk. Is that okay?' she asked still with her back to me. I ignored her – it seemed pointless answering as she merely made up the answer she wanted regardless of what I said.

I grabbed at the card, but it was securely attached to the board by a large drawing pin, as though securing it against a hurricane sweeping through the house and whipping it off. I tugged at the card rotating it back and forth trying to loosen the thumb tack. I wanted that card – it had all the information I wanted: address, phone numbers and email addresses. I knew I couldn't rely on my memory. The last thing I wanted was to get out of here only to forget some of the details; it wasn't as if I would be coming back, plus time was still ticking away and I still had to get to Cardiff and pop into the studio.

The old lady hobbled around to face me and I let go of the card and folded my arms to allay any suspicion of what I was doing behind her back; I smiled at her. She manoeuvred back around and resumed her messing about with milk, sugar and teabags, the worktop now covered in spillages as she tried to control her shaking hand.

I wrenched at that business card – I was determined I was taking it whether it liked it or not. It came away in my hand; however the drawing pin pinged out and hit the floor before bouncing several times along the ceramic tiles. I watched its progress and listening to it rattle. I was certain the old lady would hear it and I would be busted, but she never batted and eye. I stuck the card in my pocket and went over to the worktop.

'Sorry I can't stay for tea Mrs Rosser, but I have to dash.'

She looked at me with disappointment as I headed for the door.

'It was nice meeting you.'

'But what about your tea. Who is going to drink it?' she enquired incredulously.

I didn't have time to explain; I had to be off. But I felt guilty about suddenly leaving the lady; what if she got suspicious and suspected me of having pilfered her jewels or money? She might phone the police or tell Rita when she returned, about a strange man with a funny accent being in her house. It wouldn't matter that Mrs Rosser had invited me in; I would still be the guilty party.

She held the tea cup out towards me with her shaking hand. The steaming liquid was juddering around in the cup and I was concerned it would spill over her hand or the floor; this was a potential accident waiting to happen. So I acquiesced and took hold of the proffered cup. She gestured to the table at the side of the kitchen and we both sat down on hard wooden seats resting our mugs on the tabletop. I began to sup quickly, hoping to finish the tea as soon as possible and be on my way. Lee must be wondering what I was up to. I thought of phoning him but again did not want to arouse any suspicion.

'So you know my grandson Dale?' She asked as she stared at me through her cataract-glazed eyes. I thought how best to answer this, and decide to go along with her assumption.

'Yes, we're friends and I'm just on my way to see him in Cardiff.'

'Marvellous!' she exclaimed, 'he'll like that.' She managed to draw out the word marvellous in her strong Welsh lilt, so it lasted about three seconds. I supped again burning my mouth in the process; that was the problem with 'red milk': it never cooled your tea very well.

'Did you hear about Dale's father?' old Mrs Rosser said. I nodded as if in sympathy.

'Yes, I did and I'm sorry for your loss.'

'Well Charles Hannagan got what was coming to him,' she said as her voice rose in pitch at her agitation, 'he was a drug addict you know.'

This was a tad unfair, but I reckon Chas and his mother-in-law probably had the bog-standard relationship that these two relatives tend to have; and she wouldn't be mourning his death too long. I thought a compliment was in order.

'He was a very good musician,' I offered. She didn't like that much and resorted back to her negative attitude of the man.

'No, he was a drug addict. He's a disgrace to this family.' I didn't bother pursuing the argument any further.

I slurped my way through the remainder of my drink finally reaching the sweet dregs at the bottom of the cup. I hadn't a clue how many spoonfuls of sugar she had added, but I felt my teeth starting to slowly dissolve. I sprang up from my seat.

'Thanks for the tea Mrs Rosser, but I have to dash now. I'm going to see Dale and I want to catch him before he finishes work.' I gave her a little wave as I walked to the door.

'You be sure to tell Dale you had tea with his grandmother,' she called.

I assured her I would as I turned the handle and stepped outside. Thank goodness I was now free – I thought I would never get away, but at least I had the information I came for.

It was now beginning to get dark as we drove along the M4 towards Cardiff. The seventy mile journey was likely to take us over an hour. At least we were back on a motorway; it seemed an age since we drove on one having to endure the arduous slow twisting roads most of the way through Wales.

The *Mazda's* powerful headlights lit up the road ahead like aircraft landing lights and the interior emanated a pleasant bluish glow from the illuminated dashboard instrument cluster.

Lee laughed for a few miles when I regaled him with my encounter with Dale's old muddle-minded grandmother. He whooped for joy when I produced the business card I had pilfered from the notice-board as I set about programming the postcode into the satnav.

'Well that was a result,' he congratulated.

'Yeah, but I had to work for it,' I said with a laugh. 'I think I deserved it.'

This was not my first encounter with elderly demanding ladies. In my police days I had my fair share of this type.

I once responded to a call where the householder wished to report someone trying to break into her home. My colleague and I rushed to the address hoping to find a housebreaking in progress. When we arrived the street was empty and the neighbourhood quiet. We spoke to the elderly woman who invited us inside and offered us a cup of tea. We declined her offer and tried to ascertain her cause for alarm. We examined her locks, check all windows and tried to coax a description of the perpetrator from her; however it soon became clear it was a false alarm and the woman had imagined the whole thing. She begged us not to leave and craved the reassurance of a police presence.

One hour later we were called back to the same paranoid lady at the same address. This time she had a different story: gangs of youths were running wild in the street, smashing windows and fighting. We raced to the locus and found the street deserted and pacific. There was no shred of evidence to substantiate her claim; as before she clung on to us preventing us from leaving. It soon became clear that the pensioner was a closet police fan and was going to great lengths to compose stories to obtain police attention. Adhering to the 'cruel to be kind' philosophy, it was later explained to the woman that she risked being charged with wasting police time; in addition she also risked not getting an urgent police service in a genuine emergency. This seemed to do the trick and that was the last we heard from Strathclyde Police's biggest fan.

The dashboard clock declared the time to be 1900hrs. I was feeling drained from all our running around, but irritatingly Lee looked fresh and alert – and he had been doing all the driving. We located the embarrassingly titled Dale's Music Box on a busy thoroughfare and found a place to park about fifty metres from the building. This time Lee decided to accompany me. We both discussed how hungry we were as it had been some time since our last meal.

'Hopefully we won't be too long in this studio and we can grab a fish supper or something when we're done,' I said optimistically. Lee nodded agreeing that my suggestion sounded like a plan.

The streetlights were casting all manner of shadows on the lonely pavement as we strolled along the street past shops providing a wide range of goods and services from bakeries to banks and chemists to clothing outlets. The usual assortment of fast food takeaways was busy doing battle for the hungry person's money. The street was devoid of pedestrians and only the occasional bus, taxi or car passed along.

We were soon at the main door of the silly-sounding studio and noticed a door intercom system.

'Here we go – hopefully a result,' I said trying to conceal my eager anticipation. I pushed the button and the speaker buzzed in my ear.

'Yeah?' asked a puzzled sounding Welsh accented male voice.

'Hi, I'm looking to speak to Dale Hannagan please,' I shouted into the microphone smiling and trying to look official. I didn't know if they had a CCTV camera on the door; I couldn't see one as we approached the building but I had to assume they were watching me.

'Sorry. Dale's busy at the moment,' came the abrupt reply.

'Is there any chance I can speak to him – it won't take a moment.'

'No chance, boyo. I told you he's busy.'

This was annoying. I now knew Dale was inside but was prevented from speaking to him because of this 'jobs-worth' on the intercom. I forced myself to remain calm and tried again.

'Look I've driven all the way down from Glasgow to speak to Dale. Can you just let me in for a minute?'

There was silence whilst the gruff male voice considered my request. The delay was good – perhaps he was going to fetch the boss. I turned to Lee and saw him pointing to himself. I thought he wanted to try his hand at talking us inside, but he was merely correcting me in stating that he was the one who had driven from Glasgow and not me. I dismissed him with an annoyed hand and face gesture, to which he laughed. The speaker hissed and the irritating voice returned.

'He can't see you without an appointment.'

I sighed long and loud; this guy was testing my patience.

'How do I get an appointment then?'

'Through the website or phone here tomorrow during business hours,' I was told.

'Look, I've just arrived after a long trip from Glasgow. I'm only in Cardiff tonight. Is there any chance you could...'

With that he cut me off and reiterated his request for me to book an appointment.

'Them's the rules boyo.' The intercom went dead.

'Want me to have a go dad?' Lee asked. I shook my head.

'Nah, there's no point. That half-wit in there,' I said pointing into the building, 'is not going to budge an inch.'

We stood there for a minute each of us trying to compose an alternative strategy. I was determined I wasn't going to let the small matter of an appointment keep me from speaking to Dale who I knew was inside. If only I could get access, I could be in and out in a matter of minutes. I pressed the intercom button one last time but it had been muted or disabled.

I walked away disgusted and gestured for my son to follow. In contrast he thought it was mildly amusing – the fact we had traversed a large part of the country taking most of the day, to find the guy we came to see, but couldn't actually speak to him because of some pedantic rule and annoying gatekeeper.

'Them's the rules, boyo,' mocked lee in a surprisingly good Welsh accent. I had to laugh; if I didn't I may just go crazy.

Chapter 19

'Come on, let's try round the back. There must be a fire exit or something,' I said.

We strolled through a narrow alleyway keeping an eagle eye out for watchers, especially the police. We located a heavy steel door to the rear of the premises. Here we could make out the sounds of bands practicing inside the studio. Most of the noise was drums however interspaced with the odd howling vocals from people who evidently couldn't sing. The area was littered with all shapes, sizes and colours of wheelie bin.

I took hold of the door edge and tried to prise it open, but it had no intention of giving me any leeway; besides its solid heavy appearance convinced me that it was fruitless even attempting to open it from the outside. Lee was busy scanning the building for any means of entry; I don't know what he was thinking. Even if we spotted an open window, it's not as if we could climb in:

'Oh hi there. I'm here to see Dale.'

'Yes, no problem; I'll just go and get him. I hope you didn't hurt yourself climbing through the window!'

We withdrew back through the alleyway. The last thing we could afford was being stopped by the police for loitering and acting suspiciously in the area. Lee suggested we simply admit defeat and come back the next day, but I reminded him of our early start in the morning to ensure I made my 1315hrs flight. No I was determined to speak to Dale, even if I had to wait outside in the cold until he finished for the night.

Then I had a brainwave. I consulted my watch: it was now 1940hrs. If this studio operated like every other studio I knew of, we could simply stroll into the place whenever there was a session turnover. The industry standard was three hour blocks and generally: 12 – 3pm; 3pm – 6pm; 6pm – 9pm and 9pm – midnight. There should be a changeover of bands at 9pm! I told Lee my theory and he smiled at my plan. He looked at his watch and shrugged.

'Still got quite a bit of time to kill. Might as well go and grab something to eat,' He suggested.

I was fairly confident in my theory and timings, but still retained some element of doubt in case they operated different booking slots. I wanted to keep and eye on the place and be prepared to move in as soon as I spotted the door opening. That seemed like the only way we were going to get into the studio tonight.

Across the road was an Indian three-in-one takeaway establishment. I pointed it out to Lee and we crossed the road between a couple of taxis plying their trade up and down the street. This was an ideal place - it had a large bench in which we could sit, eat and still keep a watchful eye on the studio directly across the road.

We entered the place; it was deserted but had quite a few staff members on duty. I pondered how a business like this manages to make a profit when the staff outnumber the customers! The smell of cooking was a delight and my stomach rumbled as if to announce it needed filling.

Two chicken barbeque kebabs were ordered along with a large box of chips and we sat on the bench to wait its preparation. We positioned ourselves so we had a panoramic view of Dale's Music Box, but could see no hint of that main door opening anytime soon. The turbaned male Indian server promised us our food would be ready soon, but we told him there was no hurry – we had plenty of time to whittle away.

I was happily munching my way into the kebab, sauce dripping down my chin and pieces of cabbage, lettuce and tomato spilling onto my lap when I saw Lee freeze and stare out the window. A group of people were walking along the pavement and stopped just at the door to the studio. I put down my food and wiped my mouth. We had to be ready to make that dash across the road if the door opened. Lee was poised ready to run out the takeaway as well. Still we watched; I could sense the Indian behind me watching and wondering what we were up to.

The gang moved on – it was a false alarm. They had simply stopped outside the studio to chat. We relaxed and continued stuffing our faces. A quick look at my watch and I saw it was now half past eight. Things could get interesting in the next half an hour; just as long as we didn't encounter the local police or get involved in a fight with the guys inside and find ourselves unceremoniously chucked out onto the street.

By 2045hrs we had finished our food and felt we had overstayed our welcome. We thanked the assistant for his hospitality and went outside.

'Might as well have a little stroll down the street to walk off all those calories,' Lee remarked.

So we walked briskly down one side of the street, always watching the studio door for any signs of movement, then we crossed at a set of traffic lights. As we reached the other side we caught sight of a group of young guys coming towards us – two of them had guitar gig bags on their backs; another was carrying a large guitar case which I assumed contained a bass guitar, and the other male was waving a set of hickory drum sticks in the air as though trying to swat a fly. I looked at Lee; he looked back and we smiled. My theory was correct: here was a band about to rehearse on the 9pm to midnight slot. Now it was simply a case of following these characters right in through the door to the studio – and with any luck meeting Dale Hannagan.

We tracked the group keeping a short distance behind so they didn't think we were stalkers or groupies. Sure enough, they stopped at the entrance and one of the crew pressed the intercom button. I couldn't make out any communication between the guy speaking and the intercom voice, but I heard a distinctive clunk and the door opened. We moved forwards behind the guitarists. They seemed unaware of our presence right behind them, as the last guy in let the door go.

'Hold the door would you mate,' Lee shouted. The guitarist turned his head and nodded.

'No probs.'

Lee and I followed on and were soon inside the studio – now that was easy.

The corridor turned to the right and we let the group walk on ahead as we waited round the corner out of sight. Loud voices rang out as the group were greeted by the guy in charge – I

wondered if it was the same obnoxious voice
from the intercom earlier, but I couldn't make out
the voice clearly, owing to the mumbled
conversation and the muffled noise of a band still
playing.

'What do you want to do? How are you going
to play it?' Lee whispered in my ear. I turned my
head to whisper back.

'We'll wait until these guys have been seen to,
then we'll waltz up and demand to see Dale –
simple.'

I sounded confident but I wasn't feeling it.
Anything could happen and all manner of things
could go wrong. The adrenalin was pumping and
my heartbeat was racing like my son's driving;
and still we waited until the clamour died away
and the band disappeared inside a rehearsal room.

Soon the group who had just completed their
session walked past us on their way out. I
surveyed each as they passed and couldn't work
out what sort of band they must be or style of
music they played: one was dressed and made-up
like a Goth, another like a rocker with long hair
and denim jacket and the other two males had
very short cropped hair – maybe a hybrid Goth/
Rocker/ Pop group? Wouldn't it be interesting to
hear them play?

We waited like a couple of assassins ready to
move in for the kill – silent, un-moving and
holding our breath. We could now hear the band
starting to set up for their practice session in one
of the rooms; faded and muffled voices were
audible as they got sorted out with microphones,
guitar leads and the like. There was still much
movement in the hallway just around the corner;

people shuffling around, in and out of rooms; we were still invisible but could detect the movement, and so we waited for the hustle and bustle to die away.

Now the drum kit was being tested. The bass drum boom-boom boomed away in a steady rhythm and the drummer began a roll on the side and floor toms ending in a loud cymbal crash. Next the bass player joined in and practiced a few scales; but still no guitars. This always amused me: the fact drummers simply turn up for rehearsals and gigs with very little by way of equipment – a couple of pairs of drumsticks at most and they're instantly ready to play. Bass guitarists are similar – they plug their bass into the amplifier, crank all the knobs up full and they're also ready to play, hardly bothering to tune their instrument assuming it would always be in tune.

Guitarists by contrast are pedantic and slow. They waste a fair amount of time messing about with their axes; tuning it, then re-tuning it, setting up their chain of effect floor pedals, then messing about with the settings on the amplifier heads, trying to get that ultimate 'Hendrix' or 'Clapton' sound. Me personally, I always took a note of my preferential settings on each amp and kept the small scrap of paper in my guitar case. That way it was quick and easy to set up without undue delay; maybe I should copyright or patent my methods!

We heard the door to the studio closing as, instantly the sounds became muffled and quieter. They band were now onto testing and adjusting the vocal PA system.

181

'One two, testing one two three,' called a reverberating voice. Silence followed as no doubt a few adjustments and fine tuning were made to the mixer amp, then the voice was back with more counting and muffled laughs.

The hallway had now died down and I indicated for us to move in. We strode with purpose around the corner and came face to face with a Bob Marley clone; behind and hunched over the small reception desk was a young guy, mid twenties wearing long flowing dreadlocks. We startled him and he bolted upright, a blend of shock and surprise on his face. His eyes looked like they might just pop out of their sockets. I wondered if this was my obstructive friend from the intercom.

He looked up at us – our six foot four inch frames towering over him causing maximum intimidation. He tried to look calm and in control but his face said otherwise. I'll bet he was puzzled as to how we managed to get in undetected.

'Hi we've come to see Dale Hannagan,' I announced looking Bob directly in the eye. His expression then altered slightly as he recognised my voice from earlier; and it was the same guy I spoke with. He was content to be tough behind a secure entry door, but now being confronted by the very man he had denied entry to, his demeanour changed. He darted round from the desk nodding his head and causing the dreadlocks to swing around like jungle creepers.

'I'll just go and tell Mr Hannagan,' he said in a quavering voice. 'Who will I say wants to speak to him?' I thought about this one.

'Tell him we're friends of Danny Carter and Andy Brookes.' I didn't know if this would ring any bells with Dale, but it might spark his curiosity. Bob rushed off down the hallway where I presumed was an office or sound production suite. I could see him mouthing the names as though trying to memorise them so he could pass on the message to his boss.

I looked at Lee and was trying hard to contain a laugh.

'Yaah, man. I lika de Bob Marley,' Lee said in an exaggerated Jamaican accent, wriggling his fingers in front of his face to simulate a head full of dreadlocks. I had to suppress a laugh; we were behaving like a couple of children, but this was probably down to the fact we had actually achieved entry to the place at long last. Lee was about to sit down on a nearby grubby sofa whilst we waited on Bob returning. I shook my head and indicated for Lee to remain upstanding – I wanted to maintain our air of intimidation in the event Bob came back with some unwelcome news and asked us to leave; not that we intended leaving without a fight.

The Bob Marley look-alike was back; behind him was a young man with long wavy hair tied in a ponytail. He strode towards us purposefully wearing a curious expression on his face. This, I was certain, was Dale Hannagan – he was a clone of his father in his younger days: the same wavy long hair, square masculine jaw and pale blue eyes. He surveyed me and Lee as he approached.

'Hi, Dale Hannagan?' I asked as I extended my hand towards him. He nodded, still curious as to our unannounced visit.

'I'm Tony Caulfield,' I said as we pumped hands, 'and this is my son Lee Caulfield.' I broke off the handshake and gestured to Lee. Dale went through the same ritual with Lee. Meanwhile Bob was standing behind his boss as though seeking protection from the two Scottish giants.

'Can we have a couple of minutes of your time please Dale?' I said; then I eyed Bob.

'In private, if you don't mind.'

Dale nodded and gestured for us to follow him. He still maintained a puzzled look as though quietly trying to work out why we were here. I didn't know if Bob had mentioned the names of Carter and Brookes, but Dale gave no hint of recognition. He led us into a small lounge area with a sofa and a couple of armchairs. We flopped down onto the sofa and Dale perched on the edge of the armchair, the rips on his jeans opening like the mouths of hungry chicks. I didn't want to keep him in suspense much longer so I launched straight into my spiel without preamble. I had rehearsed this line for the past few hours.

'I am managing a project to try to reunite the Faceless Legions,' I said in a clear and professional tone. 'The idea is to get them back together for one last reunion concert.'

I watched him as I spoke. As soon as the words Faceless Legions were out of my mouth, his expression changed as though a switch had been flicked. Gone was the puzzled look to be replaced by a very interested one. I could see an insipient smile forming with his mouth. I went on.

'I have heard you are a bass player like your father and wondered if you would consider being his replacement in the band?'

Dale sat back in his chair, a grin now wide on his face.

'Absolutely!' he exclaimed. I could see his eyes darting around as he envisioned playing on stage with his father's former band. 'That would be a dream come true.'

Success! This was looking good. I felt like a mountaineer having scaled a lofty peak following a series of mishaps on the way.

I provided Dale with a summary of my mission so far: having tracked down and spoken with Andy Brookes and Danny Carter, who were both in agreement and enthusiastic about a comeback gig. Dale looked thoroughly impressed with my hard work and intrepid management skills. He was over the moon that both Carter and Brookes were alive and well and were endorsing the project. He voiced a volley of questions pertaining to the up and coming gig, and I had to halt him and try to calm him down in the event he hyperventilated. I cautioned him that I still had to find and convince both Dixon and Walker to join in, but was fairly confident I could do it – I had achieved quite a lot so far.

We left the studio an hour later after exchanging phone numbers. Dale presented me with a business card through trembling hands and I accepted it – I didn't have the heart to tell him I already had one of his cards, in case I had to admit the unscrupulous methods I used to obtain it.

Chapter 20

The atmosphere inside the *Mazda* was electric as we motored towards the *Travelodge* in Cardiff. I was elated and Lee was proud of me; I could tell. I couldn't believe we had done it. We analysed and discussed the long day which was by now rapidly drawing to a close: the highs and lows, the trials and triumphs. We had prevailed – our persistence and determination to win had paid off. We laughed like idiot schoolboys at the look on the Bob Marley clone's face when we simply materialised out of nowhere like a pair of ghosts.

Walking into the hotel like a couple of zombies, we quickly carried out the check-in formalities before finding our room and choosing a bed. We were out for the count and slept like a log almost instantly.

My phone alarm went off at 0600hrs and I had to check it was correct. This couldn't be morning already; it seemed like we had just dropped off. I clicked on the TV - for two reasons: firstly to check my phone hadn't decided to play tricks on me and, secondly to as a means of waking the still sleeping Lee. He cursed me and turned over in his squeaky bed.

'Come on Lee, let's get a move on. I've a flight to catch remember?' All I got in return was a muffled grunt and a few indiscernible words.

I went in for a quick shower and ran the timetable through in my mind as I lathered shampoo through my short hair: the flight left Heathrow at 1315hrs and I would require being at the airport three hours in advance, so that made it 1015hrs. I winced as a drop of shampoo got in my eye and I rubbed like mad to eradicate it, tilting my head into the hot streaming flow to wash it

186

out. I recalled checking out the journey time on Lee's satnav last night which was calculated as two hours and twenty minutes. That meant we would have to be out of here by about 0730hrs to give us time for the journey. Mind you, that didn't take into account minor emergencies like a flat tyre or road works; I would just have to trust Lee to get me there on time and hope nothing or no one was out to stop me.

When I came out of the shower, towel wrapped around my waste, Lee was up, though as yet undressed. I coaxed him on and reminded him of the strict time schedule I required. He dismissed my concern telling me it would present no real problem; I only wished I had his optimism.

We went to the restaurant for a quick breakfast, here we were offered but declined a cooked breakfast and opted for the help-yourself continental buffet. We sat at a table in the corner and wolfed down a plethora of pastries, waffles and pancakes, all washed down with several mugs of coffee. As we were about to leave the restaurant, Lee went back up to the buffet and filled a couple of napkins with even more croissants, crepes and cakes.

'That's for the road,' he said smirking.

I couldn't believe it - we were on the road by 0715hrs and the roads were relatively clear – long may this continue, but I had my doubts. Soon we were heading across the Severn Bridge on the M4 and the traffic was starting to build up exponentially at each junction as we neared Bristol. Still Lee moved the *Mazda* with impressive speed and admirable technique, overtaking whenever possible and changing lanes when the pace slowed. I checked the satnav and saw we were still on schedule.

'So how long is the flight to Perth?' Lee asked. I laughed and snorted in derision.

'Have a guess,' I challenged. I watched him calculate in his head before providing his estimate.

'About twelve or thirteen hours?'

I laughed at his paltry guess.

'Would you believe it will take nearly 17 hours?' I asked with incredulity. At this revelation, he turned his head and gazed at me to see if I was serious.

'Seventeen hours! You've got to be kidding.' I could see Lee was happy he wasn't going with me.

'Are you going by propeller plane?' he enquired with a laugh.

'No, apparently onboard a state-of-the-art *Boeing 787 Dreamliner* – non-stop as well,' I said as though announcing the big prize on a game-show. Lee's head was shaking wildly and he was giggling at something; his shoulders bounced up and down and air was expelling from his nose in pulses.

'What? What's up with you?' I said with mock annoyance.

'Seventeen hours stuck in a metal tube with nowhere to go,' he said. 'What if you get a seat next to a lunatic or somebody with irritating habits?'

Those were my thoughts exactly; ever since I found out the duration of the flight, I had thought the same thing and dreaded that nightmare coming true. I was secretly hoping the flight would be quiet and I could get a row all to myself

– but that was something from fantasyland; highly improbable.

After a quick refuel of the *Mazda's* tanks at a service station just outside Chippenham, we were back on the motorway. The London bound traffic increasing as more and more cars, lorries, buses and vans joined the M4 at each junction. The satnav display was constantly revising the ETA as we slowed down and speeded up, but we were still within the predicted timeframe.

Heathrow Airport was now tantalisingly close. The road signs were advising us which junctions to use for each of the airport's terminals. I reminded Lee that I required terminal three – that was where my epic journey to the other side of the world would begin.

The low flying aircraft in the vicinity signalled we were nearly there; a plethora of planes were on final approach to one of the easterly runways, their landing gear extended and flaps hanging off the trailing edge of the wings like broken parts. We still had to negotiate all manner of junctions, roundabouts and slow traffic. Lee and his *MX-5* had performed effortlessly and I was proud of both.

I sat in the departure lounge of Heathrow's terminal three and gazed around at the bored faces all hunched over a paperback book, tablet or phone, busy whittling the hours away until their flight.

I had said goodbye to Lee and thanked him for his chauffeur services. He told me to let him know when I was back in the country and keep him abreast of my progress. He was now a fringe member with a vested interest in Operation Lazarus.

After checking in at the *Qantas* desk, I headed to the shops to but some supplies. I needed some more shaving supplies, new underwear and a whole lot of snacks to see me through on my epic non-stop flight. I also needed a change of clothes but was happy to purchase these in Australia; besides I wouldn't be away for very long – this would be just a short business trip.

As I had some time on my hands I decided to update Andy and Danny on my success with Dale Hannagan in Wales.

'Hi Andy, its Tony Caulfield here.'

As before a pause as he ran the name through his memory. I wished he would just up update his phone entry so my name came up when I rang him, this may remove the uncertainty. He was a bit quicker on the uptake this time.

'Oh Hi Tony, how's things?' the Brummie accent asked.

I told him that I had met Chas Hannagan's son and he was very enthusiastic about joining the resurrected band as a replacement for his father. I could hear a note of triumph in Brookes' voice; clearly the excitement was infectious.

'That's fantastic news,' he beamed. 'You know I think we may just pull this reunion thing off.'

'Yeah, I hope so, but there's still a bit of work to do,' I responded.

I told him I was on the verge of jetting off down to Perth, Australia to follow up a lead on Paul Dixon. To my surprise, he remembered my previous call when I mentioned going to Australia.

'Perth?' he exclaimed. 'that's a coincidence - my brother lives in Perth.'

He offered to call his brother and arrange for me to stay with him, but I was way ahead of Andy.

'That's good of you to offer Andy, but I've got a hotel booked. Besides, I'm only going to be away for five days.'

Brookes passed me his brother's name, address and phone number and told me to look him up if I got the chance. I said I would but knew it would be unlikely; still it was good to have a friendly contact in country should I need it. I promised to update him upon my return and I terminated the call.

Next I updated Danny Carter; his enthusiasm was as wholesome as ever. He reckoned Dale would make a welcome addition in the band and looked forward to meeting and hopefully playing alongside him. I promised to keep him abreast of any developments.

As it turned out the dreaded non-stop marathon flight to the end of the earth was not particularly busy. I entered the vast aircraft and was directed to my seat by a smiling Aussie female flight attendant looking proud to be wearing the garish red, pink and black uniform. The three rows of three-abreast seating in the economy cabin seemed cramped although I had read that these seats provided 'above average legroom' according to *Qantas*; above average for a normal-sized person – but I was six foot four inch tall!

My seat was at the window in the front row as I entered the aircraft door. So far no one else had claimed my row; hopefully no one would. I was quite happy to be a sad old loner for the rest of the day and into the night; Lee had struck fear into me with his suggestion of a nightmare travelling companion sitting next to me. Luckily I saw the seats had USB ports as I had brought my laptop but it was in need of a charge. I was settling into my seat whilst keeping an eye on the boarding passengers. Each time someone walked past my row and stopped, I froze thinking they were about to squeeze in beside me, but they frowned and walked on scanning the row numbers for the one to match their boarding pass.

The cabin was now filling up, but not every seat was taken, I observed. Then a middle aged man dressed in a navy pinstriped suit stopped, looked at my row of seats then dumped his carryon bag on the seat nearest the aisle. He reached up and opened the overhead locker, lifted his heavy bag up and thrust it into the locker, giving it an extra hard push for luck, as though this would prevent it from falling out. He looked at me, nodded a brief greeting then settled into the seat at the edge of the row. I now had a neighbour albeit with a seat to separate us. I supposed it could have been worse – he might have sat right next to me and we could have battled for control of the shared arm rest.

I was relieved when the doors were closed; that was it – all passengers had now boarded and I didn't have someone right next to me about to use my shoulder as a pillow. The business man removed his tie and stuffed it into his pocket and sat back closing his eyes – perhaps he was thanking God for the very same reason as me. The fact he wasn't in the mood to converse was fine by me; I didn't fancy swapping life stories with the guy over the next seventeen hours.

No sooner had the captain switched off the 'fasten seatbelt' sign when the cabin resounded with a series of clunks and many passengers popped up and headed to the toilets, desperate to sample the *Dreamliner's* on-board facilities. My row buddy kept his eyes closed all during taxiing, take off and climb out. I couldn't tell if he was asleep, praying or just running a video of a pleasant place through his mind. He too released his seatbelt and stood up opening the overhead locker and tugged out his bag, dumping it on the floor. I extracted my bag from beneath my feet and pulled out my laptop, powered it up and got to work with some writing.

My plan was to record all my exploits and adventures so far with Operation Lazarus. It would be in the form of a report, detailing all my research, conclusions and successes. Who knew, if I managed to pull this reunion concert off eventually, then my written record may make for an interesting read.

Mr Pinstripe produced an Apple Mac, powered it up and got into whatever would get him through the long flight without having to make conversation with the other guy. I could see spreadsheets and the like on his screen and was glad we weren't buddies – I would hate to have him bore me all the way to Australia with discussion, analysis and commentary about facts, statistics and data.

After a few hours of typing and mouse pad sliding I closed over the lid and put the laptop in my bag. It was now time to sample the in-flight entertainment that the Aussie airline had to offer. I navigated through all manner of channels feeling overwhelmed with the sheer choice of things to view or listen to. I began to watch a film with Gerard Butler in it, but the action wasn't quite doing it for me as I dozed off only waking to find the credits rolling up the screen. I turned to see Mr Pinstripe out for the count, his neck at a crazy angle and saliva trickling down his chin like a drooling dog; I was relieved he wasn't in the seat beside me.

Over the ensuing hours my life consisted of a perpetual cycle of eating, drinking, watching, sleeping, waking, going to the toilet – and back to the beginning again. The darkness outside gave way to a brilliant glorious sunrise and I celebrated by munching a handful of *Jelly Babies*.

Mr Pinstripe had now woken, cleaned his face and got to work yet again on his really important business stuff. I compiled more of my record of events pertaining to my little quest.

I lay back, closed my eyes and considered my successes so far: despite having initial reservations whether I could pull his thing off and wondering if it was a crazy waste-of-time notion, I now had scored three out of five, which was not bad at all. I was pretty confident I would find Paul Dixon, but I knew he may be the toughest nut to crack. Carter and Brookes stressed concern about Paul not wanting to be part of the band, but that was decades ago. I hoped he had changed and would welcome the unique opportunity to reunite and play on stage one last time.

Then there was Mick Walker. So far I had not the slightest clue as to his whereabouts on the planet, but considering how I managed to track down the others, I reckon I had the necessary skills to detect and locate the keyboard player; but that would be the next phase after finding Paul Dixon.

So far my research had not revealed that Mick Walker was deceased, so I had to assume he was alive and well and living out there somewhere. I only hoped it was not some other far flung place like his colleague Dixon. I doubted I could suffer another long range flight, and I'm sure my credit card would protest if I pushed it towards its limit.

I was glad Dale was on board with the project; hopefully the others would accept him as the perfect replacement for his deceased father. He certainly looked the part – just how his dad looked in the band's hey-day; but would he stand out like a sore thumb on stage alongside a bunch of aging men? He certainly appeared to have no qualms about sharing the stage with his dad's old mates. I had yet to hear young Hannagan play but I assumed his father had taught him well, after all Chas would be a hard act to follow with his unique and talented playing technique.

Mind you, how would the others get on with being back in a professional band and playing onstage? As far as I could see, most of them were no longer in the music business and probably hadn't performed professionally for quite some years. Of course, Brookes owned his own guitar store and played regularly, but this was a far cry from performing on stage in front of a mass audience who expected quality entertainment. Danny Carter also wasn't in the business and as far as I could gather, had not sung in a band for years. I recalled from our day together on Skye he still had the charisma and charm of a seasoned performer, plus a good strong voice as far as I could tell.

Either way, even if this gig happened, it would require an intense rehearsal schedule to get everyone mentally and physically prepared for a return to the professional music industry. They may not look as fresh and energetic as in their former days, but I hoped they still had their musical abilities and entertaining stage presence.

Chapter 21

The *Dreamliner's* ten tyres touched down on Antipodean soil right on schedule at 1300hrs local time; my life had fast-forwarded one complete day – seventeen hours of travel plus the seven hours time difference. As soon as we docked at the gate, the engines shut down and the seatbelt sign pinged off, all passengers sprang up like coiled springs relieved to be free from their seats. Limbs were stretched and muscles rubbed vigorously as the cabin looked like a huge physiotherapy treatment room. No sooner had the cabin crew opened the doors then there was a stampede; everyone keen to get off their metal prison as soon as possible. Elbows were used to good use to secure a prominent position at the front of the queue and carry-on baggage was swung into the faces of would-be over-takers. Now the aircraft interior resembled a herd of antelope all pushing and shoving to secure an ideal position at the muddy watering hole.

I followed the rest of my weary travelling comrades as we trundled along the maze of long corridors leading to immigration. Virtually all were still unsteady on their legs after the mammoth journey and teetered along like new-born lambs trying out their legs for the first time. Many of the elderly passengers wore worried looks as though fearful they may have contracted deep vein thrombosis during the long skyward trek, and have to sue the airline.

Fortunately the Aussie immigration service was super efficient and got through the long snaking queues in a timely manner, much to the gratitude of the masses. Being in the enviable position of not having to wait for any hold luggage, I bypassed the area and went straight outside to look for a taxi. The air was warm and moist and smelled exotic: a blend of pungent plants and fragrant flowers all foreign to my nose, permeated the atmosphere – but I was glad to be finally on terra firma and breathing in the southern hemispheric air.

Looking pretty much like many other airport buildings, Perth International was just as boring, although the clean white façade of the building did contrast nicely with the cloudless azure sky. I stood among the throngs of tired and bewildered passengers as they tried to orientate themselves and work out how to get to the taxi ranks, bus stop or car pickup points.

Once again I hadn't made any firm decisions yet – on our final approach I had considered how I would get from the airport to my hotel in the Guildford area of the city – taxi or bus? Both had their pros and cons: the former being more expensive but convenient and faster, the latter being cheaper but would probably take me on an unwanted mystery tour of the city. I really couldn't take much more sitting today, so I opted for the taxi route. Luckily I had exchanged some sterling for Australian dollars whilst at Heathrow, but I still had a limited amount and was hoping this would last for my short trip and I wouldn't have to visit another bureau de change.

I located the taxi rank and joined yet another queue. I was glad to see a constant supply of taxis and didn't have to wait long. I slid into the back of a spotless white taxi – it looked more like a police patrol car than a taxi with its blue and red cheat line running along the sides. I had to perform a double-take to ensure I was in the correct car.

That reminded me of a time in my policing past: I was monitoring the spilling-out of a crowd from a night club – it looked like the zombies had been release from their prison. I sat with my colleague in our high visibility marked police car and laughed at the staggering inebriated masses as they came to grips with the end of night and how they would get home. A long irregular queue then formed along the pavement but the constant stream of taxis made quick work in swallowing up the revellers. The odd scuffle broke out between two alpha males, but as we were in a prominent position right outside the nightclub door, they seemed to sense our presence and quickly desist to avoid the risk of an arrest and night in the police cells.

The usual show of passion ensued between couples and we watched in quiet amusement at the loner males, desperate for a date, try their hand at wooing virtually every single female in the crowd, but faced constant rejection.

Now the supply of taxis had dried up and the queues had grown considerably. Females attired in short skirts and dresses, and males in sweat-soaked t-shirts shivered as they waited in the cool night for their turn of a taxi. Without warning we were aware of our rear passenger door opening and someone getting in. I spun around to see a dolled-up woman slide across the seat and announce her destination. I looked at my constable colleague and we both laughed.

'Sorry Mrs, but this is a police car and not a taxi,' I informed her with a grin. The woman gazed at me through bleary eyes and thick makeup as though I had just insulted her. She looked at my uniform with metallic shoulder numerals, then to my colleague just for confirmation. Then she clutched her face in embarrassment as she realised her mistake. I was expecting her to hurry out of the car with a quick apology, but she sat there defiant.

'Can't you just give me a lift home anyway?' She pointed to the long snaking taxi queue, 'I'll have to wait ages on a taxi.'

'Sorry, but there is only one place we take people in this car,' my colleague announced.

'Well you're not taking me to the jail,' she shouted and hurriedly exited the car.

Guildford was closer than I had realised. I thought the Asian taxi driver was kidding when he told me it would only take about ten minutes. This was very welcome news as my legs were beginning to seize up through lack of use and being in the one position for so long. I asked the price of the fare and, following a quick mental calculation I worked out it would be the equivalent to about ten or eleven pounds, which was about average for that length of journey I reckoned.

We drew up outside the *Southern Welcome Hotel*, I paid and tipped the taciturn driver and extracted myself and bag from the interior. Again I struggled to get my legs working having spent the last hour or so rubbing and massaging my legs to rejuvenate the muscles and encourage the blood to flow.

I joined the short queue at the reception desk and awaited my turn. There was only one member of staff serving and I figured I may be another ten minutes before the Japanese couples in front of me were served and booked in. Then a tall skinny smiling woman appeared from a side door, approached the reception desk and efficiently got through the queue in no time at all, thoroughly showing up her male colleague who was taking an age processing his guests; perhaps he was new to the job, or just incompetent.

Soon it was my turn. The woman gestured me forward and smiled showing a mouthful of pristine shining teeth. She looked in her early twenties and wore her long blonde hair pulled back severely into a high ponytail. Her nondescript uniform fitted her slim frame neatly and she exuded an air of confidence and competence. With a series of rapid clicks on her computer keyboard and the odd confirmatory question, I was all booked in and ready to enjoy my stay in the four-star hotel; and still the bored looking Japanese couple hadn't been checked in yet; they looked at me with envy.

For the remainder of that day, I did very little. Feeling totally exhausted and suffering the effects of jet-lag, I showered, shaved and went down to the hotel restaurant for dinner, after which I retired to bed. In testimony to the comfort of the bed and my need for a long period of rest and recuperation, I woke late in the morning; in fact it was nearly lunch time when I got up, dressed and planned my day; I was feeling suitably refreshed and raring to go.

I went out to explore my immediate area, but keeping an eye out for a suitable place to have lunch. I located a fast food burger joint nearby and gave in when the appetising smell of food wafted out of the buildings vents and straight into my nose. I went inside and mingled with the spotty-faced teens and hoards of dirty workmen as we queued to be served by equally spotty and dirty looking staff.

As I munched my way through my chicken burger and fries, I got out my folded map of the area which I liberated from the hotel. I located the street where the Johnny B Goode Bar was located and reckoned it would take me about ten minutes of casual strolling to get there. Given this was now Thursday, I reckoned I wouldn't make my first sighting of Paul Dixon until the next night when no doubt his resident band would play. This was assuming my hunch about Dixon was correct and he still played in a band in the Johnny B Goode. For all I knew this may turn out to be a complete waste of time and money. I would be livid if I found out I was wrong about the Paul Dixon connection and he, in fact lived much closer to home. Although Perth looked a nice and interesting enough city, I was not here for the sightseeing – I was here on business.

Finding the bar was easy enough as the big bold lettering above the door told me I had reached the blues-themed establishment. I stepped inside half expecting it to be like the bars in your quintessential western movie: where the music suddenly stops and all heads turn to face the intruder with cries of 'Gee, there's a stranger in town!'

The place had obviously had a bit of a makeover since the photograph I was given by rocknroller332; it smelled faintly of fresh paint and the décor looked new or spruced up, but the same old photos of the famous blues men still adorned the walls. The ceiling and walls were lit by cleverly concealed multi colour LED lighting, sweeping through a spectrum of blue and purple hues creating an interesting homely and hypnotic effect. On one wall was a huge LCD television showing a football match in progress, albeit with the sound muted. A series of square tables with accompanying vinyl-covered chairs littered the floor space creating a rather claustrophobic effect; it appeared the owners packed as many tables into the place as possible – probably to accommodate as many patrons as they could during the busy weekends and when the live band was playing.

I spotted the small stage area over in one corner with two wedge monitors on the floor and a pair of extra large speakers on stands at each side of the wooden platform. At the rear was a reasonably sized drum kit with more cymbals than were probably needed, flanked on each side by a selection of guitar and bass combo-amplifiers. Beside the drums were a number of empty guitar floor stands and at the front of the stage stood three boom microphone stands. The stage was closed off by the careful placement of three bar stools.

The place was by no means busy – only about eight or ten other individuals within, all male; most were sitting around tables drinking and chatting, and one guy was trying his luck on a games machine, his fingers pounding at the buttons like his life depended on it. He wore an intense look of concentration on his face and obviously took this particular game seriously. I awaited the imminent rush of coins to spew from the machine which would signal that the guy knew what he was doing. No one paid me any attention and the quiet background music didn't stop.

Locating a vacant table in the corner, I sat down to survey the place and tune in to my new environment. I watched the lone barman busy himself by cleaning the long wooden surface, trying to eradicate the plethora of stains, spillages and greasy handprints. I could see a young girl milling around in the background but could not see what was keeping her busy.

Leaving my jacket over the back of the seat, I rose and wandered over to the bar. It would look odd and I would draw attention to myself if I sat with no drink. The barman saw me coming and stopped his labours to give me his undivided attention.

'Hi there. What can I get you?' he asked with a genuine enough smile. I surveyed the bottles lining the back of the bar and optics as though looking for inspiration, before ordering a soft drink. He clocked my 'foreign' accent immediately.

'You here on holiday then?' he said with a thick Australian accent. I considered the question: if I told him I was here on business, no doubt he would want to know more and I didn't want to discuss that with him.

'Yeah, sort of,' was my half-hearted answer. He fetched my drink and I could see him trying to work out my accent.

'Came down from Britain, then?' he probed.

'Yeah, Scotland actually, although I few from Heathrow.' He nodded his interest.

'The guy who owns this place is English actually,' he responded. Now it was my turn to look interested.

I surveyed the place scanning the walls for posters or looking for leaflets which may indicate who the resident band were or when they would be playing next. Finding nothing of any assistance, I would just have to ask.

My drink was placed on the counter, the barman quoted the price and I dug into my wallet to extract some Aussie dollars before handing them over and pocketing the change.

'Do you have live bands playing here then?' I asked indicating to the stage in the corner.

'Oh yeah. Every Friday and Saturday, Sport. We have a resident band with the odd guest band playing as well.'

I nodded and looked keen. This was good confirmation of my research; they still had a resident band playing, but was Paul Dixon the band's drummer, I wondered? I didn't want to come straight out and ask in case I ended up having the same evasive experience I had in

Birmingham with Wayne while trying to get to Andy Brookes. I thanked the barman, picked up my drink and went over to my table. I continued to survey the place as I considered my strategy; it would probably involve coming back to this place tomorrow evening, where with a bit of luck I would witness Paul Dixon rattling those drums on that stage.

Then a figure emerged from through the back. I could only see the back of him but he looked older, exuding confidence and a slight air of arrogance – I reckoned he must the shift manager, or maybe the English owner the barman was talking about. He wore slightly long grey hair, which looked almost white in the light of the illuminated bar ceiling. He beckoned the girl forward and I watched him lambaste her for something or other. I couldn't make out anything of the conversation but it looked heated, with him pointing his finger at the girl and mouthing off loudly, shaking his head after virtually every sentence. The girl looked shamefaced as she bravely took his tirade of abuse; I wondered if her incompetence were sins of omission or sins of commission – was her admonishment for something she did or didn't do?

Whatever it was, she was getting the third degree and the guy was loving his power over her. The barman kept himself busy, tidying up and staying out the way of the argument; I formed the distinct impression he had seen this all before, and most probably had been in the same position as the girl at some point in the past. I could see the other patrons look up from their drinks and conversations to watch the spectacle behind the bar. I felt sorry for the girl but annoyed at the guy's arrogance and lack of diplomacy – it was very unprofessional to reprimand a member of staff in front of the clientele.

This type of behaviour certainly was not alien to me – being in the police for thirty years and having worked alongside many an arrogant supervisor, I had seen this kind of thing many a time: sergeants and inspectors criticise and chastise a constable in front of the public, much to the poor cop's humiliation. Once I was promoted, and whenever I had to reprimand one of my team, I would always do it tactically and in private. If an officer had made a bad decision or done something wrong, then more was to be gained in pointing out the error as a learning curve than humiliating the person and having them detest you and you lose respect.

I considered whether I wanted to sit here and continue to patronise the premises given the questionable conduct by its supervisory staff.

Chapter 22

The show abruptly stopped and the girl hurried off through the back. I was hoping she wasn't going to empty her locker and grab her coat. Mind you, I hadn't a clue what she had done – for all I knew she had been dipping her hand into the till or maybe secretly supping the bar supplies.

The man turned and glided over to the busy barman. I thought this was going to be round two of staff appraisals, but the two engaged in light-hearted banter with both laughing. Then I heard them lower their voices and lean in towards each other as though discussing some conspiracy theory. There was a bit of thumb pointing in my direction by the barman and the grey haired guy looked up and straight at me. I stared back at the guy – and knew instantly it was Paul Dixon.

My heart raced as I recognised the same guy from the photo I obtained from the Legions of Fans website – and I was confident it was the same man. He ducked under the bar and headed in my direction. I calmed myself; I had to remain professional. I looked away as though not noticing his approach.

'Hi there, I hear you've come all the way from Britain?' he asked, now looking calm and relaxed after his aggressive and abusive tirade a few moments ago – perhaps he was a schizophrenic! I looked at up him and smiled.

'Yes, that's right. I'm from Glasgow. He looked at me through his purple tinted glasses and returned my smile.

'I'm actually from England.' He thrust his hand outwards, 'Paul Dixon. I'm the owner of this joint.'

I felt elated - final confirmation at last – and a surprise: Paul actually owned the place. I shook hands with the once famous Paul Dixon and told him my name.

'Mind if I join you Tony?' Paul asked indicating to a vacant seat beside me.

'No, at all. Be my guest.

He sat and down and cupped his hands in front of him, his elbows resting on the tabletop.

'So what brings you all the way down here?' Paul said. I wished I could just come right out with it, but felt it would be more prudent to ease into the conversation.

'Well, it's more of a business trip than a holiday actually.' I replied. His eyebrows rose beneath his glasses; I had aroused his curiosity.

'What line of business are you in Tony?'

I pondered my options and how best to reply, then decided to ease into the reason for my being here.

'I'm in the music promotions business,' I replied. His curiosity remained heightened. Then he smiled and pointed over to the stage area.

'I play drums with the resident band here. Maybe you could promote us?'

I smiled candidly as though promoting small-time pubs bands was way beneath me.

Then I decided while I had the guy's undivided and curious attention, I would go straight to the point. This may be my big chance – the very reason I had endured a long overseas flight to come here. I relaxed, leant towards him and asked.

'Tell me Paul, do you miss being in the Faceless Legions?' His face altered abruptly from one of calm curiosity to instant suspicion.

'What? What are you talking about?' he said, his voice rising in volume as annoyance took hold of him. I could tell he was irritated that his cover had now been blown and I knew exactly who he was.

'Come on Paul. You were the drummer with the big and famous Faceless Legions in the seventies, right?'

It was more of a statement than a question. He averted his gaze as he decided on the best course of action. His hands opened to reveal clean

208

calloused hands - evidence of a lifetime of gripping drum sticks. He let out a long tired breath, which seemed to last about three seconds and shook his head slowly.

'Okay, you got me. Yup, I was that sad freak who was a member of the Legions.' I let him continue without interruption. 'So how did you know it was me?'

I explained my previous life as a police detective and the fact I managed to piece together fragments of data and information to trace him here in Australia. Despite his defeated demeanour, he looked impressed. His theory was probably: moving to the other side of the world would provide the ultimate anonymity and privacy, and he would never have to speak about the Faceless Legions again. Now I had tracked him down and confronted him with questions of his past life.

'Do you ever miss that period in your life Paul?'

He sat back in his seat and I could see his eyes glaze over as he ventured down memory lane.

'The Faceless Legions!' he exclaimed, 'That was a pretty stupid name! Do you know how we ended up with that as a band name?'

I nodded; apparently it came out of some obscure book by Poe or HP Lovecraft or other, no one seemed to know exactly. It was also rumoured by some fans to be a lyric from the Led Zeppelin song, *Carouselambra*, but this was only released in 1979 – the year the Legions disbanded, so it couldn't have been the origin.

'I hated that name, but the others thought it was great – creative and clever,' he lamented.

'But you enjoyed playing in the band?' I asked. He considered this and composed a suitable answer.

'Oh yeah, it was alright.' Then he clarified, 'At first it was great, then as time went on I was growing a bit bored.'

I could tell he was viewing a videotape of past performances in his mind; his eyes were glazed over. I let him recollect for a moment before I asked.

'Paul, why did you all more or less disappear after disbanding?'

He had a ready answer.

'I think we all had had enough of the music business. Don't get me wrong we all made a packet out of being in the band,' he turned in his seat and swept his hand around in a horizontal arc, 'I mean I came out here and bought this place with my savings.'

'But none of you ended up playing with other bands or forming a new one,' I pointed out. Paul shrugged his shoulders quickly.

'I don't know about them mate, I just know I was happy to be out and starting a new life, so to speak.'

This was a common theme - I recalled pretty much the same answers from Carter and Brookes; the consensus appeared to be they were all fed up and wanted a bit of peace and quiet following an intense, exhausting work regime for many years – I supposed I would be the same in their shoes.

'But the band seemed to split-up quite abruptly, did it not?' I probed, curious for an answer to burning questions. He snorted in derision and shook his head.

'Yeah, that was all down to the lycra and leather gang.'

I faked confusion, prompting him to explain; I had a fair idea who his rant was aimed at, but I wanted to hear his explanation.

'You know the…what do you call them?' he struggled to recall the sobriquet. 'The new wave of British heavy metal,' he said his voice heavy with sarcasm and a hint of jealousy, I detected.

'Bands like Iron Maiden, Judas Priest, Motorhead,' here he thought hard to augment his list, 'Def Leppard and…Saxon, I mean what were Saxon all about?'

He was now laughing at the absurdity of all these bands that effectively popped up out of nowhere and became very popular in the British rock and metal music industry. I thought it best not to wind him up by telling him that most of the bands he mentioned I was big fans of at one time and went to many of their concerts – including Saxon.

'So you didn't like those bands?' I asked knowing this would wind him up.

He snorted in derision yet again as though I had said something absurd.

'Oh those bands appeared and then no one wanted to know us anymore,' he admitted sadly. I let him continue.

'You know, our manager suggested we don the lycra and leather and join the nancy-boys playing pop-rock music,' he said laughing at the absurd notion, 'we all told him where to stick his spandex.'

'So the new-wave bands effectively put an end to bands like the Faceless Legions?' I said.

'Yup, pretty much, although by that time we were all running out of steam and wanted out, but to ousted by that gang was embarrassing,' Paul lamented.

'I mean we were a good old fashioned rock and roll band playing quality music, then the spandex and lycra-wearing boys arrived and suddenly this was the new fashion!'

It was good to hear him ranting and raving about the past, and revealing the real reasons for the sudden demise of the Legions; however I wanted to steer him back on track and get to the crux of the matter.

'So let me ask you this Paul,' I said leaning forward and pausing to let the anticipation grow. 'What would you say to a reunion of the Faceless Legions, would you be up for it?' I watched his face change from mild amusement at his lament, to derision.

'What are you talking about? That would never happen.'

'Well, the real reason I'm here Paul, is to ask you if you would consider being part of a reunion of the band with view to playing a one-off comeback concert?' There I had said it – and now I would let the cards fall wherever they may. He flopped back in his chair and let out a laugh.

'You're having a laugh aren't you – reunite the Faceless Legions!' he said this as though it was an impossible task. I shook my head to enhance my serious expression.

'No Paul; I'm serious. What do you say?'

His head was shaking vigorously and his face was not registering any interest in my proposal; this was not good. Perhaps I should now reveal my trump card – the Brookes and Carter cards.

Paul rose to go as though the conversation was now over and the whole discussion ended.

'It's a nice thought, but it'll never happen Tony, I'm sure of it.'

I grabbed his arm to detain him and hope he resumed his seat – maybe be was done discussing, but I sure wasn't.

'Paul, please give me a minute to explain.'

I pointed to his chair urging his to sit down, but he remained standing.

'Look Tony, it was nice meeting you but I've got to get back to work – I've a business to run.'

With that he walked away and was soon back behind the bar conversing with his barman, probably discussing the madness of the Brit in the corner with his absurd suggestion of resurrecting a dead band.

Over the years in my police career I had to deliver an inordinate amount of death messages, and I came to predict the usual array of responses. It seems to be a typical human trait whenever some one is told of the passing of a loved one, they lapse into denial.

'I'm afraid I have to report that your husband had been killed in a road traffic accident, madam.'

Her response would be something like this: 'You're kidding!'

'Sorry to tell you that your son died as a result of being stabbed.'

He would reply, 'No, not my son – it can't be him. You've got it all wrong.'

And so it became predictable. Whenever I was the barer of sad and tragic news, I would be regarded as a joker sent to wind them up with reports of fake deaths. This is how it was with Dixon – I had made a legitimate suggestion and offered him a chance to reunite with his former band, but he had me down for a time-wasting fool. He had simply dismissed me and went about his business like I had just wasted his valuable time.

I rapidly downed the remainder of my drink, grabbed my jacket and rushed over to the bar.

'Paul, can I just have a second please.'

He looked at me with disdain and shook his head. I could see the barman looking curiously between me and Paul – he was anxious to know what was going on.

'I don't want to discuss the matter any more, Tony. I'll see you around.'

I wasn't finished with him yet – this may be my only opportunity and I couldn't risk blowing it.

'Paul, please hear me out. I've come all this way to speak to you; just give a minute,' I reasoned.

He consented and ushered me over to the other side of the bar, out of earshot of the nosey barman and the other patrons.

'You've got two minutes then you'll have to go,' he said holding up two fingers as though I needed that confirmation.

'As well as tracing you all the way to here, I've also traced Danny Carter and Andy Brookes.' I let the information register and watched his response. Sure enough his hostility gave way to curiosity. His eyebrows behind the tinted lenses rose.

'You spoke to Brookes and Carter?' he enquired as though I was teasing him.

'Yes indeed. Both alive and well, Paul.'

Still he was interested. I was glad I brought them into the conversation otherwise he may be forcibly ejecting me from his bar. He shook his head as though stunned.

'Wow – Andy Brookes and Danny Carter, that's a blast from the past. How are they? What are they up to?'

I explained that I had painstakingly traced both; Brookes who owned his own guitar shop in Birmingham and Carter who was living a peaceful life up in the Isle of Skye. Dixon laughed as though the lives of his former colleagues were absurd. I thought I would keep up the pressure and feed his curiosity; now was the ideal time to play my trump card.

'You know what Paul?' I said as I looked him in the eye to show I wasn't bluffing. 'Both are totally up for a reunion. Both said yes they want to do it.' I let this significant revelation sink in.

'So what do you say, Paul? Are you up for joining them for a Faceless Legions reunion?' The look he gave me betrayed his answer.

'No, I told you already. I'm not interested but thanks anyway.'

'Oh come on Paul, this is a huge opportunity,' I reasoned.

'Sorry to disappoint mate, but that's my final answer.'

With that he turned his back on me and made his way through the back of the bar and into a door marked 'private.' So that was it? Dixon was out and couldn't be persuaded? I thought not. I would simply try again later. He would not be getting let off the hook that easily.

I explored the area, wandering down many streets, gazing into shop windows and watching people drinking coffee at roadside cafes and bars. I was annoyed at Dixon's refusal to consider my proposition but I was not unduly concerned. I reckoned with a little persuasion, I could get him to agree and sign up for the gig. I still had a few more days in which to work my magic and finesse him into saying yes; however the pressure was on me to get a result. I had come here with the express intention of finding Dixon and getting him to agree to reform the band; I did not travel from the other side of the world to get an answer in the negative.

As I couldn't concentrate on the sights and the muggy heat was affecting my mood, I decided to retire back to my hotel room – besides I had yet to adjust to the new time zone and was still suffering the effects of jetlag; and so I lay down on top of my bed and was out for the count in moments.

When I came to, I fired up my laptop to check on emails. I had one from Danny Carter asking me if I had gone to Australia in search of Paul Dixon and if so, how was I doing with that particular quest? I returned his email but didn't reveal my failure with Dixon so far; I just stated I was hoping to speak with him in the next day or two. He wished me luck and requested me to update him as soon as able.

Next I emailed Alison to tell her where I was and how my mission was progressing. Given the time difference, I knew she would be asleep and did not expect a reply until later or tomorrow. To my surprise, she sent a reply immediately as though she was up and about. As it turned out she had just come home following a night shift and was not feeling tired at the moment; so she had decided to spend some time checking emails and messing around on *Facebook*.

Alison was surprised to hear I was thousands of miles away in Australia and I detected a hint of annoyance that I hadn't told her I was going. To be honest it was a bit of a rush and impromptu decision, but that was just the nature of the mission. My priority was to rush off somewhere whenever I got a hunch about finding one of the former Legions, and update people later.

Then Alison asked me if I was equipped for, and able to setup a *Skype* link between us. I agreed this would be more conducive for having a proper face to face conversation instead of the slow and tedious type-send-read-reply system we were currently engaging in.

I found a garden area at the rear of the hotel which was empty and quiet. So I took my laptop and placed it on a picnic table, set up the *Skype* connection and was soon conversing with my ex-wife like old pals.

'So you found Paul Dixon? What's he like?' Alison said.

'Looking a lot older. Grey hair, wrinkles and the same old grumpy demeanour and bad temper,' I replied.

I told Alison about his behaviour towards the female staff member then his lack of cooperation with me when I got to the heart of the matter. Alison laughed at that; she was well aware of Dixon's choleric personality when he was with the band.

'What are you going to do now?' she enquired.

'I'll pay him another visit and pile on the pressure. I'm not taking no for an answer.'

I explained that I was reasonably confident I could get him to agree as I detected some interest in his face and predicted he was just playing hard to get.

We moved on to other discussions and spoke about Lee's recent visit to Aberdeen. Soon the conversation turned back towards Operation Lazarus as I narrated our recent trip and adventures in Carmarthen and Cardiff, leading to finding Dale Hannagan and getting him to sign up for the reunion gig.

'So you're almost there then?' Alison asked.

'Well even if I get Dixon to agree, I still have to find Mick Walker, and right now I haven't a clue where to start with him.' Alison said she would carry out some research and let me know should she uncover some fragment or clue. As we were both yawning now, we decided to terminate our conversation and promised to speak later.

Chapter 23

The band launched into a fantastic cover of the Dr John song *Right time, Wrong Place*; I remembered the original version but much preferred the cover by BB King and Bonnie Raitt – and this was the version the band were performing. The female singer's melodic voice contrasting with the guitarist/ singer's baritone vocals making for a very impressive rendition of the famous song. Their harmonies and interactions enhanced the duet considerably. My gaze turned to Paul Dixon as he pounded out a

218

rhythm on the ride cymbal, performed a roll along the side toms ending in a tap on the eighteen inch crash cymbal. Paul looked content sitting behind his drums and playing along to blues hit after hit. Still I could easily envisage him playing along to the old Faceless Legion hits on some big stage. I hoped it could still happen. It wouldn't be the same if we had to recruit some other drummer simply because Paul was being difficult in refusing to support such a venture as a one-off reunion concert.

My plan was simple: wait until the band stop for a break or intermission then home in on Paul and continue where I left off. Hopefully he had time to think about my offer and had chewed it over – for all I knew he might approach me and instigate the conversation.

I sat at my table near to the stage, drink in front of me and my phone nearby. I was taking the occasional photo of the band just to convince those who may doubt I had indeed found Dixon. Whenever the opportunity was presented to snap Paul in an unobstructed pose, I took it. I was unsure if he saw me sitting there; if he did, he made no attempt to acknowledge me.

The Friday night crowd was large and more and more patrons spilled in through the doors no doubt attracted by the loud but pleasant music emanating from the Johnny B Goode Bar. Soon all seats were taken and it was standing room only. One or two couples danced to the music and a group of middle-aged females performed some embarrassing air guitar moves, to much cheering and applause from the raucous crowd; it seemed anything was acceptable to this rowdy bunch of alcohol-fuelled fans.

I ended up with a bunch of ladies sitting at my table. The usual question was proffered whether the seats were taken or being kept free for someone perhaps at the bar or visiting the toilets. My first inclination was to deny them the use of the seats, but they might take umbrage to me guarding a couple of seat that no one would use, especially when the place was hectic with no spare seats.

The three overweight and heavily done-up ladies squeezed their plump figures into the chairs and began discussing the drinks order and who was going up for it. They had to shout to be heard over the loud din of the band's rendition of ZZ Top's *Tush* now being performed.

Two of the plump threesome got up dumping their handbags on the chairs, and excused their way through the throngs as they headed to the crowded bar. The one remaining friend made eye contact with me; I think she felt compelled to speak to me out of pure politeness.

'Do ya like the band?' she hollered in her thick Aussie accent. I nodded.

'Yeah their top quality,' I shouted back.

Her expression changed as she clocked my accent. I could see her trying to work out and place my nationality.

'Are you American?'

'No, no, I'm from Scotland actually,' I replied with a laugh.

Her thin carefully plucked eyebrows shot up in amazement – perhaps they didn't get many Scots in this place.

'Wow – Scotland!' she shouted in reply as though it was on some other planet. Didn't she know that Australia had a large Scottish population?

'That's amazing – you've come all the way from Scotland? Did you fly here?'

I nodded; what else did she expect me to say? No, I actually paddled all the way here in a canoe! Now she had just revealed her intelligence level – and it was not impressive.

I turned away to watch the band, but could not see much on account of the masses swaying to the beat and milling around. I was not interested in having a conversation with this lady or her mates – I was here to speak to Paul once the opportunity arose.

Soon her friends returned cradling lots of bottles of beer in their arms – they had obviously stocked up on enough drinks to last a while given the queue at the bar. The bottles were dumped on the small table and the plump ladies flopped onto the chairs after shoving the handbags onto the floor. Soon I was being smothered by the three as they moved even closer to each other so they could chat without having to resort to shouting. In addition, the standing patrons surrounding our table continually bumped into us causing the ladies to move their seats closer to the table to provide that extra buffer space; soon I was their new intimate friend.

I looked at my watch and saw the band had now been playing continuously for forty five minutes, so I figured they were due to take a well-earned break. I sprang up causing my new lady friends to recoil in fright at the unexpected move.

'Excuse me ladies, but I'll move and give you all some space.'

They looked up at me confusion etched on their white-powdered faces; that's when I realised they probably didn't understand a word I had just uttered. No sooner had I vacated the seat when someone sat down on it, looking exhausted as though having been standing for hours on end and badly in need of a sit-down, thankful at my good deed.

I shoved my way through the crowd excusing myself in a bad Aussie accent, thinking this may help me to be better understood. Most patrons just looked at me as though I was the rudest guy in the place. I found a vacant spot near to the stage and watched the band wind down to the closing bar of the song. Paul finished the number with an impressive multi-beat roll using all the side and floor toms before whacking the large crash cymbal to end. A deafening roar of applause went up and I felt my ears tingle.

'Thanks so much,' the elated female vocalist shouted into her microphone. 'We'll be right back after we've had a short break.'

This generated more applause, whooping and cheering. Clearly this band was popular and, judging by the numbers packed into the place, was also a very healthy money earner for Paul and his establishment.

The band members left the stage after placing their instruments on stands and ensuring the microphones were turned off. Paul was the last to go after making some adjustments to his bass pedal. I moved forward to be in a good position to intercept the man. He shuffled around from behind the drums then spotted me watching. I could see his eyes tilt upwards and his face turned sour as he walked towards me.

'Hi Paul, great show,' I offered.

'Thanks, Tommy,' he returned. I felt the need to correct him to avoid any misunderstanding.

'It's Tony. Have you thought any more about what we discussed earlier, Paul?'

Here he nodded but his face did not alter its choleric expression at all.

'Same answer as before, Tony. I'm not interested.'

With this he brushed past me and squeezed his way through the crowd as he headed to the bar, ducking underneath the counter before disappearing through to the back private area. I was gutted; I was expecting him to express an interest having been given time to consider. Apparently he had made his mind up.

I had no option but to wait for him to reappear then hit him with the question once again. I was not prepared to give up that easily; I was determined to persuade Paul to agree to the reunion before I jetted off back home, whatever it took and by whatever means. I had to maintain the pressure on him; every opportunity I got to speak to him, I would take.

Why was he being so obstinate? I was offering him an opportunity of a lifetime and he was rejecting it. This could be his only chance to reform for a one-off live concert; it was not as if he was being asked to write and record an album or get cosy with his former band-mates. It was simply a chance to recapture a slice of the past and thrill countless numbers of fans. After that, he could disappear into oblivion and never play with the band again if he so wished.

I once had a prisoner who totally refused to cooperate with any instructions given to him. My colleague and I were arresting him for a domestic violence incident and were expecting him to resist arrest and possibly fight with us. He certainly resisted arrest, but not actively - through passive resistance. He lay on his belly on the ground and refused to put his hands behind his back so the handcuffs could be applied, and kept them firmly in his pockets. This involved us having to prise them out and practically break his arms as we forced then around to the rear, before painfully clasping the cuffs around his red and swollen wrists.

Next he refused to get up from the ground, necessitating us hauling him to his feet and practically dragging him to the awaiting police van. Once again he stood there as though awaiting instructions. We commanded him to step into the cell in the van, but he refused, so we had to push the guy inside before slamming the secure steel door closed.

It was a repeat performance upon arrival at the police station resulting in a team of officers who practically dragged him from the van and frogmarched him along to the charge bar to be processed. As predicted, he remained taciturn and made no reply to the questions from the custody sergeant. Having no other option, the sergeant ordered him to be thrown in a police cell until such times as he decided to be more cooperative. When it was explained to him that because we had no details of him, a prosecution report could not be sent to the Procurator Fiscal, therefore he would have to remain in police custody until he decided to talk. Fearing an indefinite stay in a cold, hard, dark cell, he wasn't long in breaking his silence and offering to answer almost any question posed to him.

The band soon returned, walking purposefully to the stage to resume their performance. Paul was last to arrive and as he trundled past me I called out to him.

'Paul, can you just consider again please? Just think about it mate,' I reasoned.

He ignored me and brushed past and onto the stage. I knew that was the best shot I would get for the moment.

The music fired up again and my ears began to itch as though in protest to the great many decibels entering their delicate inner structure. My option now was to hang around and wait for the band to finish, then home in on Paul once again, but the music was too loud for me and the crowds too close for comfort. The place was hot and sweaty and I craved some fresh air outside, so I left.

Upon stepping out the main doors, I was glared at by a couple of burly bouncers. They studied me as though I had a gun and a knife secreted on my person. Both were around six foot in height, highly muscular with bulging biceps and closely shaved heads. Given the muggy atmosphere they had no use for jackets, which I reckoned they preferred as they were able to showcase their burly physiques and big broad arms, both to impress and intimidate.

Even though I towered over them by at least three or four inches, they didn't look at all daunted – this was safety in numbers with this pair; separate them and you would probably give yourself a distinct advantage. I brushed past them and out onto the street which was busy with people going about their business. Most were dressed up as though going to a nightclub or bar and all seemed in good spirits at the though of a whole weekend of drinking, revelling and socialising.

It was good to be out in the relative cool and quiet of the street. My ears were buzzing and sweat was running down my back causing an itch which I couldn't quite reach. I pondered my next move – do I wait until a bit later when Paul's band were done then attempt to speak to him again, or do I just retire for the night and try again tomorrow? I weighed up the options as I trundled along the streets a few blocks from my hotel. I was conscious of the evaporating time and the pressing need to have a positive answer from Paul before I boarded the plane back to Heathrow on Sunday afternoon.

As I was still suffering the effects of jet lag and the balmy weather was adding to my constant feeling of fatigue, I decided that enough was enough for the evening and so I proceeded back to my hotel.

I went online to check emails and see if Alison was around so I could provide an update of today's failed attempt with Dixon. There was no response from Alison, so I added a little more to my memoirs before powering the laptop down, showering and going to bed.

Saturday brought a big change in the weather – rain, although it was still warm and clammy. The roads and pavement smelled of that universal scent whenever it rains after a prolonged period of relative drought; the subtle blending of rainwater with tar and other chemicals used to pave a road or sidewalk. It was strangely appealing and reminded me of home.

Saturday was also my last day to do what I came here for, so it was with increased purpose that I strode towards the Johnny B Goode Bar where, hopefully I could secure Paul's backing with my mission to resurrect his old band. In twenty four hours time I would effectively be boarding the flight for my long arduous voyage back to the UK, and I hoped I would have Paul Dixon's excited agreement to be part of what could potentially be a very big deal.

I entered the bar unhindered. Clearly the big burly goons were only employed and required in the evenings where the influx of boisterous patrons needed careful control. As before the place was fairly empty – a major contrast to the heaving atmosphere of the pervious night. Paul clearly employed a team of efficient cleaners as the place was spotless. Any liquid spillages or glass breakages had been tidied up. The vinyl flooring had been mopped and vacuumed and displayed no trace of the hundreds of feet which had traversed and danced across it only twelve hours previously.

The same barman was on duty, but he was joined by the same girl I had seen being chastised by Paul yesterday. I was happy to see she had retained her employment here; perhaps she was on her final warning and this was why she was industriously scrubbing at the bar and draught handles.

I approached the bar and the barman acknowledged my presence with a nod of his head. He didn't seem to register any recognition, but I supposed he saw a wealth of faces on a daily basis and could not be expected to remember everyone he encountered.

'Is Paul Dixon available at the moment?' I enquired.

He shrugged as he dried a pint glass with a dish towel, his hand rocking back and forth as he aimed to polish it to a shine.

'I think he's busy at the moment, sport.'

'Is he through the back?' I said indicating to the private door behind the bar.

He shrugged once again. This guy was beginning to irritate me; he was being rather unhelpful – of course he must know where his boss was.

'Well could you go and see where he is. Tell him it's Tony Caulfield and I won't keep him long.'

The glass polisher stared at me as he hurried to think of a reason not to comply.

'I dunno, Paul said I hadn't to disturb him.'

'Could you do me a favour? Just go and tell him Tony's here to see him before he goes home to Britain.' I attempted to keep the annoyance from my voice. This guy was the gatekeeper and if I treated him with politeness, then maybe he would permit me access to his boss. Cross him or be cheeky then I might as well just walk away.

At last he had completed the drying and polishing of the glass and placed it down on the wooden bar top. He leaned forward and made direct eye contact with me.

'Look Paul said he doesn't want to speak to you. He told me that if a tall Scot called Tony Caulfield came in here looking for him, I was to show you the door,' he said lowering his voice to a conspiratorial whisper. 'He doesn't want to see you or speak to you, I'm sorry sport, but you'll have to leave now.'

He pointed his long bony finger at the door.

I was rapidly loosing my cool; the adrenalin was beginning to course through my veins preparing me for the fight or flight. I took a long deep breath and let it out slowly before I spoke again.

'Please go and ask Paul to give me just thirty seconds of his time, that's all I'm asking.'

I spoke in a calm and controlled manner and actually impressed myself with my cool headedness. The barman stood stock still staring at me. I could see he was wracked with indecision: should he go and tell his boss or attempt to do his master's bidding and eject me from the premises? His obstinate manner told me he had decided on the latter.

'Okay,' I said striding towards the end of the bar, the access point through to the back office, where I guessed Paul was hiding. 'I'll just go and get him myself.'

Chapter 24

This was where my six foot four inch frame was advantageous. I towered over the obstructive barman and he backed down.

'I'll just go and get him, please wait here,' he said through quivering lips.

'Fine, I'll wait here, but be quick about it and don't mess me around.'

My threat was designed to carry menace and reinforce my no-nonsense approach; I didn't intent to get embroiled in a fight nor did I want to sample the hospitality of a local Perth police custody cell.

The barman hurried through the back closing the door behind. I looked up and saw the girl eye me closely. When we made eye contact she looked away and continued with her chores. I wondered if she was nearing closer to the staff telephone in the event she would have to summon the police.

I heard the sound of raised voices from behind the closed door. No doubt the barman was getting much the same treatment as his female colleague the previous day, and facing the wrath of Paul.

Soon the door opened and the barman walked out looking embarrassed and red faced. Behind him strode Paul with the usual sour look on his face. He ducked under the bar and summoned me to a table in the corner away from the other seated patrons. I followed and was about to speak when he silenced me with an outstretched vertical hand.

'Listen Tony. I've had enough of this. I've given you an answer and I'm not changing my mind, now that's it. You'll have to leave now.' I let him calm down a bit before I spoke.

'Paul, I endured a seventeen hour flight to get here for one reason and one reason only – to get you to say yes to a one-off reunion with Carter, Brookes and Hannagan who are all totally up for this gig by the way.'

He opened his mouth to speak, but now it was my turn to silence him with an even larger hand.

'It would be much appreciated if you just agreed to it Paul, it would mean a huge deal to the others and all the Faceless Legion fans who would pay a fortune to see you guys on stage again.'

'What do you mean fans – we disbanded over thirty years ago,' he replied with an incredulous tone.

'Well Paul, the Legions have a fan website with thousands of dedicated fans desperate to see a comeback.'

I had no idea if this was true, but it helped to bolster my case. Any way, it seemed to calm him somewhat and get his attention. He sighed then explained.

'Tony, I'm totally honoured at you having come all the way down here to ask me, and I have thought about it, believe me, but my instinct is to say no. I'm sorry to disappoint you and waste your time, but that's my decision unfortunately.'

He raised his hands in a dismissive gesture as though the decision had been made for him and there was nothing he could do about it; like an appeal lawyer having to explain to his client that the death sentence was still on and nothing further could be done by way of mercy.

Fair enough, I thought – if that was his final answer then I could no do nothing but respect his decision. I stared at him trying to gauge if this really was his definitive answer and whether I should admit defeat. Behind his tinted lenses I could see defeat, not defiance. I reckoned he still fancied the idea but he had now committed himself.

'Okay Paul, thanks anyway. It was a pleasure meeting you.'

I extended my hand towards him and smiled despite feeling totally annoyed at him. He returned my handshake and I walked swiftly off towards the door. I was determined to show no hard feelings. Then I remembered something, spun on my heel and walked back towards him. I extracted a leaflet from my jacket pocket and thrust it towards his open hand. This was a leaflet for the hotel I was staying in and I had scrawled my room number along the bottom just below the hotel's telephone number and contact email addresses.

'That's the hotel I'm staying at until tomorrow, if you happen to change your mind, just give me a buzz.'

I did not wait for an answer and was out the door before he could say anything in reply.

So that was that; Paul had failed to commit to be part of the reunion, which was very disappointing, but not the end of the world. I had tried my best but that seemed wholly inadequate. The only option was to replace him with another drummer; I had no doubt there would be a multitude of drummers who would gladly jump at the chance to replace Paul and be part of the reunited Faceless Legions; however would this be an agreeable option for Brookes and Carter? I would have to break the news to them and hope this did not diminish their enthusiasm much, let alone dash all hopes of the project happening.

I spent the remainder of the day wandering the streets and exploring the area in a sulk – like a child who's fallen out with his parents after not getting his own way. It was the helplessness I felt and the lack of being in control. I felt I had wasted my time and money coming all the way out here – and all for nothing. The phrase 'so near yet so far' was totally apt in this instance. I considered myself a failure – like a student having piled all their time, effort and energy into preparing for an exam only to fail miserably.

Back at the hotel following a quick dinner, I began to pack my bag in preparation for my departure tomorrow afternoon. I just wanted to be out of here and would have taken an earlier flight if I thought it was possible – but no doubt that idea would have conspired against me as well.

I sent Alison an email in which I ranted and raved about having wasted my time and why Paul Dixon was so irritatingly uncooperative. Within an hour she had replied and tried to calm me by praising my motivation and ingenuity which led me to here. Like me, she too had a phrase of the moment: some you win, some you loose.

Just when I thought my day couldn't get any worse, I got an email which just lowered the day and my mood even further. I felt like giving up completely on Operation Lazarus. The message sent from Dale Hannagan read:

'Hi Tony, hope you're well. I am sending this message to let you know that unfortunately I have to pull out of being part of the reunion gig of the Faceless Legions. Although I'm totally up for this and was really excited about being asked, I spoke to my mother about it and she was dead against it. She thinks that it would impact negatively on the death of my dad by reminding people that he had a drug problem. She has spend all of her time and energy fending off the press and nosey parkers since the death of my dad and she's only now enjoying the peace and quiet in which to mourn in privacy.

'I have to respect her wishes and it is for that reason that I have to decline your kind offer. I can only apologise for letting you and the rest of the band down and hope you manage to find a suitable replacement bass guitarist and I look forward to see my dad's old band performing on stage one day in the not too distant future.

Cheers, Dale Hannagan.'

I re-read the message hoping to find something positive within. I couldn't believe this – things were going from bad to worse; this was a major set-back. If things continued like this, then I wouldn't be surprised if Brookes and Carter also pulled out. I couldn't blame them if they did.

Then all the negative thoughts filled my head making me feel like I was on a losing streak and completely wasting my time. The bricks and mortar of the entire operation seemed to be crumbling around me, and I was standing in the wreckage. Perhaps this was not to be – maybe it was never going to happen, and I was just wasting my retirement years with a useless white-elephant of a project. Now I couldn't wait to get back home and return to reality.

I ranted again about Dale's email and pondered whether I should even bother to respond – was there any point in trying to persuade him when if seemed he had already decided? The main thing that was bothering me was the fact I sensed his mother was too much in control; certainly I could see her point and respect her opinion, but Dale was a growing man and could make his own decisions, even it they went against his mother's wishes. I had no doubt he had made such decisions in the past which were not exactly approved by his family, but had gone ahead anyway; so why not now? He was obviously still keen to be part of this project, but was being prevented by an intense sense of loyalty and intention to please his mum.

I had made my decision: I would reply to Dale's email with the intention of persuading him to alter his opinion and change his mind. I felt I had nothing to loose – I didn't want to regret not trying to reason with him; I felt I had to make that effort – just like the great effort I had made in attempting to get Paul Dixon on board.

With shaking hands I composed my message in reply to Hannagan's. I would remain calm and in control. I would consider what I had written before I sent it. I tried to recall which famous person once said that when replying to a letter (or in this case an email) that has infuriated you, you should always leave it twenty four hours before sending a reply. This ensured you had the chance to calm down and reword the message where possible to avoid saying things that you would inevitably regret.

'Hi Dale, I'm sorry to hear you have decided to pull out of the Faceless Legions reunion project. I totally respect your decision and that of your mother; however after careful thought I am convinced that this reunion could be a great thing for the memory of your father. It could be used to bring awareness of the problem which unfortunately plagues this country leading to many premature deaths; don't forget that your dad had admitted his problem and was actively seeking professional help and not simply ignoring the issue. Who knows, but perhaps a portion of the proceeds from the concert could be donated to an appropriate charity? I also believe that having you on board would be a very positive sign that although your father had a drug addiction, it does not necessarily run in the family; you could be the beacon of hope to the population of drug addicts, not just in this country but worldwide.

'I urge you to at least consider your position Dale and discuss the potential advantages with your mother. I speak for the rest of the band by saying you would be warmly welcomed on board a reunion of the Faceless Legions and I have no doubt you would make the perfect replacement bassist for your dad and a credit to his memory.

'Look forward to hearing from you. All the best, Tony.'

I read over my reply several times before clicking the 'send' button. I was pretty happy with my diplomatic response and cognitive reasoning. He had to admit: I had made a good point or two. But I was not getting my hopes high – I would hope for a change of heart, but expect the status quo.

Needing to clear my head, I went out for one last wander around the area. I figured I would try some other bar rather than patronise Dixon's establishment, besides I fancied listening to some other music and not more rhythm and blues covers from Dixon and Co.

The rain had now stopped and the streets were drying up as though trying to erase all trace of the earlier rain shower. I heard music emanating from a few bars I passed, but couldn't get into these places owing to a full house. It seemed that the Johnny B Goode Bar was not the only one in the vicinity playing live music to sell out crowds.

Although I tried hard to avoid it, my route back to my hotel took me along the street and past Dixon's bar once again. I could hear the loud music spilling out of the semi-open windows and the door anytime a customer opened it to enter or leave. The two giant goons were there looking lean and mean, flanked either side of the door like a couple of Corinthian columns. They were both locked in conversation with each other and didn't notice me stroll past. I don't know what came over me, but I decided to stick my head inside the bar to see if there was any possibility of attempting to speak with Dixon one final time before I jetted home the next day. I was not feeling hopeful, but figured I really had nothing to lose.

I had my hand on the big brass handle and about to tug it open when the bouncers clocked me. Their jovial grins from the joke they had just shared suddenly changed like a switch had just been pressed. Their calm confident demeanour transformed into one of hostility and menace when they saw my face.

'You're not going in there sport,' growled one of the bears. His partner folded his chunky arms to make himself look bigger and more threatening. I saw tattoos on his arms – impressive drawings of pistols and skulls with some wording in an impossible-to-read gothic type font.

'Why not? Am I in breach of the dress code?' I said standing up to them to show I was not intimidated. As before I towered above them, but the two against one philosophy was no match for my tall stature.

'Look mate, you're not wanted in there, so get going,' the second goon spat. I could feel droplets of his saliva pebble-dash my face and caught a whiff of tobacco on his breath.

Before I knew what was happening, I was harshly grabbed by two pairs of bear-like arms and wrestled away from the main door. I tried to struggle but was held too tightly to free my arms. My feet dragged on the ground as they marched me faster than my legs wanted to go. I tried kicking out at their legs, but they had anticipated that, and simply moved their legs out the way. I tried to shout out to attract attention to my plight, but one of them put his huge smelly hand over my mouth, and mumbled something about me shutting up otherwise I would regret it. I spotted a group of people walking purposefully down the pavement across the road and hoped they would spot me and come to my rescue; no one came – either they hadn't seen me or simply didn't want to get involved. For all I knew this was a common occurrence every weekend in this neighbourhood.

Now I was in a dark alleyway; it had to be just to the side of the bar as I hadn't been frogmarched very far. I felt an intense pain as I took a hard blow to my solar plexus. My instant reaction was to double up, but was prevented from doing so by the monster holding my arms as he pinned me up against the wall. I exhaled all the breath in my lungs and tried to tense the muscle up in anticipation of another stomach blow. I wriggled and squirmed trying to free myself, but another blow hit me in the ribs, this time I was released and I fell to the ground landing heavily on my left arm. Instantly I curled up into a ball to protect my head and vital organs. I felt kick after kick from pairs of heavy boots into my back and kidney region and the pain was so intense I feared I would pass out. I just lay there unable to fight back as the wind had been driven out of me, hoping that the attack would end soon. I noticed a shadow over my head and felt a face draw near to my ear. I tilted my head slightly hoping to cradle my ear into my shoulder to offer some protection in the event the beast was going to chew it off.

'Stay away from Paul Dixon. He doesn't want to see you ever again. You understand?' he balled in my ear. I nodded as best I could despite resembling a foetus.

'You sure you understand sport, or do we have to persuade you more?' a second and louder voice barked. Again I nodded and mumbled something resembling 'yes.'

I received another couple of blows to my back before hearing the sounds of the booted bears hurrying off back to the door of the Johnny B Goode.

I uncurled my aching body and slowly rose to my feet. The pain in my back and stomach was acute and I rubbed at my left arm half expecting to feel a break or fracture. I rubbed at my stomach trying to ease the pain, and then transferred the rubbing to my back. I staggered out of the smelly alley which was pungent with the scent of urine and discarded fast food packaging .

All in all I had faired not too badly – it could have been a lot worse. As far as I could tell, I was just bruised and battered but I'd be sporting black and blue patches along my body for the next couple of weeks. I was sure I had no broken bones, and fortunately my head had not been struck with either fist or foot.

I hurried back to my hotel trying to conceal the fact I was still in pain and hardly able to walk properly. I passed many people who saw me staggering and probably assumed I had consumed one too many drinks; not surprisingly, they avoided me like I was a leper.

Back in my room I ran a deep hot bath and let my wounds soak. They stung like an attack from a hive of angry hornets, but gradually calmed down as the soothing water gently caressed them. Looking at them in the mirror, I could see bright red marks on several places on my back, and my stomach was bruised in a couple of places.

I replayed the series of events in my mind and thanked God I had survived the ordeal with only minor injuries. It was clear that Dixon had instigated the attack as a way of warning me off. At first I thought the goons had attacked me simply after taking a dislike to me and anxious to display their aggression and muscle; but I was not just an unfortunate victim – I had been marked for a beating. The burly bouncers had been briefed by Paul to scare me off to stop me annoying him any further. Granted, I had been relentless in my quest to speak to and convince Paul to be part of the reunion, but to have me brutally attacked simply to send home a message was wholly unacceptable. He knew I was leaving town soon, so could easily have endured me for a short time longer.

The sleep I had that night was not exactly peaceful. I couldn't get comfortable as my back, sides and stomach still ached and I awoke with a start anytime I dozed off, the events of the attack returning in my mind to haunt me.

Chapter 25

I was packing the remainder of my things into my bag when the telephone rang. I tried to guess who it could be as I trundled around to the bedside to answer it. It would probably be reception confirming I was checking out today and if I wanted to leave a great big tip!

'Hi, Mr Caulfield here,' I said into the mouthpiece. I listened to the voice of the caller – to my surprise it was not an Australian accent, but a rather familiar male English accent.

'Hi Tony, it's me, Paul Dixon.' I froze; what did he want? Was he calling to arrange another boxing match between a defenceless guy and his couple of bully boys?

'Yeah, Paul. What do you want?' I asked with not a hint of friendliness in my voice. The reply came back full of pity and regret.

'Look Tony, I've just heard and I'm so sorry.'

I said nothing and let the silence hang until he felt obliged to speak again.

'I told them just to give you a warning. I never mentioned giving you a beating. I'm so sorry about that.' Again I remained taciturn.

'Are you all right?' he enquired, 'you're not seriously injured are you?'

Was he mad? If I was seriously injured I would be in a hospital ward and not a hotel room.

'I'm okay, I think,' I confirmed. 'Just battered and bruised a bit, but I'll live.' Again he repeated his apologies on behalf of his bouncers.

'You haven't reported the incident to police have you?' Paul asked cautiously. I pondered his motives for asking; then I figured I might just have an advantage here. I felt an air of optimism creep over me.

'No not yet,' I said cryptically, 'but I'm seriously considering reporting the matter.' He was quick with his reply.

'Oh Tony, please don't go to the cops. My boy will get the jail. He's already been done for assault and if he gets convicted, he'll be inside for a while.'

So there it was – the reason Paul was phoning me: to try to dissuade me from going to the police as his son, who must have been one of the goons, would not doubt go down for assault. I was in the perfect position to manipulate and even blackmail Paul. I maintained my pretence of intending reporting the crime to the police.

'Well it was an unprovoked attack, Paul. He and his mate really do deserve to be prosecuted for it. I'm duty bound to report crimes like that.'

I could tell Paul was growing desperate; his pleading on behalf of his hired hands was not working.

'Oh please Tony, I'm begging you not to do that. I'll do anything you want.' Then out of sheer desperation he rambled on.

'I can pay you. Just tell me how much and I'll give it to you, no problem. Just don't go to the cops please.' I had him exactly where I wanted. This was much better than revenge.

'Well you know what you can do for me Paul,' I let the question hang and awaited his answer. I could hear him sighing long and loud.

'Okay, Tony. You've got me; I'll do it. I agree to be part of the comeback of the Faceless Legions.'

But this required a bit more manipulation. I had to ensure he was genuine and not just agreeing to fend me off.

'Do you really mean that Paul? You have to convince me you really mean it so I don't go to the cops.' He was quick with his reply.

'Yeah, I know what you're thinking, but honestly I do mean it. I want to be part of the comeback. I mean I've been thinking about it a lot since you came here and I quite fancy doing it.'

'But you were pretty sure you had made up your mind only yesterday,' I pointed out.

'I know I said that, but I didn't mean it. I just wanted to play hard to get that's all, but seriously I do want to do it, so please sign me up Tony.'

I considered his words and felt he was convincing enough, but I was not 100% sure. I needed a bit more clarification that he was genuine and not trying to keep his son and his mate out of prison.

'All right Paul. I think I believe you but listen to me,' I paused to get his undivided attention. I put on my policeman's head.

'Even after I leave Australia, I can still report the assault to police in Britain. I'll give them a full witness statement and they'll fax the thing over to the cops here, then they'll probably launch an enquiry. So your bullying bouncers could still be prosecuted, do you understand?'

'Yeah, I know what you're talking about, but Tony, I am totally serious here. Forget what I said to you over the last couple of days, I really am

243

excited to do this and I can't wait to meet Carter and Brookes again.'

It was with an excited air of elation that I replaced the telephone handset and flopped down onto the bed. For some reason, the news had been somewhat therapeutic as my injuries felt a little better. I was pretty convinced of Dixon's change of heart. He did give the impression he had made his mind up and was wanting to say yes last time I spoke to him, but his moody nature and lack of humility prevented him from agreeing. All it took was the thought of visiting his son in a Western Australian prison to jolt him back to reality.

I felt the beating I had taken was not in vain; it had worked out to my advantage in the end. I had literally taken a hit for the team. All I needed now was a change of heart from Dale Hannagan and we were moving forward with an impressive pace.

In order to cement our agreement and offer his apologies in person, Paul had agreed to meet me here at the hotel later just before I left for the airport. If he failed to turn up, I would assume he had recanted on his agreement, but I was certain he would show up.

I checked emails once again – nothing by way of reply from Dale Hannagan. I decided to update Alison with my success in finally persuading Dixon to come on board; however I didn't mention the beating I had endured – she would worry and ask all manner of questions. Despite us being divorced and not having seen each other much, I believe she still liked me and cared for me; I know I did for her – every since our meeting in Aberdeen, I felt like I wanted to reconnect with her and perhaps rekindle some sort of flame. Alison certainly gave me the impression of wanting much the same.

I carried out a quick calculation and figured it would be the early hours of the morning back in Britain, so I didn't expect a reply any time soon from either Dale or Alison. Next I booked a return flight from Heathrow to Glasgow being careful to select a flight which would give me plenty of time to disembark through passport control and find the appropriate gate for my Glasgow flight, without rushing around like a madman.

Running through a mental checklist to ensure I had covered everything I would require for my journey from here to Glasgow, I suddenly remembered I would have to book a taxi to convey me from here to Perth International Airport.

I descended the stairs to the lobby at the prearranged time to meet Paul. There was no signs of the man and I felt a slight feeling of despair at the thought that he had stood me up in the hope I wouldn't carry out my threat to report my ordeal to the police. I checked my watch and decided to give him the benefit of the doubt and wait for another five or ten minutes maximum.

I approached the reception desk and asked if they could furnish me with the number of a taxi firm that could take me to the airport. The girl on the desk was very obliging and after a few questions and a rapid fire phone conversation in strong Aussie dialect, she reported that I would be picked up by taxi in good time for my flight. That was it – I was booked up and my mental 'to do' list was now complete.

I turned away from the reception desk to see Paul walk through the revolving doors. I felt my good mood swell; He had turned up and looked in a good mood also, which was not something I had witnessed since meeting the guy.

We shook hands again and he apologised for being late for our meet. We spotted a vacant leather sofa in the corner and flopped down on it. Paul yet again offered his sincere apologies and offered to compensate me with some Aussie dollars, to which I refused; I didn't want his money - just his word and commitment.

By the end of our chat, I was convinced beyond all doubt of Paul's unswerving dedication to the quest to be part of the reunited band. I was excited and elated at the change of heart and demeanour of Dixon.

'Just let me know where and when rehearsals are and I'll be there,' Paul stated. Then he felt the need to clarify. 'Just because I'm at the other side of he world doesn't mean I can't get to London for a rehearsal or a gig. I'm happy to travel as and when needed.'

I formed the impression he was feeling slightly nervous at the thought that perhaps we would decide to replace him given his distance from where all the action would be; but that wouldn't necessarily be a problem – we now had email, *Skype* and a regular airline service linking Australia with Britain, plus I had an inkling he made quite a tidy profit from his business, so probably wasn't short of a bob or two.

We parted after shaking hands like businessmen cementing a multi-million pound deal. I had all his contact details and he had mine. Now I couldn't wait to get home to tell Andy,

Danny and Alison. With a stroke of good fortune, maybe even Dale Hannagan would reconsider his stance and join the good ship Faceless Legions which hopefully would set sail very soon.

The flight back to the UK was going to be even longer than the trek out here and I wasn't looking forward to it – especially with my back and side injuries. My stomach muscles still ached like a perpetual cramp and my back was tender when it came into contact with any moderately hard surface like a seat back. I settled into my window view seat and stuffed an extra cushion behind my back to provide more support to alleviate the pain.

Just like my journey out to Australia, I dreaded the thought of being seated next to a raving lunatic or exceptionally garrulous passenger who wanted to tell me his or her complete life story. To my pleasant surprise, I ended up in a row of three as before being separated from my fellow passenger by one whole seat. This provided the necessary buffer to ensure a bit of privacy, plus we could share the spare seat by putting our junk on it.

The guy must have been about mid fifties, clean shaven with slicked back salt and pepper hair. He looked like he could be Harrison Ford's stunt double, so uncanny was the resemblance. I made a conscious effort not to mention this fact as he was probably sick of hearing it on a regular basis. He wore a pale blue shirt and plain red tie, which he swiftly removed once he settled into his seat carefully rolling it up and placing it in his laptop bag. I watched him out of my peripheral vision and saw him look at me as if sizing me up as a potential friend or foe.

'Will Pearson,' he said offering his hand to me. I was left with no option but to acquiesce and return the shake. This was it – I now had a new friend and would feel obliged to talk to the guy now all the way home; only eighteen hours to go!

I introduced myself and we engaged in the usual chit-chat about the dauntingly long voyage which lay ahead, how we had enjoyed ourselves in Australia and plans for when we landed back on home soil. He was quiet spoken with a definite London accent which I detected he tried to mask a little.

Before we knew, the *Dreamliner's* port and starboard engines had been started, the aircraft taxied out to the active runway and we were airborne, the big *Boeing* banking to the left to fly up the western side of Australia before heading out over the Indian Ocean.

The very interesting fact I learned about Mr Pearson was that he was a freelance events promoter and had just returned from Australia where he had helped to arrange an exhibition of kitchen gadgets on behalf of his client: a UK based innovative design company. As he told me all about his work and experience, he had me riveted. I was thinking this guy might be ideal for advice on how to plan and execute a music concert.

We were passing the coast of Sumatra before I felt able to reveal details of Operation Lazarus to Will. I told him of my quest to locate the missing Faceless Legions with view to persuading them to reunite, and my successes thus far. He was stunned by my audacity and guile and spellbound by my detecting abilities which had led me half way round the world. I explained the ultimate

248

goal was to arrange a concert for the reformed band to play, but admitted this was way out of my league as far as skills and planning was concerned. This is when my new friend offered to lend a hand; he had a fair bit of experience in all aspects of events planning including the arrangement and promotion of numerous music concerts for bands and artists. This guy was a godsend and a thoroughly valuable contact – I felt like a Conquistador finding gold after a long and arduous trek through the jungles of South America. Not only was he able to explain the procedures and intricacies of planning and promoting an event such as the one I envisaged, but he was keen to be a big part of such an endeavour. He thought my idea to reunite the Legions after decades of silence was very commendable and worthy of success.

At just over 0515hrs on a damp and dark English morning, we descended out of a thick layer of nimbostratus cloud and landed on Heathrow's runway 27 left, and taxied to terminal three. Stiff, sore and desperately in need of a proper meal and bed, I shook hands with Will Person. I ensured his business card was safely in my wallet and promised to make contact with him as soon as Operation Lazarus moved into its next phase. This would follow the finding of the final man on my list – Mick Walker; and I had no clue whatsoever how to find him; I tried hard not to dwell on the negative.

By the time I finally stepped into my house, I felt totally drained of all energy and craved copious amounts of quality sleep. I was feeling like a world traveller having been in two taxis and two planes in the last twenty four hours and having traversed a total of over 9200 miles.

The house seemed strangely unfamiliar – the feeling you get after returning after a long holiday and everything in your domain seems oddly vague and foreign; but I hadn't been away for that long.

I wasted no time in undressing and climbing into bed; it seemed I hadn't slept or been in a proper bed for days, which was partly true I supposed. I had a lot of sleep to catch up on and jet lag to overcome. My bruises were healing nicely, though still rather tender.

Much, much later when I awoke and oriented myself with reality, I fired up the laptop once again, remembering to remove the voltage adapter so I could pug into a good old fashioned three-pronged British socket. There was something comforting and reassuring about the large three-prong mains sockets in the UK compared with the flimsy fragile looking two prong efforts of other countries which tent to spark and buzz whenever a plug is inserted or removed.

So far I had managed to keep my mission journal up to date, although given the intense and interesting discussion with Pearson on board the flight, I hadn't got as much typed as I had hoped.

Sifting through my emails, I systematically directed all junk and spam messages straight to the bin. I was instantly suspicious at the fact whenever you make a purchase from an online company such as *Ebay* or *Amazon*, shortly after you find your details on a hundred databases and become the irritated recipient of unwanted offers from all manner of companies. Sure you can easily unsubscribe, but that shouldn't be necessary as you didn't sign up in the first place! It seems that names, addresses and email contact details are a valuable commodity and unscrupulously traded without your permission.

I experienced a jolt of excitement when I noticed a reply from Dale Hannagan; I was anxious to open and read, but feared it was just a reiteration of his earlier decision. My hand shook as I clicked the mouse to open the message. I couldn't believe what I read.

'Hi Tony, further to my previous message, I have now thought long and hard about my decision and the points you raised in your reply and I am happy to say I have changed my mind and have now decided to be part of the reformed band, if you'll still have me.

'I discussed the matter in detail with my mum and other family members and they are all 100% behind me and are willing to help with planning and finances where possible. If you need me to sign a contract or whatever, I am quite happy to come up to Scotland to meet you, otherwise you know where the studio is in Cardiff – so feel free to pop in anytime. By the way, Owen apologises for being rude to you and your son (he's the guy with the dreadlocks you met at the studio!)

'Please keep me up to date with all progress and arrangements, and remember that Dale's Music Box is available if the Faceless Legions want to practice for their big reunion gig – plus I won't charge them!

'All the best, Dale.'

This day was improving exponentially. My mission was progressing much better than I had envisioned or planned. I was glad I took the decision to reply to Dale to convince him to think again, as it had paid off nicely. Now it was time to update the other members of the band with my successes. I telephoned Andy Brookes first and told him about my successful trip to Perth, Australia.

'That's totally fantastic news, Tony,' he roared excitedly into the receiver. 'I can't believe Paul Dixon is happy to be part of the band. I thought you would have a problem convincing him.'

'Well now that you mention it, he was totally obstinate at first but then I forced him to change his mind,' I said. Andy was curious.

'How did you manage to do that?'

'Well let's just say I had to endure a beating to manage it!'

Andy commended me on my bravery and audacity in pursuing the issue especially in the face of threats and menace at the hands of a pair of Aussie apes.

I promised to keep him updated on a regular basis; then I terminated the call. Now it was the turn of Danny Carter to hear all about my Antipodean adventures.

Danny was over the moon with the news of my accomplishment.

'Four out of five – only one to go,' he said with all the excitement of a child on Christmas morning. 'You know Tony; I do believe we can pull this thing off. I think it could really happen.'

'Well now it gets tricky as I haven't a clue where to start with finding Mick,' I admitted with a hint of frustration.

'I have every confidence in you mate,' Danny commended, 'that you can do it. I mean look how you found me way up in the middle of nowhere, then Andy in deepest darkest Birmingham, then you flew to the other side of the world to find Paul. That, mate is the sign of someone who knows what he's doing.' I felt good about his praise; he was correct, I found the others with only fragments of information, so I felt I could do it with Walker – but where to start?

Chapter 26

I couldn't wait to speak with Alison; I guessed she would be overjoyed at my accomplishment at managing to achieve the seemingly impossible. The last update she had was that I had persisted, tried and failed to persuade Paul Dixon to agree to be part of the band. My last email was a rant and rave at Dixon's irritating stubbornness causing me to regret travelling so far to convince him. Now she would be thrilled at my resourcefulness in getting the man to reconsider and change his mind.

Alison didn't answer the phone so her answer service invited me to leave a message after the tone. I kept the message brief and asked her to call me as soon as she was able. I assumed she was working, but didn't know what shift and when she would terminate duty.

Later the home telephone rang; I was outside washing my car at the time and only heard it at the last minute. I scrambled inside to hear the answer machine click on and now it was my phone's turn to invite a message to be left. The beep sounded then Alison's voice sounded.

'Hi Tony, it's me, Alison. I'm just in. Could you give me a ring as soon as you can? I've got some exciting news for you with your big quest.'

She sounded out of breath, but highly excited. I did as she requested and soon the phone-lines were buzzing with eager exchanges of welcoming news.

'Okay, you first. What's your news?' Alison asked.

I told her all about my last encounter with Dixon and his big change of heart and mind. Again I didn't mention my beating which was instrumental in forcing Dixon to rethink, just in case she chastised me for taking risks. She whooped and cheered with delight as though I had won the jackpot on the lottery. I also told her about Dale Hannagan's surprise u-turn.

'So now we have four out of five – not bad eh?' I said beaming.

'If you were here in person, I would give you a big hug and a kiss,' Alison said. I told her she could owe me those when we next met.

'But now the problem is finding Mick Walker,' I said, 'I don't know where to start with him.' Alison was silent for a moment, letting the anticipation grow as she prepared to share her big news with me.

'That's where I can help you,' she replied.

'Go on – you have my full attention,' I invited.

'I've been doing a bit of detective work myself,' she said cryptically. I let her continue uninterrupted. 'And I think I might know where Mick Walker is.' I couldn't contain my intrigue and urged her to share her story. She enquired if I was sitting comfortably before she began, but I with mock impatience and sarcastic tone told her to start talking otherwise I would hang up.

'Well, I was in a music shop in Aberdeen with Isobel, my friend. Her daughter is learning clarinet at school and she needed a music book, so I went with her to the shops. Now I started browsing the music shop while Isobel was talking to one of the assistants about clarinet reeds and all that stuff.'

I stayed silent to let her continue unhindered with only the occasional 'Yup' and 'Okay' to let her know I was listening.

'So I was looking at the pianos and keyboards and that stuff when I noticed a music book on the shelf. I can't remember the title, but it was one of those teach yourself to play keyboard books, but it was written by a Mick Walker.' Here Alison paused to let the gravity of that statement sink in. I was intrigued and wanted to hear more.

'Now I leafed through the book to see if it told you anything about the author, and it did – although not very much. It said something like: Mick Walker is an experienced piano and keyboard player having played professionally for a number of years...he resides in Mallorca with his wife.'

'So you think it's the same Mick Walker?' I enquired. She might be on to something but it was still a long shot. There must be a multitude of Mick Walkers who play keyboard instruments.

'That's what I asked myself, so I took a note of the publishing company's website address and phone number. When I got home I checked out the website to see it they had any info on the author of that book, but nothing really.'

'So I phoned the publishing company and asked them if it was the same guy who played in the Faceless Legions years ago.' Again she paused to let me digest the information so far. I was totally curious to hear what happened next. She continued with her account with the publishers.

'They were a bit guarded about telling me much, so I lied and made up some story about researching for my university degree and this information would be very useful in helping me to pass my degree,' Alison said with a slight laugh at her own audacity.

'So what happened?' I asked impatiently.

'Well they hummed and hawed a bit. But eventually put me through to the guy's agent and he told me it was definitely the same Mick Walker with the Faceless Legions.' My heart was off on a race like an excited Whippet after a rabbit.

'That is absolutely amazing, Alison,' I praised, 'You have been a very busy girl.' Now it was my turn to promise affection when we saw each other.

Once I had my excitement under control, we discussed the next step. It was fantastic to know we had pinned Mick Walker down to the Spanish Island of Mallorca, but it would still require a fair bit of detective work to narrow the search down to a specific area on the island.

'There's only one possible snag,' Alison informed cautiously, 'the book was published about eight years ago, so I don't know if he still lives there.'

I pondered this and was reasonably certain he would still be residing there. It sounded like Mr and Mrs Walker had retired to the island to settle down – and it was an ideal place to do this: nice all year-round climate, lovely scenery and all the rest. I couldn't envisage the couple suddenly getting up and leaving all that behind. Of course it was just a hunch, but I thought it worthy of further research and most probably, another field trip.

Then Alison stunned me by offering to accompany me to Mallorca should I require an assistant. I leapt at the chance to have her come with me. Besides, she had earned herself a place in Operation Lazarus with her research initiative. In addition, she reminded me that she was about to stop for a couple of weeks annual leave and that she had made no plans for the break. This seemed to be confirmation that we should do it.

Not long after we married, we had spoke about taking a dream holiday to the island of Mallorca; we planned to fly out, hire a car then spend a couple of weeks touring the island stopping where we fancied and just doing as we pleased with no fixed itinerary. Needless to say, that holiday never happened on account of the work schedules of us two workaholics. So it was an exciting prospect for the two of us to be planning more or less the same trip decades later – we would treat the voyage as part holiday and part business trip, working our way around the island until we found Mick Walker. To top it all, I would have someone to protect me should I get into yet another scuffle with the natives!

Alison was due to finish up the next day, following an early shift at the hospital, and planned to drive down to Glasgow sometime after this, expecting to be here around evening time.

That gave me a day to conduct more research which would, hopefully narrow the net somewhat and assist our quest in finding Walker. I also intended booking a flight out to Palma de Mallorca so we could leave shortly after Alison's arrival.

The next couple of hours were a frustrating series of blind alleys and roads to nowhere; I tried desperately to find some connection with a Mick Walker in Mallorca, but yielded no results – not even possible fragments. I trawled through online phone directories with a negative result; this was not completely unexpected as I reckoned someone like Walker would be ex-directory. I then tried searching for businesses relating to pianos and keyboards – shops, tuition and even piano tuners! Still nothing of any help – like many of the other ex-legions they weren't making themselves easy to find, but I enjoyed the challenge no matter how frustrating. I needed something a bit more concrete otherwise we would simply be touring the island blindly hoping for some sighting of Mr and Mrs Walker.

It was as though he sensed my growing frustration and had waited until just the right time. Maybe it was luck, providence or even the hand of God, but the ringing phone soon elevated my mood from the doldrums to the Dolomites.

'So how was your trip down under, sport?' Lee asked in a mock Aussie accent. I filled him in on my successful trip to Perth, regaling him with tales of my frustrating daily pilgrimages to the Johnny B Goode Bar and practically having to twist the arm of Dixon so he would agree to my demands. Lee was livid when I told about the beating I had endured by the bullying bouncers.

'Should have taken me with you dad, that wouldn't have happened if I was there,' he announced. There was a great deal of truth in that statement – both of us were way over six feet in height and would have towered above the bouncers and I had no doubt that Lee would have stood up to the goons had he been there. No doubt there would have been a confrontation and I would have been issued my warning to stay away from Dixon, but I was sure no battle would have ensued.

'So who's the next target on your list?' Lee enquired.

'I have only Mick Walker left to find, then we have the old band back together,' I replied.

I told him about his mother's industrious research and commendable detective work in tracing a possible Mick Walker to the island of Mallorca. There was a pause on the line as Lee was evidently pondering something.

'Mick Walker?' he repeated the name over; then like a shock, his memory had been jolted and gave up its secret.

'I knew that name was familiar,' Lee explained. I wondered where this was going. Would the discussion yield anything concrete?

'I worked with a guy recently who claimed his girlfriend went to school with Mick Walker's daughter. We were discussing old rock bands at the time, then we got onto the subject of the Faceless Legions and he came out with that.'

I thought about this; was there any value in pursuing this line of enquiry?

'Do you think the guy's girlfriend would be able to tell us anything?' I asked.

'I dunno, but I can ask him if I speak to him,' Lee replied.

I felt this was worth a bit more investigation; any fragment may just help narrowing down the area to at least a town on the island.

'Any chance you can speak to the guy soon?' I asked, a hint of desperation creeping into my voice; I was well aware of my pending trip to the Spanish island and wanted any information sooner rather than latter.

Lee was unsure how he could get in contact with the guy as he no longer worked with him, but was sure one of his colleagues was friendly with him and had his mobile number.

'Leave it with me and get back to you as soon as I have anything,' Lee replied.

I urged him to hurry with his enquiries and stressed the need for information before heading over to Mallorca on what might just turn out to be a wild goose chase.

I spend the remainder of the evening checking out flight times between Glasgow and Palma de Mallorca and even prices and availability of rental cars at the airport.

I studied a map of the island: it seemed to be double the size of the Isle of Skye with a lot more towns. The population was given as about 900,000 inhabitants – no doubt a sizeable proportion made up of ex-pats, the island being a favourite destination for retirees, criminals and tax dodgers, according to one website! This seemed like a tall order – to find one man in an island of so many people when I didn't even have an area narrowed down.

I went ahead and booked a couple of seats on an *EasyJet* flight to Palma; we were committed to going anyway. If nothing else it would be a well deserved holiday for Alison and me, and I would just see what research could be done when we got there. Who knew, with Alison's newly discovered detecting skills, between the two of us we might just be able to find the missing keyboard player.

About twenty four hours later, Lee phoned back with some welcome news, although not as rich in fact as I would have liked.

'The guy's girlfriend still keeps in touch with Sarah Walker, that's Mick's daughter, through *Facebook*,' Lee informed, 'So she asked her where her dad was living. She was a bit unsure as she doesn't really keep in contact with her old man and hasn't visited him for a while, but she's sure he lives in a place called Cala Algar.' I noted this down as my son spoke.

'She doesn't know much else but described his big white house which apparently is very distinct and sits all by itself on top of a hill overlooking the sea. It has bright red shutters over the windows.'

'Sorry, dad but that's about all I could get, the girl was a bit vague,' Lee apologised.

'No problem son,' I admitted, 'It's more than I already had. At least I now have a town I can aim for.' Then Lee said with a laugh.

'Apparently Mick Walker's been living in Mallorca for about twenty five years but has never learned to speak Spanish.'

I laughed along with this absurdity. It was typical of some ex-pats living abroad – making no real efforts to integrate into the ways and customs of a foreign country and expecting the locals to do all the talking in English.

Lee apologised again for the lack of information, but I assured him it was of some use, and might be more helpful than he imagined. I was more than happy I had a location pinned down and could at least aim to explore this town for any sightings of Mr and Mrs Mick Walker. I promised I would keep my son updated on the progress of his detective parents when they flew out to the island to do a bit of quizzing and probing.

The flight was over before I realised; compared to the marathon flights I had been on lately, this was a very short-haul flight indeed. Alison and I extracted our carry-on bags from the overhead lockers and joined the queue of holiday makers and boisterous groups of loud females, intent on letting everyone know they were here for a hen-weekend, and the island was warned to lock up all its male citizens.

The heat was pleasant enough, though not excessive as we had been expecting. The air-conditioned terminal was spacious and bright, though we moved along with rapid pace to be out of the building and into our hired car as soon as possible. Unfortunately our baggage trolley had a mind of its own and was trying to take us to the departures area instead of out of the terminal.

Soon I had completed the paperwork and the tall skinny Spanish man handed me the keys to my hired *Citroen DS3*. I mentally prepared myself for the cognitive demanding task of driving on the other side of the road. This was easy enough until roundabouts were encountered, then panic tended to set in.

We had spent most of the flight pouring over a map of Mallorca, planning the locations we intended to visit and in which order. We located the town of Cala Algar over on the south east coast. Although there was a main road directly from Palma to the vicinity of the town, we opted for the more leisurely and scenic coastal route. We planned to spend the day on an unhurried drive along the coast, stopping at Cala Santanyi and booking into a hotel for the night. This would enable us to be fresh for the short drive up to Cala Alga and hopefully, to find Mick Walker. Who knew, maybe we could be supping Margaritas or Piña coladas with the great man and his wife.

The deep azure Mediterranean Sea was a distracting sight as we drove along the 6014 road which took us past a number of quaint towns proudly displaying their Moorish influences and Roman heritage.

The island appeared smaller than I had imagined as, before we knew it we were nearly on the south coast. Alison suggested stopping for a bite to eat somewhere so I steered the *Citroen* towards the nearest town which was sure to offer a variety of eating establishments. Parking in Colonia de Sant Jordi was problematic, as all available parking places seemed to be taken up by new cars sporting all the usual hire company logos; this was proving to be a popular place for all tourists.

After a lunch of baked potato and salad, we wandered down to the marina. Alison took hold of my hand and I felt like a teen on his first date;

263

my stomach fluttered and I smiled like I'd just had a handful of happy pills.

Chapter 27

We explored the vast marina and admired its fleet of expensive looking boats all moored up and bobbing in the gentle swell of the turquoise sea. It seemed odd that on such a nice sunny day as this with calm seas and gentle breeze, more of these boats weren't out cruising around the Med and exploring the coves and small islands which dotted the coast – I knew I would if I owned a boat.

We were mindful of the parking restrictions in the town, so we headed back to the car so we didn't end up having to negotiate with a Spanish traffic warden to avoid getting a ticket.

During the drive, Alison and I spend as much time catching up on each other's lives: the period between divorcing and finally meeting again after a hiatus of many years, when I called into Aberdeen on my way back from Skye. Apart from her brief marriage to the deranged doctor, she had just been plodding on with her simple life: working and socialising with her small circle of friends and colleagues. Understandably being put off men for a period following the locking up of her violent husband, she had contemplated emigrating to Canada where she had some distant relative and fancied the idea of a new life in a new country. I told her I was glad she hadn't gone through with her plan and expressed pleasure at our opportunity to effectively start over again with our relationship; this too was her opinion.

We found a nice hotel in Santanyi and booked a room for the night under the name of Mr and Mrs Caulfield. Alison had no objections to this and the idea of still being married to me seemed to make her smile like a Miss World contestant.

The hotel room was immaculate and we wondered whether we were the room's first inhabitants such was its level of cleanliness with no hint of having hosted many other residents in the past. There were two single beds separated by a bedside cabinet, and we giggled like schoolchildren to see the setup.

'We could move the cabinet and shove the beds together if you prefer,' Alison suggested. I nodded.

'Yeah, we'll see!'

Luckily the hotel had *Wi-Fi*, so we took full advantage of this and I fired up the laptop. Alison got to work researching the area of Cala Algar; I was relieved to see it was just a small town, perhaps it could be classified as a village – so finding a particular house in the place was a bit easier given its size. It would have been a whole lot more problematic if it was in a larger town. It might take ages searching for a house and location like the one supplied by Lee.

Google Earth maps proved invaluable in our research here. Following a couple of mouse clicks, Alison had zoomed in on the town, then the area as described by Lee, then she found a photo of the house: a big white affair with bright red shutters flanking the windows, perched alone and atop a hill boasting a cracking ocean view. She scribbled down the address and sat back looking proud at her handiwork. I draped my arms around her and we hugged, before letting out lips explore each others.

'Another day in paradise,' I mused when we stepped out of the hotel and into the warm humid morning.

'Yes, it's a great day for finding a missing ex-rock star,' Alison returned and we walked hand in hand towards the hired *Citroen*.

The drive to Cala Alga was pleasant and the traffic light. We had the blue expanse of the Med on our right and an imposing mountain range on our left. Regular road signs announced the way and distance to the many nearby towns.

Once in the town of Cala Alga, we had no difficulty in finding the target house. It looked just like the one in the *Google Earth* photos, so the picture must have been fairly recent, or the house hadn't undergone a major exterior decorating since the man in the satellite had taken the photo.

Despite only two-up, the little car struggled to ascend the steep hill leading to the Walker's house. It protested when I changed down a gear, but refused to gather much momentum when I changed up. I considered abandoning the lethargic car by the roadside and walking the rest of the way, but eventually we got there and drove up and stopped just before the large driveway. Stepping out of the car, the sea breeze had transformed into more of a gale, owing to its high, exposed location; mind you, the views were stunning, providing a panoramic vista for miles across the wide open Mediterranean Sea. There was a pristine white coloured *Freelander* parked in the driveway, it seeming to blend in with the bright whitewashed exterior of the house, like a chameleon.

Alison and I walked towards the stout big red wooden door which was framed by a neat row of bricks; if it had been round-shaped and painted green, it would resemble the door to Bilbo Baggins' house way down there in the Shire.

With a feeling of slight nervousness, I pressed on the gold coloured button of the doorbell. It ding-donged loudly and we stepped back to listen for approaching footsteps. The car in the driveway was a good indication that someone was home. Soon the predicted footsteps arrived and the door swung open to reveal a middle aged foreign-looking woman. I knew nothing about Mick's wife, but something told me this was probably the maid or maybe an acquaintance. She wore a light coloured dress which sported orange and blue flowers in pastel shades, a drab grey cardigan and white slippers. Around her tanned neck sat a golden crucifix, it glinting in the intense sunlight. She stared at us both with a perplexed look etched on her pleasant, weather-beaten face.

'Hello, I'm looking for Mr Walker?' I made the remark sound more like a question. Her head shook vigorously and she spoke in very poor English.

'No, no. He no here.'

I pondered the meaning: was she implying he was currently out or he no longer resided here?

'Mr and Mrs Mick Walker live here?' I asked slowly pronouncing all the words for the benefit of the foreigner. Again her head shook and her dark eyebrows lowered into a frown.

'No. Mrs Walker, she is…' she searched for the equivalent phrase in English. Then she crossed her arms over her chest to signify the position of a corpse in a coffin.

'Mrs Walker is dead?' I ventured as though I was playing a game of charades. Her head nodded in agreement; then she tugged at her crucifix necklace and silently mouthed something. This was unexpected news.

'Is Mr Walker still alive?'

'Si, si. He no live here.'

'Do you know where he is now living?' I enquired combining slow deliberate speech with a few charade-style hand movements. This was a blow, locating the house in question but finding it was no longer the residence of Mick Walker. Evidently this lady was now the new tenant of the big house. I hoped she could point us in the direction where we could continue our enquiries.

'Meester Walker, he is in…' here she searched her memory bank of rudimentary English.

'He is…no well,' she finally offered.

'But he is alive, is that correct?' I asked for confirmation. Her head nodded vigorously.

'Si si. He is in…' another pause, another confused look. I looked at Alison and could see her trying to think of something to help the poor lady out.

'Hospital?' I ventured. She thought this through before shaking her head.

'No, no ospital. He is in…'

'A nursing home? An old folks home?' Alison suggested. This seemed to be the correct answer. She pointed at Alison and gave her head an animated nod. I reckoned I already knew the answer, but I asked anyway.

'Do you happen to know where this home is?'

'No, no, sorry,' was the expected reply from the helpless looking Spaniard.

'Is it here in Mallorca?' I asked, pointing to the ground.

'I don't know, sorry,' she said with a deep shrug of her broad shoulders.

I was confident we were now finished here; there was nothing further this lady could offer. We thanked her for her time and trundled back to the car, both of us feeling dejected and defeated.

We debriefed in the car. The facts of the matter appeared to be thus: Mick's wife had passed away, recently as far as I could gather, and Mick not being in the best of health had ended up in a nursing or old folk's home where he could be looked after. But where was the home? Was it nearby? Was it still on the island? Too many questions and no one to answer them.

'That's a pity,' Alison remarked, 'we were so close as well.'

'That's been pretty much my experience so far with this mission,' I returned with a laugh.

We sat in silence and gazed out across the blue sea watching the occasional sailing boat cruise around the jagged coastline. Each of us lost in our own thoughts and trying to find a solution to our dilemma.

'So where do we go from here?' Alison broke the silence. I shrugged and exhaled.

'Well it'll take an age trawling through all sorts of care homes in Mallorca,' I said, 'that's assuming he's still living on the island.'

'If he's lived here for, what was it, twenty five years, don't you think he would choose to live in a home still in Mallorca?' Alison reasoned. She had a good point and was probably correct.

'Yeah, I suppose, but there's bound to be quite a few here.'

'So let's head to a hotel with *Wi-Fi* and run a check of care homes in Mallorca,' she said with an optimistic smile.

I was correct with my estimations that there would be quite a few care homes in Mallorca; however Alison as industrious as ever, replaced my pessimism with a healthy doze of optimism when she produced a short-list of possible care homes. With a bit of discussion we whittled the list down yet again. In the end the only possible place where Mick could be, we reasoned, was a retirement home in the town of Manacor; this, the website informed, was a care establishment especially for ex-pats living on the island. I recalled what Lee had said about Mick having lived in Spain for twenty five years yet never bothered to learn the lingo.

'That has got to be the place where Mick is, I'm sure of it,' I said, my mood lifting once again.

'Yeah, it has to be; he's not that old, so an old folks home wouldn't be appropriate, and unless he is seriously ill, he'd unlikely to be in a nursing home,' was Alison's educational reasoning.

'Plus he'd be surrounded by fellow retired Brits and they could all gab away in English,' I added.

So it was unanimously agreed to pay the retirement home a visit the very next day, where we were hopeful of finding Mick Walker; if not, we would just have to rethink our theory.

We strode towards the big glass fronted door of the sleek modern building. We had dressed appropriately, not in our shorts and t-shirts but more on the formal side. We had discussed and identified a possible problem: the home may not permit us access unless we either had arranged an appointment or were a member of the resident's family. Alison had earlier suggested phoning to enquire if Mick was indeed here, but figured they probably wouldn't pass that sort of information on easily; besides, Manacor was not that far away.

So it was agreed we would attend posing as family members in order to get access to the place, and the dress code had to be appropriate in order to impress the staff and make us look presentable.

'Do you want me to do the talking?' Alison asked, her hand poised on the door entry intercom button. Just then, the door opened with a loud buzz and an old woman in a wheelchair emerged with a young lad pushing her down the small ramp. I seized the door and held it open for them to pass then we hurried inside.

'That was a stroke of luck,' Alison said with a smile once the wheelchair and pusher were out of earshot.

'Yeah, we're passed the first hurdle easily,' I said in reply.

The next obstacle was a tall reception desk where a slim be-speckled black woman sat behind it. She eyed us suspiciously as though wondering how we managed to penetrate the first line of defence to the place. Her look wasn't long in turning to a warm smile as she looked us both up and down taking in our smart clothes. We probably dressed completely different from many of the visitors who came here; the dress code seemed to be baggy shorts, loud Hawaiian shirts and flip-flops judging by the folk milling around the car-park and grounds.

'Good afternoon,' said Alison with a smile to match the receptionists, 'we were wondering if it was possible to visit Mr Mick Walker?'

Now this was the make or break moment; this would tell us if we had the correct place or had come to all the wrong conclusions. I was proud of the way Alison had worded the question: if she had come out and asked it Mick was resident here, no doubt the lady would have become guarded and probably admit she couldn't reveal that information, so we would be none the wiser.

'Mr Mick Walker,' the receptionist said as she clicked on her concealed keyboard and squinted at the screen, the bright display reflecting in the huge lenses of her glasses. I spotted a name-badge on the lady which gave her name as Francis. She too was a Brit; no doubt the entire staff would've been imported from Britain.

'Yes, Mr Walker is currently at home,' she said as she looked up at Alison, 'shall I see if he is in his apartment?'

'Yes please, that would be great,' Alison chirped, trying to keep the excitement out of her voice.

Francis displayed her efficiency by lifting up a telephone handset, pressing a button or two and listening for a reply. After a minute, she frowned and replaced the handset.

'I'm so sorry, but there is no reply from Mr Walker's apartment. Perhaps he is in the recreational area.'

A secure entry door swung open and a staff member appeared holding a stack of files. Francis seized the woman before she could head to a door marked private.

'Tracy, could you check if Mr Walker is through in the recreational area?'

Tracy looked slightly annoyed at this request, but quickly changed her expression to a smile when she saw Alison and I.

'I'll just go and check, give me a minute.' With that Tracy hurried through the door she came still clutching the files.

'Are you both family members of Mr Walker?' Francis asked looking at each of us. Now it was time for a little white lie. I hoped we could pull this off given how close we were to seeing Mick. Alison nodded then bowed her head as though saddened.

'Yes we are,' she said with a sniff, 'I'm sorry, I'm still quite upset about the death of poor Mrs Walker. We've just flown in from Britain this morning.' With this she wiped a fake tear away from her eye. Francis looked at us both in sympathy. I felt the need to be part of this charade, so I too bowed my head solemnly and sniffed.

Tracey was soon back with the welcoming news that Mick was in the games room and currently playing a game of chess with another resident. I felt elated, but continued to mask my true feelings; we had to gain access into that room.

Francis seemed to survey us for an exceptionally long moment as if trying to work out if we were genuine and if she should permit us access without an official sanction. She reached a decision and instructed Tracy to escort us through to where Walker was. We thanked her and tagged on behind Tracy through the secure door and into a large room. We were in – I couldn't believe it was that easy to breach the security of a guarded complex; any dubious person could easily finesse their way in.

Tracy opened yet another door and held it open for us. Soon we were in a smaller room which smelled like boiled cabbage mixed with some antiseptic solution: what was that smell: was it *TCP* or was it *Detol*? Whatever it was it reminded me of my granny's house.

We shadowed Tracy as she glided over to a table where two men sat, both frozen in deep concentration. A random scattering of game pieces decorated the black and white chequered board. I wondered how long this game had been going on. Had it just began today or was it one of those epic matches which goes on for many weeks, months or even years?

For an instant, I thought Tracy had led us to the wrong table as none of these old men hunched over the board looked like they could be the famous keyboardist Mick Walker. Tracey spoke to the man on her left.

'Hi Mr Walker, you have visitors just arrived from Britain,' she said cheerily. Fortunately she didn't bother to ask our names assuming we were family and Mick would recognise us. Our luck held when Tracy abruptly turned and left us with the chess players, still intent on her original destination, before she was intercepted by Francis at the reception.

I turned to the man who Tracy had addressed as Mr Walker. He was a thin frail looking man,

274

balding with a neatly trimmed grey beard and slightly sunken eyes. His skin was deeply tanned as was expected from living in a Mediterranean climate for so long. I struggled to see any resemblance between this old man and the energetic organ player I had seen so many times on stage with the Faceless Legions. Perhaps Tracy had got the wrong Mr Walker; there were bound to be other residents with that fairly common surname.

'Mick Walker?' I enquired.

'For my sins,' the man replied, 'and who exactly are you?' he asked looking mildly puzzled.

'Tell me, are you the man who played with the Faceless Legions?' I said. I studied him for a reaction. His face turned form puzzlement to pleasure. He nodded his head slowly and laughed.

'Yes, that's me.' Then he sat back in his high-backed chair and gazed up at the ceiling.

'The Faceless Legions,' he announced, 'yes I was once their keyboard player.' With that he shook his head as he pondered the past.

Chapter 28

I thought back to the many concerts I had attended, especially the Legions. I recalled seeing Mick as a young man in his late twenties; long sleek black centre-parted hair, droopy moustache and intelligent keen eyes. He was always energetic and animated as he rocked and rolled to the music that he was a big part of. His long bony fingers would caress the keys of his two Hammond organs with such precision and dexterity that one would have suspected he was merely miming along to a backing track and not actually playing. But every fan knew the extent of the man's talent and the praise and admiration was justly deserved. Mick was a true musician and an invaluable contribution to the band.

Now the figure who sat across from me was a veritable shadow of the man he once was. He had aged, lost the vast majority of his hair and looked haggard and ill; weary and worn out. Somehow I couldn't picture the man on stage behind his organs and pianos; I doubted he could ever be an integral contribution to an energetic rock and roll act ever again.

Mick had excused himself from his chess-playing mate and shuffled over to a long sofa where he flopped down on one end, I on the other and Alison perched on the edge of a worn armchair. Curiously he hadn't asked exactly who we were despite us introducing ourselves and my enquiring about his past heritage.

'I'm just glad of the company actually. I don't really care who you are, I'm happy to chat about anything. I don't get many visitors,' he said with a self-conscious smile.

'I'll tell you why we're here Mick,' I replied.

He sat back and listened with interested curiosity. Although he looked poorly, his mind was still very much active and he exuded intelligence.

'We are managing a project to reunite the Faceless Legions,' I began. I watched to see if his expression would change at this news, but he remained calm, relaxed and in good spirits.

'So far I have traced the other members of the band and asked them to consider reuniting.' I detected a hint of intrigue in his face. He remained reticent so I continued.

'Andy Brookes, Danny Carter and Paul Dixon have all agreed to reform and play a reunion concert.' Mick's eyebrows shot up.

'What about Chas Hannagan? Is he not playing?' Clearly the man was on the ball; it proved that you certainly cannot judge a book by its cover - or think someone looks tuned to the moon when in fact they are more alert than you.

'You haven't heard?' I replied; Mick shook his head.

'I'm sorry to tell you that Chas passed away a few years ago.' I said employing the clichéd euphemism in order to avoid upsetting Mick.

Mick shook his head slowly and pondered this revelation.

'I might have known Hannagan would die prematurely. He dabbled with every drug under the sun. We used to tell him he had to quit and get help, but he kept going as though he was invincible,' Mick reminisced. I nodded in agreement. I looked at Alison who was studying Mick as though he was one of her hospital patients and she was attempting to diagnose him and work out what medication he should be having.

'That's a pity. Chas was a talented musician,' he admitted as he exhaled a long breath. I was quick to fill the temporary void with some cheery news.

'Well, Chas's son has agreed to be the replacement for his father. He too plays bass guitar.' Mick looked pleased at this notion.

'That's fantastic news. When do they play?' he enquired. I don't think he got the picture clearly.

'The Faceless Legions can't play without their star keyboard player, Mick,' I said with all the flair of a TV presenter, and pointed straight at the man.

'Me?' he exclaimed. 'I'm too old and frail for that.'

'Nonsense. The band can hardly reunite without you,' I returned. He sat back in his seat and smiled; only now did it dawn on him. He obviously thought he wasn't going to be part of the reformed band.

'I'd love to do it,' Mick said looking like an excited child. 'That's made my day folks.'

I felt so elated, not just at having heard Mick agree to join the band, but the fact he was so enthusiastic about it. The very thought seemed to transform him; in an instant he looked healthier, happier and high as a kite. I hoped he didn't have a heart condition as this might well trigger an episode.

'I hope I'm able to do it,' he stressed, 'you know I don't keep too good and I'm on medication.'

Alison had at last completed her diagnosis and gave her opinion.

'Did you have cancer Mick?' she asked. Mick nodded.

'Stomach cancer?' Alison continued. Mick nodded again. He was probably thinking she had read his file or spoken to his nurse.

'You've had treatment but your now in remission, right?' He looked surprised.

'How did you know?'

'I'm a nurse, Mick. I've been doing this job so long I can tell a lot by looking at people.'

Mick smiled at her. I could tell he had taken a shine to her; not surprising given her calm and reassuring bedside manner and her kind and caring nature. In addition, she was pretty to look at.

'I have good days and bad days. I don't want to agree to this gig then let everybody down because I've fallen ill.'

Alison was quick to reassure.

'You'll be well taken care of and I'll make sure you get your medication and you're not overworked.'

'Remember Mick, the rest of the guys are not as young and fit as they once were,' I added.

This was largely true with the exception of Danny Carter – I saw the way he practically raced up that mountain on Skye.

Mick seemed reassured by our reasoning. He still sat there looking relaxed and smiling like lottery winner.

'Yes indeed. I'd love to reunite with the Legions. Where do I sign?' he asked with a laugh.

'That's fantastic Mick. I'll tell the others that you are as keen as them to get going,' I said.

Mick then frowned. I could tell he was in deep thought and troubled about something.

'I doubt I could stand for any length of time at a keyboard.'

Both Alison and I shook our heads. This was very minor point.

'So we'll get you a seat. There's loads of keyboard players sit down to play.' He seemed reassured by this point.

'What's the next step then?' he enquired still exuding excitement and keen interest.

I sat back content that we had got this far. On first sighting I was convinced Mick wouldn't be able to participate; then I figured he would refuse on numerous grounds including his heath, but to see the man rejuvenated by the offer to reform the band he was a big part of many years ago was a delight to behold.

'I've just finished searching for your colleagues,' I explained. His keen look urged me to continue. 'I found Danny way up on a Scottish island; Andy in Birmingham and I travelled all the way to Australia to find Paul Dixon.' Walker looked impressed; then at the mention of Paul Dixon, he scoffed.

'Paul Dixon!' he said the name as though it was an expletive. 'Do you know me and him used to argue and fight like cat and dog?' I nodded. I was well aware of the tension and conflict between the two.

'Just make sure you don't put us near each other on stage!' he joked. 'I didn't think Paul would be up for a gig like this; he was pretty fed up with the whole thing.'

Now it was my turn to laugh; I considered my response.

'Let's just say Paul was a bit difficult to convince,' I said with a conspiratorial wink. I still hadn't told Alison about my injuries. Mick nodded; he had a fairly good idea how awkward Dixon would have been, based on his experience with the drummer.

'So now that I've got the go ahead from you, the faceless Legions are effectively back together,' I declared. Alison smiled, and Mick shook with excitement.

'When we get back to the UK, I'll tell the others it's a go for launch for a comeback gig.'

Mick began to clap; this was the best medicine he had had in ages.

Suddenly Mick's happy demeanour changed - he had thought of a problem and wanted to voice his concern.

'There's one little problem folks,' he said to set the scene. We both looked at him curious to know what his other problem could be. He continued.

'I relied on my wife to look after me, and after she died my son put me in here so he wouldn't have to take care of me. He also sold off my house – I owned a lovely big house over on the coast and my boy was keen to sell it, so that's why I ended up in here,' he said with a sweeping hand gesture.

'But you're free to leave at any time, right?' Alison asked. Mick shook his head emphatically.

'I'm afraid not. I can only get out of here with the written permission of my next of kin, who is...have a guess.'

'Your son,' Alison and I answered in unison. Mick nodded and pointed at us.

'You got it.'

'So you doubt your son would sign you out if you wanted to leave to say, rehearse with the band?' I enquired. Mick nodded this time.

'He never really comes to visit; only about once a year; he still stays in England. I'm pretty sure he would refuse to sign me out just to be awkward. That's the kind of boy he is unfortunately.'

I pondered his dilemma – and decided an insignificant problem like that could easily be circumvented.

'Do you think if we spoke to him and explained the reason, he might cooperate?' I asked. Mick shrugged and looked uncertain.

'You could try, but I doubt it – I know what he's like and he just loves being in control,' Mick replied. 'It was him who negotiated that clause with staff, so he always knows where I am and he doesn't have to look after me.' A hint of annoyance was creeping into his voice.

'I'm sure there's a way around that clause if he refused to sign,' I said, 'like if we say…faked his signature,' I said with a conspiratorial wink at Mick. He liked that one and laughed.

'Yeah, that could work!' he admitted, 'I'd go along with that.'

'And if that failed, maybe we could just break you out of here.' I said with a laugh. Mick was very supportive of any idea if it meant being released from his relative captivity. I could see his eyes glaze over as he pictured the scene:

The night was dark, being only partially lit by a waning moon. A man lay in bed, apparently fast asleep. He awoke with a start upon hearing an owl hoot and cautiously eased himself out of bed – but he was fully dressed and now looked alert. He grabbed a heavy suitcase and edged towards the window, being careful not to create any undue noise. He eased the window open and stepped out into the still humid night. The only sounds apart from the creaking window were the crickets frolicking in the nearby grass. A man and woman appeared from the shadows; the woman offered her hand and helped the old man step over the window ledge and onto the ground. The man took hold of his suitcase and the three hurried towards a waiting car, partially hidden behind a clump of bushes. The car's doors were eased open; the man dived into the driving seat whilst the woman helped the old man into the back seat after placing his suitcase in the boot.

The noise of the starting engine broke the silence of the night; the car was flung into first gear and took off like a startled mouse running from a pursuing barn owl. The hurried departure was masked by a cloud of dust kicked up by four wildly spinning tyres as the car and its excited occupants headed to the local airport for a flight back to the UK.

It was a delight to meet and talk to Mick Walker. To see the man transform from an old infirm looking pensioner into a keen and more youthful version bursting with energy and optimism was a tonic. I was exultant at his enthusiasm and willingness to be part of a reunited band, despite my reservations at first sighting of him; and my invitation for him to be part seemed to work a miracle with his disposition.

We left Mick to resume his chess game after agreeing to keep him informed of the progress with planning a reunion concert. He gave me his son's phone number and I promised I would telephone Michael when back home, with view to explaining the situation and requesting him to sign his father out of care as and when needed. If he was found to be as difficult as his father suspected, then we would consider plan B which might involve a bit of skulduggery by way of fake signatures or even arranging a stand-in Michael

Walker who would happily sign the release forms. I didn't consider it prudent to resort to busting him out of the care home as this would cause all sorts of untold grief with the authorities.

Back in the car, Alison and I hugged for ages; both of us delighted at the result. Alison too thought Mick a hopeless cause when first meeting him and predicted we would be out of the place in double time when the crazy notion of him taking to the stage once again was suggested.

'So you've finally done it – you've reunited the Faceless Legions, you clever boy,' Alison said, her voice filled with triumph.

'No, we've done it!' I returned, 'I couldn't have pulled it off without your help and encouragement.'

We drove out of Manacor and took the road towards Capdepera driving at an easy and contented pace; we were in such high moods, it seemed nothing could spoil our day; even the rude drivers who tooted us and gestured for us to move aside and let them pass as we drove like a scene from Driving Miss Daisy, didn't bother us. We were as happy as children being permitted free reign of a sweet shop.

Our first sighting of Capdepera was rather a let down; it seemed the impressive fourteenth century castle with its long snaking defensive walls was let down by the shanty town-style dwellings which littered along the base of the walled town. We found a nice restaurant and dined al fresco on the balcony overlooking the old town with striking dark green foliage-lined hills in the distance, leading down to the dark cerulean sea. It seemed all the clouds had gone away on holiday leaving behind an empty expanse of clear deep blue sky.

We discussed the next phase of Operation Lazarus and what shape it would take. To be honest, I hadn't really thought that far in advance. My main priority since beginning the mission was to locate and present my proposal to the five men; that had now been completed despite many doubts of my abilities, and had been done in record time. Now the next chapter required a bit of planning and structure, and I was sure this was somewhat out of my league – this is where the expertise of others would kick in. I had utilised my set of skills in detecting, locating and persuading, but now the arrangement of a come-back concert would require a different set of skills and experience – not something I had much knowledge of; however I was quite prepared to lend a hand where possible.

It was fortunate my meeting with Will Pearson on the return flight from Australia; no doubt he would play a pivotal role in the arrangements of the next phase, but I suspected I would have to put together a team or committee in order to delegate and manage the various and complex steps involved in such a large project.

'So what's the next step?' Alison asked as we strolled hand in hand through the old town.

'First step is to update the rest of the band and let them know it's a go. Second stage is probably to get everyone assembled for a get-together and discussion, then…' I let the sentence fade as I pondered the next move.

'I'm sure it will all come together nicely,' Alison offered, sensing my intrepidation at the next phase. I nodded slowly.

'I can't believe it's happened – I doubted I could do it. And now it has actually happened and the next part of the operation is really out of my depth. That's where I have to rely on the expertise of others.'

Now Alison nodded as she fully understood my concerns.

'Well, let's not trouble ourselves with those details; lets just enjoy the rest of our little break together, after all, you deserve it.'

We did just that – we continued our tour of Mallorca exploring the eastern and northern coasts, visiting towns big and small and even venturing off the beaten track once or twice to experience 'essential Mallorca' with its primitive houses, dirt track roads and locals who stared at us as though we were visiting aliens. This side of the island seemed much greener and vibrant than the interior and the south. Other parts of the island we had seen were less aesthetically pleasing – barren rocky hills scarred with occasional patches of foliage clinging like barnacles to a ship's hull. Some parts were rocky wastelands and looked like the surface of the moon or some other planet – perhaps where NASA faked the moon landings!

We even joined the sun worshipers and spend the odd day lazing on sun loungers, then a quick dip in the sea followed by more lounging around. As planned, we stopped wherever took our fancy and booked into small inexpensive hotels and guest houses – mind you, some of the rooms we had to cohabit with large hissing cockroaches and small darting lizards who took to running up and down the walls in search of tasty insects. We had to agree – we got what we paid for.

The first time I removed my top to let the sun's rays get to my back, Alison noticed the bruises and marks on my back and recoiled in mild horror at the sight. Being an experienced nurse she knew instantly what had made the marks; I knew it was pointless trying to explain away the blemishes by lying about their origin. So I felt compelled to explain what had happened in Perth with Dixon's henchmen. She was full of concern and compassion, then set about performing an investigation of my back to check for underlying damage. I detected her attention and concern went much further than that of a professional and caring nurse. I wondered if she was violating the nurse-patient ethics code. In the end she declared nothing but superficial marks and reprimanded me for not telling her sooner.

Despite my enjoyment of my holiday with Alison, I was still anxious to get back home to begin the planning of the next phase of operation. I felt I had to maintain the momentum and continuity to keep all those involved motivated and raring to go. I feared one or other might just change his mind and pull out, leading to a strategy rethink, or abandonment of the entire project.

By the time we pulled into the car hire return complex at Palma airport, I was looking forward to returning home. Alison was keen to stay for a little longer but knew it was time to go home. Not only had we both enjoyed the tour of the Balearic Island, but we also thrived in each other's company and cultivated our relationship. Whenever we met another couple or family, Alison would be quick to introduce us as Mr and Mrs Caulfield.

During the return flight to Glasgow, Alison assisted with compiling a 'to do' list. We considered every task big and small which would now be required to consolidate the mission's accomplishments so far. The long bullet-pointed list comprised many items including: informing the band members and also Lee, arranging a meeting with Will Pearson, posting information on the Legions of Fans website in order to gauge interest, and thinking of ways to generate income in order to fund the whole project. I was well aware that to arrange a live concert would involve finance – concert venues, equipment and personnel wouldn't come cheap.

It was great to hear the positive responses from everyone I phoned to update, upon my return to Glasgow. All were excited at the prospect of getting back together. All previous doubts and concerns about it ever happening had simply vanished. Danny sounded like a big-prize game-show winner; Brookes was so delighted I'm sure if I has saw him he would have a tear in his eye. Dixon was all set to book a flight to the UK as soon as we had arranged a date to meet, and even stated he had purchased several sets of brand new drumsticks for the gig – wow: he really was taking this thing seriously! Dale Hannagan sounded as keen as ever and again repeated his offer of his studio should it be required.

As I was busy on the home phone, Alison called Lee on her mobile and updated him; he congratulated us both and offered his assistance with the next phase of operation as and when required.

As predicted, the toughest call to make was to Mick Walker's son, Michael. I dialled and got no response, but declined the offer to leave a message; I would just call back later. This went on several times until I eventually got a human voice on the end of the line.

'Hi, Michael Walker?' I enquired.

'Yes it is; who am I speaking to?'

'My name is Tony Caulfield and I'm a friend of your father,' I went on.

There was silence as Michael tried to place me. No doubt he knew everyone his father was acquainted with, but he clearly didn't recognise my name or my accent. I felt compelled to explain.

'Well, I just met your dad recently in the retirement home in Manacor.'

Still he remained taciturn, pondering who I was and what my motives for calling him could be. This guy was annoying – he was leaving me to all the speaking; I had intended on a bit of interaction here.

'We discussed a little matter which needs your consent, Michael.'

At last, this aroused his curiosity.

'What matter?'

I told him about the reunion of his father's old band and Mick's willingness to participate.

'You've got to be kidding, my dad's ill. He couldn't possibly play in a band again,' Michael replied with incredulity.

'Well he told me he feels fit and able enough to do it,' I said. I felt like bringing up the fact that if Michael visited his father more often then maybe he would be better able to gauge his state of health.

'I'm afraid not – I can't allow him to do that, it'll probably kill him.'

Here it was – as Mick had foretold: his son was a control freak and enjoyed being awkward.

'Listen Michael, this is your dad's decision. I discussed the matter with him and he is well aware of what it would entail and he really wants to do it. He is of sound mind and well able to make his own decisions,' I replied. I could hear a note of annoyance creep into his voice as his agitation rose.

'Well if he's daft enough to want to play in a band again then I guess I can't stop him.'

I felt the need to point out the fact that Mick still needed his son's permission before he could legally leave the home.

'I'm not prepared to sign him out. He might not make it back – this crazy concert thing could kill him.'

I had to carefully word my replies to this negative guy. I could easily have pointed out should Mick die, then Michael would no doubt reap the benefits from the life insurance as he did with the sale of his parent's big house on the hill.

'Look, all we're asking is for you to let him leave as and when he needs to. He'll be well taken care of and will be brought back to his residence when he's done; besides this could be very beneficial for his mind and soul.'

Michael seemed to chew that one over, and for a minute I thought he was going to relinquish his control.

'No, as his next of kin I cannot allow him to leave the place where he lives and gets well cared for. He has nurses and doctors who give him his regular medication. I don't think it's a good idea for him to go trying to be a rock star again; he's just not that young anymore.'

I could see it was pointless trying to get through to Michael, so I thanked him for his time and hung up. Perhaps with a bit of time to consider, Michael may just change his mind in due course, although I wasn't living in hope. I was rather annoyed, but not surprised; the only thing which kept me going was the thought that there were many other ways and means of getting Mick out of that place whenever the time came; I would not trouble myself with Michael's obstinate attitude.

Chapter 29

I sent Will Pearson an email detailing the success of the mission to reunite the Faceless Legions. His reply was positive and congratulatory. He was still enthusiastic about being part of the planning and organisation of the next phase of operations. We decided that a formal meeting would be the best way forward. As Will was going to be up in Edinburgh in the next few days on another matter, I planned to drive across and meet with him. We arranged a time and venue and I felt good about the mission's continuing momentum.

The tricky thing now would be to arrange a meeting of the band-members; but given they were all scattered around the world, this might be problematic finding a suitable location. Granted, Dixon had agreed to travel to wherever he was required, but the venue would still have to be central for all the rest. Considering we had Carter up in Skye; Brookes in Birmingham; Hannagan in Wales and Walker in Mallorca, the logical location would have to be London – possibly even Heathrow airport, that way Dixon could make it easily enough. I sent out a standard email to all involved seeking their opinion on the suggested venue and for them to nominate a convenient time and date. Once the results were in, I could consolidate the data and hopefully we could all agree on a definitive arrangement.

Alison had returned back to Aberdeen but promised she would do what she could, albeit remotely, as part of the ongoing operation. I missed her, having spent an intimate week in her company; she felt the same as it was with a tear-filled eye she departed for her home in Aberdeen. It had been a surreal experience – effectively dating again my divorced wife! I had no idea what the future held, but I wouldn't be complaining if it involved Alison; in fact I would welcome it and her with open arms.

Now it was time to reveal to the world (or the fan club at least) the possibility of reuniting the Faceless Legions with view to playing a come-back concert. I brought up the Legions of Fans website from my saved bookmarks and logged in. I navigated to the forums and began a discussion thread entitled 'Bringing back the Faceless Legions'. Here I hinted at the possibility of the band reuniting and asked for a show of interest should this venture happen. I was cautious about revealing too much and merely wanted to test the waters and gauge response.

As it happened, the response was phenomenal. Over the next few days I was inundated by fans desperate to know more and eager to get themselves involved in whatever way they could if it meant turning this into a reality. Hundreds more were asking where they could purchase tickets from, thinking the live gig was about to happen.

It was with a sense of excitement and high motivation that I drove along the M8 towards Edinburgh Airport. My meeting with Pearson was in just under an hour but I allowed plenty of time for any unscheduled stops such as heavy traffic or mechanical malfunctions – not that I got many of those with my reliable *Hyundai*.

I watched for Will entering the large spacious reception in the hotel; right on time, he entered and I waved to him. I had secured us a location in the rear corner of the room with two leather armchairs around a square coffee table as the ideal spot for our confidential meet. As he glided over, I indicated to the hovering waitress to bring a pot of coffee.

We shook hands and lowered ourselves into our plush armchairs and discussed trivial matters initially before getting down to serious business. By this time the smiling waitress had returned with a tray containing a large pot of aromatic coffee, two cups, jug of cream and a pot of sugar cubes. The waitress, obviously keen to impress and secure herself a healthy tip, offered to pour the coffee for us, and we let her. We waited for her to depart then dived straight into the planning strategy of the mission. Will had prepared well for our meeting and produced a pile of papers and printed documents from his briefcase.

'So I had a word with a few contacts and done a bit of phoning around,' Will said leafing through the sheets, 'and I have a few ballpark figures for you to chew over.'

'Excellent work, Will,' I replied.

'So it all depends on the type of venue you want to have this concert.' He sifted through his pile and extracted a couple of printed sheets.

'Here we have some rough prices for a few select venues in London,' he pointed to the figures and I leant over to read them.

'The O2 Arena is pretty expensive and would cost about eighty grand for a day, but this has a capacity of up to twenty three thousand.' He let the information digest. That was a lot of money and would require a heck of a lot of fund raising to secure that venue.

'Then I looked at Wembley Arena but I think it is way out of our league. The likely cost would be somewhere between a half and three quarters of a million quid.'

I admired his optimism and confidence in our enterprise but knew that was not even a consideration; even if it housed about ninety six thousand people.

'And what about an old classic venue like the Hammersmith Odeon?' I asked. This was more the type of venue I had in mind, and one in which I reckoned the band would prefer to perform. Will smiled and held up his hand to silence me.

'I'm just coming to that one,' he said with a laugh, 'now that is more in line with reality.' He read out the information on the sheet.

'To hire the Hammersmith Odeon; or to give it its new name, the Eventim Apollo, would cost about twenty eight grand including all sound, lighting and promotion of the event. Its capacity is about five thousand three hundred bodies, part standing part seated.' He sat back to study my reaction. I nodded and smiled.

'That's a bit more do-able,' I said, 'and I reckon a more appropriate venue for the comeback concert of an old rock band.' Will was in full agreement.

'What's more, I may be able to negotiate a discount and so reduce the price a bit.'

This was sounding better and better by the minute. Suddenly the whole crazy idea of reuniting the Faceless Legions seemed less of a pipe-dream and more of a possibility. Sure it would still require a bit of planning and fund raising, but it did have potential.

'Have you any idea of the numbers who would buy tickets?' Will asked. I shook my head.

'I don't know yet but I've already been swamped by requests; too numerous to count but probably around three thousand so far.' Will looked impressed.

'So you reckon you could fill the Hammersmith easily?' Will enquired.

'Yeah I think that would be easy enough. If the requests for tickets keep building as it has been, yes I'm hopeful.'

Will agreed with me on this. Given his experience with this type of work, no doubt he would have told me if he thought the idea didn't stand a chance. As it stood, he was not charging me a fee for his services and had already done a fair bit of research. His eagerness and professionalism was commendable.

We discussed other costs which would be required including promotion and payment for other services and individuals. In the end we agreed on a bench-mark figure of about forty grand to make the concert a reality; again Will reiterated the possibility of negotiating discounts in order to get the costs lowered where possible. We examined all other tasks which would require to be done and other agencies that may be required to assist with both the planning and the execution of the live event. Will was happy to recruit and source all the help needed from his vast industry contact database. I had much faith in Will; he was definitely the best guy for the job – enthusiastic, knowledgeable and eager to make this whole venture a success.

Within the week, the floodgates had been truly opened and the *Legions of Fans* website was going into overdrive. I now had definite replies from over six thousand fans who promised they would purchase tickets as soon as they were available. It this was true then selling out the old Hammersmith Odeon was going to be easy, although I had the sneaky suspicion we might have to consider two nights or perhaps a bigger venue in order to accommodate all interested fans.

At my urging and encouragement, the fans declared it a great idea and vowed to arrange various forms of fundraising in order to help share costs for hosting such a momentous event. There would be sponsored activities and donations sought from all supporters. This was very encouraging as I initially feared I would have to fund the event all by myself.

I also had a list of available dates from all the band members along with approval for hosting the reunion meeting in a hotel or other venue near to Heathrow Airport. This made sense and would be a logical place for such a rendezvous. Dixon would fly into Heathrow as would Carter on a shuttle flight from Inverness; whereas Brookes and Hannagan would simply drive into London. The only problem that remained was in getting Walker from Mallorca to London despite the insistence of his son not to sign him out of his residential home.

When I telephoned Mick to discuss the matter, he was excited about the prospect of coming to the UK and meeting up with his old band-mates. To top it all, he told me about his recent visit from Michael who, after a bit of negotiating, had agreed to let his father leave and return without his express permission. The conditions being he had to be taken care of by a competent person who would ensure he was given his medication and looked after. This was very welcome news and saved us resorting to improper means to help him escape from his care home.

Previously I had discussed the matter with Lee and had agreed to attend the home with me posing as Michael Walker in order to sign Mick out for a time; ironically Mick was happy to participate and go along with the charade if required, stating as his son only occasionally visited, staff were unfamiliar with him, so any young man identifying himself as Mick's son would be accepted without question. So now we could legally remove Mick to London and wouldn't have to worry about getting caught and ruining the whole plan.

The scene resembled a surprise party, but rather than have one victim, there was a room full of surprised guests. Hugs and handshakes, tears and tales was the order of the day as the Faceless Legions gathered after nearly four decades of separation. I stood back to watch the emotional spectacle. Alison held my hand and whispered yet more congratulatory praise into my ear.

Earlier that day, Alison and I had flown out to Mallorca, hired another car and drove over to Manacor where we collected Mick along with a box full of his medication – enough to last the weekend. Staff were reluctant to let him go at first, but Alison was quick to put them at ease when she identified herself as a vastly experienced nurse and liaised with the resident doctor regarding the care and medication of her new patient. Mick was still looking as rejuvenated and healthy as when we last saw him. Clearly the thought of getting back into the music business was doing wonders for Mick; even his doctor told Alison his heath had improved dramatically as a result of our last visit.

During the flight Mick had surprised us by admitting he had began his own rehearsal by practicing daily on an electric piano in the music room of his residential complex. He claimed he was able to play any Faceless Legions song we requested.

'It's like riding a bike,' he told us with a laugh.

Even Paul was behaving himself despite the jetlag he was invariably suffering from; he actually looked thrilled to see his former comrades although at the time of the break-up he had stated he would be happy never to see anyone again. He removed his glasses several times during the meet and greet and I'm sure it was to wipe away a tear or two.

Dale Hannagan was well received by his band-mates and virtually all remarked on the uncanny resemblance to his father in his youth. Dale looked awestruck to be in the company of, and indeed part of the band that his father was a big part of and spoke with fond memories prior to his passing. Although Dale looked the part, I only hoped he could bass guitar as well as his father – it would be embarrassing for everyone if it turned out he lacked the necessary competence to be part of a professional rock and roll band. Looking like his father was one thing but playing like him was another thing completely.

Mick was overjoyed to see everyone again; this was clearly a dream come true for the man. I think he had resigned himself to living in obscurity in a residential home in Mallorca and would remain there until his dying day. I was his life-changing angel who had descended upon him presenting him with this once-in-a-lifetime opportunity – and he had embraced it with wide open arms. He looked well which was very encouraging; well may it continue. I still had little nagging fears in the back of my mind that Mick would fall ill at the last moment and put the whole project in jeopardy. Despite reservations by both men, Mick and Paul looked pleased to meet once again – hopefully they would maintain their cordial friendship and not resort back to their former strained relationship. Again, a persistent doubt rattled around my mind that during the build-up to the concert with the pressure of intense rehearsal and preparation, no doubt there would be friction and the odd fall-out – not just between Dixon and Walker, but between all members. The health and well being of all would have to be carefully monitored and managed.

Danny, still every bit the true leader arranged a series of photographs of the group and individuals. Snaps, clicks and flashes filled the small conference room and whole host of grins were presented to the camera lenses. Danny called me over and inserted me into the group photo; I protested that I wasn't actually part of the band, but the rest demurred stating as I was the one who had actually brought the band back again, that made me an honorary member.

I took the time to introduce Alison and Lee; both were warmly received by all. When I informed them that Alison and Lee had been an invaluable part of my team, there was much back slapping and handshaking. Will Pearson also made the homage to witness the big reunion; if was him who had secured us the use of this conference room for a couple of hours – for a hugely reduced charge, on account of his expert negotiating skills.

Soon I called the meeting to order and we all slumped into chairs around a shiny teak oval table, grins as wide as the Thames estuary, and everyone looking relaxed and happy in old familiar company.

For the next hour or so, Will and I took turns discussing the forthcoming concert, the research we had carried out so far and the planning still to be done. It was unanimously agreed to secure a booking at, and have the band play their reunion concert at the old Hammersmith Odeon (now the new Hammersmith Apollo); certainly it would be great for them to play to a mass crowd at the O2 Arena or Wembley, but an old haunt like the

Hammersmith Odeon was the preferred place to play.

'That's one of the first places we ever played,' Brookes pointed out.

'And one of the last before we disbanded,' observed Walker.

This was the most prudent choice and seemed to be within our budget. The capacity of five thousand three hundred bodies would surely be easy enough to fill judging the response of fans so far. A quick mental calculation showed that if a capacity crowd paid say, £20 for a ticket, then the earnings would be over £106,000 – more than enough to pay all estimated costs and have some left over; any surplus I was happy to donate to a charity, perhaps one in connection with drug rehabilitation as discussed with Dale.

Given we had pretty much decided where, now the question was: when. How long would it take the band to be well enough prepared and rehearsed to provide a quality show? Would six months ahead be adequate or was that too optimistic? Certainly there would be a fair bit of work to do; many hours of rehearsal not only to recap on songs they hadn't played for years but to effectively work at coordinating once again as a music group. They had done it very well in the past, but how well could they do it now after decades with no practice?

Eventually the time period of six months was decided; all agreeing that with intense regular practice, they could be ready to play at the Hammersmith Apollo – assuming Will could secure a booking for the chosen date in six months time. A deposit to secure our booking would no doubt be required and we conferred about how to raise the money to pay this. It was unanimously decided that we as a team should contribute a modest amount to pay the deposit. We each pledged an amount which could be easily withdrawn from the bank and given to Will to make the booking official.

'Now you guys,' said Will pointing to the band-members, 'will require to get yourselves a manager.'

Good point and one I hadn't really thought of. Will would be the overall manager and organiser, but it would be too much to ask him to manage the band as well; hopefully he would have someone in mind who he could contact – better yet if that person was inexpensive. All five men nodded at Pearson.

'So I think your manager should be Tony, here,' Will said turning to look at me. What was he talking about? I was no band manager; I had been barley able to manage Operation Lazarus! I laughed at his absurd suggestion, convinced he was having a joke.

'I think you'd make a great manager, Tony,' Will continued looking serious. I shook my head and offered my defence.

'I'm not a manager Will; that job should be left to the experts.'

'But you spent thirty years in the police and were promoted, what, twice during your career?' Pearson said. I nodded – and suddenly realised where he was going with this.

'So obviously you've had extensive experience managing operations, teams and departments?' Again I nodded slowly – he was correct. As sergeant and inspector I had indeed ran my own departments, managed my own teams and planned a great many missions.

'Yes, but managing a music group is quite a bit different,' I protested.

'I suppose,' Will conceded, 'but you do have leadership and management experience, and I reckon you have the ability to adapt or evolve your role slightly.'

I could see the Carter, Brookes, Dixon, Walker and Hannagan all nodding in agreement. I supposed there was no way out of this new position. I pondered the responsibilities and tasks involved and had to agree that Pearson had a fair point; I probably could be a band manager if I wanted to.

'What's involved in the job?' I addressed Will.

'Nothing much to it; you just make sure these guys are doing the right things in the right place at the right time. You monitor their progress and liaise with me. Any problems, you contact me and we can discuss the solutions.'

I nodded, but under duress. I was happy enough to give the job a go, but apprehensive about failing or letting the team down.

'So, all in favour of Tony being your manager for the reunion project? Will announced.

A sea of hands shot up – all the band-members were in agreement and even Alison and Lee raised their hands. It seemed everyone had faith in me and confidence in my abilities – I only hoped I could live up to their expectations.

Chapter 30

My first promotion in the police was after about ten years; my sergeant and inspector both encouraged me to apply to take the qualifying exams. I was actually quite happy being a mere constable with little responsibility and low pressure levels, but felt it was inappropriate to betray their faith in me, so I demurred and applied for the promotion exams. For the next few months I had my head in books studying such dry and uninteresting subjects such as General police duties; Crime, and Road policing. I had to effectively relearn all the things I had forgotten since graduating from Police College.

I sat and passed the exams with impressive results and sat back to await an invitation to a promotion panel interview. By now my confidence had grown and I had extensive experience under my belt. My supervisors still saw great potential in me and continually urged me forward towards the all important interview.

I sat before a panel with similar austere faces as my police panel interview ten years previously. This time the questions were more about my potential as a manager of a department than my prospective ability to make a good police officer. I answered truthfully all simple and implied questions put to me; they presented me with a host of moral dilemma situations to test my mettle as a manager and I returned with carefully thought out answers.

Before I had time to consider my future, I had been awarded my sergeant stripes and panicked at the new and added responsibility those stripes would afford. Despite intrepidation and doubt in my own abilities, I actually enjoyed and found it a pleasant challenge in managing a shift and department. In the end I couldn't wait to climb another rung on the promotion ladder – it seemed the power of promotion agreed with me.

As Dale had offered the services of his well equipped studio for the band's express use, it was agreed to utilise this at least for initial rehearsals. A date was agreed where the band would descend upon Cardiff and begin getting back together as a working band. Dale had also offered to supply some of the back line amplification and a drum kit for the future live concert and Andy offered to augment any equipment from his music store. This was very good news and went some way to keeping costs down. Danny said he would contribute financially where possible and Dixon vowed to arrange a series of fund-raising initiatives at his bar back in Perth, to help top up the project funds.

After the initial meeting in the conference room, we all descended on a nearby pub where we had a meal and continued our discussion over rounds of drinks. It was great to see the band in good spirits and all still relaxed and enjoying each other's company. Even Dixon and Walker were behaving like best of friends.

I embraced my position as Legions manager and soon got into the swing of things. I updated the website with the pertinent details of the reunion meeting and even posted some photos just to prove it was official and the Faceless Legions were indeed back together again. Still the response from interested fans was overwhelming. I now had a virtual show of hands totalling nearly ten thousand – including fans from all over the world; some of them vowing to purchase more than one ticket to the forthcoming gig. I now feared we would we swamped with enquiries effectively with demand for tickets outweighing quantity – and capacity.

Will had phoned me back the very next day to proclaim the good news that the Hammersmith Apollo was available for our requested date and he had provisionally booked the event. He had paid the modest deposit on credit card and we arranged to reimburse him from our gradually growing funds. To my surprise, he admitted he had also booked a second night at the venue as he suspected demand would be huge requiring a second performance. This was a fantastic insight on Pearson's part, as I was just about to suggest the same thing. Judging by the demand, we both agreed that the band could easily sell out two shows.

When I sent a blanket email with the update to the band, they were in wholehearted agreement that a second night would be beneficial and were excited at the prospect. Even Mick foresaw no real problem with this, as long as he had a seat at his keyboard, his meds were up to date and he didn't suffer too much pain from his arthritic hands.

The day before the first rehearsal, I spoke to Dale to ensure his best rehearsal studio was available and had all required equipment in place – a large drum kit set up to Paul's specification; a couple of quality keyboards for Mick (along with a comfortable stool); a long boom microphone with a *Shure* SM58 microphone for Danny to scream into and a *Marshall* vintage stack to satisfy Andy's guitar playing style. Dale assured me all was in place and that he had recently re-equipped the room with a top quality PA system and microphone stands for all backing vocal requirements.

On the day, Danny took a flight down from Inverness to Cardiff; Andy drove down from Birmingham and Paul had arrived from Perth a couple of days before and stayed with a family member in Bristol. I feared I may have the laborious task of going back over to Mallorca to collect and escort Mick, but his now super-helpful son, Michael had offered to do the necessary. I reckoned he had sensed big potential in his father's endeavour and now wanted to be part of it, hence the drive to helpful; he probably saw the change in his father's health and how much improved his condition now was as a result of his new lease of life. Michael had collected his father and transported him to Palma, dropping him off at the airport. I collected Mick at Cardiff airport and drove him the short journey to Dale's studio.

Despite it only being two weeks since the meeting in London, the guys were all over each other again like they had been apart for another bunch of decades. Dale and his studio minions worked industriously in setting up all pieces of equipment to exacting standards before shuffling out of the room and leaving me to conduct the band. The cheeky dreadlocked guy from my previous visit to the studio with Lee was not to be seen; I wasn't sure if he still worked here, was off duty, or was simply staying out of my way; I thought it best not to enquire.

After a few false starts while equipment was adjusted and levels tweaked, the Legions were playing together once more – after decades of silence and lapses into obscurity, the fabulous four plus the newly recruited Hannagan were performing like they had never been apart. Memories came flooding back as the set-list Danny had compiled was worked through with all the classic Legion hits of the past being played in reasonably tight musical formation. As to be expected, the performance was imperfect but all musicians made an effort to recall each song and play with an air of professionalism.

A credit to all members, they had evidently prepared for this moment and each seemed to produce sheets of paper with notes and memory jogs for each song. No doubt they had listened to their former selves on CD or perhaps a back-catalogue on *YouTube*; such was the quality of the rehearsal after such a momentous gap in playing together. As their manager and fellow musician, I was truly impressed and longed for the up and coming concerts.

As the next rehearsal was scheduled for a week's time, Paul decided to extend his stay with his family in Bristol and Mick took Danny up on his offer to accommodate him at his B&B in Skye. Young Michael had no objections to this knowing that Danny was a former colleague of Mick and, now a very close friend.

Will and I liaised closely with each other, sending emails on a regular basis or conversing on the phone every other day or so. I updated him on the progress of rehearsals and how impressive the reunited Legions were now sounding. By now, the deposits had been paid to the Apollo and Will suitably reimbursed. Tickets had been printed and were now available for distribution with the concert venue providing the primary vending source. The fans website was doing a commendable job of promoting the up and coming event.

Will had directly liaised with Dale and Andy regarding the supply of equipment and discussed the necessary logistical arrangements to get the equipment safely to London in time for the gig. Will had also made contact with department heads at a few colleges running sound engineering courses looking to hire volunteers to work as engineers, roadies and technicians in exchange for quality experience working in a famous concert venue with a big live band. He was inundated with requests from eager under-graduates wanting to take part; in the end, with help from a couple of contacts in the industry, he carried out an interview procedure in order to separate the chaff from the wheat. In addition, Dale would supply experienced sound engineers from his studio and other contacts and Andy vowed to send a few of his shop assistants who would jump at the chance of being a drum and guitar technician.

Response from the Legions website was encouraging; money was being raised by a variety of ingenious and thoughtful ways – from sponsored walks to parachute jumps; and sales of valuable guitars and merchandise. Money was flowing in to the specially set-up account and ticket sales were speeding along like an unstoppable juggernaut. It was very encouraging to see all fans rally round to make this event happen and do so with ease. As this project was a non-profit making endeavour, all costs were kept as low as possible with many people voluntarily becoming involved by donating time, money and other resources when, where and whenever they could.

Despite the ongoing project taking up most of my time, I still managed to play my regular slots with Experience Counts. When I jokingly suggested that we play as a support band for the future Legions concert in London, the guys leaped at the chance urging me to attempt to make this a reality; this, they agreed would be dream come true. It was one of those moments when I wished I had kept my mouth closed – but the more I thought about it, the more I fancied the idea of playing the Hammersmith Apollo in the build-up to the main band.

I ran the idea past Will who thought it a fantastic proposal and saw no objections to it happening; after all it was us who were paying for the hire of the venue, so we could effectively do what we wanted. Dale also recommended a few top quality acts that regularly utilised his studio for rehearsals and recording, for consideration to join the billing of support bands.

I travelled down to Cardiff with Stevie and Phil from my band and we auditioned four or five bands who Dale nominated. In the end only one band was deemed professional-sounding enough to be given the coveted position on the billing. A few other bands were good enough, but lacked the dedication and professional attitude; we felt it only right to have quality bands take part in the event; a classic band like the Faceless Legions deserved no less.

The website was a hive of activity with fans heavily promoting the event through all the common social media outlets, printing and distribution of leaflets and even the sale of custom-printed t-shirts with big bold logos such as 'Return of the Legions' along with the concert dates.

I visited the Apollo along with Lee and Will just to get a feel for the place. Its plush interior had been renovated and modernised and seemed be too clean and lavish for an old fashioned rock and roll concert; still it was the ideal place as it had a well-established heritage and had been well used by a great many big and famous bands all through the ages.

Although the place was empty, I could imagine the hall bustling with excited fans, the eager anticipation heavy in the air as the masses waiting patiently for the arrival on stage of their long lost heroes.

Band rehearsal was going well; but now it had become routine and I only attended on occasion to check the progress. The guys were working their way through the Legions back catalogue making every effort to reproduce each song as it had sounded all those years ago and to which all fans would be expecting. Paul, by now had altered his routine and was still living with his relative in Bristol and only making the occasional trip back to Australia to check on the progress of his bar. Given the high cost of his long-range commutes, we made some of the funds available to pay for his flight tickets.

Will informed me that we had now sold 80% of tickets for the first night, and about 70% for the following night's performance. We had full confidence we could sell the remainder of the tickets and be in a financially viable position.

Mick was still in good health and Danny appeared to be his new carer with Shona providing the nursing services when he returned to the Isle of Skye. Mick and Paul were getting along much better than they used to do and often went off together for drink in the local pub after rehearsals.

Dale was loving his dream job playing with his dad's old band and was just as good as, if not quite as slick as his father on the bass guitar. Curiously he played a Fender Jazz just like his dad played, although no one could come up with a nickname to match his predecessor's sobriquet 'Chas the Jazz'.

Alison had now reduced her working hours at the hospital and had so much more time on her hands – so she made regular visits to my place, and I, in turn visited her in Aberdeen. I sensed she was slightly envious of the freedom I had due to retirement and craved the release of the working rat-race. The strategy, she later admitted was to pave the way to early retirement and more time to do the things she wanted. When not working she was kept busy with assisting me in my capacity as band manager – she had effectively become my unofficial secretary and personal assistant, a job which she performed with great aptitude, efficiency and without as much as a grumble when problems arose or I was having a bad day.

Regular meetings with Will ensured everything was going according to plan and any problems identified could be dealt with before they festered and became a major issue. We arranged a photo shoot and the band reluctantly done the bidding of the charismatic photographer without too much grumbling; a far cry from their previous band days when they craved the publicity and camera lens; but they were much younger, fitter and tolerant in those days; plus they were much more photogenic back then.

Interviews were arranged with a number of major newspapers and magazines and the guys coped admirably with some tricky questions, whilst being guarded about their private and personal lives. I was well aware this was one of the issues which had originally led to the band's break-up, so I displayed caution with regards to public relations and promotional matters. Still, it was required as an aid to making the forthcoming concerts a success, and I was duty bound as their manager to ensure they received the promotion and credit due.

Dale reported a massive increase in his studio usage and therefore, income due the fact the famous Legions were regular users of his establishment. He was kept busy with running his facility at more or less full capacity and intensive rehearsing with the band in between promotion events. Fortunately his mother maintained her support of her son's endeavour and was actively seeking to promote awareness of drug abuse and rehabilitation, working with a number of charities.

Andy was in a similar position: his music store was busier than ever leading him to consider opening a second shop somewhere in the country or moving to a larger premise. He even reported having to take on more staff to meet the growing customer demand. No doubt his business would benefit even more when the band played on stage and his shop branding was prominently displayed on the backline equipment. Dale would probably do the same with his business which I had no objections to; after all, between Hannagan and Brookes, they would be supplying all of the backline amplification plus drum kit and keyboards. Both businesses could be considered sponsors of the event.

Lee also maintained his interest in the project, assisting whenever possible. Given his location in London, he became invaluable in providing transport to and from many of the London airports for any member of our team. He even spoke to a friend who owned his own printing business and secured us a very nice discount on concert programmes which would be printed and sold on both the performance nights. Any surplus would be sold through the fans website or other online retail outlet.

I was really pleased with how things were progressing and with my new-found abilities as a music promoter. I thought back to not so long ago when I first set out on this quest to find the missing Legions. I practically started with very little information, but with a little patience, skill and persistence, I had found Brookes, which then led to Carter. Dale Hannagan was easy enough to find, but persuading him to join was not so easy. Then there was the problem with Paul – a mammoth and expensive trip to the other side of the world nearly proved a waste of time and money, plus I was forced to endure a beating, but in the end, it all turned out right. It was Alison I had to thank for helping to trace Mick in Mallorca and despite my initial concerns about his health and reluctance to participate he too had come up trumps.

I couldn't believe I had achieved all I set out to do, and in record time as well. As a bonus, I had more or less restarted my relationship with my ex-wife and we were getting on exceptionally well. I also got to spend more time with my son as he was as keen to help out as his mother. It was the police service I suppose I had to thank for equipping me with the skills and experience needed to succeed with Operation Lazarus – plus the benefit of early retirement providing the much needed time on my hands.

Chapter 31

It was now only one month to go before the big concert and I felt the anticipation grow within me. I pondered the whole project trying to work out if everything had been done and what still had to be done to make the two-night performance a roaring success. I feared there was some box still un-ticked or some glaring detail left undone, but my regular talks with Will assured me all had been taken care of – anything still outstanding would no doubt be quite irrelevant or minor in nature. I was reassured by Will's confident nature, but still had slight doubts as to my own abilities as a manager. My biggest nightmare was for the whole project to fall through on account of my inadequacies or negligence.

The telephone rang and I guessed it would be from Will or Alison.

'Hello, Tony here.' I recognised the caller's voice immediately and his apprehensive tone triggered alarm bells ringing in my head.

'Hi Tony, it me Danny. Listen, Mick's in a bad way – he's ended up in hospital.'

'Hospital!' I repeated, 'What's happened to him Danny?' I sensed reluctance from Carter.

'Well he collapsed this morning from a suspected heart attack.'

I was shocked at this news; I could feel my own heart racing as though in sympathy at Mick's condition; I wanted to know more.

'Heart attack! How did that happen – he's been doing really well lately?' I remarked. Again I could feel the tense apprehension from Carter.

'I took him for a little hike in the hills and it must have been too much for him. When we got back he just collapsed and I had to summon an ambulance,' Danny revealed.

'You're joking Danny,' I said, my tone harsher than I had intended. 'You didn't drag Mick up a hill did you?'

'He wanted to go and I thought it would be good for him, you know, build up his muscles and stamina.'

This was typical of Carter to drag the elderly and infirm Walker up a hill as though the two of them were youngsters at the prime of their lives, and not men in their mid to late sixties. How irresponsible Carter was – I had seen the way he raced up the hills when I accompanied him in Skye and clearly the man was fit and healthy, but to have Mick running all over the Scottish hills like William Wallace and his band of outlaws was just plain reckless. Carter was jeopardising the whole endeavour and might be the means of driving Mick to an early grave.

'That was pretty irresponsible Danny,' I said, unable to keep the annoyance from my voice. 'You're gonna kill the guy – you know he's nowhere near as fit as you.'

'Sorry mate. I know it was my fault and I can only apologise.'

I was still livid with carter, but now my immediate concern was for the health and well being of Mick.

'So what hospital is he in? How is he anyway? Is he going to live?' My words were tumbling out as I fought with the forces of anger, panic and concern.

'Listen, just calm down mate,' Danny said. This was not helping at all.

'Don't you tell me to calm down; you're responsible for Mick's condition – if he dies it'll be on your conscience,' I blurted out. For a brief second I contemplated hanging up on Danny just to show how annoyed I was at him, but I needed to know more.

'Look I'm totally sorry. I think he'll be okay. The paramedics put him on oxygen and raced him to the hospital,' Danny tried to console.

'So where is he? What hospital – Inverness, Aberdeen…?'

'No there's a hospital here in Skye – The MacKinnon Memorial Hospital.'

I was unaware of such a facility on the island and assumed Mick would have to be taken to a hospital in the nearest large town; I was somewhat comforted by this news knowing he was in a hospital close by. In my experience, many a heart attack sufferer had died in the back of an ambulance on their way to hospital; I knew paramedics were highly trained operatives and ambulances well kitted out, but neither were substitutes for doctors and hospitals.

'So what did the paramedics say? Is he going to live?'

'I'm in the hospital at the moment and he's in a stable condition. Staff say he's probably going to be okay.' I heard the relief in Danny's voice as he fought to console himself with this news.

'Okay, I'm coming up Danny. I'll leave shortly but it'll take me a few hours to get up there.'

I could tell Danny was about to protest that it was pointless me driving all the way up there when there was nothing I could do, but he refrained. I just wanted to see Mick – it might be the last time ever.

I hung up and immediately called Alison to disseminate the news. She was as shocked as I and agreed to head over to the hospital in Skye where we would rendezvous. Interestingly the journey to the hospital in Broadford was virtually the same distance from Glasgow as Aberdeen and would take us both about four and a half hours of continuous driving. Still we were determined to make the homage to check on Mick.

I set off right away, determined to reach Skye before nightfall. I drove fast but remained vigilant of police cars and speed traps.

Despite it being about thirty years since I sat my standard police driving course, it remained etched deep in the contours of my memory. It was more of a talking course than a driving one: you were expected to speak your thoughts out loud so the instructor was aware of each and every hazard you were perceiving and anticipating, rather than second guess you. It required an intense level of concentration to be able to dive correctly and safely plus commentate on the road and traffic ahead of you.

They had a series of systems for all phases of driving and all had to be learned verbatim, otherwise the austere and sadistic instructor would reach out and strike your hand with a long steel ruler. It was a steep learning curve and you constantly fought feelings of despair and incompetence in order to succeed and pass the dreaded test so you wouldn't have to do this ever again.

The driving test was a serious affair and you sweated and worried for days prior to the big day. You poured over books and hand-outs making an intense effort to consolidate all you had learned during the many weeks of training in order to be suitably prepared to pass – failure was not an option if you wanted to keep your job as a police officer – and your knuckles in tact!

I drove the police car along the road with all the skill of an advanced driving instructor, speaking my thoughts and performing the verbal systems as diligently as possible trying to impress the examiner.

Suddenly the loud crack of his ruler struck the top of the dash board and he called out in his loud schoolmaster's voice.

'Right – you have received an urgent radio call. Officer in need of assistance – go, go, go.'

I needed no urging and flicked on the blues and twos. The wail of the siren was deafening in the confines of the car, but I tried to ignore it and concentrate on the road ahead. I could feel the adrenalin flood through my bloodstream and I instantly became as alert as I'd ever been. First I had to perform an overtake manoeuvre system, which seemed to come from my subconscious as I didn't have to think too much about it. Then we approached a traffic light controlled junction, so I launched into this verbal system, before easing through the gap in the traffic and accelerating away at speed.

'Come on, come on. Your colleague is receiving a beating at the hands of a gang of yobs,' the examiner yelled, his clipboard vibrating on his knee.

By now I was already doing about 70mph in a built up area and was apprehensive about going any faster. Rows of dilapidated tenements lined each side of the street and I feared a child or dog would run out in front of me at any moment forcing me to perform an emergency stop. Still I was urged on; the faster I drove, the quicker I had to speak in order to get all my thoughts and words out for the guy next to me to hear. I could see out of my left peripheral vision his pen darting crazily across the clipboard – I was hoping they were ticks and not crosses.

I voiced my concern of potential hazards and conflicts as we raced along the narrow street, avoiding potholes and discarded litter on the poorly maintained roadway. Kids waved to us and some even gave us a rude gesture or two. Adults just stared at the sight of the high speed police car with its huge blue lamp on top flashing like a lighthouse beacon and wailing siren warning everyone in a two mile radius to get out the way. I think many expected to see us chasing a car full of crooks – little did they know this was no real emergency.

Sweat was trickling down my back and I felt drained as we eventually pulled into a lay-by a few miles out of town and following an intense drive lasting about thirty five minutes. I flicked off the siren and lights and the car fell eerily silent. I glanced across to the examiner who sat stoic and calm as though we hadn't just been through a potentially life-threatening drive through the suburbs of Glasgow's east end. His face gave nothing away and he instructed me to drive back to police headquarters where he would reveal whether I had passed or failed.

It was with a feeling of triumph and achievement when I left the building with a pass certificate clutched in my hand. Of course the ascetic examiner took great pleasure in criticising my driving and highlighting my failings, but admitted I had done enough to pass. That was a period of my police career where I wouldn't wish to repeat; it was probably the toughest course I had endured. The only way I would ever have to do this again would be if I crashed a police car and was deemed incompetent and required to re-train and be re-examined. Fortunately I had got through my entire career without having to endure all this again.

I made good progress and only encountered the occasional tourist on the A82. All my overtaking manoeuvres were performed with skill and care, and without as much as a verbal system! After all this time, I still recalled parts of the systems I was taught, proving how deeply rooted in my subconscious memory they were.

At six o'clock I pulled into the car-park of the MacKinnon Memorial Hospital in Broadford, found a vacant space and clocked the driver in the car next to me – it was Alison, having arrived just moments before me on her marathon drive over from Aberdeen. We got out, locked our cars and embraced for a moment or two, before heading into the building. It was good having Alison with me as she seemed to know exactly where to go despite never having set foot in the place before – such was her nurse's instinct.

The sight of Mick lying there in his bed, tubes and cables springing out of virtually every orifice was a depressing sight. He was on a drip and hooked up to a few machines which were no doubt monitoring his heart's condition and blood pressure; however he was awake. I went over to him and smiled down at the fragile man.

'All right Mick, how are you feeling?'

'Yeah…I'm fine…but I've been better,' he said, clearly battling to speak through the manifold of tubes from his nose.

'You'll live, Mick – I have no doubt,' I said with a smile. He returned my smile despite his obvious discomfort.

Alison was studying Mick and his myriad of machines like an anthropologist studying a fossil, trying to gauge the extent of his condition. A nurse came over and Alison seized the opportunity to talk business with her as I continued to assess and console Mick.

'Don't know…if I'll be able…to perform…at the concert,' Mick managed to say, 'sorry to…let you down.'

'Don't be daft, Mick. It's not your fault. Don't you worry about that; you just concentrate on getting better.'

At the sound of a raised voice, I spun around to see a middle aged man standing just feet away, a paper cup of steaming coffee in his hand. He was staring at Alison who was trying to calm him. He turned to me.

'What are you doing here? You've done enough to him, I knew this mad idea of yours would kill my dad,' the man said in an accusatory tone; I guessed I had now met Michael. He sallied towards me, but the nurse stopped him with an outstretched hand.

'Look, this is a hospital. If you lot want to argue and fight, I suggest you do it outside,' the young nurse said looking between me and Michael and pointing to the exit.

I gestured for Michael to accompany me outside and he obliged. We walked towards the door and Alison stayed behind with the nurse.

'I'm sorry about what happened to your dad, Michael, but this was nothing to do with the up and coming concert,' I explained. He didn't seem convinced.

'Sure it was. If he had just stayed put in his residence back in Mallorca, this wouldn't have happened.'

I wanted to point out that Mick's heart attack could have happened anywhere, including his former home in Manacor.

'Yeah, but his heart attack was as a result of pushing himself too far on a hike, and nothing at all to do with rehearsing for a concert performance,' I said.

Mick stared up at me as he supped noisily from his cheap drink. He took a moment to calm himself and rehearse his reply.

'Well he can't perform now. I'm taking him back to Mallorca as soon as he's discharged from here.'

Michael downed the last of his drink, tossed the cup in a nearby bin and went back into the ward. I remained outside. I didn't want to antagonise the guy nor resume an argument. I was feeling defeated and depressed. This truly was the end of a dream, after achieving so much and getting so near to the prize – suddenly it was snatched away.

I sat at a table in the canteen across from Alison. We eyed one another pondering each other's thoughts and feelings.

'You okay, Tony?' Alison said, reaching out and taking my hand.

'Yeah, I suppose,' I admitted, 'seems I wasted my time with this whole mission though.'

I could tell she was struggling for the correct words to console me.

'I spoke to the nurse and she's confident he'll make a quick recovery, it was only a mild heart attack.'

I shrugged and exhaled deeply. This was comforting news but still a large question mark stood over Mick's ability to get up on stage.

'Still, he's not going to be able to participate now as Michael is going to whisk him away back to Mallorca. The whole project is up in the air – it's pretty much over now.'

'Is there no one else who could take his place?' she asked with a hopeful look. I returned her look with one of incredulity.

'Are you mad? We can't replace Mick, not at this late stage. It's over; we just have to accept it.'

We sat in silence for the next ten minutes or so. I couldn't mask my feelings of despair and defeat, coupled with annoyance at Danny for pushing Mick too far.

My phone buzzed and I extracted it from my pocket – it was Danny calling.

'Hi Danny. What's up?'

'Are you at the hospital just now?'

'Yeah I'm here with Alison.'

'Okay, I'll be right over. Give me ten fifteen minutes,' Danny replied.

'Don't know if that's wise, Danny. Mick's son Michael has turned up and he's on the warpath.'

'Okay, thanks for the heads-up, but I'm on my way.' With that he terminated the call.

I met Danny at the main door and steered him towards the canteen and away from the ward where Michael was still loitering. He sat and the three of us talked. Danny reiterated his apologies for the problems he had caused. I expressed my apologies for being a bit harsh with him earlier. There was nothing to say about the subject – it had happened and now we had to move on with our lives. When Alison repeated her conversation with Mick's nurse, Danny looked hopeful as though in a few days time, Mick would be as right as rain and ready to resume with rehearsals. I dashed his theory when I told him about his son threatening to fly him back to Mallorca as soon as he was discharged. Danny suggested having a chat with Michael, but Alison and I warned him off this notion. It was better just to let tempers cool and a chance to let everyone get their sensible heads back on; this was a testing time for all.

'So I phoned the other guys to tell them what's happened,' Danny announced. This was good, for I feared I would have to spend the next day or so doing all the calling and spreading the tidings of bad joy.

'And what were the reactions?' I asked. Danny considered his answer.

'Pretty much as we feel – devastated and disappointed at the gig not happening, but concerned for Mick's welfare.'

I was mindful of a scheduled rehearsal for tomorrow and had an idea: rather than cancel, it might be best for us to gather for a bit of a crisis meeting. I aired my proposal and it was met with approval from Alison and Danny. We reasoned that as everyone was planning on being in Cardiff tomorrow, we might as well use the time to talk things through.

Danny was back on his phone and sent a blanket text message to Brookes, Dixon and Hannagan requesting them to still attend the studio. Replies came back confirming they would be there as planned.

Danny accommodated me and Alison in one of his vacant rooms for the night and next day we drove over to Inverness where we boarded a flight for Cardiff. Alison continued her journey back home to Aberdeen and urged me to keep her up to date with progress. She told me she would keep in contact with the staff in Mick's ward to keep tabs on his wellbeing and would update me with any changes, good or otherwise.

The Faceless Legions sat around looking grim faced and moody; an air of despair was palpable. I had contacted Will Pearson and updated him on events and he said he would make every effort be here for our extraordinary business meeting. I was about to begin, assuming Will couldn't make it when the door to the studio lounge opened and Will entered, apologised for his lateness and sat down on a vacant seat. I stood to address my audience.

'First of all, just to update you on Mick's condition. He's stable and being monitored by staff, who expect him to make a full recovery shortly,' I paused to gauge the response. All looked pleased at the news, but still disheartened by the future.

'But even though he may be out of the hospital in the next day or two, he's not going to be able to part of the band now, I'm afraid.' No one responded, so I continued.

'So as far as I can see, we have three choices. One: we abandon the whole project and loose everything we've worked hard for. Two: we postpone the gig and hope Mick recovers enough to join in again, then we schedule for sometime in the future; and three: we continue as planned without Mick and no keyboards, or we look for a replacement keyboard player.'

I sat back to let the arguments and opinions flow. I searched all faces: Danny was in deep thought, his hand stroking his chin; Andy was frowning as though considering all the options; Dale just sat there with an air of disappointment; but Paul's face said it all – he was livid. He sat rocking around in his seat in an agitated state and his head continually shaking.

'Well I favour option three. I think we've all toiled so hard to see our big chance just evaporate,' Danny said.

'I think if would be wise to postpone and try to reschedule the gig in say six month or a year's time,' was Andy's opinion.

'I was really looking forward to doing this, guys,' Dale said looking at each of his comrades in turn. 'I favour just going ahead with maybe a replacement keyboard player.'

Paul was still fuming; now he seized his opportunity to voice his viewpoint. He spun towards Danny, his finger pointing straight at the vocalist.

'First of all, let me say that you are a total idiot, Carter. You've been irresponsible and Mick's lucky to be alive because of you,' Paul ranted.

I interjected with an outstretched hand and called for calm. I was in wholehearted agreement with his opinion, but now was not the time for a quarrel; besides Danny had apologised profusely to all and seemed genuinely repentant.

Paul realised that his rant was not going to do himself or the others any good at this moment and forced himself to calm down.

'I think it would be a disgrace to continue without Mick, or even consider replacing him. The only option as far as I'm concerned is to abandon the whole thing,' said Paul, still agitated but more pacific.

Now it was the turn of Will to discuss his thoughts. He composed himself and nodded. I thought for a moment he was going to side in with Paul.

'I agree with Danny. You guys have all worked so hard turning this reunion into a reality and it would be a great shame to throw it all away now. Besides, we will disappoint nearly ten thousand fans who've paid good money to see you guys and are looking forward to it. Every one has dedicated a huge amount of time, money and resources to this project and I'd hate to see it go up in smoke.'

There were nods of agreement from everyone with the exception of Paul who sat grim-faced and staring at the carpet.

'My thoughts exactly, Will,' I said, 'I think we should plough ahead without Mick; I'm sure he'll fully understand. Let's face it, we'd loose a lot of money in cancelling and we'd leave a whole truck-load of fans bitterly disappointed and feeling ripped-off.'

'Yeah, I suppose it's the best option out of a bad lot,' Andy ventured, 'I'm sure Mick would want us to keep going. I know he was excited about doing this, but he'd not want us to cancel, I'm sure of it.'

'I'm in favour of keeping going. I too am desperate to perform with you guys – this is a dream come true for me and I want to do it, but I think to get a replacement keyboard player ready and rehearsed in a month is a tall order, so I reckon we should just go without keyboards,' Dale added.

I was happy with the way the discussion was going; I felt it was the most reasonable and sensible option to keep going with or without Mick. But Paul was the awkward one – it would take a power of persuasion to turn him around. The surprising thing was: in the past Paul and Mick never seen eye to eye and were constantly grating on each other, but now Paul seemed to consider Mick his new best friend and was vigorously defending his honour.

'I can't believe you guys. I can't believe you want to go ahead without Mick. He's worked just as hard as everyone else.' Paul spat. 'You lot are a disgrace, at least you can do is to postpone the concert until a later date.'

I could see the uneasiness and the potential for a major argument, so I charged in ahead of anyone else.

'Postponing is not really an option, Paul. Mick's son is at the hospital and he's all set to whip his dad back to his home in Mallorca as soon as he gets out. Plus he blames us for causing his dad's heart attack, even although I told him this was nothing to do with it.'

'Yeah, his son is never going to allow him to perform ever again,' said Will.

Again a strong argument had been put forward in favour of continuing. I could see nodding heads; well, all except Paul's which was still shaking.

'So, all in favour of plodding on to perform the two nights at the Hammersmith, without Mick and keys, raise your hand,' Will said.

Three hands plus mine and Will's rose high in the air. Paul observed the vote and shook his head in disgust.

'Sorry mate, but a vote's a vote. We all agree to carry on,' Danny said turning to confront the sour-faced Dixon. He received nods of approval and support.

330

Paul suddenly sprang up from his chair.

'Well if you're opting to go ahead without Mick, then you can do it without me as well.' With that he raced out of the room and slammed the door leaving a sea of shocked and furious faces.

Chapter 32

Danny and I boarded the flight back to Inverness. We said little to each other during our taxi ride to Cardiff airport. There appeared to be nothing left to say; the gig was now over and all the planning and hard work was for nought. Without having Mick in the band was disappointing enough but we were confident we could still perform as a band without the keyboards, but now that Paul had pulled out, we were left with no other option but to disband. It was inconceivable to contemplate replacing them both – with only one month to go. Even if we succeeded in finding a replacement drummer who was competent in playing all the songs, one month in order to rehearse and integrate with the band was far too great an expectation. We had to admit we had been beaten and take it on the chin; that was just life.

Danny had tried to go after Paul when he stormed out the studio, but we held him back reasoning it would be pointless trying to talk sense into the enraged Dixon, and better to try again when he was calm and hopefully, had time to consider the logical choice. However numerous phone calls had been made to his mobile all of which went unanswered. I tried as well only to receive the answer service; Will had tried with the same result and Paul appeared to answer then immediately hang up when Andy phoned him earlier. For all we knew he was probably on a plane and heading back to Australia, his tail between his legs.

When we landed, I powered up my mobile and found I had a call from Alison. I duly called her back. She was anxious to find out how our group meeting had gone.

'Not good. Not good at all. We were all in favour of carrying on, except Paul, who stormed off in a huff. He wanted to abandon the gig altogether,' I told Alison, my voice laced with sadness and despair.

'That's a pity. Everyone has worked so hard. Oh well,' Alison replied. 'I spoke to Mick's doctor and he's happy with his progress and reckons he might be fit to be discharged tomorrow.' That was good news for Mick, but I could see him being rushed away towards the airport by Michael as soon as his discharge papers were signed.

Danny and I drove back to Skye and popped into the hospital to visit Mick. The nurse in charge tried to be officious and block our visit stating it was out-with visiting hours; we told her we had come all the way up from Cardiff out of concern for Mr Walker and demanded to see him. I think the no-nonsense look on our faces convinced her to change her mind, and she backed down.

Mick was looking very well; all his tubes had gone and the heart monitor had been disconnected. He sat up in his bed looking radiant as though his heart attack had been a false alarm. I was pleased to see him looking so fit and able; perhaps we had a chance yet to get him back into the band! There were no signs of Michael which was good as neither of us wanted another confrontation with the miserable guy. Mick looked elated to see us both.

'Listen guys. I've had a word with the doc and he reckons I'm fit enough to continue with the band rehearsals, as long as I don't overdo it.' I didn't want to burst his bubble but I felt compelled to tell him of Michael's ruling in the event he was ignorant.

'That's great Mick, but the problem is, Michael is going to take you back to Mallorca and he's adamant you're not continuing with the band. I'm sorry mate,' I said. Mick stared at me incredulously as he shook his head.

'No. I told Michael I want to do this concert, it's my decision not his. He wasn't happy but he had no choice. He said it may kill me, but I just told him,' here Mick chuckled at his recollection, 'if I die doing this, then I'll die happy and doing what I enjoy.'

I looked at Danny who wore an enormous grin. I was beginning to smile as well as I felt my spirits lift. This was indeed fantastic news. It seemed all the problems of the last couple of days had been solved: Mick was now willing and able to resume with the band and his son no longer had the control over him; Mick had stood up to his son and was now free to do as he pleased.

Then I remembered the Paul problem. If we were back on as a band, then we'd better herd Paul back into the fold; but what if he was no longer in Britain? If he had headed back down under, chances were he'd never return. We explained the situation to Mick and he offered to phone Paul.

One week later, the Faceless Legions gathered in studio one of Dale's Music Box. Andy tuned up his *Stratocaster* and tested his backing vocal microphone; Dale fine-tuned his *Mesa/Boogie* bass amplifier and Danny counted into his microphone and listened for a realistic reproduction of his voice. Over on the left sat a sprightly Mick Walker at the keyboards. He was excited to be here and raring to go; I only hoped he took it easy and did not suffer any further attacks; I would have to keep an eye on him.

A burst of drums shattered the relative silence of the room and all heads turned to witness the drummer rattle all toms and cymbals in an impressive rhythmic pattern. The guy waving the hickory drum-sticks wildly in the air was none other than Paul Dixon – and it was good to have him back.

Mick's phone call to Paul was a success; when Mick explained he was back on board and ready to press on with the rehearsal schedule, his optimism and enthusiasm infected Paul and he agreed to return to the fold. Luckily he had not yet left the UK shores but was busy packing his suitcase when the call came through; a couple of hours later and it would have been too late. Within minutes, the Legions were back in business and aiming towards the goal they had set out to achieve.

I felt exhausted at all the running up and down the country; my mood levels had been on swings and roundabouts, and my temperament severely tested over the last week; but now I was delighted to see the band back together and progressing towards the reunion concert. With only three weeks to go, we could afford no further setbacks. As the band's manager, I didn't know how far my duties extended – did it cover each man's personal life? I wasn't sure, but I knew I would have to keep a close eye on everyone and try to anticipate any problems and conflicts before they could became major issues.

Alison was keen to keep a watchful eye on Mick and would regularly take his blood pressure and check his pulse. She ensured he kept up to date with his medication and urged him to let her know as soon as possible if he felt unwell.

So far, nothing further had been heard from Michael. Apparently he had gone back down to Leeds where he resided and had as yet not made contact with his father – not even to check on the man's health and wellbeing. This, I thought was a poor show; he might not agree with his father's decision, but the least he could do was to take an interest in his state of health and be happy for him.

The week before the big day was hectic: so much to do and so little time; so much stress and pressure and not enough relaxation and down-time. But this was what is was all about – and no one said it was easy being in the music business.

Rehearsals were going well and there were no major fall-outs – just the occasional minor one which was easily resolved. Alison took the week off work to dedicate full-time care to Mick, who loved the attention she was giving him; she was happy with his progress but restricted his time playing, insisting on regular periods of rest where she monitored his blood pressure for any abnormalities.

Dale had temporarily closed his studio thereby permitting exclusive use for the Legions to rehearse unhindered. We had booked the band into a hotel in Cardiff for the last week to avoid any unnecessary travel; however Paul insisted on staying with his relative in Bristol and commuting daily into Cardiff. Rather than antagonise him and create a problem I conceded and let him do his own thing. Dale who had a flat nearby didn't require any hotel accommodation, which saved us some money.

Alison and I shared a room which was next door to Danny Carter. We regularly heard him singing in the shower, and recognised every one of his songs – pretty much all Legion's songs, all performed with impressive gusto and enthusiasm.

Andy's wife Wendy had arrived to provide some moral support for her husband. She and Alison got on well and kept each other company when the men were busy doing band things.

I checked with Dale and Andy to see if all was well with the equipment both had pledged to supply. Vans had been booked and the equipment was on schedule to be delivered to the venue on the Friday morning, the morning of the first concert.

I had designated Lee the man in charge of the sound crew. He accepted the job without question and was happy to be an integral part of the project. His duties, I explained, would be to coordinate and supervise all the volunteer would-be sound engineers and roadies who would arrive on the Friday morning to assist with moving and setting up all the equipment.

I conferred with Will and we tried to ensure we had everything covered. Will had a checklist and worked his way down the list and between us; we managed to tick almost every box. I was still concerned that something had been overlooked. It was a similar feeling when you go on holiday and are convinced you've forgotten something essential – in the end it turns out to me something irrelevant and all your fears were for nothing. But this was much more than a holiday – this was a huge deal; the comeback concert of the year and it had to go well. Will informed me that virtually all tickets had now been sold for both nights and that we could expect a healthy profit. I reminded him that after all expenses had been covered then the profits would go directly to one or more charities. We had discussed this with the band and each had nominated their own choice of deserving charity which we would pledge some money to when the event was over.

The Legions of Fans website was experiencing heavy traffic as fans were raving about the up and coming concerts. Many had vowed to film the event and produce a live DVD for prosperity's sake. Dale had arranged for a feed to be taken from the enormous mixing desk and fed to some digital recording equipment where his studio guys would record the concerts. After some editing and mastering he would make a live CD available for purchase.

I had to head back up to Glasgow in order to meet with my own band to discuss a set-list. We would go on first and be the initial warm-up act before the band from Dale's studio came on; then, of course – the main head-lining Legions. The two warm-up bands would get a slot of no more than half an hour; then the roadies would move in and fine tune some equipment for the next band; we had agreed to utilise the same equipment to minimise turnaround times and on-stage disruption which may have a knock-on effect for the Legions.

Phil, Stevie and Darren were energised and couldn't wait to get on a real stage and play some good old classic tunes in a famous rock and roll venue. As we performed regularly and were competent musicians, we decided that a rehearsal wouldn't be required – not for a thirty minute set list, which worked out at about five or six songs. Once we got access to the Hammersmith on the Friday morning and set the equipment up, we would use the sound check period as a mini-rehearsal.

The legions rehearsed until they knew their own songs backwards and could play almost blindfolded. It was amazing that after such a long period of time since these songs were last performed, on hearing them played they sounded fresh and contemporary. It was almost impossible to capture that same sound of the seventies due to a variety of things including newer equipment and sound processing, but all were happy enough with how the band sounded.

I had a daily meeting with the Legions just to check how everyone was doing and to identify any problems any of them were having. All were happy and keen to play; Mick was still keeping well; Paul looked happy enough with only the odd grumpy face, generally when he was getting tired; Andy seemed calm, relaxed and itching to get on that stage; Dale was like an excited child filled with nervous energy, which seemed to infect Danny as both of them took to gong for an early morning run each day. I made sure Danny didn't extend the invitation to Mick!

Will had raised the issue of a stage manager – one to coordinate the bands to and from stage. After a brief discussion, we decided that to hire one was superfluous; given there would only be three bands playing on both nights, we reckoned I could perform the role of stage manager along with my band manager duties, and save us the additional expense of hiring someone.

So now I had inherited extra duties all of a sudden and had to get my head round what this would entail – nothing too taxing it would seem. It would simply be a case of clock-watching and ensuring the bands went on stage at the right time and exited at the prearranged time. I would also have to anticipate and identify any problems which may crop up, and liaise with the other departments to find a solution. I only hoped there would be none, as I didn't want to be the cause of the gig not going smoothly.

Then the first major hiccup arrived. Will phoned me in a panic to inform that the company he had hired to supply the sound reinforcement system had let him down; he had began a frenzied series of phone calls to other companies, but none so far were able to supply at such short notice. The basic PA system in the Apollo would be inadequate for the sound levels required for a rock concert. Not that we required anything major – after all this was not going to be an AC/DC or Iron Maiden concert, so power levels could be a bit more reasonable and tolerable.

I remember in the early eighties when there was a battle of the power levels by many of the leading rock and heavy metal bands at the time. Each band would crank up the power levels to say 20,000 watts; another band wanting the honour of being the loudest would play at 30,000 watts, the next 40,000 watts; and so it went on rising higher and higher until the noise levels were unacceptable and bands were made turn down to more sensible volumes. In fact, it was rumoured that the structure of the Glasgow Apollo was weakened through years of excessive noise levels from the many loud bands that played on that huge stage, leading to it being demolished back in 1985.

I got hold of Dale and Andy and explained the situation to them to see if they could offer an alternative solution. Neither was able to supply any more equipment than they had already pledged – sound reinforcement equipment was a much more specialised field. Both promised to do a bit of phoning around to see if they could secure something suitable.

Eventually the problem was solved as a relieved Will found me in an agitated state fearing the whole gig could be over before it had a chance to begin. He had found another company who had experienced a last minute cancellation and were only too happy to step in to our rescue. I felt the lifting of my burden of despair and thanked Will for his industriousness. It was only now I was experiencing the thrills and excitement along with the pressure and pains of organising and planning for this event; I would be glad when it was all over.

Chapter 33

The day before the big night was hectic: many people running around like madmen with checklists and clipboards. In the afternoon we all re-grouped and had a meeting chaired by Will. He consulted his clipboard and announced the plan of attack to his eager audience.

The main sound equipment was scheduled to arrive at about 1000hrs just after the Apollo was opened for access. The additional equipment supplied by Dale and Andy was due shortly after that, so it would require a bit of slick choreography to avoid clashed with a number of different teams all vying for access to the building. Once the equipment was delivered, the appropriate sound technician teams would begin assembling the rigs and all cabling. Both teams would be working in separate areas: the main PA roadies would be at each side of the stage stacking speaker cabinets and running cables from amplifier racks and to the mixing desk in the sound control booth. The backline guys would be working to the rear of the stage setting up amplifiers and speaker stacks; assembling the drum stage and drum kit; positioning the keyboards, and finally, setting up the microphone stands and cabling to interface with the mixing desk. Lee would be supervisor and liaison between the various groups and companies.

Sound-checks were scheduled for late afternoon when, hopefully all gear had been set up and ready for use. As they would be on last, the Faceless Legions would sound-check first, so all equipment could then be moved and levels reset before repeating the procedure for the second band. All levels and settings required by Dale's studio band (who had the curious name of Job for Life) would be noted, then Experience Counts would perform a sound-check last as we would be the first band on stage later that evening. Given there would only be three bands taking part, a decent time to sound-check would be provided, as long as there were no major problems in the setting up.

In my experience as an amateur musician, I had played numerous venues and faced all manner of problems from poor equipment to obstinate band members. One memorable gig saw us nearly fighting with another band as they had messed around so much that they had used up all the available time to sound-check and left us having to tweak levels whilst performing, which was not ideal.

Another gig saw us sitting around in an agitated and stressed state whilst we waited on the sound engineer arriving to manage the sound-check. He strolled in over an hour late, without a care in the world and we ended up having to check levels in front of the audience. A sound-check is supposed to be a chance to set up and make all adjustments prior to your big entry onto stage, in relative privacy and not in sight or earshot of your audience!

At the conclusion of the meeting, I was reasonable happy everything was in place and good to go. I felt at peace having worked our way through our long list and managed to tick all the boxes; however I was a realist and was well aware of the old adage: if something can go wrong it will. The secret lay in anticipating any problems and seeking solutions as soon as possible to minimise stress and prevent the predicament from getting out of hand. I was also content with my team and felt confident in their abilities, and knew I could rely on them to get this project running smoothly.

We all descended on a nearby restaurant and harassed the staff into moving tables so we could all sit together. I was curious to their expressions of annoyance as they would be benefiting financially from our large group.

Wendy Brookes sat with her husband looking slightly intimidated at the sea of unfamiliar faces. Andy sensed her panic and began the introductions. Mick looked content and healthy enough – which was a good sign; Danny, as usual was the life and soul of the party, chatting with everyone in his usual extroverted manner; Dale sat beside his girlfriend: a small nervous looking girl with long blonde hair and numerous facial piercings. She held Dale's hand discretely under the table and looked proud to be the girlfriend of a rock star. Paul was chatting away to Lee; and the two support acts were engaged in light-hearted conversation, do doubt about music, gear or the state of the music industry in general.

I had Alison on one side and Lee on the other. Lee had brought along his girlfriend and this was the first time we had met her. Initial introductions had not gone well as Alison had goofed by calling her by the name of a previous girlfriend of Lee's. It seemed Lee had a new love interest every week and the last name he quoted was Abbi: apparently she was The One and their future together was looking good. So it was not unreasonable for Alison to greet the tall skinny girl with,

'Ah, you must be Abbi? Lee had told us all about you.'

An embarrassed silence, then Lee dived in to the rescue.

'No mum, this is Jessica. Abbi is long gone.'

'Oh I'm so sorry Jessica; pleased to meet you.'

The embarrassed pair shook hands then hugged, whilst Lee and I just laughed the awkward moment away.

After a rowdy couple of hours, we felt compelled to leave the restaurant. Will paid the large bill and left a reasonable tip for their troubles – this would go through the books as a business expense.

Spirits were running high and a party atmosphere was in the air. Experience Counts and Job for Life were threatening to hit the town and party until morning, but Will and I frowned upon the idea and insisted all headed back to the nearby hotel, so all were fully rested for a busy day tomorrow. Grudgingly, they all acquiesced and we trundled along the street en masse towards the hotel where we had taken a large portion of their rooms.

Following a long hot shower, I retired to bed and fell asleep almost immediately. I awoke with a start several hours later and sprang upright as though having been hit with a cattle prod. Alison consoled and calmed me; then I told her about my crazy dream:

The massive hall was jam-packed; not a single bit of floor was visible. I surveyed the masses from centre stage and jerked in horror when they all stared back at me with nefarious grins on their faces; some had blood-shot eyes, some with deep sunken eyes looking like zombies but all were scowling at me. Fingers began pointing and soon a volley of boos and hisses were launched directly at me. I tried to calm my audience down, but I only succeeded in antagonising them. Objects began to fly through the air in my direction forcing me to dart off to stage right to avoid the missile attack. That was the moment my incubus ended, and I was thankful for it.

I was well aware of the origin of my nightmare – it was all the stress and apprehension of the last few weeks culminating in an intense uneasy dream. Forget all those pointless dream dictionaries and books which con readers into explaining the deep and mystical meanings of their dreams – I knew exactly what triggered mine, and in a couple of day's time, it would all be over and I could rest easy.

By morning I had managed to accrue a few hours of quality sleep, once I managed to relax enough to drop off. Feeling energized by the adrenalin and pressure of the task which lay ahead, I rose, dressed and checked my mobile – good: no urgent messages and no one running around in a blind panic just yet. I left Alison to sleep on while I went down to the hotel restaurant to partake of a quick breakfast. Here I met Will who was munching on a croissant with his coffee. He too had the tell-tale bags under his eyes through lack of, or interrupted sleep.

'You worried about the event Will?' I enquired as I sat down across from him.

'Just a bit,' he admitted.

'But I thought you did this all the time?' I said, 'does experience not make you less prone to worry?'

'It does to some extent I guess, but I still get concerned about details. It's my reputation that's at stake – one cock up and I could be out of a job,' Will said with a laugh, 'no one would want to hire an incompetent.'

We ate, drank and talked shop for the next half hour. Despite my nervousness, I was looking forward to the day ahead – and the evening which would be the zenith of all my pondering and planning. I couldn't wait to see the Legions back on stage after their long hiatus.

I was at the stage access door to see the arrival of a couple of lorries. As soon as the parking brake hissed on three burly men stepped down from the cab and opened the rear doors. Soon a minibus arrived on the scene, parked near to the truck and disgorged its load of reinforcement personnel. Like a hive of worker bees, the team then set about unloading the truck and wheeling the equipment inside. I approached the guy who stood about monitoring the men – I guessed he was in charge. We made the necessary introductions and I left him to it.

I looked around for Lee – he was missing in action; no doubt having one of his usual lie-ins. I had told him to be here for the arrival of the equipment, so he could begin his role as supervisor, but was either running late or had forgotten the prearranged time. I dug out my mobile from my pocket and was about to dial him when a cheery voice called out from behind.

'Hi Dad. You're up bright and early.' I spun around and pointed to my watch.

'You should have been here ten minutes ago,' I said with sarcasm.

'Why, what happened?' was Lee's witty response. He sensed my annoyance and tried to comfort me in my unique way.

'No point in getting stressed dad, it won't make the day run any smoother.'

As usual he had a point; there was no benefit in getting agitated and worrying about what would happen over the course of the day. This day had been well planned and we were confident all details had been taken care of. I would just have to trust in the mercy of the teams to ensure all went according to plan. Any problems identified, we would simply thrash out a solution.

We went into the arena through the stage door and Lee approached the roadies, introduced himself and explained his role in the operation. I watched the gang work impressively hard moving speaker cabinets and huge power amplifier racks into position, running long lines of cable from the racks to the speakers, and making the connections between the mixing desk and the amplifiers. I stared up at the speaker stack – impressive though no quite as big and powerful as the stacks the Legions used to use back in their prime. I chuckled at the old adage in the rock and roll business: if it's too loud – you're too old! There was some truth in that, although loud volume wasn't necessary required to make you sound good. It was all down to the skills of the musicians on stage. In addition, high sound levels had been proven to be damaging to one's hearing – so it was sensible to keep volumes down to reasonable levels, at the risk of being branded an old-timer.

The hall echoed with the voices of the roadies shouting instructions at each other and the noises of the squeaky castors as flight cases and cabinets were dragged across the stage. I surveyed the thousands of empty seats and knew the hall would sound so much different when bums were on these seats tonight. Sections of seating areas had been removed from the rear of the stalls and circle to accommodate some standing viewers. I tried to envisage over five thousand people crammed into this auditorium tonight; the heat from the mass of bodies; the hustle and bustle of the excited crowd and the eager anticipation for what was being billed as a memorable night – I only hoped it all went to plan otherwise it might be duped disaster of the year.

I saw Andy rushing across the forecourt with his mobile clamped to his ear. He saw me and came towards me, breathing heavily with the exertion; he terminated the call and spoke.

'My guys are just around the corner and will be here in a couple of minutes.'

This was good news; so far there was no sight or sound of Dale's lot. I looked at my watch – it was now eleven o'clock.

The truck manoeuvred into position, the brakes hissed on and three guys emerged from the cab. Andy approached them and all engaged in a ritual of hugging and back slapping. Andy introduced each man to me and I pressed the flesh.

The tail lift was lowered and all disappeared into the rear of the truck. Soon all manner of combo amplifiers and stack systems were wheeled out onto the lift, and transported into the arena. The equipment kept coming, so much so I actually thought the truck was a *Tardis*. When I surveyed the equipment all laid out in neat rows at the rear of the stage, I was amazed that it had all been inside the vehicle.

'So where's Dale's crew?' Andy asked. I shrugged and looked at my watch again.

'No sign of them so far; hopefully they'll be here soon,' I replied trying to keep the annoyance from my voice.

'Otherwise they'll be no drums or keyboards to play,' Andy said with a laugh.

Andy's guys had divided the backline equipment into two sections leaving a gap for the drum stage and drum kit right in the middle; the gap was glaringly obvious - like a missing tooth in an otherwise perfect mouth, and I hoped the drums and keyboards Dale was supplying turned up soon.

I was mindful of the time way back in the seventies when Status Quo played a gig in Glasgow. According to legend, both Rossi and Parfitt had their guitars stolen, and had to make a frantic last minute dash to a famous music shop in the city to purchase replacement instruments. I only hoped we wouldn't have to do likewise in search of a drum kit and keyboard.

I gave Dale a call and he answered immediately.

'Hi Dale, any signs of your guys and the equipment?'

'Hi Tony. I'm just off the phone to them. Apparently their held up in traffic but say they'll be here in an hour or so.'

'Okay. Keep me updated will you?' I said struggling to keep the frustration out of my voice.

I updated Andy and he just laughed and shook his head.

'You'd think they would have left earlier. Everybody knows the traffic into London is murder at this time of day,' Andy lamented.

I nodded – these were my thoughts exactly. I remembered the heavy build up of traffic on my journey from Cardiff to Heathrow recently.

I was having lunch with Alison in the hotel restaurant when my mobile vibrated into life. I looked at the display – it was Dale.

'Hi Tony, my team are at the service yard with the gear.'

'Okay I'll be right over; someone should be there to let them in and show them where to put the gear,' I replied. I terminated the call and turned to Alison.

'Only about three hours late!'

'Better late than never, eh?' she responded with a smirk.

Despite my promise, I was in no hurry to go back over to the venue until I had finished eating; who knew, perhaps this would be my only meal of the day. Besides, they hadn't been in a hurry to get here.

I sauntered back to the Apollo half an hour later and was relieved to see the drum stage in place and the drums being positioned upon it. Another guy was setting up a double keyboard stand; I hoped they had remembered to bring along a stool for Mick to sit on whilst he played.

By three o'clock all equipment had been set up; now it only required to be switched on and tested. This would be the big make or break event: if some of the equipment failed to work, this would require a frenetic investigation by all the sound-tech guys to solve the problem.

I wandered through to the backstage dressing rooms – the venue had no less than ten such rooms. The Faceless Legions were using two of the rooms and the other two bands one each. I knocked on a door sporting a hand-written sign which read 'Grumpy musicians inside – enter at your peril!'

'If you're the invisible man – I can't see you,' the unmistakable south London accent of Carter cried out. I pushed the door open and entered.

'Tony me old mate, come in,' Carter drawled.

There the Legions sat all sprawled over sofas and feet resting on tables and other furniture.

'Your door sign was right, you all look miserable,' I joked.

'Nah, we're all sparked up and ready to go,' Mick said.

'So you all ready for a sound check then?' I asked, surveying the group. They all whooped and cheered as if they had been waiting this moment for weeks – well actually they had.

I sat on the front row of the stalls with Lee and we watched the Legions set up their equipment and sound-check the levels. Paul banged away on the drums; Andy played a selection of scales on his guitar and made some adjustments to his bank of floor pedals; Dale performed a series of pentatonic scales by running up and down the frets; Mick sat on his high stool and messed about with the Korg's various settings and voices; and Danny was deep in concentration whilst adjusting the boom microphone stand to an appropriate height and angle to match his tall frame.

Thankfully the drums had been 'miked-up' and the tedious task of sound-checking each drum and cymbal had been performed by the drum technician earlier, so we didn't have to sit through that.

The long-haired and goateed engineer on the mixing desk indicated for them to play something so he could begin to make the necessary adjustments to the settings and controls on his huge thirty-two channel desk.

The band composed themselves then began playing an old Legions classic. I sang along with Carter as I swayed to the beat in my seat. At first Carter couldn't be heard, but the efficient engineer was soon on the faders and Carter's vocals rang out loud and clear. A few minor adjustments to the guitar and bass feeds and the sound was nicely balanced. I could hear the pounding beat of the bass drum and considered it a bit too loud in relation to the other drums and cymbals, but reckoned the slick engineering team would soon suss out the imbalance; besides it wasn't my place to interfere with the sound levels was it? Or, in my capacity as band manager, could I insist on having the levels tailored to me and my client's taste? In the end I sent my associate to speak to the guys on the mixing desk; Lee glided over and within a minute or so, the bass drum was sounding better and the band were sounding very fine indeed. At the end of the practice song, Andy called for a slight increase in his backing vocal microphone and Danny requested the stage monitors to be turned up so he could hear himself; this was done and Legions performed another song before declaring themselves pleased with the set-up and the overall sound balance. I was well aware of Carter's concern about the on-stage monitoring levels: there was nothing worse than not being able to hear yourself singing; all musicians have been there at one time or another – and tend to sing out of key purely because they can't hear what is actually coming out of their own mouths!

Next up was Job for Life: the drum tech raced onto stage and began to move some of the drums and cymbals around to suit the new drummer. Drummers were a curious lot - insisting that the various drums and cymbals had to be in certain positions to match their playing style; unlike guitarists who can simply pick up any guitar regardless of make or model, and play it, whereby demonstrating their versatility and skills.

We listened to Job for Life as they performed a few of their own songs; I couldn't place their sound exactly. After listening for a few minutes, Lee suggested they sounded like The Clash or The Cure.

Soon we were joined by Stevie, Darren and Phil who were all anxious to get on stage and start setting up. Stevie had brought along my Jackson Performer in its fur-lined hard-case. We all listened to Job for Life as they finished up their final test-song and the drummer went mad on the cymbals as though completing the final song of a gruelling tour, or maybe he was trying hard to impress.

'Hope he doesn't crack one of those Zildjian's,' Phil said with a concerned look etched on his face.

We all climbed onto stage and I left Lee in charge of ensuring our levels were adequately balanced – we wanted to sound at our very best.

Again a few adjustments were required by Phil behind the drums, and the rest of us tuned up our instruments and tested the microphones. A nod from each other and the engineer on the mixer, and we were off. We played a few bars of the start of a song and Phil suddenly stopped playing, cursing the previous drummer for having messed around so much with drum and cymbal stands, necessitating him moving things back into position. I asked for the monitors to be increased in volume and Darren his bass to be turned up slightly.

Ten minutes later we had adequately sound-checked and were reasonably happy with the sounds we were producing. I knew that there was a huge difference in sound and hall acoustics between an empty auditorium and a jam-packed one; no doubt more adjustments would be necessary before we kicked off the event later this evening.

Chapter 34

I was talking to Will about the door opening times when my mobile rang. I fished it out of my shirt pocket and looked at the screen. What did Danny want now?

'Yo, Danny. What's up?'

'You better come quick Tony. It's Mick – he's in a bad way.'

'What do you mean? What's up with him?' I asked as I felt my mood drop like a stone.

'Well it's him and Paul. You see Paul's been at him all afternoon challenging him. Mick finally gave in and now they're both going at it to the death. Mick's lost the will to live.'

I couldn't believe what I was hearing. This was serious stuff. This could possibly be the end of the gig before it got started. What was Paul thinking about goading Mick? I knew we shouldn't have left the two of them together. I hung up and raced over to the dressing room, Will running after me.

'Should I call an ambulance?' Will asked as he struggled for breath.

'Hopefully someone has already done that,' I called back.

My heart was racing – and not just from the exertion of running; I felt it might rip right out of my chest. If Mick had indeed taken another heart attack, it was doubtful he would survive, and this time Paul was responsible. It seemed that all the band were having a go at trying to kill poor old Mick.

We reached the door and I burst inside, Will hot on my heels. Five faces looked up at me. I stared at Mick who sat at one side of a card table, Paul at the other. Mick looked absolutely fine to me, except he wore an irritated look on his face. On the table sat a game of *Scrabble*, the board full of lettered tiles. Mick looked up from the board and spoke to Paul.

'Oh, well, you've got me beat this time mate. The game's over.'

Then it dawned on me. Now I got Carter's meaning. I let out a deep relieved breath and laughed along with the others.

'Very, very funny guys,' I said my voice loaded with sarcasm, 'it was me nearly having the heart attack.'

I strolled along the front of the Hammersmith Apollo hand in hand with Alison and we gazed up at the illuminated signage above the main doors announcing 'The Faceless Legions – a reunion to remember!' It gave the dates of the two performances, but failed to list the names of the support bands, instead simply stating 'plus support acts'.

'You've done it Love. You managed to make it happen – just like you set out to do,' Alison praised.

'It's not started yet,' I cautioned, 'let's wait until then.'

The plan was for everyone to go out for a quick meal prior to preparing for the gig, but Alison and I opted for a quiet dinner together. I knew the after-gig party, would no doubt get very rowdy and we probably wouldn't get quality time together. Besides, I feared that if the audience didn't take to Experience Counts then they might just launch missiles at us or storm the stage and lynch us!

Will had earlier voiced concerns about lack of security and stewarding for such a large expected crowd. He had discussed this with the Apollo's manager, leading to a series of hurried phone calls to a friend in the business. In the end his mate supplied a dozen or so solemn-looking security personnel who attended as promised all dressed in high-visibility jackets and sporting their identity cards and license on their sleeves. Will had them all briefed and at their respective posts prior to the doors opening at 1830hrs.

Backstage was a hive of nervous activity. Arguments were starting to break out over trivial matters and minor irritations were rapidly becoming big problems. I went between the various dressing rooms checking on progress and enquiring if anything was required. I had to intervene on a few occasions to prevent a few of the Job for Life guys from squaring up to each other. Roll on the event, then everyone can get a chance to work off their nervous energy.

Alison was giving Mick another check of his vitals and pronounced him fit, well and remarkably calm for a man of his age about to go on stage and play to a packed auditorium. I checked my watch: the doors had just opened and we were due on stage in half an hour; time to change and mentally prepare for the task ahead.

I went into the Experience Counts dressing room and began to change clothes. We had opted to go on stage in smart shirts and denims; we wanted to be casual but not too sloppy. Phil sat drumming on the furniture, Darren looked lost in thought and Stevie was in the middle of the room performing star jumps and squats.

'Come on Stevie, its not a gym were in,' I joked. He liked that one and laughed as he increased the pace of his vigorous exercise regime.

'You'll be sweating buckets before we even hit the stage,' offered Phil.

'Don't you know you have to warm up before a gig?' Stevie asked.

'We are the warm-up act you Pratt,' was Darren's offering of wit.

357

I faced the audience: a vast sea of eager faces stared back. Mind you, I could only see those in the front few rows, the blinding stage lights preventing me from seeing further afield. Although this evening was virtually sold out with only a handful of tickets remaining, I knew we didn't have a full house just yet. Crowds were still spilling into the arena and finding their seats.

Phil counted us in with a click of his drumsticks and we launched into an old rock and roll favourite: *Rockin' all over the World.* At fist I struggled to hear what I was playing on the guitar and I could tell Stevie was also straining to hear his lead vocals, but the efficient sound crew on the desk soon sorted out the inconsistencies and we were back in action.

After we completed the song with a big drum roll finish, the crowds cheered and clapped their appreciation; only then did the nervousness disappear, to be replaced with a feeling of euphoria. Wasting no time, we went straight into another of our rock cover classics: *Born to be Wild.* We had deliberately restricted our set-list to shorter songs thereby maximising our short time slot.

By the time we were finishing our final number, it seemed only a few minutes had passed; I wanted to play for longer and was just getting into it, but I caught sight of the weird guys from Job for Life off to stage right and knew they were itching to get on stage.

The crowd went wild and we got the impression they had really enjoyed our short performance. This was indeed the biggest audience we had ever played to and it was a fantastic response. We left the stage waving to the applauding crowd and were high-fived by the other guys. I eased my guitar off of my shoulder and placed it on a nearby guitar stand and was heartily embraced by Danny, Mick, Paul, Andy and Dale. All sung our praises and stressed how good we sounded – evidenced by the euphoric response from the audience.

It was cool drinks all round from backstage and a quick change of shirt - I was glad to dispense of my sweat soaked one. Alison was there to assist and lavish high praise on me; apparently she was extremely proud of my performance not having seen me play in years. Lee was obviously busy doing his job liaising with the roadies somewhere in the auditorium. Will shook my hand so vigorously I thought he might injure me and render my hand useless for our next night's performance.

We could hear the next band playing, but they sounded rather bland in comparison to our energetic and raucous performance; we moved to watch them from the side of the stage and laughed at their on-stage antics. The lead singer was egging the crowd on as though this was a *Monsters of Rock* festival and he the singer of the headline act. The bassist was trying hard to replicate Flea from the Chilli Peppers' playing style and the guitarist clearly thought he was a cross between Jimi Hendrix and Pete Townsend. I only hoped he wouldn't start smashing up the backline amps as we needed those.

Luckily their thirty minutes of fame soon ended and they trooped off stage to a lukewarm response from the audience. I peered out into the auditorium and could see a packed hall. Every seat looked filled and the standing areas were crammed with excited bodies. I even spotted a few wheelchairs in the reserved area.

I went to the Legions dressing room. They were all dressed and ready to go. They too had opted for a smart but casual dress code. Danny looked good in his crisp black shirt and black denims which perfectly complemented his slim figure; Mick wore a white shirt and dark denims; Paul a denim shirt and matching jeans and Andy's long dark cotton shirt perfectly concealing his bulging belly. All looked calm and keen to get going. I glanced at my watch to see it was now 2020hrs; good everything was going according to plan. All stage changeovers had been done in an efficient and professional manner and so far no equipment hitches.

'Looking good guys. All ready for this?' I asked.

They all looked at me as though I was the lottery prize giver confirming if they really wanted the million pounds. Danny approached me; I could see a tear in his eye which he brushed away as though a speck of dust.

'Look man, we really appreciate this opportunity you've given us; we won't let you down.'

'Yeah, if it wasn't for you we wouldn't be here right now,' Andy added.

'No problem guys, it was a pleasure,' I replied. 'Now get out there and do the thing you came here to do. There are over five thousand folk out there waiting to hear from you.'

'Yes sir,' said Paul giving me a mock salute.

I followed the band out along the snaking corridor towards the backstage area. I could feel the excitement and eager anticipation emanate from them like a tangible entity. Lee was there to greet them just behind the stage.

'Couple of minute's guys then you're good to go,' Lee said watching the roadies adjust and fine tune the onstage equipment and drum kit.

Alison took hold of Mick's wrist and felt his pulse. I watched her face – and it didn't change expression. Was that a good or a bad sign? She seemed to frown briefly before her face transformed into a warm smile.

'Okay Mr Walker, you're all clear.'

'Thanks nurse,' Mick replied with a smile.

My watch told me it was now 2030hrs. Lee got the thumbs-up from the lead roadie and he turned to the Legions.

'Okay guys, you all ready?' He received nods of approval all round. 'Right I'll just go and introduce you.'

Lee strode onto the stage and squinted at the bright spotlight which shone directly onto his face. He approached the centre microphone, took a deep breath and began his speech.

'Ladies and gentlemen; now is the moment you have all been waiting for. After a period of nearly forty years, here they are back together and on stage again. Please give a huge welcome to…' here he paused for emphasis, 'The Faceless Legions.'

The crowd went wild; five thousand voices whooped, cheered and the volume of applause was deafening.

The band strode purposefully onto the stage, waved at their audience and took up their respective positions.

'Thank you so much, Hammersmith,' Danny screamed into the microphone, as the rest of the band sorted themselves out. Danny looked over his shoulder at Paul who gave him a nod of approval. Paul then started playing a rhythmic beat on the drums, before Dale entered with a pounding bass line a few bars later. Andy and Mick were soon contributing to the well known song and the audience soon recognised the distinctive intro of the Legions classic *Livin' life and rock 'n' roll*. This was a very good choice of an intro song – catchy, rhythmic and loud. Danny raised both his arms high in the air and began clapping in time to Paul's beat - this in turn encouraged the crowd to join in. Mick's unique keyboard playing was audible and distinctive and Andy's melodic riff performance was a delight to the ears.

After a minute or so, Carter closed in on the microphone. His characteristic powerful voice soon got the song charging ahead like an avalanche. That voice was still fantastic despite years of non-use and four decades later. I reckoned Carter had been secretly practicing for years when no one was around. Perhaps he did this on top of the many mountains he climbed up there in Skye. I stood mesmerised watching the band and recapturing precious memories. They sounded so fresh – if I didn't know better I would have insisted they had never been away.

Alison and I moved off stage and down into the circle in order to get a better view of the band. We stood there arms wrapped around each other and smiled. This was pretty much the position we had been in way back in 1978 at the Faceless Legions gig at the Glasgow Apollo. How our lives had gone around in a massive circle and it seemed we were back to where we first started. We had fallen on love after that memorable gig, got married four years later. Unfortunately our affection for each other had cooled on account of our hectic work/ life balance; being more work than life. We had separated then divorced and gone on to live individual lives.

Now here we were back together and most definitely in love and watching the band that had united us and to whom we probably would never have met had it not been for them playing the Glasgow Apollo on that night. The other major thing that had changed for the better was the fact I was no longer in the job which had formerly owned me and was instrumental in robbing me of precious family and social life; plus Alison was on the cusp of retiring from her life encompassing career. Maybe we could start again – and make it work this time around – things were looking promising so far.

I studied the band and remarked to my companion how good they looked back on stage. Paul looked relaxed and content back behind his large drum kit; Andy seemed to have a permanent smile on his face – as though he just couldn't erase his feeling of euphoria; Mick, despite his fragile health state and recent scares, clearly was enjoying himself; I wondered what his current pulse rate was at. Dale looked as much at home on this big stage than his father did, despite him never having played such a large auditorium. He certainly didn't look intimidated at being the youngest band-member. It was uncanny how much he resembled his father back in the days when the Faceless Legions were doing this on a regular basis. Finally Danny – he looked like he had never been away from this job. He still had those youthful looks, cheeky smile and charismatic personality which drove the crowds wild. He sill had the knack of controlling his audience and making them beg for more; plus he still retained his youthful energy as he raced back an forth over the stage inciting the crowds to sing, dance, clap or cheer. Clearly his exercise regime in running up and down Munros kept him in good physical shape.

After about six songs, all musicians with the exception of Andy left the stage for a well-earned breather leaving Andy with the audience's undivided attention. He spent the next ten minutes showing off his slick guitar work as his hand seemed to float up and down the fret-board at impressive speed and ease as he pounded his sunburst *Gibson Les Paul*. He demonstrated minor, major, pentatonic, chromatic and even the obscure Phrygian major modal scales with all the finesse and accuracy of a seasoned guitar player. No doubt all his years running a guitar shop had been beneficial in keeping his guitar playing hand in.

I surveyed the vast crowd: they were transfixed with the guitar guru's impressive playing. Andy may not look like your typical rock guitarist – with his short, tubby stature and receding hairline, but they couldn't fault his playing.

Dale, Mick and Paul arrived back on stage, returned to their positions and began another number. Danny ran onto stage at the end of the intro to the song, grabbed his microphone from the stand and sang. This one was a classic

Legions song. When the chorus arrived, Danny coaxed the audience into singing along.

'What goes up?' chanted Danny before pointing the microphone towards the crowd; they dutifully responded with 'must come down'.

Each time Carter encouraged his choir to sing louder; again they needed no prompting and sang with fierce determination as though in a singing contest. Danny was loving all the attention, and at times, seemed to forget he had a full band behind him. He even divided the hall up into sections and encouraged a full-on singing contest to see who could chant the loudest.

Next it was Paul's turn to display his dynamic drumming talent to the captive audience. He drummed continuously for ten minutes in a rhythmic pounding of the toms and cymbals, speeding up the tempo towards the end of his solo performance into a crescendo of crashing cymbals and frantic thrashing of the drum skins. The crowd went wild, cheering the energetic performance and a grinning Paul waved his drumsticks in the air to acknowledge his gratitude.

There followed another string of Legion's hits before Mick finally got his instrumental slot. Once again the rest of the band departed stage left leaving a contented and relaxed looking Mick alone on the platform. The crowd waited with bated breath on Mick beginning as he composed himself.

Suddenly he launched into a rendition of a classic piano concerto; his fingers an impressive blur as they darted across the ivories hitting each in a relentless salvo. For a man who had earlier admitted problems with arthritis in his fingers, there was certainly no trace of the illness now as evidenced by his polished performance.

To continue his demonstration, he merged the ending of the concerto into a honky-tonk style piece. The mesmerised audience watched the elderly maestro pound the keys and occasionally glance out to the watching crowd with a wry look on his face; he was enjoying himself just as much as these folk.

After an impressive hour and twenty minutes of exciting performance, the Faceless Legions ended their set with a characteristic rock and roll ending, which saw Paul nearly destroy his drum kit; such was the pounding it was taking. Andy has his *Les Paul* held high in the air and Danny was standing arms outstretched like Christ the Redeemer on Mount Corcovado; a broad grin covering his face. He thanked his audience for their support and praise before joining his comrades and walking off stage waving frantically to the cheering crowds.

Alison and I exited and moved towards the door to gain access backstage. We were stopped by an austere woman in high visibility jacket. She was about to speak and probably tell us we were not permitted backstage, when she caught sight of our backstage passes pinned onto our trouser waste-bands. Her officious face turned to one of mild apology and she stepped aside to permit us access.

The air of triumph through here was unmistakable; whoops, cheers and clapping sounded in the confines of the small area where the band gathered and congratulated each other on a successful performance.

We hugged the band-members in turn, feeling the wet perspiration from their clothing and heat from their bodies. The guys from Job for Life and Experience Counts were there to offer their congratulations through manly handshakes, teenage high-fives and boisterous back-slapping.

Lee appeared from the stage area and hushed the gathering. We could hear the crowds cheer and chant 'Legions, Legions, Legions.' Some were even wolf whistling along to the chant.

'I think they want an encore, guys,' Lee said.

The Faceless Legions looked at each other and Danny gestured to the stage.

'Well I'm up for it if everyone else is,' Danny said edging closer to the curtain. The rest nodded their approval. Alison moved forwards and approached Mick. She gazed into his face trying to ascertain his health state.

'How are you feeling Mick?' Alison asked. Mick smiled at her.

'Never better nurse.'

'Well let's just check your pulse, shall we?' Alison said reaching for Mick's arm without waiting for a reply.

Mick looked slightly apprehensive as though his nurse may detect an anomaly with his pulse rate and prohibit him from returning to the stage.

I indicated to the band to wait until Mick was given the all clear. They were all anxious to get back on stage and perform one last number to their eager audience.

'Okay, you're good to go,' Alison declared as she let go of Mick's warm arm.

We watched them head back to the stage like excited puppies; this truly was an impressive sight. After nearly an hour and a half of solid performance, they still had enough energy to tackle an encore. Soon the chanting for the return of the band gave way to a crescendo of cheering – the crowd had got what they wanted.

I stood with my ex wife and son, as we admired the band playing another two songs, from the stage left.

'Did Mick seem alright then?' I asked Alison. She nodded.

'Yeah he seems fine and his heart's holding up okay.'

'Let's hope he'll be fit for one more performance tomorrow night,' Lee added.

After the final encore performance, the band left the stage to a standing ovation from an appreciative crowd. Again the congratulatory ritual was repeated as though the first was simply a practice. Lee indicated to the roadies to terminate the power feeding the backline amplifiers so the crowd would see the red illuminated lights extinguish and know the band would not be back out. This was a wise move; I had been to many a gig where he crowds cheer relentlessly for ages after a second encore expecting the band to return to the stage if they shout loud enough.

The after gig party took place in a near riotous atmosphere. A sense of achievement was felt by all and drinks were downed in true celebratory fashion. I found myself at the centre of all attention, much to my consternation and embarrassment. I was hailed the hero for managing this whole project to bring the band back from the dead and providing a stage for them to show the world that they still had the ability to perform. I was happy with the outcome and thought they pulled it off admirably.

Chapter 35

Dale was anxious to see me early next day. He left a panicky message on my mobile requesting me to call him back as soon as I received the message.

'Hi Dale, what's up?' I asked pondering the urgency of his call.

'Sorry about this, Tony,' Dale said with genuine apology in his voice, 'but Job for Life say they don't want to play again tonight.'

That was it? This was the near-emergency Dale was reporting? I waited on some other fact to justify his panic such as his decision to pull out of tonight's performance, but there was nothing further.

'Why's that Dale?'

'They said they didn't think the audience liked them and felt out of place playing to them.'

I felt like telling Dale I agreed with them and didn't much care for them myself, but instead I put on my professional, caring band-manager's head.

'That's a pity. I thought they were quite good.' I felt my nose to see if it was growing.

'Yeah I did as well. They played well and I'm proud of them,' Dale said.

'Can you not persuade them to do another set tonight? It'll be a different audience,' I returned.

'Nah, I've tried Tony. I'm sorry to let you down, man. They're planning on hitting the road back to Cardiff by lunchtime.'

I terminated the call and arranged a minor crisis meeting with Will and Lee. We decided that we could easily combine a meeting with breakfast, so we met in the hotel restaurant and discussed the departure of Job for Life from the billing.

'So what are we gonna' do?' Will asked through a mouthful of toast. I shrugged in a perfunctory manner.

'To be honest, I'm not that bothered that they've thrown in the towel; I didn't think much of them and agree that they weren't the best choice of support act,' I admitted. Lee nodded in agreement and Will looked undecided.

'I think it's too late to arrange an alternative band,' Will stated the obvious.

'I suggest we just put on the one support band, so they and the Legions get a bit longer on stage,' Lee said.

This was exactly what I was thinking, but reckoned it would be better coming from someone else. As usual Lee rose to the challenge. Will nodded as he pondered this suggestion.

'Yeah, you're right Lee,' Will said looking at him before turning his attention to me.

'Is that going to be a problem for you and your band?'

'No. It'll be no problem. I'll run it past the guys but I think they'll be totally up for it.'

Totally up for it was an understatement. Phil, Stevie and Darren were thrilled with this news; we would be the one and only support act for tonight's gig and our slot time would be increased to fifty minutes. We had a large portfolio of songs in our repertoire, so to play a longer set would present no problems whatsoever.

Will was concerned that the ticket holders would feel cheated as the tickets implied supports acts – plural, and not just one, but I succeeded in reassuring him that the ticket holders were actually here to see the main band and probably didn't care particularly for the support; in fact most people arrived and found their seats during the warm-up band's performance.

As before, we had to undergo the sound-check regime, but this time after the Legions checked, we set up and all equipment and levels were left ready for us to go on stage later.

I was strolling along corridor leading to the dressing rooms when I came face to face with a figure I thought and wished I would never see again. The burly, shaven haired brute of a man eyed me curiously before shooting out his hand towards me. I recoiled thinking he was ready to pound me once again just like him and his crony did in Perth, Australia a while back.

'No hard feelings man,' the brute said in a thick Aussie accent, a friendly smile now covering his face. I took his hand and we shook.

'Yeah, no hard feelings,' I returned.

'Sorry for the beating. We got a bit carried away,' he admitted. Then as an afterthought he offered, 'I'm Paul's son – Jerry Dixon.'

'Pleased to meet you Jerry,' I returned. I had long forgiven the guy; I had taken a hit for the team and it had paid off. I had no intention of making friends with this guy, so I excused myself and hurried off towards the dressing rooms.

'I've just met your boy, Paul,' I said as I entered.

'Uh oh. Tell me he didn't hit you again,' Paul said in mock horror.

'Nah, he actually apologised, so I let him off,' I replied.

The rest of the afternoon was spent bumping into and being introduced to old and new friends: I met dopey metal-head Wayne from Andy's guitar store who practically bowed before me like I was royalty; then Danny's wife Shona turned up with Wendy Brookes. We engaged in the usual greeting regime then Lee approached me with mischievous look on his face.

'You'll never guess who I ran into?' he said grabbing my arm.

'I dunno. Mick Jagger?' I ventured. Lee shook his head.

'The dreadlocks guy from Dale's studio. You remember - the cheeky guy?' How could I forget the Bob Marley clone?

'Oh, where is he? Maybe I'll go chuck him out of here,' I joked; Lee laughed. That guy too had been forgiven. His arrogance was annoying, but in the end our perseverance had paid off and we got to speak to Dale – and here he was: playing in the band.

Dale said he had invited his mother and grandmother to witness his big moment, but both had declined fearing it would be too loud and boisterous for their liking; besides both had a newly painted wall to watch drying.

By 1950hrs, Experience Counts were ready to rock the Hammersmith once again. We had a set-list of good old favourite rock and roll hits to cover, making a veritable A-Z list: from AC/DC to ZZ Top.

The slight feeling of nervousness from the previous night seemed to vanish now that we had grown accustomed to the hall and stage. The odd on-stage acoustics was now predictable and we seemed to hear ourselves and each other better. This made for a tighter and more professional, polished performance which we were all proud of.

As I played and sang, I couldn't help a feeling of accomplishment: here we were – just a typical common rock covers pub band, but now playing on stage at the world renowned Hammersmith Apollo – such a far cry from The Regent in the south side of Glasgow.

We exited the stage in a euphoric mood, but feeling slightly saddened at the end of it all. The roadies congratulated us and we engaged in the ubiquitous ritual with high-fives, knuckle bumps and the rest. Yet another change of clothes was called for and we headed back to our dressing rooms.

The door to one of the Legion's changing rooms was slightly ajar and I could hear raised voices from within. I froze; this was not what I wanted to hear. I knocked on the door and eased it open.

'Only me guys. Everything all right?' I enquired looking around for the source of the raised voices.

I spotted Danny pacing the floor. His face was livid and his body language screamed anger and annoyance. Dale, Andy, Mick and Paul all sat around on sofas, their faces displaying a mixture of irritation and disappointment.

'That's it. I've had enough of you lot. Call yourselves musicians?' Danny roared as his head swung wildly from side to side.

'So what are you gonna do about it, Danny – cry like a baby?' Paul asked, his voice dripping with distain.

Carter lunged at Paul pointing his finger only inches from Dixon's nose. Paul rose to his feet and both squared up at each other. Fearing a fight was only seconds away, I rushed towards Danny to pull him away from Paul in an attempt to separate both parties. This was not looking good at all. It appeared the pressure had finally got to them and they had all erupted into loathing for each other. As if they couldn't have just kept it together for one more night – that was all I was asking; then they could fall out and never talk to each other again.

'Well I'm out of here. You lot can go on stage without me,' Danny screamed, his pointing finger now aimed at Andy.

'You're useless anyway Carter. On you go – get out of here. We don't need you,' Andy said returning Danny's pointed finger.

Danny spun around and spotted me right behind him; now it was my turn to feel the wrath of the enraged Carter.

'And as for you, Caulfield. I wish I had never met you.' I could feel flecks of spit erupt from his mouth.

I was conscious of a rush of movement behind me and turned to see Lee, Alison and Will at my back. All had evidently overheard the shouting and come to investigate. Alison looked shocked,

Lee confused and Will looked like he was ready to run away from the impending battle. Danny brushed past me and headed for the door. I knew it was all over; the final reunion gig was in tatters. I knew it was too much to hope for. My mood descended like a fat polar bear on thin ice. The disappointment was so strong and bitter I could almost taste it, and felt nauseous at the thought. Now someone had the unenviable task of going on stage and telling five thousand three hundred expectant fans that the show was now over. I feared that candidate was going to be me. I wished for a large hole to appear before me and open to swallow me up.

Then a roar of laughter erupted into the air. I turned to see Danny with a huge grin on his face and the rest of the Legions rolling around on the sofa with hilarity, giggling like mischievous pranksters.

'Got you again, eh Tony?' Danny said grabbing me and giving me a bear-like hug. I shook my head. They had indeed got me – their prank the night before had me believing Mick was ill and having to pull out, now this fake argument had me thinking the show was over.

'You lot need to grow up!' I laughed as I exhaled a lungful of anxiety. Alison put a comforting arm around me and Lee joined in the laughter. Soon my breathing and heart-rate was more or less back to normal.

'Come on guys, you're on in two minutes,' Lee cried looking at his watch.

'No way. Not after that little prank,' I shouted in mock incredulity, 'you lot can go busk in the streets for all I care.' I gestured outside.

Once the laughter had faded, the guys composed themselves and headed to the door. Lee and Will followed the troupe to the stage and I walked along hand in hand with Alison. As before, Lee waited on confirmation from the sound crew that the stage was all set and ready for the Legions. He walked onto the stage and took up his position at the centre microphone stand and made pretty much the same short speech he had the previous night. The crowd this evening seemed more excited than the previous and Lee had to wait on a bit of silence before resuming his introduction.

Then they were on. The audience erupted with an ear-shattering applause with accompanying cheering; this crowd were definitely a whole lot noisier than last night. Danny waved at the ocean of excited faces as he approached his microphone stand and made a few minor adjustments before speaking.

'Good evening Hammersmith,' he cried in a sing-song voice. The crowd responded loudly, but Carter in true showmanship fashion responded, 'I can't hear you. I said good evening Hammersmith Apollo.'

This time the noise was near Earth shattering. Danny grinned and nodded his approval. Meanwhile Paul was getting comfortable behind his kit; Dale and Andy slinging their instruments over their shoulders and adjusting the strap for maximum comfort, and Mick was perching himself on his stool whilst flicking a few switches on his keyboard.

Andy kicked off the show with a well known riff on his cherry-red *Gibson SG*. Within a few bars, the audience had recognised the song and erupted with cheers. Next Paul joined in with a bass and snare drum rhythm interspaced with a ride cymbal beat. Eight beats later Dale entered playing the same riff as Andy but one octave lower. Soon Mick's distinctive organ was heard complementing the instrumental. Danny rocked about in front of his microphone stand and swayed his hips to the rhythm – then launched into the song with a piercing scream which triggered the crowd into frenzy. People on the balcony stood up and began to sway along to the beat; the ushers were quick to pounce and order them back into their seats, which they reluctantly did. The crowds to the rear of the circle and stalls had no such restrictions and were free to boogie to their hearts content.

Once again I stood with Alison and we watched the famous band doing their thing which had made them famous all those years ago, and showing they could still perform. The sell-out ticket sales over two nights were testimony to the band's ability and popularity. Who would have guessed after all these years that the Faceless Legions could still put on a spectacular rocking performance plus sell out the place?

Near to us stood Wendy Brookes, Shona Carter and Lee's girlfriend, Jessica. They were deep in conversation and seemed more interested in discussing a whole host of irrelevant topics than watching the band. I felt like directing them through to one of the spare dressing rooms where they could have themselves a coffee morning in peace and quiet.

Chapter 36

Towards the end of the band's set, Danny spoke to the audience. He wore a serious face and looked out at his audience like he was about to deliver a eulogy.

'Ladies and gentlemen, I'd like to take this opportunity to introduce to you the man whose idea it was to reunite us, and has worked tirelessly for many months to make this event happen.' I heard Carter's words but didn't actually register.

'Would you please welcome Tony Caulfield,' Danny cried like a game-show host introducing the grand prize. He glanced to the side of the stage and I stared back. He was pointing straight at me! Alison released my hand and spoke into my ear.

'Go on Tony. Say hello to the crowd.'

With that she gave me a gentle push towards the stage. I panicked; I had not anticipated this moment; I wasn't even mentally prepared to go back on stage and be showcased like some circus exhibit. I reluctantly moved onto stage and towards Danny who stood with open arms like the prodigal son's eager father. Danny lunged towards me and we embraced to a raucous applause. I was about to turn and head back off stage, but Danny had other ideas. He approached the microphone and kept one arm firmly around my shoulder, probably to keep me from escaping.

'Go on Tony, say something,' Danny invited. Then as if on cue, the audience started chanting 'speech, speech, speech…'

I was left with no option; the pressure to say something was immense. I silently cursed Carter for putting me into this situation – he might have prepared me and I could have written something down on paper, or else mentally prepared something to say. I felt the flutter of butterflies in the pit of my stomach and a strange tingling in my legs. Evidently the adrenalin was coursing through my veins preparing me for the good old fight or flight response; I desperately wanted to do the latter, but felt compelled to stay – five thousand voices urging me to speak, left me with no choice.

I was not averse to public speaking – I had done many interviews in front of TV cameras during my career in the CID, but I always had time to prepare what I was going to say. Plus I had been playing and singing in front of audiences for many years in my capacity as amateur musician, but that was different – for some reason a microphone stand and guitar provide some sort of psychological sword and shield which seems to make appearing in front of vast crowds easier. I composed myself and attempted to slow down my breathing as I gazed out at the watching faces. I was impressed to see a variety of age ranges – from children right up to elderly people; who knew the Legions would appeal to such a wide and distinctive age span; mind you I had witnessed a similar audience at Status Quo concerts.

'Thanks Danny,' I began as I thought ahead what I would say next, 'and thank you Hammersmith for coming out to see the best band in the world.'

This had the desired effect and drove the crowd wild and they clapped, cheered and whistled their agreement; it also bought me a few precious seconds in which I mentally prepared the next part of my impromptu speech.

'Well, it's been a long and tiring journey, but it was well worth it.' A small burst of applause mainly from the middle of the stalls and I let it pass before continuing.

'Like Martin Luther King, I also had a dream. I wanted to see these guys back together and playing the music that made them famous and which they do so well.' My captivated audience was enjoying this; and so with improved confidence I continued waffling on.

'Finding these guys was just the first challenge, and I had to travel half way round the world - mind you I've managed to collect a fair amount of air miles,' I said with the flair of a comedian. A mild eruption of laughter at my daft joke; even Danny giggled at it, but I reckon he was doing it to be polite.

'But convincing them to reunite for one last gig was like drawing beer from a stone.' A mild ripple of laughter for my efforts - either the rest didn't like my jokes or they couldn't understand my Scottish accent; I continued.

'I wasn't prepared to take no for an answer; I wanted to see the band back together again and I was sure they could do it. So I bullied and begged until they said yes.'

'I'm convinced my persistence paid off as tonight's performance is testimony to the fact these guys have still got it and can still sell out the Hammersmith.'

The entire hall cheered and applauded; Danny thumped me on the back and nearly knocked the wind out of me. Paul hit a few crash cymbals to acknowledge his agreement.

'I'd like to thank everybody who have worked like Trojans behind the scene making this moment possible. I'd like to thank Alison and Lee Caulfield and Will Pearson especially, for their assistance and moral support during all the preparation for this concert. And lastly, I'd like to thank all you people for supporting the project and buying tickets – without you this wouldn't have been possible.'

Over five thousand voices roared their agreement and appreciation for my ill-rehearsed speech. I reckoned I had said enough and taken up sufficient time, so I waved to the audience and hurried off stage left; I could tell the band were itching to get on with the remainder of their set list.

Backstage I was congratulated on my fine bit of impromptu public speaking which seemed to go down a storm. The band blasted into another song and our little group consisting of me, Alison. Lee, Jessica, Shona and Wendy stood watching the band complete their set and leave the stage. As before, the crowd had decided that the hour and a half long performance was not quite long enough. They protested by cheering and chanting 'Legions, Legions, Legions.' This continued for a minute or so, the band taking the opportunity to rehydrate and mop the pools of perspiration from their faces and necks before dashing back on stage to perform an extension to their set list.

'Mick's looking a bit tired,' Alison said with a concerned look on her face. I turned to look at her.

'You think he's okay?' I asked.

'Yeah, but I think he should call it a night after this encore. I don't want him pushing himself too much.'

I agreed with her, but I doubted we could stop him if he decided to go back on for a second encore. I looked over at Lee; he checked his watch and shrugged.

'Plenty of time,' Lee shouted over the music; so it was not as if we could use that as an excuse.

Last nigh the band had performed two encores, so I reckoned they would probably do likewise this evening; the crowd seemed very receptive and no doubt would want their money's worth; but how could we stop Mick from going back on?

Two songs later and to rapturous applause, the band exited the stage once again. I caught sight of Alison scrutinising Mick up close - he did look tired and worn out and I considered it a risk if he went back on.

As it happened, the rest of the band had sensed Mick's flagging energy and had a quick conference to discuss going back on. The band were very much up for it, even Mick, but Alison intervened and explained her concern for his health if he drove himself too far.

Meanwhile the chants and cheering were getting louder putting pressure on the band to return for one last encore. I could see Danny itching to get going; Andy and Dale were also poised ready for the indicative nod. Paul approached Mick and put his arm around him.

'We can do the last couple of songs minus the keys, mate. Why don't you have a bit of a rest?'

'Yeah, it's no problem, Mick,' Danny added.

'You can come back on after the songs and we'll do the curtain call thing together,' reasoned Andy. This seemed like a sensible solution to me.

'I think it would be best if you had a wee sit down and rest, Mick,' Alison said, trying to steer Mick away from the direction of the stage and towards a row of seats.

'No. I want to do this,' said a defiant Mick shaking his head vigorously, 'I've said it before and I'll say it again – I'll perform if it kills me.'

So that was it – the last word from the rebellious king of the keyboards. Now the pressure was on the band – do they cancel the final encore, or go on as a complete band, even with the risk of Mick keeling over?

Still the audience chanted for more from the Faceless Legions. Lee peeked out and reported that people had begun to rise from their seats thinking the show really was over. I looked at each member of the band: their faces said it all – they were quite prepared to go back out, all five of them. Alison and I watched them shuffle onto the stage, to raucous applause and take up their respective positions.

'Thank you so much Hammersmith. You've been great,' Danny shouted into the microphone. The response was immediate and encouraging.

'Who wants another song then?' he continued with his well-known catch phrase. The daft question needed no answer, but Carter was loving the attention.

'Hammersmith, I can't hear you. I said who wants another song?' he shouted an octave higher and with more volume in his voice. The rhetorical question was met with even louder applause, cheers and whistling. Carter got the message and turned to face his band. Following a quick nod, the band began the final number; an apt song for the setting and a good going number to end a momentous occasion.

'We will meet again in rock and roll heaven,' sang Danny with an enormous grim on his face. The line was echoed by Andy and Dale on backing vocals; both augmenting with a third and fifth harmonic respectively and swelling the power of the song. The crowd sang along too, although in a less melodious monotone. I watched thousands of arms punch the air in time to the beat, their heads back as they screamed the lyrics, giving it their all knowing this was the probably the last time they would get to sing along with the classic band.

The guitar solo was up now and Andy moved to the front of the stage and let rip with a fast run on the rosewood fret-board, amazing the audience with his arsenal of techniques as his frenetic fingers ran amock up and down the neck bending the strings at crazy angles.

'The amazing Andy Brookes,' Danny announced as the crowd went crazy.

Then the keyboard instrumental section was up – the exhausted but resilient Mick rose to the occasion with an impressive burst of energy. His dextrous hands moved almost as quickly as Andy's a minute ago as he graced the keys with his well honed techniques causing a blur of musical notes to blast from the loudspeakers. He was loving this and wore an enormous smile, in competition to Danny's.

'The king of the keyboards, Mr Mick Walker,' Danny proclaimed gesturing with a wide open arm towards Mick.

Danny continued to announce the other band members, each receiving a loud crack of applause. Then Andy approached his microphone and spoke as he continued to play.

'Ladies and gentlemen, the fantastic voice of Danny Carter.'

A massive smile broke out on Carter's face as he bowed low to his audience and gave them the thumbs up.

The song then wound down to the closing bars and ended with the ubiquitous rock and roll ending: Paul pounding the drums like he was intent on breaking them; Dale was thumping the strings of his bass; Andy's fingers sprinting up and down the fret-board and Mick's arms were all over the place as he made sure each and every key was hit with vigour. Danny stood legs apart and arms outstretched waiting on the final note.

After what seemed like a never-ending conclusion, the song drew to an abrupt halt; the crash cymbals ringing out on the stage. The audience were on their feet now as they showed their appreciation with a standing ovation. They clapped, cheered, whistled and called for more, but the show really was over – two encores were more than enough; some bands only did one!

The five musicians stood at the edge of the stage, arms around each other and the widest grins I had ever seen. They looked tired and exhausted but ecstatic and euphoric. Danny saw me lingering at the side of the stage and beckoned me to join the band on stage. My instinct was to decline – I wasn't part of the band, however Carter left me with no choice. He bellowed into his microphone for me to join his team upstage. I may not be part of the band, but I was instrumental in bringing them back from the dead, so to speak.

I strode back onto the stage to loud applause and was quickly inserted into the line-up, between Danny and Mick. I put my arms around their sweaty backs and could feel the pulsing heat from their bodies. The blinding intensity of the spotlights gave off its own heat and the temperature soared. The noise from the five thousand-odd audience's clapping hands, cheering voices and stamping feet was truly deafening, but it did confirm the success of the event. All my hard work, aches, pains and persistence had paid off. At times I had doubted the feasibility of this project, but now I had witnessed what the power of perseverance and dogged determination could do. I set out to find and reunite the Faceless Legions and had done just that – and it turned out much better than I could have ever have imagined.

Epilogue

I stepped down from the witness box feeling confident; I had presented my evidence in a clear and concise manner. The look on the faces of the jury confirmed my confidence, and the Procurator Fiscal looked jubilant.

I was just one of many witnesses in the case against the notorious Frankie 'Lanky' Langham. A couple of years previously Mr Langham had murdered his wife following an alcohol fuelled burst of domestic violence. He dumped her body in wasteland miles from civilisation, and then reported her missing, telling the police she had walked out on him after an argument. He was very believable according to the police officers who took the details for a missing person report; they had searched high and low, visited all her relatives and acquaintances and studied numerous CCTV recordings, but could not find the women – she had simply vanished.

A year later, a driver lost control of his car whilst driving along the road near to the resting place of the murdered woman. His car rolled down the steep embankment through a forest of thick bushes and scrubland and finally came to rest within metres of the decaying corpse of the late Mrs Langham. There followed an intensive manhunt for the killer, the prime suspect being Frankie. But Lanky Langham had absconded when he heard his wife's body had been discovered and he was wanted for questioning.

I was the detective allocated to the case and I embraced it with eager expectation. Although Mrs Langham's body was in a very advanced state of decay, the forensic team were still able to identify the tell-tale signs of strangulation from a pair of large male hands. Again the evidence pointed to Frankie who sported such large hands.

It took almost a year of intensive searching, gathering of evidence and interviewing witnesses before the case could be presented to the Procurator Fiscal. Frankie Langham was eventually traced living in a homeless centre. A team of six officers, including myself pounced on him in the middle of the night and he was arrested and dragged kicking, screaming and protesting his innocence all the way to the police station charge bar. I interviewed him, put immense pressure on him and he eventually caved in and admitted his guilt.

The whole courtroom erupted into cheers when the Judge declared Frankie guilty and sentenced him to life imprisonment. All the hard work and perseverance had come to fruition. At times I doubted I would ever be in a position to bring the suspect to court such was his elusiveness, but painstaking detective work by a dedicated team had indeed paid off.

That was a similar feeling I had when we finally exited the stage of the Hammersmith Apollo. The weary warriors trooped off in triumphant spirits. The back-slapping and high-five ritual began in earnest and we all engaged like tribal combatants. The atmosphere was electric and everyone buzzed with energy despite the hectic performance.

The after gig party was wild: liquor flowed in torrents down thirsty throats, and praise was lavished on all those who had taken part, both on stage and behind the scenes, making it such a success. Mick, despite his obvious exhaustion looked in good spirits and Alison assured me he was in good health, his heart standing up to the rigours of two nights solid gigging with impressive might.

The next day, hangovers aplenty, we all parted and went our separate ways; the Legions were keen to continue as a band and wanted my managerial skills, but I declined their kind offer. I was happy enough to be their manager just for the duration of the planning and preparation leading up to the event, but I would now be glad to detach my managerial head and finally relax. Protests from all led me to defer my decision and admit that I would think seriously about the job. I certainly didn't want to be a full time manager, but the consensus seemed to be that the band would be more of a part-time affair, with only the occasional gig and perhaps a session in the studio to record a brand new album. This appealed more to me and I said I would give them a decision in due course.

Paul returned to Perth to resume his running of the Johnny B Goode bar, but now with celebrity status. Andy went back to demonstrating and flogging guitars and other musical equipment, but was now seriously considering a move to a larger store, such was the popularity of the shop now that the owner was revealed as the famous Legions guitarist. It seemed that there was only one place in the area in which to procure a guitar or drum kit – and the man who would be taking your hard-earned cash would be none other than Andy Brookes.

Dale was tearful when the moment came to leave – he had enjoyed himself so much he didn't want it to end and aspired to touring the world with the band his father had once been part of. He was overjoyed at the opportunity to be part of the Legions and expressed his gratitude at how easily he had been accepted into the brotherhood. The guys had joked that it was only on account of his resemblance to his father that he got the job.

Mick had enjoyed his time with Danny in Skye so much he decided to move there permanently. He was loathe to return to a retirement home in Mallorca, despite the much warmer and dryer climate than that of north-western Scotland, but he reckoned the scenery made up for the weather.

I warned Danny not to pull another stunt having Mick among his band of merry men trundling over the heather like a scene from *Braveheart*. Danny assured me that he would take good care of Mick and Shona reiterated the message.

Will looked relieved that the event was finally over – it had clearly tested his resilience and resourcefulness to the limit judging by the haggard look on his face and deep shadows under his eyes, but he had done an impressive job and I was proud to have met and worked with him. Will was so impressed with Lee's professionalism and organisational skills that he offered to find him a job in the industry, promising to put in a good word with one of his many industry contacts. Lee jumped at the chance of a career change – anything was better than lugging bricks and mortar around a construction site.

Alison and I returned home in jubilant spirits; she lavished praise upon me all the flight home saying how proud she was at my creativity and sheer nerve in actually going ahead with my crazy quest in the first place – to succeed in such a momentous manner. I actually surprised myself at how I had actually pulled it off; but it just goes to show that if you want something bad enough and are prepared to stick at it despite a plethora of problems plaguing the project, then you might just surprise yourself and others with success.

Not long after Alison returned to the Granite City, she had accepted early retirement and was now a free woman, keen to make the most of her retirement while she was still relatively young, fit and healthy. However she had a dilemma – to invite me to start a life together with her in Aberdeen, or to sell up and move back to her old house in Glasgow and retire gracefully with me. She chose the latter and now we were back to where we started, but minus all the trouble and strife which had originally driven us apart. If felt as though someone had turned back the hands of time.

I never imagined it could happen, but here we were now back together, reunited and enjoying being a couple once again – and feeling much the same as the guys from the Faceless Legions must have felt. I had succeeded in turning around not just a band from long ago, but also my previous life – and I was content with how both had turned out. I was getting good at this resurrection business.

Printed in Great Britain
by Amazon